Perfect
Lies

Perfect Lies

A Novel by

Liza Bennett

HarperCollins

HarperCollins

10 East 53rd Street, New York, NY 10022-5299

ISBN 0-7394-0687-6

Cover photograph © Tony Stone Images

Printed in the United States of America

For my sisters
Kate and Emily
and, as always,
for W.E.B.

Thanks to Police Chief Carl Cooper, who kindly shed light on the workings of a small town police force and how it coordinates its efforts with state detectives to solve violent crimes... Supreme Court Judge Nicholas Figueroa who took time out of his busy schedule to explain the dynamics of the courtroom and the intricacies of the legal system... Maurice Sieradzki who gave generously of his time, experience, and sheer love of the law throughout the conception and writing of this book. His enthusiasm for the project and for reading in general have been an inspiration.

Perfect
Lies

1

Running usually cured just about anything that ailed Meg Hardwick. A new business presentation that wasn't coming together, say, or a morning alone after another disappointing date, and all she needed was that three-mile run along Riverside Drive and into the park, looping down to the boat basin and along the river. Often, by the time she had returned to her co-op at Eighty-sixth Street and Riverside, sweating, breathing hard, Meg would have to ask herself: What had she been worrying about again?

Not that Meg was ever trying to run away from her problems. One of the main reasons for her success was her determination to face every challenge head-on. She'd seen what self-indulgence could lead to when she was growing up, how her parents lives and dreams had slowly dissolved in a haze of alcohol and denial, and she vowed that she would never end up like that. However, she'd long since realized that life was not going to simply hand over the goods. She'd have to make things happen on her own. Grab the initiative. Seize the moment.

And she had. Created her own good looks. Built up Hardwick and Associates from nothing. Overseen every photo shoot, watched every line of copy. She'd pored over balance sheets, prayed for checks to clear. Pushed for profits. She'd made it all work through sheer force of will and the unstoppable momentum of someone who didn't register the word "no" as an answer. Meg was all about "yes," and "now," and "not a problem." She was about getting it done right. And in doing so, she'd developed a kind of emotional muscle—a tautness, an alertness, a hunger to keep going. Give Meg Hardwick a challenge—as any one of her fashion accounts would attest—and she would wrestle it to the ground and have it pinned in no time.

But even Meg had to admit that she was a great deal better at handling business concerns than personal ones. And the particular problem troubling her that morning was just about as personal as a problem could get. When it came to matters of the heart, she too-often discovered that her mind—usually so sharp and decisive—simply clouded over. Strong emotions meant big trouble for Meg. And her feelings that morning were at a high-water mark.

As Meg started off slowly on her run, it occurred to her that the weather, at least, was responding sympathetically to her mood. Thunderstorms were forecast for the afternoon; she could feel the air thickening with ozone. The sky had a greenish, underwater cast to it. The leaves of the majestic plane trees that lined the drive, already dry after the long hot summer, rustled like newspapers in the rising wind.

Concentrate, Meg told herself. Think it through, slowly, methodically as you would anything else. She could feel her pulse rate start to pick up as she hit her stride. She heard the even rhythm of her breathing. She was in very good shape, able to pass easily for someone a decade younger than her thirty-seven years. Her looks, her stamina—she worked just as hard at these as she did everything else. She enjoyed the effort of achievement, she loved reaching the goals she set for herself.

But neither hard work nor heavy thinking would solve this problem. This was like a natural disaster, an earthquake. It had hit her without warning. And now, trying to sort through the rubble, she had no idea how to begin to repair the damage. Or what dangerous aftershocks might await her.

Maybe, if it was just her life that was affected, the whole thing would be easier. She'd know what to do, how to end things, put the wrongs right. But when it came to seeing her younger sister Lark get hurt—or her three little nieces—Meg lost her common sense. Her practical instincts deserted her when she felt that those she loved the most in the world were being threatened. Meg realized as she sprinted for a quarter mile that she was just too angry at Ethan to know how to handle the situation. And her decision to keep Lark safely out of it had been well-intentioned but ultimately futile.

Thunder rumbled somewhere to the south over New Jersey. The sky to the west glowed with the greenish purple hues of an unripened eggplant, and the air smelled sulfurous as Meg made her way out of the park. A heavy rain was coming. The run solved nothing, but it solidified a growing unease in Meg. She had no choice, really. She had to tell Lark.

As she got off the elevator at her floor, the Edleson twins nearly mowed her down. In-line skating was her neighbors' children's latest craze; a Saturday rarely went by without Meg running into them.

"Sorry!" they cried in unison as they dived past her.

"It's about to pour out there—" Meg started to tell them, but the door closed before she could finish her warning. Not that it would have stopped them. They were both headstrong and inseparable. In many ways, they reminded Meg of herself and Lark when they were growing up. Loving, dependent. Each other's best friend. Closest confidantes. Staunchest supporters.

She had been planning to change and shower first, but the Edleson girls and their giggling lightheartedness changed Meg's mind. She could do nothing to repair the damage, but the emotional crisis wasn't confined to Meg's life—it was about to shatter Lark's as well.

Her hand was reaching for the receiver to call her sister when the phone rang.

"Meg?"

"I don't believe this—I was just going to phone you." But, there had been something odd about Lark's greeting. "Is everything . . . okay?"

"Oh, Meg." Lark started to gasp as though trying

to catch her breath, an indication, Meg knew, of extreme distress. "Meggie."

"Lark. Baby, come on now. Just tell me. Just talk to me."

"Meg . . . It's Ethan."

"Yes." Meg steeled herself for what she knew was coming. Ethan had gotten to Lark first.

"He's dead."

"What?"

"Ethan's been murdered. This morning. Janine found him in the studio. In front of the ovens. Someone had driven a burning pontil rod . . ." Lark's voice started to trail off, but then she added with sudden vehemence: "Into his heart."

"No—"

"Lucinda was there. She was curled up in the corner of the studio, holding the rod. They've taken her into custody."

"Lark—"

"I've got to go now. There's so much to do."

"I'll be there as soon as I can."

"Meggie," She started to cry. "I'm scared. I'm just so . . ."

"I'm leaving right now, baby," Meg told her, as an angry streak of lightning lanced through the dismal afternoon and, with a clap of thunder, the storm finally broke over Manhattan.

It had always been Meg's job to protect Lark. Whether the threat was as amorphous as ghosts in the dark, or as real as their parents fighting in the kitchen late at night, Meg was the one who came up with the comforting words, the calming reassurances. Now, lightheaded with panic and a growing sense of unreality, Meg again promised Lark what she had so often promised during their childhood, "Everything's going to be all right."

But even as she said the words Meg knew how flimsy and hopeless they sounded.

2

Meg and Lark's parents had what was called in the 1960s an "open marriage." Though Frank and Sara, both from fairly conservative, middle-class families, had met and married at the end of the 1950s, they came of age as a couple in the midst of the sexual revolution, and had joined the counterculture with the whole-hearted, unabashed enthusiasm of religious converts. Meg, who was born in 1963 and whose first memories were hazy fragments from the Summer of Love, could distinctly remember her dad saying, with the rapt seriousness of the true believer: "Let it all hang out."

For several years after the infamous festival, the family lived in a hippie commune near Woodstock, New York, where Frank designed psychedelic posters and record covers for a small design firm above a head shop in town. The whole area, by that time, had become overrun with dropouts and has-beens and scores of homeless teenagers looking for love and finding mostly lice and sexually transmitted diseases. It was—Meg realized when she was much older—a confusing and demanding time for young parents across the country. The lure of marijuana and the siren song of unrepressed sex must have been potent and easily addictive. But most hippies eventually matured, finished college, and moved out to the suburbs to raise their children. Meg's parents were never able or willing to outgrow the '60s; Frank went to his grave with a peace symbol tattooed on his right bicep.

Growing up, Meg always tried to come to terms with the fact that her family was different. Hers was the only household she knew of that had a hashish bong on the coffee table. Frank was the only father at her junior high school graduation who still wore his hair in a ponytail. That her mother believed in the healing powers of crystals and her refusal to take her daughters to a G.P. for checkups was just one of the many familial quirks Meg learned how to handle emotionally—and sometimes practically. When Lark's measles turned to mumps and then into a frightening, ongoing listlessness, it was Meg who finally picked up the phone and made an appointment with the local health clinic. And a good thing, too: the doctor diagnosed Lark with severe anemia due to a diet of Sara's nutritionally unbalanced vegetarian fare. Other than vegetables, the family subsisted on pizza, grilled cheese sandwiches, and ice cream.

Frank and Sara were never intentionally negligent or uncaring. There was a lot of love and humor and good times in whatever run-down house or apartment the family currently occupied. And Meg loved them both, dearly. But, as the years passed and Meg grew up while her parents didn't, she began to realize that she didn't approve of them. The mind-bending, culture-changing ideals that had formed Frank and Sara's thinking when Meg was a baby had, by the time she was in her early teens, deteriorated into feeble excuses for selfish and often self-destructive behavior.

"I'm not stoned," Sara would irritably inform Meg as she lay in her darkened bedroom at three-thirty in the afternoon, the breakfast dishes still unwashed in the kitchen sink. "I'm meditating."

Meg learned how to handle the drugs and the alcohol; her parents were sleepy and contented when stoned, boisterous and happy when drunk. They were, really, like children who wanted to be left alone with their playthings. Meg learned to take over the day-to-day running of the house, and she didn't mind letting them be, so long as they were together. What made her crazy was when one or the other of them drifted back home with a stranger.

"Hey, girls, this is Cheryl," Frank would announce at the breakfast table with a proud grin the Saturday morning after a long night out carousing. And there, across from them, would be some plump, pasty-faced redhead with smeared eye makeup and an overly revealing tube top. Sara would join them later, smiling and seemingly cordial to Frank's conquest.

"Wow, you guys really have a good thing going here," the clueless Cheryl would enthuse. "I've never met such a cool couple."

And though the Edenic atmosphere would last until Cheryl finally pulled herself together and stumbled out the door, the trouble often began before Cheryl got her key into the ignition of her Ford Fairlane. The walls of the rented house were so thin that even from their upstairs bedroom, Meg and Lark could hear their parents fighting.

"Jesus, Frank," Sara would say. "Where'd you find that? Under the bar at Storey's?"

"At least I found some. What happened to your cowboy with the silver earring?"

"Wouldn't you like to know? And let me just point out that I have a little more decency than to bring trash home and make the girls sit down and eat with it at the same table."

"Oh, fuck you." And Frank would slam out of the room and out of the house.

Frank and Sara claimed that what they were practicing was free love. What they ended up with, however, as far as Meg was concerned, was nothing more than cheap sex. What did it say about the family—about a marriage—Meg would ask herself, if one had to search outside it for stimulation and approval? She would look around her at the lifestyles of some of her high school friends and long for what she saw there—a placid, churchgoing wholesomeness. She didn't care that Frank would scoff at her friends' parents' conservative politics, or that Sara would call the mothers "Stepford Wives." Meg would have given anything to live the "boring, straight, repressed, and capitalistic" way that her friends did. Instead, she did what she could—learning how to cook and drive, helping Lark with her homework, shopping and cleaning—to make the household at least *look* normal. She also did her best to put a good face on their home life for her younger sister.

"Who is that man in Mommy's room?" Lark would ask Meg during the night as they both lay awake listening to the sounds coming from the bedroom next to theirs.

"He's a friend. Just go to sleep now."

"Why was he yelling like that?"

"It's a grown-up thing. But it means they're having fun."

"So he's not hurting Mommy?"

"Oh no, baby, he's making her happy."

Perhaps Meg had sheltered Lark too much from the sordid side of her parents' lives. She would make Lark go outside and play or go up to her bedroom when her parents fought. Later, she would drive Lark and herself to the movies or just cruise aimlessly down back roads when one of their parents' "friends" came to visit.

"Why can't we stay here when Carl comes to play with Mom?" Lark asked Meg once as they headed out to the car.

"Well," Meg explained, automatically putting a soft spin on their hard reality. "Mommy doesn't make *your* friends play with *her*, right? I mean, they're your friends. Carl's her special friend now. It's just nicer for them if they get to be alone."

"Is Carl a more special friend than Daddy?"

"No, baby, Daddy and Mommy are very best friends, no matter what. Remember that, okay?"

Meg had sugarcoated it all for Lark, making it palatable, making everything seem okay. Making it easy, natural even, for Lark to believe that what her parents shared was something to be proud of—even to emulate. If Lark had been given the time and opportunity, Meg believed, she would gradually have come terms with the very real problems in her parents' marriage. But Lark was only thirteen when Sara and Frank were killed in a car accident and their deaths placed them, in Lark's mind, forever beyond reproach. For this—as for so many things about her younger sister's upbringing—Meg felt responsible.

If Meg had often acted as a surrogate parent to Lark when Sara and Frank were alive, she stepped firmly into their shoes after they died. And like many people thrown into roles of responsibility before their time, Meg tended to be personally conservative and overprotective of her charge. With the help of a small nest egg left to her by her late grandmother, Meg put herself through Columbia University. She then insisted that her younger sister attend college as well, though Lark had found even the ultraliberal Bennington "way overstructured and stifling." When Meg heard that Lark, in her sophomore year, had moved into an apartment off campus with an adjunct professor in the art department, she had been furious. She turned murderous when she learned that he was married and had a young child.

"And you actually believe him when he tells you he's going to get a divorce?" Meg had screamed into the phone from her office at Y&R. She'd been an up-and-coming junior account executive by that time, fresh out of college and wired for success. The pressurized world of advertising was the perfect conduit for her energies and ambition. She looked and acted smart, knew how to make her points in meetings, and had a knack for pleasing clients. It didn't matter to her then that she didn't have much of a social life, not to mention a love life.

"I'm coming up there this weekend," Meg had announced. "And you both better be prepared to explain a few things."

Bennington, Vermont, in February was a Currier & Ives print of snow-laden mountains and smoke-plumed chimneys. The New England college town moved at such a slower pace than Manhattan that it seemed to Meg to exist in a different century entirely. By the time Meg finished the three-hour lunch with Ethan and Lark she sensed that what bound them to each other was also of a different time and place. Even Meg, who considered herself the furthest thing from a romantic, could see they were in love. They could hardly take their eyes off each other, let alone their hands. They were constantly touching and kissing as if to reassure themselves that the other was real.

It was more than physical, though Meg at first wanted to write it off as such. No one knew Lark better than Meg—her fierce independence, her artistic yearnings. Lark had always been the "creative one"—making up poems, putting on plays, designing and building elaborate houses for her family of beloved dolls. Since girlhood, she had been determined to be an artist of some kind. She had gone to Bennington to discover her *métier*. What she seemed to have discovered instead was Ethan and the promise of more than just existing as an artist. She found she could create and sustain an entire artistic existence.

"You know who you sound like, Lark, with your talk of freethinking and self-exploration?" Meg said. "Just like Mom."

"And nothing could be worse than that, could it?" Ethan had asked, turning to her. Meg was usually suspicious of the probing look common to certain therapists and EST devotees. Ethan's unwavering gaze held some of that unnerving quality—intimate, demanding, and altogether too knowing.

"I don't believe I was addressing you."

"I know—but you were trying to intimidate Lark, and I don't like that. Besides, this isn't about Lark, is it? It's about me. You don't trust me."

"You're ten years older than my sister. You're married. You have a stepchild to care for. You're an assistant professor who makes what? Thirty thousand a year?"

"Lord, if only!" Ethan laughed. "Tell me where they'll pay me that kind of money. But no, you're perfectly right. I'd distrust me, too, if I couldn't see into my heart and know—absolutely—that there is no better person in this world for Lark than me."

"Fine. Then I suggest you file for divorce immediately."

"It's a little more complicated than that."

"Why? I'm sorry, but if you love my sister, you'll get a divorce and marry her. I think that's pretty simple."

"You don't know the full story."

"Please—this is ridiculous. Lark, can't you see you're being taken for a ride?"

"No, I don't see that. I feel that I've found the other half of my soul."

"Oh, for heavens' sake!" Meg threw down her napkin and pushed her chair back. "Do whatever the hell you want. Give me a call when he breaks your heart."

3

It was hard to remember those early days very clearly—back when Ethan first emerged as a major player in Lark's and Meg's lives, and when Meg disapproved of him so vehemently. Of course, even then she knew that a big part of her problem with Ethan was that he had come between the two sisters. Until Lark met Ethan, Meg was the one Lark sought first, loved most, and clung to in times of need. When Ethan arrived, Meg experienced what every mom naturally feels when her daughter leaves home: the sharp, sad pain of separation. And also, like a stereotypical dad, Meg examined her little girl's selection of a mate and found him wanting.

Tall, broad as a linebacker, and with the flowing locks of an unrepentant hippie, Ethan generated a slightly out-of-control virility. A don't-give-a-damn charm that sprang generously from his Irish genes and that he had carefully groomed into a highly individu-alized charisma. When Lark met him he was thirty-five and already as much his own creation as the blown-glass sculptures he'd long believed would make him famous.

Ethan was an Artist—an artist with a capital *A*. And if there was any one thing that irritated Meg most about Ethan, it was the arrogant self-absorption of that temperament. The other thing, the overly obvi-ous sexual electricity that Ethan gave off, bothered Meg less over time. The constant undercurrent of Ethan's masculinity eventually faded into so much background noise.

Slowly and with obvious determination, Ethan won Meg over. Two years after Lark and Ethan first met, he obtained a divorce from his first wife. The compli-cations Ethan had tried to explain to Meg in Bennington were very real: Ethan's ex, Mimi, was an alcoholic with a young daughter Ethan had adopted. The courts ruled that the girl was to stay with her mother. According to Lark, Ethan was torn about leaving Lucinda, a difficult seven-year-old at the time of the divorce, in the hands of her unstable mother. But Meg's concerns were for Lark, so when the divorce came through, she paid little attention to Lark and Ethan's long discussions about how to get cus-tody of Lucinda.

That sort of talk died down soon enough when Lark found out that she was pregnant herself. The marriage ceremony was quickly moved up three months. They'd hoped to hold it outdoors in June at the farm they'd just bought in the small upstate New York town of Red River, but opted instead for a chilly indoor affair at Red River's First Congregational Church. Meg remembered being impressed by how many people attended—how many friends Ethan and Lark had already made in a town they'd so recently adopted.

At that point Meg could count on one hand the people she considered her real friends in Manhattan. She may have wanted a wider social life, but she just didn't have time for it. The same year Ethan and Lark married, Meg was promoted to account supervisor—the youngest woman to receive that title in the history of the agency. It was an honor that brought with it fourteen-hour workdays and almost weekly trips to Chicago.

Meg was somewhere over Illinois heading to the Windy City the morning Lark gave birth to her first daughter. The parents named her Brook Megan McGowan in honor, they told Meg, of the two people who meant the most to them in the world: Ethan's mother and Lark's sister. With Brook's birth, one of the last layers of concern Meg felt about Ethan melted away. Now it was not so much a question of Meg allowing Ethan into her life as Ethan welcoming her into his and Lark's growing family. And he did, with open arms.

It probably didn't help Meg's love life that she spent every other weekend in Red River. But Brook's birth was followed two years later by Phoebe's, and Meg took such pleasure in her towheaded, laughter-prone nieces that she had a hard time staying away. Actually, Meg herself didn't do much to help her love life. She was certainly pretty enough, and many men told her she was beautiful. They took one look at the soft, honey-colored blond hair; the reflective green-and-gold-flecked eyes; the slim, well-cared-for body; and mistook Meg Hardwick for someone who needed their protection. It never took long for the steel resolve, the take-no-prisoners ambition shimmering just beneath her surface loveliness to shine through.

"May I get a word in edgewise here?" The magazine sales representative (a dead ringer for Richard Gere) had asked her on their second date. "You know, I've had a day, too."

Well, that was always the problem—Meg had little interest in sharing. She wanted to be admired, desired, and then pretty much left alone. For the first five or six years of her sister's marriage Meg went through men faster than she did pantyhose. After one or two dates, she'd simply lose interest and find a way of disposing of the relationship. She was never less than kind, and often stayed friends with her growing cadre of former boyfriends; it was just that her heart never seemed to be in it. Sometimes she felt that most of her emotional life resided at her younger sister's upstate household, and she didn't really have enough left over for her time in New York City.

Meg founded her agency the year Phoebe was born. With her small savings, the profit-sharing proceeds from Y&R, and a carefully monitored line of credit from the bank, she opened up a one-room, two-person agency with one fashion account—a disgruntled ex–Y&R client who'd always liked her chutzpah. For the next year or two, so much of her energy was taken up with getting Hardwick and Associates off the ground that she barely realized how solitary her life had become, though she never felt lonely. With the exception of Lark and a few close friends, she had no one with whom to share her life, and her growing success. Before Fern was born, it didn't matter. And then, for reasons Meg couldn't rationally explain, even to herself, it suddenly did.

Lark and Ethan's third daughter was born six years after Phoebe and, while not a mistake, she was certainly a surprise.

"Meggie, I'm pregnant again. Can you believe it?" Lark had confided one weekend when Meg was visiting. One long look at her glowing younger sister made Meg wonder why she hadn't noticed Lark's condition herself. Lark never looked lovelier than when she was pregnant.

"I'm so happy for you!" she had cried, hugging Lark to her. But her joy was weighted with a sadness that she couldn't immediately identify. "Is Ethan thrilled?"

"Oh, of course," Lark told her. "He's sure it's going to be a boy. But I know we're going to have another girl. . . . I can always tell."

During Lark's pregnancy with Fern, Meg felt her depression deepening, and finally faced up to what was really bothering her: This time, experiencing a birth and having a child through Lark was not enough for Meg. She wanted a baby—no, more—a good man and a family of her own. Typically, as soon as she identified a problem, she started to search for a solution. And, as usual, she welcomed her younger sister into the process. With Lark's eager advice, Meg began to look around for an established, successful alpha male with whom to build a long-term relationship and, she hoped, a family. What she discovered, as had the multitude of single thirty-something women before her, was that once one seriously started to hunt for a man, the older, marriageable ones had pretty much become an endangered species.

There was the magazine senior editor who looked like Clint Eastwood, but who had the emotional maturity of Pee Wee Herman.

There was the television producer who, though recently divorced, spent most of his evenings with Meg talking longingly about his ex-wife and two kids.

And there was the sportscaster who advertised himself as single and available but who was not only married, Meg discovered, but appeared to have a girlfriend in every Major League city in the country.

"Ears as big as what?" Lark asked when Meg replayed for her yet another disastrous evening—this time a blind date, the cousin of a client who had been billed as "adorable."

"Saucers. And not espresso either."

"Doesn't that supposedly indicate that something else is big as well?"

"No, baby, I think that's the hands. Or feet. In any case, believe me, it was not worth sticking around to find out."

And then Meg met Paul Stokes, and her long losing streak seemed to have finally come to an end.

"I know I always say this, but he sounds perfect for you," Lark told her during one of their almost daily phone conversations. Ethan made fun of them for talking so much—"like teenagers, for chrissakes." Lark, like every other happily married woman Meg knew, kept pushing her sister toward conjugal commitment, but she was as choosy about the potential mate as Meg was. "'Lawyer. Millionaire. Philanthropist. *Divorced'*—I like that last attribute the best," Lark had said, reading from the *Wall Street Journal* profile on Paul that Meg had somewhat proudly sent her.

Yes, things were going very well until Paul invited her to the annual corporate dinner of Straithorne, Riddick, and Cowles, the firm at which he was a managing partner. Black tie at one of New York's top restaurants. She'd been treated with bland courtesy by the men who small-talked her about the fashion industry and with almost rude curiosity by the women, almost all of them full-time wives, wanting to know where to find Donna Karan wholesale. But then, over coffee and cigars (Meg was tempted to ask for one as a joke because the whole evening seemed so humorless), the talk veered suddenly to police brutality and Meg heard Paul say something about "the liberal press stirring up trouble yet again."

Nobody seemed to find the comment offensive. Not the woman next to her who smiled sweetly at Meg and asked her how much she'd paid for the lavender strapless Scaasi she was wearing. Nor any of the men who nodded sagely into their tobacco smoke and pointedly ignored Meg's angry retort.

"The fact is they shot a totally innocent young man who, not coincidentally, happened to be black!"

"Meg, I forgot to tell you—no liberal flag-waving at Partners' Dinners," Paul had told her with an apologetic laugh and a "When will they ever learn?" shrug to his colleagues. In the taxi afterward, it had taken exactly ten seconds for her to tell Paul what a bigoted ass he was and for him to tell her what a loud-mouthed, bleeding-heart cunt she was. She asked to be let out at the nearest corner—Madison and Fifty-ninth. She was so angry that she walked all the way up to her co-op at Eighty-sixth and Riverside in her three-inch black velour Susan Bennis heels. The next morning, her toes were in tatters, but her heart was intact.

She was not exactly in a party frame of mind the following night for the opening of Ethan's exhibition at the Hannah Judson Gallery in Chelsea. Ethan was pumped up with excitement about his first Manhattan showing and, Meg decided, would probably have enough enthusiasm for everyone. It didn't help her mood that she had promised Lark she would be bringing Paul Stokes with her to the event. She wasn't sorry that she'd kissed the son of a bitch good-bye, but at the same time she wasn't looking forward to disappointing Lark again.

Deciding that all she really needed to do was put in a quick appearance, she worked until past seven o'clock and took a taxi downtown from the office. When she arrived at the Hannah Judson gallery at Eighteenth Street and Twelfth Avenue that evening she was still mentally rehearsing just how she was going to explain things to her sister. She knew that she'd built Paul Stokes up in Lark's mind, as she had in her own. That she'd been so wrong about him revealed a serious flaw in her judgment, as well as an all-too-obvious eagerness to, *this* time, make a relationship work. She had always enjoyed her role as the older, wiser sister, the dispenser of advice, the woman of the world. Now, Meg worried that Lark was starting to guess how fragile her ego could be when it came to men. Worse, she dreaded the thought that her younger sister might actually start to pity her.

She wasn't thinking about Ethan at all.

4

At first she actually didn't recognize the man, dressed all in black, with the thick gray-streaked blond hair and Hollywood-style stubble of beard. He stood on the far side of the dimly lit and now nearly empty gallery, holding an Ethan McGowan original white-wine glass in his right hand. His left arm moved abruptly from the waist of the tall, platinum-haired woman standing next to him and he waved eagerly to someone. To her. What had she been thinking? It was Ethan, of course. She threaded her way toward them through the forest of black aluminum pedestals displaying Ethan's primary-colored contortions of blown glass.

"I was afraid you wouldn't make it." When Ethan kissed her on the forehead as he always did, she realized why he looked so different. He wasn't wearing his round, rimless Lennon-style eyeglasses, without which

he was basically blind. Obviously he'd switched to contacts at the same time he'd shaved his thick beard to get
the younger-looking sandpaper affair he sported. Well,
he definitely looked hipper if that was what he wanted.
Meg was tempted to laugh and call him on this obvious
bit of vanity. But this show of his "art pieces," as he
proudly called them, meant so damned much to him.
Despite her irritation—after all, it was ridiculous for
such an already good-looking man to preen—she kept
her mouth shut.

"Sorry. It's been one of those days. I was lucky to—"
She'd been glancing around the two-room gallery.
There were less than a dozen people left. "Where's
Lark? And the girls?"

"Fern's sick again. Lark decided they should all stay
home."

"Damn," Meg said, thinking first of herself. She'd been
looking forward to having Brook and Phoebe stay with
her. Ethan, Lark, and the baby Fern were to stay at the
Windsor. They rarely came down to the city from Red
River because of Lark's feelings about the pollution and
noise in Manhattan. But whenever Meg was able to get
the two older girls to herself, they had an hilarious free-
for-all. Meg delighted in indulging them with the Big
Macs and Disney videos they were forbidden at home.

"But Fern's okay?" Meg added.

"Of course. You know Lark." Ethan smiled and
shrugged. Yes, they both knew Lark. The original
mother hen. Squawking with alarm at the least sign of
danger to her chicks. Especially the youngest. Meg
returned Ethan's conspiratorial smile, thinking that
he'd been right about the beard. He had a good strong
jaw line and chin.

"Hannah, this is my sister-in-law, Meg Hardwick." Ethan took a step back so that Meg now faced the woman whose waist Ethan had been holding when Meg first arrived.

The woman's appearance gave her pause. Although Meg knew she herself was considered beautiful, she also knew that a lot of her allure was the result of hard work, an excellent fashion sense, and utter self-confidence. She started with what God had given her—a rather typical, fair-haired American prettiness—and augmented it with every trick known to woman. It took a good two hours every other week for Manuel to maintain her hair's deceptively casual, honey-colored look. A daily forty-minute work-out had become a form of religion. And so accustomed was she to seeing herself in full-court makeup, that she was often surprised to notice how wan and insignificant she looked in the mornings when her face was bare.

Hannah, on the other hand, though easily ten years Meg's senior, was to the real thing. She was innately, hauntingly beautiful, with almond-shaped eyes and high, rounded cheekbones. Her hair, a shock of silver cut short against her skull, emphasized the expressiveness of her brows and the extraordinary sea green of her irises. Her long, athletic body was tailored in a severely cut black wool suit, the top two buttons left open to offer glimpses of the delicate apricot-colored lace of her camisole. If there was one flaw, it was her mouth. Her lips were thin and flat, and she did nothing to disguise the fact.

"Ah, yes ... The beautiful Hardwick sisters," Hannah's handshake was strong to the point of pain, her voice plummy with lockjaw snobbishness: *Haaaawdwick.*

"You make us sound like a song-and-dance team," Meg said, laughing.

"Well from what Ethan tells me you two *could* do just about anything. I've heard of your agency. Philip Jonas is a dear friend of mine."

Meg's biggest and most demanding account was Jonas Sportswear. *You're not really dressed unless you're in a Jonas.* She'd met the multimillionaire chairman Philip Jonas only twice in the five years she'd handled the account, and both times he'd been dismissive to the point of being rude.

"Brilliant mind," Meg said, her standard comment for people impossible to work with.

"Oh, Jonas is full of crap. But he does know how to pick talent. He has some wonderful designers. And I think your work is just extraordinary."

"Why, thanks." Meg responded well to flattery, even when she felt—as in this case—that it was condescending and possibly insincere. She noticed that the gallery was empty now except for the wait staff, who were starting to clean up. "I'm sorry I ended up being so late," Meg apologized, though it occurred to her that perhaps the crowd had left a little early.

"How did the opening go?" she asked, turning to Ethan. The contacts gave his eyes a startling blueness.

"Great. At least, that's what Hannah was telling me when you came in. I sold only two pieces."

"Sales are not the point," Hannah said. "Notice is. And just about everyone of value was here. The *Times.* The *Voice. Paper.* By representing you, I've told them you're important. Someone to watch. Even if they don't understand your work—even if they don't particularly like it—they'll have to *notice* it.

And once your name's in the right kind of print, sales follow. Cause and effect. Not to worry, darling."

"I'm not worried, Hannah, believe me. This has been the most amazing night of my life. I suppose I should attempt to be more sophisticated and urbane about it, but screw that. Just to see them all out there, finally . . ."

Ah, his sculptures. They were crafted from blown glass in what seemed to Meg an endless and arduous process of turning and firing, cooling and shaping. Ethan made his living selling the table glasses and paperweights that he and his assistants Clint and Janine Lindbergh turned out every morning in the Red River studio. But his heart and soul went into the sculptures—free-form masses of swirling glass that he worked on every afternoon. He'd been at it for more than a decade now, honing his style, perfecting techniques, mastering the problems of pigmentation and balance. Meg was vaguely aware that over the past three years Ethan felt he'd made some kind of breakthrough. That the pieces he turned out were—as far as the process would allow—everything he wanted them to be.

Once, years ago, when Ethan had first got the studio up and running, Meg endured one of his ardent dissertations on glassblowing—how it all begins with the biscuit-shaped piece of colorless crystal, called a gob, which is flamed and transferred to the blowing rod, or pontil, and then placed in one of the gas-fired furnaces and periodically removed to be turned, tempered, blown, and shaped. What happened next depended on what was being made—water tumblers, paperweights, wineglasses, or (and of course this was what Ethan really cared about) a section of one of Ethan's flamework sculptures.

"Glass is totally unforgiving and limiting," Ethan had explained. "One mistake—one crack or fissure—and days of planning and work can go down the drain. But that's what makes it exciting as well. The limits. The demands. I mean, you can do any fucking thing you want with oil or acrylic, stone, wood. But glass—it's molten, mercurial, dangerous."

Meg would never admit this to another soul, but she thought Ethan's sculptures were hideous. If anything, they reminded her of those long, thin, colored balloons, twisted into shapes that were supposed to resemble schnauzers or giraffes, that were handed out at county fairs and children's parties. Except that Ethan's pieces were larger, grosser, and made of glass. That anyone would actually want to display them—let alone buy one—was beyond Meg's comprehension. But then so was the work of Basquiat and Clemente, not to mention practically the whole school of abstract expressionism. Meg knew she was no judge of modern art—she could only assume that Ethan's work fell roughly into that category—so she'd learned long ago to keep her unvarnished opinions to herself.

Ethan had walked over to one of his pieces—a towering mass of oranges and reds that looked to Meg vaguely like a giant torch.

"That's one of the ones he sold," Hannah told her.

"Who bought it?" Meg asked.

Something in her voice must have revealed how she felt about Ethan's work because Hannah replied, "A collector. A very prescient one. Ethan has a real future in front of him. I hope you all recognize his potential. I'd hate to think of him turning out wineglasses for the rest of his life."

"Of course, we all support Ethan," Meg replied, insulted. She thought of the various odd jobs Lark had taken on so that Ethan could devote half his day to his damned "art." Lark put up her own preserves and baked organic breads and muffins, which she sold through a local farmers' market. She worked several afternoons a week as a masseuse in the Whole Life Healing Center in nearby Montville. For years she'd been writing and illustrating children's books. None of them was ever picked up by a publisher, but Lark had a local printer run off three of her stories, which she sold at the general store in Red River. The way Meg saw it, Ethan was not so much supported as indulged.

Over dinner, Meg began to see Ethan from a slightly different perspective. Later, when she tried to reconstruct how everything had happened, she realized that she had probably been looking at Ethan through Hannah's eyes that night. They'd walked to a restaurant three blocks from the gallery—a small French bistro, run by a gay couple who were on a first-name basis with Hannah.

"So, dear heart—how did it go?" one of the owners asked as Hannah as Megan and Ethan followed her into the restaurant.

"Henri, you remember Ethan?"

"Of course. Our man of the hour. How did it *go*?"

"I sold two pieces," Ethan said.

"Lovely. But I meant the hors d'oeuvres, dear." Ethan's face fell. "David spent all morning on those tiny olive tarts."

"They were unbelievable—disappeared in a flash. Henri and David cater all my openings," Hannah explained as she slid into the banquette beside Ethan.

Meg faced them across the candlelit table. Between them on the white paper tablecloth sat a glass of crayons for doodling and a latte cup spilling over with tea roses. Ella sang somewhere nearby with loving regret. *You're going to turn me down and say can't we be friends. . . .*

"I went to the Biennial after all," Ethan told Hannah, referring to the Whitney Museum's showcase for emerging artists, which was held on odd-numbered years. "And it didn't much matter. I looked at the stuff, and thought I must be living on a different planet."

"But in a way you are," Hannah replied, sipping wine that one of the owners had poured without being asked. "Your influences are totally different. So much of what you see at the Whitney is from the urban-angst school."

"It all just seems so—dead. Self-referential."

"Well, of course. But you're a romantic. Unlimited horizons. Nature's wild child. It's very fresh."

Ethan looked down at his glass and his hair, Meg noticed, fell across his forehead, glinting in the soft light.

"Please. No puffery. Save that stuff for your critic friends and clients."

"I'm not flattering you, Ethan. I'm helping you define yourself. You've been out in the damned woods for twelve years now. It's important for you to understand your context."

"Why? As you said yourself I don't really *have* a place in the art world that the Biennial defines. Do you know who my two biggest influences are? Auguste Rodin and Louis Comfort Tiffany. Now if I could somehow combine the power and genius of Rodin's sculpture with Tiffany's mastery of glass—well . . ."

"Personally—and I beg you not to jump down my throat because this sounds vaguely like a compliment—I think that's what you're doing."

"Please, Hannah." Ethan, laughing and shaking his head, held up both hands in a mock attempt to ward her off. "That sort of thing goes straight to my head. I'm really better off working alone in the wilderness and feeling unappreciated."

"Somehow," Hannah replied, signaling Henri that they were ready to order, "I doubt that."

Ethan's and Hannah's conversation continued over an excellent dinner of artichokes vinaigrette and poule grille, but Meg didn't bother to follow the actual words. She was listening instead to its deeper, surprising context—Ethan was being taken seriously as an artist by the owner of one of the leading galleries in Manhattan. *Lark's* Ethan, *her* Ethan. She was impressed and more than a little ashamed of herself for not having believed in him until now. She'd always assumed his work was amateurish, something akin to a hobby. She'd even dismissed the Judson Gallery opening as a fluke. In fact, she'd been worried that at the opening they would all have to watch in embarrassment as Ethan was humiliated by a mocking Manhattan art establishment. This was obviously far from the case.

"Luigi wants to meet you." Meg caught Hannah's lowered reverential tone.

"Not . . . from the SoHo Guggenheim?"

"Just to meet," Hannah replied, leaning forward to spoon the lemon peel out of her espresso. She tapped it off on the rim of the tiny white saucer. "Perhaps over dinner sometime. I might put something together at my place in a week or two. But I make no promises."

"Hannah . . . I'm so grateful."

"Understand something, Ethan. This is not just about you anymore. It's also about me. My eye. My judgment. Ultimately, my reputation and the success of my gallery. I do absolutely nothing out of the kindness of my heart."

Though Meg was tired and tried to beg off, after dinner Ethan insisted that they all go to a jazz club in Tribeca he'd heard about.

"You've got to help me celebrate," he'd urged Meg when Hannah had gone to the ladies' room. "I need you here—I just can't process this kind of happiness on my own."

And celebrate they did. Ethan ordered a bottle of champagne as soon as they arrived at the black-painted basement that constituted Voulez Vous. Two dozen beat-up looking tables were scattered around a small room that stank of dead cigarettes. A raised wooden platform against a far wall promised a small combo band; a bass leaned against the keyboard of an upright piano. But they were the first to arrive and Meg could feel Ethan's disappointment that the evening had come to a sudden standstill. Though ordinarily she would have refused champagne at ten o'clock at night, she'd caught some of Ethan's ebullient mood. Hannah obviously had as well because, though the champagne was terrible, they made it through the bottle by the time the band started to play.

The small combo played old standards riffled through and reshuffled like a deck of well-thumbed cards: "Autumn Leaves," "Stardust," "Night and Day." Another bottle of champagne materialized in Ethan's hands. He couldn't hear Meg saying "no more" over the music. He refilled her glass. And filled it again. The band was surprisingly good. At some point, Meg realized that she must be slightly drunk because the champagne had started to taste better. She found herself smoking a cigarette. She looked across the table and saw that Hannah and Ethan were gone. No, they were dancing. Her arms were around his neck, and he was whispering something in her ear. He took a small step back and looked at Hannah in the slightly mocking way Meg knew so well. She couldn't see Hannah's face, but she could hear her strange, carrying laughter.

They're writing songs of love, but not for me. . . .
The Gershwin lyrics seemed to have been written especially for Meg, but what had she done to deserve them? Why had Lark been so lucky—the first time out—when it came to finding the right man, and Meg had failed more times than she cared to count? Feeling very tired and sorry for herself, she watched groggily as Ethan guided Hannah around the now crowded little dance area. It seemed to her that they were holding each other much too

close, Hannah's lithe body a smooth fit against Ethan's large, powerful frame. At one point she thought, but couldn't be sure, that she saw Ethan kiss Hannah on the forehead. She told herself that this was something he did to his daughters and to Meg herself all the time. It was a gesture of pure, impulsive affection that certainly didn't mean much of anything. And yet, Meg's last conscious feeling was one of floating unease.

"Hey, there, baby," someone was rubbing her shoulder and smoothing back her hair. "Time to go home." Oh, Lord! Meg sat up abruptly—she'd fallen asleep, her arms cradling her head on the tabletop.

"Ethan . . . I . . . must have . . . What time is it?"

"Two A.M. You're a regular party girl."

"What did I do?" The room had cleared out.

"Honestly?" Ethan sat down next to her. "Are you sure you want to hear?"

"I'm not used to drinking so late. . . ."

"That you made pretty obvious."

"Tell me—what happened?"

Ethan laughed, leaned back, and ran his hands through his hair. "You snored."

"Oh . . ." When she turned her head to look around, the room spun at a sickening angle. "Where's Hannah?"

"I put her in a cab. They're closing up here. Let's get you home."

She nodded off again in the taxi, her head bobbing against Ethan's shoulder until he finally put his arm around her to steady her, and she slept in the crook of his arm.

"Home again, jiggedy, jig." A door opened and light spilled into the cab. "Let's go, bright eyes."

Her head cleared a bit in the elevator, which was a pity because she could a painful drumming was starting to build behind her eyes. The overhead lights in the hallway were trying to pierce her cranium.

"Should I help you with the keys?"

"I'm not entirely incapacitated," Meg said as she fumbled with the lock. Her apartment door swung open.

"Will you be okay?"

"I'll be fine. I'm sorry if I made a fool of myself in front of Hannah—I was just trying . . ."

"Meg . . ." His right hand touched her chin. She looked up at him.

"I think I'd better come in," he said.

Why does it happen? How does it start? What force—fierce, gravitational, blind—draws one body to another? There was certainly no thought involved. She didn't turn on the light. The door closed behind them. She leaned against it. He stepped toward her. His body pressed against hers. His lips were in her hair. He was kissing her.

"Ethan." She stepped back abruptly. "What's going on?"

"You know." He moved toward her again.

"Please . . . I think you'd better go."

"Meg, come on," Ethan said, his arms sliding back around her waist. He had an erection; she could feel it against her hip. "You know it's what we've always wanted."

"Jesus, Ethan! Don't be ridiculous!" She pushed him away. He leaned against the wall, facing her in the dark.

"I'm not afraid to say it, Meg. I've wanted you from the moment I saw you."

"*Wanted* me? What the *hell* does that mean?"

Ethan stepped forward and pulled her to him with such force that her head snapped back. She struggled against his grip, but it was as if she had lost her footing. She couldn't breathe.

"No!" She wrenched herself away and stumbled down the hall. As she turned on the living-room light she realized her hands were shaking. She stood swaying in the middle of the room, her arms cradling her elbows. She heard him come up behind her. She could feel his breath in her hair.

"I want you to go now," she said. "We'll forget this ever happened."

"We'll never forget. And it's not over."

"Yes, it most definitely is."

"I'm not sure we have that kind of say in the matter."

5

"Ethan said he wasn't there."

The voice on the phone woke Meg up abruptly. For a disoriented moment she thought Lark was telling her Ethan had denied being at Meg's the night before.

"Who?" Meg raised up on one elbow, then slid back down, cradling the phone against her ear and chin. Her mouth was so dry she could hardly speak. And when she moved, she felt a listing nausea. She'd fallen asleep on her living-room couch and now the morning sun shone full-force into the room. She closed her eyes.

"What's the matter with you? Paul Stokes, that's who. I asked Ethan for a full report when he got back this morning, and he told me he wasn't even there."

"Paul . . . Oh, yes. No. I was going to explain, but . . . How's Fern? Is everything okay?"

"I could ask the same about you. What the hell happened last night? Ethan has been uncharacteristically closemouthed about everything. He's in bed asleep now, so I thought I'd see if I could get anything out of you."

"The show was a big success," Meg tried to keep very still and concentrate on forming simple sentences.

"Well that, of course, I did get to hear about. Tell me about Hannah. Is she as brilliant and beautiful as Ethan says?"

"Is that what Ethan said?"

"Also cold and calculating and thoroughly ambitious."

"Yes, all those things. Very chic and cool in a downtown kind of way. But no spring chicken."

"And speaking of which, older sister—just what the hell happened to Mr. Stokes?"

"He went sour. Very fast I'm afraid."

"Permanently?"

"I'd say so. He called me a cunt."

"Oh, then he's a dead man for sure."

Lark talked on about Fern, who was much improved but still congested . . . about Brook who was asking if she could start shaving her legs, though Lark could see no discernible signs of body hair . . . about the ever troubled and troubling Lucinda, a constant source of worry for Lark . . . about the long Columbus Day weekend coming up and what Lark had planned for them all. It seemed to Meg that Lark would go on forever while she slowly died on her own couch of a combination of dehydration and an all-encompassing sense of guilt and shame.

But what had she done? It was Ethan's fault. What

had he been thinking? He must have had too much drink—they both had—and she was so out of it herself she didn't notice until it was too late. She hadn't seen Ethan really loaded before, though she knew from experience that men could turn into total Neanderthals when under the influence. Ethan's musky aroma clung to the blouse she still wore from the night before. As Lark chatted on, Meg thought about how he'd pressed his penis against her, as though it were some prize he was offering. She felt sick to her stomach. She strained to concentrate on what Lark was saying.

"You know Rita Davenport? She has that place between Huntington and here? She's a weekender, an editor at Untenmeyer. Anyway, she took my new manuscript and drawings in to a friend of hers in their children's division. A Marcia Rubenstein—I have her name and number written down right here."

"But you probably should let her call you," Meg advised.

"She did. Left a message yesterday afternoon when I was at the clinic with Fern. I didn't even check the machine until late, though, because the girls were so crabby when we got back."

"And? The message?" It was so typical of Lark to circumvent a subject, digress in half a dozen directions before finally getting to the point. Meg, whose daily existence was all snap decisions, focus, deadlines, often found herself leading Lark back to the subject at hand.

"Marcia said in her message that she thought I had a very unique style—lovely and kind of magical."

"And she wants you to call her? That's a good sign."

"Actually, what she wants is . . . well, Untenmeyer wants to publish *Wally of Wall Street*."

"Lark, that's wonderful! Untenmeyer is one of the biggest publishers in the country. This is incredible. You must be thrilled. What did Ethan say?"

"I haven't actually had a chance to tell him yet. He was so tired when he got back. And I didn't want to steal his thunder after the show."

Meg glanced at her watch. It was nine-fifteen. Meg thought of what Ethan had been doing while his wife waited up at home with her happy news. She could imagine Lark's disappointment as Ethan begged off further conversation that morning and clomped up to bed. She could see Lark, sitting in the kitchen, watching the clock, wondering if it was too early to call Meg.

"I'm so proud of you," Meg said. "Two successful artists in one family."

"Yes . . . well, what I do is just . . ."

"Lovely and magical, I think she said."

"I guess I should call this Marcia person back. She gave me her home number and said to get back to her as soon as possible. But it's Saturday, so she probably doesn't want to be bothered. Maybe I'll just call her office and see if I can get her voice mail."

"Lark—she gave you her home number for a reason. Call her. Go on. Right now, before the kids are up and running around screaming. Do it. And call me back later and tell me what she says."

Meg was in the shower when she heard the phone ring again, but she decided to let it go. She would call Lark back after she dressed and made herself some coffee. She took her time, trying not to think about what happened the night before. She worked on keeping herself in the moment, focusing on the physical details around her.

Early autumn sun flooded her closet-size kitchen. She had a sliver of a view of the Hudson and the Palisades, a long shoulder of bright green, beyond. The sky was a brilliant blue with the kind of clouds that reminded Meg of the billowing sails of old schooners. If only she could put last night in such a ship and let it drift away. Finally she decided she could face hearing Lark's voice again. She played back the message left earlier. It wasn't her sister.

"Listen, I'm sorry. I—Meg—I don't know what to say exactly. I'm calling you from the general store. I slipped out of the house. Couldn't sleep. I can't stop thinking about you. I just want you to know. I tried for so long to keep this from happening. Then last night—oh, baby—what am I going to do? Damn—" his voice dropped to a whisper. "Someone wants to use the phone. I'd better go. I'll—what can I say?— I'll be in touch."

The teapot was whistling by the time the message ended, then it escalated into a piercing scream. Meg turned it off and was pouring water into the Melitta filter when the phone rang again, jarring her. She upset the cone, scattering grinds into all four gas burners.

"Meg? Are you there?"

"Yes . . . yes, hold on . . ." she said to the machine. "Hello?"

"Since when are you screening your calls?" Lark asked.

"I'm not," she lied. "I spilled coffee all over the damned stove."

"I just got off the phone with Marcia Rubenstein—she was *so* excited about the book, I could hardly believe it. She was going on about getting me an agent, contracts, multibook deals . . ."

"That's wonderful."

"She seems to think I have a special talent—'that certain magical touch' she called it—that children really respond to. And she discovered Isa Polidor—you know, the author of the Little Laurie books?"

"That's just wonderful."

"And those sell by the thousands, no millions. Marcia was saying that Isa and his wife just bought an island off Nova Scotia on his Little Laurie earnings. If you make it, I guess it can mean those kind of bucks—not that I'm expecting anything like that."

"But it's just great, really."

"She wants me to come down to the city this Wednesday to meet with her and the editorial director. Me—coming down for a meeting at Untenmeyer! Lord, what will I wear?"

"You can borrow something of mine."

"No, Ethan said I should buy something new."

"So you told him? He knows?"

"Yes. He's sitting here in the kitchen with me. Beaming like what—a proud husband, right?"

Meg heard his voice in the background, and then Lark started to laugh.

"Ethan says I look like a cat licking cream off my whiskers. Oh, Meggie—I'm just so happy. Somebody better make sure I'm attached to the ground."

6

Wednesday was generally one of the busiest days at Hardwick and Associates. Most print ads closed on Thursday, and there was always a last-minute flurry of type changes and color correction. At midweek, clients were wondering where media schedules stood, when they would see the next round of layouts, how much they'd spent on broadcast in the last six months. The phone rang incessantly. There was a waiting line at the fax machine. Messengers clogged the reception area, their Walkmans blaring.

"Hardwick and Associates, could you hold please?"

Meg, calling from her cell phone in the back of a taxi, imagined the chaos at the front desk as Oliver fielded the various crises and calls.

"Yes? May I help you?"

"It's me."

"She lives, thank God. People have been asking. Hold a sec."

The semimonthly marketing meeting at Eden Lingerie had run three times its typical hour. The launch for their new high-end evening pantyhose—shimmering shades of spandex silver and black—wasn't doing as well as they'd hoped. They talked of discounting inventory. Pulling the ads. Revamping the campaign. Goosing the publicity. Cooking up a last-minute in-store promotion. And then, after considering every possible option, they decided on what Meg had known they would do in the first place: nothing.

"We'll wait and see," Hilary Unger, the sales director, said at eleven-forty-five. "With all the holiday traffic over the next month or so, we'll get a better idea of where we really stand. Thanks for coming, Meg. Your input is terrific." Meg's role was essentially that of a therapist. She listened. Nodded from time to time. Pointed out that they'd already committed to a plan of action. Advised caution. Charged money.

"You have about ninety-two messages," Oliver said. "I'll give you the top ten for now." He read off the names as Meg punched them into her laptop. "And your sister called. She can't make lunch because her editor's taking her out. *Editor?*"

Oliver prided himself on knowing Meg's business—both professional and otherwise—as well as she did herself. A former Broadway chorus dancer who used to temp between shows, Oliver had been hired from an employment agency when Meg had first started her business and found that her one assistant was too busy taking phone calls to actually assist her. His career as a dancer had languished as Hardwick and Associates had flourished. The intervals between shows grew each year as Oliver's time and importance at Hardwick expanded. When he'd pulled his Achilles tendon two years ago during a summer stock performance in the Berkshires, Meg offered him a full-time job as the office manager–receptionist with benefits until he recovered. She allowed him the fiction that someday he would return in glory to the stage, that his work at Hardwick was just another temporary stint. In the meantime, he ran the agency and her affairs with skill, grace, and élan—head erect, shoulders back, literally on his toes.

"She sold her new book to Untenmeyer."

"That's wonderful! She sounded totally breathless on the phone, no wonder. And Ethan called shortly after her. He was at a pay phone. I told him you'd be back by twelve-thirty at the latest."

"Listen, if he calls again, tell him I'm swamped. I'll call them both tonight."

"Okay." Meg could hear the question in his voice.

"I've got to totally revamp the SportsTech creative. Jen and Spencer were way off on their stuff. And the meeting is what? In two weeks?"

"You know as well as I do. I'll get rid of Ethan for you if he phones back. But call Shirley right now—she sounded hysterical about getting into January *Vogue*."

Meg made her calls from the backseat as the taxi inched through midday midtown traffic. By the time she reached Fortieth and Sixth, where Hardwick had its offices, she'd connected with almost everyone she'd needed to reach. She was paying the fare, opening the door, and gathering her briefcase and shoulder bag when a hand reached in to help her out.

"Hey."

"Eth—" Her first reaction was one of revulsion. There he stood, hair flowing in the breeze, dressed in jeans and his worn leather bomber jacket as if he had nothing to be sorry about. Let along beg her forgiveness. He'd been drunk and behaved outrageously to her and then left that insinuating message on her machine. Though it had been nearly a week since his opening, he had done nothing to repair the damage he'd inflicted. Her second response was anger. How dare he show up at her agency without any warning— as though he actually thought she would want to see him there!

"Let me take that for you." He held out his hand for her briefcase.

"I'm fine on my own, thanks," she said, taking her change from the driver, and then stepping quickly out of the cab. She was astounded that he seemed so self-contained and unrepentant.

"Meg. We've got to talk." It was impossible to read the expression behind the sunglasses he wore.

"No," she replied firmly, pulling the strap of the bag up over her shoulder and stepping toward the building entrance. "Not another word until you apologize."

"Okay," Ethan threw up his hands dramatically and then fell to his knees on the pavement in front of her. The lunch-hour crowd streamed around them, and Meg heard one or two people start to laugh. "I'm sorry. I'm sorry. I'm sorry," Ethan said, looking up at her through the concealing lenses.

"Get up this instant," Meg said. "When did you start acting like an utter ass?"

"You have a bad effect on me," Ethan replied, as he slowly got back on his feet. "I really am sorry, Meg, and I did come to make amends. But the moment I saw you, I just—"

"Please, don't," Meg cut him off when she heard the note of pleading enter his voice. "You've made your apology. I'm very busy right now, and I really don't appreciate you showing up here like this."

"Like what?" he asked, folding his arms across his chest.

"Like alone. Without Lark and the girls. I won't have it."

"You won't, huh? And you are who? Goddess of the whole damn universe?" Ethan ran his hands through his hair with barely suppressed anger. "Listen, I'm sorry. I didn't mean that. I'm just . . . Meg, I'm going a little crazy here. Can't you understand? Please, can't we just sit someplace and talk quietly for a few minutes?"

The pleading was gone, replaced by what Meg heard as real pain and regret. They shared a long history together, Meg told herself, no matter how troubled and confusing the present seemed. If this had just been about Ethan, Meg might have sent him on his way. But Lark and the girls, no matter how unfairly, stood to be hurt by Ethan's bizarre behavior. They went across the street and into Bryant Park. Meg sat down on a bench facing the manicured lawn. Ethan sat beside her, looking down at his hands. Beside them on the lawn, people from nearby offices were eating sack lunches, reading paperbacks, dozing in the sun.

"I guess I really shocked you the other night, didn't I?" he said in a subdued voice.

"You know, I think it's better if we just put that whole episode behind us. You were drunk. I can understand that. Things can get out of control—"

"No, Meg. That wasn't it at all. Listen . . . I shouldn't have waited. I should have faced this years ago."

"What are you taking about?"

"Oh, don't give me that bullshit! You know exactly what I'm talking about." Meg had never heard such vehemence in his voice before; it frightened her.

"Ethan—"

"I've been in love with you for fourteen years. Don't tell me you didn't know—that you didn't feel the same."

Meg felt as though someone had punched her in the stomach, knocking the breath out of her. She stared at him. He couldn't be serious. "No. Absolutely not." she told him. "I don't know what made you think that. It's . . . it's just not true."

"Meg, please. It's okay to admit it." Ethan said, turning to her. He'd slipped off his glasses and Meg noticed that his usually clear blue eyes were threaded with red. "I've been thinking about this almost non-stop. What we have—what draws us together so powerfully—it's really out of our control. I've been trying to deny it for so many years. Then, the other, night— it just felt so right."

"Actually, Ethan, nothing ever felt more *wrong* to me in my entire life." Meg felt tainted just having to explain this to him.

"I don't believe you."

"Well, you'd better, damn it," Meg said, angry that

there was even a shadow of a doubt in his mind about how she felt.

"All these years, when you've been hanging around my family. All these years when you've been unable to find the right person ... Haven't you wondered why?" Ethan's tone was persuasively sincere. She found herself listening, though she knew she should already have gotten up and walked away.

"Don't you wonder why you never seem able to make a relationship work?" he continued slowly, sensing that he'd gotten her attention at last. "Why you pick men who are wrong for you—wired to backfire within a short time? I've been watching you play out these charades of love affairs for years. These so-called successful men—brokers, lawyers, bankers—whom you start out admiring, proceed to dominate, and end up despising. You've never been in love, Meg."

"How dare you—"

"You've never found a real partner. Someone who would stand up to you. Who refused to be controlled. Each time I see you repeat one of these ridiculous cycles, I become more convinced of what the problem is. You don't want to find the right person because, deep down, you know you already have."

"Oh, please—what self-serving—"

"Listen, to me, baby." His hand was at the back of her neck. He gathered a fistful of her hair. "This is about us. Not me. *Us.* It's real. I know you can feel it. We've got to work this out."

"Let go of me. Or I'll scream. I mean it." He released his grasp, and Meg moved away from him on the bench. "The only thing we have between us is you acting like a fool. And a bastard. Do you have any idea how deeply Lark would be hurt—she'd be just ripped apart—if she knew what you were saying to me right now."

"Of course, I know." Ethan looked up at her without remorse. "Why in the world do you think I've waited so long, why I've denied these feelings, tried to block them out? I know how badly Lark would feel—if she knew. But what about me, Meg? Do you have any idea what I'm going through this *minute*? The utter hell of it?"

"No, I don't understand," she replied, unable to feel anything but disgust. "And honestly, I don't want to. Somehow you've confused my caring about you as a brother—a brother-in-law—with something very different. And—believe me, Ethan—you're dead wrong. You've meant a great deal to me—as Lark's husband, as a great father to my nieces. I've admired your marriage. I love your daughters, you know that. I've felt lucky just being a part of your family. This . . . this fixation of yours, Ethan, it puts all of that in jeopardy. Everything we've shared. Please . . . let's not ever talk about it again."

Ethan said nothing and Meg gradually became aware again of the world around them: the grinding roar of traffic up Sixth Avenue, the distant wail of a fire engine, the rustle of sycamore leaves as the wind gusted east. When Ethan lifted his head to look at her, she saw tears in his eyes.

"Whatever you say," Ethan told her softly. "Whatever you think is right . . . But I've got to tell you that what you're asking—I just can't promise that I can do it. Don't you see, Meg? You've become a part of me. Like blood. Like breathing—"

"Ethan, I'm going now. I can't hear any more of this. You know what you have to do."

Juggling her briefcase and shoulder bag, she started to walk away, even though he kept talking, almost as much to himself as to Meg. "You've been my inspiration. My secret fire. You're asking me to put that out. . . ."

7

The Taconic Parkway in autumn was, to Meg's mind, one of the most beautiful highways in the country. Winding up through the Hudson Valley, with the blue-tinged Catskills to the west and the foothills of the Berkshires to the east, its graceful curves and long valleys retraced the path of glaciers. The Columbus Day weekend fell at the very peak of autumnal color, and the hills were a dazzling wash of oranges, reds, and golds ablaze against a thickening gray sky. It was unseasonably warm for that time of year, and the forecast promised a series of powerful thunderstorms. Meg had the passenger window halfway down, the wind whipping at her hair.

After the accident that killed her parents, Meg's confidence in her driving abilities was severely shaken. She learned to manage well enough when the weather was clear, but even now hated to be behind the wheel when the roads turned wet or icy. On inclement weekends, Meg often accepted Abe Sabin's standing invitation to ride upstate with him. A lawyer and longtime friend of Ethan's and Lark's, Abe commuted from the city every weekend to his sprawling contemporary home on a mountaintop overlooking Red River. It was there that Meg had first met Abe and his stunningly beautiful wife Becca, though it was back in New York that she had really gotten to know and respect him. When Meg was starting her business, Abe, who was going into practice on his own at about the same time, gave her free legal advice. Hardwick and Associates grew as Abe's firm also flourished, and Abe eventually became Meg's official legal counsel, guiding her with painstaking care and a well-honed cynicism over several rough business patches.

Over the course of the ten or so years that Meg had known Abe, they had made the trip together back and forth to Red River hundreds of times. Though Abe had long ago put an end to Meg's attempts to pay for gas, he did let her help replenish and recycle his extensive supply of tapes and audio books. The great thing about Abe, Meg had discovered, was that he seemed perfectly content driving the full two-and-a half-hour commute without saying a word. If however, she needed to talk, Abe listened and—in his overassured, court-appointed manner—dispensed advice. After the usual chitchat, Abe rarely initiated conversation himself and Meg sensed that he liked to use this time to unwind and mentally sort through his problems. In the past year those had included the bitter breakup of his five-year marriage to a woman who appeared to be so absolutely perfect that Meg and Lark referred to her as "Becca the Beautiful."

Meg knew that Becca weighed heavily on Abe's mind, even though he hardly ever talked about her these days, but she never pried. Lark, however, had confided to Meg that Becca had taken Abe "for everything he was worth" and that, though he had fought her each step of the way, she had recently received a very lucrative divorce settlement. Today, with Abe in a particularly quiet mood and Meg mired in her own concerns, they'd exchanged about a dozen words. Meg had bought a new Joshua Redman recording for the trip, and for the last half-hour she'd sat with her eyes closed listening to music that seemed to tap directly into the turmoil that had taken over her life.

Ethan. He hadn't followed through on his promise to forget her—not for a single day. In fact, Meg decided, he was now thoroughly out of control. For the past three weeks he had been calling her every night, late at night. Meg could tell from the sounds in the background that he often placed these calls from a noisy restaurant or bar. After the first two or three rambling conversations, Meg wouldn't pick up the phone. He just talked into her machine instead.

"I can't take this anymore," he would begin. "I have to see you. Today was utter hell. I could hardly work, thinking about you. Do you have any idea how beautiful you look when you're angry? That afternoon in Bryant Park your eyes were such an amazing green— I've been trying to reproduce that exact hue with my glass. Oh, God, Meg, it's the only thing keeping me sane. Am I sane? Perhaps, you're right, I am out of my mind. But it's you, baby, who've driven me there."

He stopped by the office three times, unannounced, bringing her ridiculously huge bouquets of flowers. At Meg's obviously perturbed request, Oliver steered him back to the elevator banks each time, apologizing about how busy Meg was at that moment, but how he'd be sure to give his boss the lovely gift.

"What's up with your brother-in-law?" Oliver had asked her after running interference during Ethan's second unexpected visit.

"Believe me, you don't want to know," Meg had responded, though she was longing to confide in someone. She was losing sleep worrying. And, as the ordeal continued, Meg came to believe that Ethan was deluding himself—living out a fantasy that he seemed convinced Meg shared with him.

Ethan had always been somewhat histrionic and prone to mood swings. He was an artist, after all, and Meg had assumed that his volatile nature was part and parcel of his creativity. But when he didn't ease off, when he refused to accept Meg's rejections, she began to think he was experiencing some kind of nervous break-down. Perhaps the whole awful affair could be written off as a male midlife crisis, a chemical imbalance in the brain, a sudden overproduction of testosterone. Whatever the case, some explanation was needed. Because someone had to let Lark know what was going on.

The week before, Meg had decided to face Ethan head-on with the problem. She agreed to have lunch with him at a very busy, very public restaurant in midtown. From the beginning, he'd been impossible. He kissed her on the cheek as he arrived and sat down next to her on the banquette.

"Sit opposite me, please," she'd said. "In the chair. And keep your hands to yourself."

"It's just so great to see you." Ethan slipped around the side of the table and settled down across from her. Meg had noticed several heads turn as Ethan, tall and magnetic, strode through the restaurant. He was now gazing at her with a look of such unabashed admiration that the woman at the next table smiled at her and shook her head with good-humored envy. If she only knew, Meg reflected ruefully.

By the end of the lunch, as she might very well have predicted, they were going over the same well-worn ground in an increasingly heated manner.

"If you don't stop with all this—the calls, the flowers—" Meg said, "I'm going to be forced to tell Lark."

"Don't do that, Meg, please."

"So, you'll stop. Today, this lunch, is the last time we discuss this madness?"

"It's the gold I can't get," he told her, with a wide grin that would have seemed disarming to anyone except Meg at that moment.

"What are you talking about?"

"In your eyes. You have these beautiful golden flecks, kind of embedded in the green."

"Ethan, please stop." But it just started all over again.

Would this have been any easier if she and Lark weren't so close? There was no one in the world Meg loved as much as her younger sister. There was nothing she wouldn't do to keep her from being hurt. And yet, telling her about Ethan would cause Lark such anguish, Meg could hardly imagine it. Lark was still so glowingly, unashamedly in love with her husband. She was such a devoted, doting mother. And, ultimately, she was so proud of the beautiful family she and Ethan had created. She'd even managed to integrate the difficult, demanding Lucinda into the household. Lark had been able to accomplish what she and Meg had always longed for as children: she'd built a real home. And now it looked as though Meg was about to destroy it.

Because she usually confided every detail of her life to her younger sister, Meg stopped phoning Lark once Ethan started his campaign. Lark, who sometimes knew Meg better than she knew herself, quickly would have been able to detect that something was wrong. But not calling her proved to be a mistake after all.

"Hey there—what the *hell* is going on with you?" Lark had left a message on Meg's machine the night before, an hour or two before Ethan called. "I know when you go into hiding like this that something's wrong. Is that snake Paul Stokes back in the picture and you're afraid to tell me? I asked Ethan how you seemed at your lunch with him the other day and you know what he said? 'She seemed fine.' Period. Men. Listen, believe me, I'm going to get it all out of you this weekend, so be forewarned. Also, it turns out that Fran and Matt are coming to dinner after all and I just don't have the time to do any more baking. Could you pick up two of those great little Dutch apple pies from Cupcake Cafe for me? Love you. See you Friday."

And Meg knew that Lark *would* come after her, probing, cajoling, unrelenting. Even as a small girl Lark had demanded intimate and direct access to Meg's feelings, a result, Meg believed, of having an older sister as quasi-parent. When Lark became a mother herself, she honed her skills of observation and emotional control to a fine art. In the past, this intense concern had been a comfort to Meg. It was Lark's way of expressing love and, Lord knew, Meg could use all she could get. But now, with the prospect of three long days under siege, she dreaded the thought of what Lark's persistent questions would force into the open.

"So? Who is it?" Abe asked. They were crossing the short bridge just below the Columbia County border; the lower Berkshire hills rolled away to the east, like so many misty, gray-green breakers.

"Pardon?"

"Who's the guy? You've had this little frown on your forehead all afternoon. In my experience that can mean only one thing." Abe himself was smiling as he asked the question—the slightly down-turning, self-deprecating grin that Meg had seen him use to his sly advantage on many occasions. Abe seemed so easygoing and harmless at times that one could easily forget the razor-sharp, unforgivingly logical mind that was constantly at work. His dark, unruly hair had started to recede at the temples and his compact frame had grown lean from years of tennis, but he could still pass at a glance for the brilliant Harvard Law graduate who had clerked for Justice Rehnquist. Until one met his gaze. Abe had the weary, slightly hooded eyes of a man twenty years his senior.

"You've been talking to Lark?"

"No, I've been talking to Paul Stokes." Abe had introduced Paul to Meg, and he had followed their burgeoning affair with a proprietary interest. "Paul said he saw you at lunch the other day with some man he didn't recognize. He said the guy looked like he really had a thing for you."

"You lawyers sure have a fine way with the English language."

"I'm sorry. Have I offended your feminine sensibilities?"

Meg considered Abe's tone of voice. "Why are you so upset, Abe? I'm a bona fide SWF."

"Me? Upset? Not at all. I was just curious. From the way you were talking post-Paul, I thought you were giving up on the male of the species for a while."

"Actually, I am," Meg said, pressing the button to roll up the window. The sun had fallen behind the larger mountains and with its departure the temperature had plummeted. Meg felt the chill on a deeper level. If other people were noticing Ethan's attraction to her, then she had no choice. She would have to tell Lark what was going on.

"Whatever you say."

"What's with you, Abe? You know, it feels like you're actually sniping at me."

"Not so."

"If you're pissed at me about Paul, just come right out and say so."

"You're accusing *me* of holding back?" Abe said, laughing. He glanced at her quickly and then turning his eyes back to the darkening road. "You know me better than that. No, this isn't about Paul. I told you before that I was a little stunned when you two seemed to take. Opposites attracting and all that. I guess I'm just puzzled these days by the whole subject of couples, and of love. You usually tell me when you've got something hot going on."

"Hot? That's really how you boys talk?" Meg asked, though she felt relieved. "I didn't tell you because, well . . . it was nothing really. Just some guy not understanding what 'no' means."

"You okay?" Abe asked, the gentleness in his tone surprising her. Though keenly observant and quick to judgment, Abe had never been particularly solicitous of Meg's feelings. He'd seen her operate in the business arena and knew her to be tough and demanding, and he gave her the same treatment in return. Which was, Meg had observed over the years, very different from the gentlemanly, almost gallant way he treated Becca, or even Lark. She sensed that Abe mentally categorized her as a guy—a grown-up kind of tomboy—and that they both enjoyed their bantering camaraderie.

"Oh, sure. I've been here before."

"I don't know why this one seems different to me," Abe said, the Saab grumbling as he downshifted for the exit that would lead them, through curving back roads, up to Red River. "Maybe because you didn't say anything to me about it."

"Oh, puh-leeze, Abe! From now on I promise to tell you the minute I so much as look at a man."

But as they made their way in silence along the glistening black river, a full moon following them shyly through the trees, the question Abe had initially asked remained unanswered—hanging delicately in the air between them: Who?

*   *   *

The smell of wood smoke and mulching leaves. The sound of the river, swollen by a midweek rain, roaring through the culvert. The last of the cicadas singing its thin, sad song. The air was so dry and clear that the whispering voices Meg heard ahead could be a dozen steps from her—or a quarter mile away. Abe had left Meg at the bottom of the drive, and she was walking up the curving graveled roadway to the house when she stumbled on an exposed tree root and fell, her left elbow taking most of the punishment.

"Damn!" she cried out.

"Who's there?" Meg recognized Lucinda's whiny voice, followed by a hurried exchange, and the sound of someone running away.

"Meg? You okay?" Lucinda crouched down beside Meg as she pulled herself to her feet and rubbed her elbow. The joint hurt like hell but didn't seem seriously damaged.

"I think so." Meg took in Lucinda's glazed expression and realized with dismay that the teenager had been drinking.

Lucinda McGowan, Ethan's stepdaughter from his short-lived first marriage was, according to the last bluntly worded report from the local high school, "Seriously Troubled." She should have been graduating this year but, at eighteen, had been so truant and inattentive that she was now flunking out of junior-year courses. Five feet nine, thirty pounds overweight with scraggly burgundy-dyed hair and a pasty, uneven complexion, Lucinda had been nicknamed "Bozo" by the local tightly knit teenage crowd.

She'd reentered Ethan's life—and invaded Lark's—a little over a year ago when the state of Pennsylvania

notified Ethan that Lucinda's mother was to be insti-
tutionalized. Mimi's alcohol and drug abuse had
reached life-threatening proportions, her real father
had deserted the family years before, and Lucinda
would have gone into foster care if Ethan and Lark
hadn't taken her in. It had been a disaster from the
moment the foul-mouthed, hostile, beer-drinking
Lucinda belligerently unpacked her dirty duffel bag.

Over the course of the last twelve months Meg
received Lark's regular reports on the teenager's
progress. The bottom line: There wasn't any. Her
room was always a mess. She sneaked out at night.
She skipped school. She was nasty to the little kids.
Talked back to Lark. Hung out with a bad crowd
from Montville, the neighboring town that was big
enough to have two movie theaters and a mall—a
magnet for teenagers all over the mostly rural county.
Lucinda had been picked up late one night by Tom
Huddleson, Red River's police chief, for peeing at the
base of the VFW monument in the center of town.
But the worst of her behavior, the distilled potent
essence of her anger, was directed at Ethan.

"It's horrifying," Lark confided to Meg after one
particularly bad fight between father and daughter.
"It's like she's possessed or something. She's totally
irrational when it comes to Ethan—screaming out the
most vile things. And poor Ethan, he tries to reason
with her. He's so patient. I know he feels guilty,
guilty for leaving her with Mimi all those years, but
what else could he have done? Mimi won custody
and, in the beginning at least, she made a stab at being
a decent mother. It went downhill after Brook was
born and we moved to Red River. I think, until then,

Mimi believed she could somehow win him back."

Meg remembered all too vividly what it was like to be raised by irresponsible parents. She could imagine the pain and confusion of a childhood marred by a single mother's downward slide into addiction. Perhaps it was this innate empathy that Lucinda sensed. Whatever the reason, where Ethan and Lark had failed to make the least impression on Lucinda when it came to discipline, the troubled girl would—and often did—listen to Meg. Six weeks ago when Meg had been visiting, she thought she'd persuaded Lucinda to stop drinking, promising to have her down to visit in Manhattan over the Christmas holidays if she could stay the course. Since then, though the teenager remained impossible on every other front, Lark had been giving Lucinda good marks for sobriety. But now Meg was detecting the unmistakable odor of beer on Lucinda's breath.

"You've been drinking, Luce. I'm really disappointed."

"No, I haven't."

"Yes, you have." Meg tried to avoid losing her temper with Lucinda.

"You're fucking wrong."

"You reek of beer," Meg said. She slung her overnight bag over her shoulder and started back up the drive. Off to the right she could see a glimmer of lights through the trees from Clint and Janine Lindbergh's small, shingled Cape house. Years ago, when the property operated as a mill and large, prosperous farm, their home had served as the hired hand's cottage. For the last decade, the Lindberghs had lived there and helped Ethan in the studio, doing the dirty work while Ethan turned out his award-winning stemware and paperweights. In the afternoons, while Ethan concentrated on his sculptures, Clint handled the studio's paperwork and shipping and Janine helped Lark at what everyone called "the big house."

"Don't, Meg, please," Lucinda whined, following her. "Don't count this. It was just this one time because . . . because Ethan got me so fucking mad I couldn't take it."

"Here, help me with these pies, though I bet that fall ruined them," Meg said, handing her the plastic shopping bag to carry so she could rub her sore elbow. "What did Ethan do?"

"He won't let me go to the basketball game in Montville Monday night."

"Why not?"

"Because he's fucking irrational, that's why. Just because I got into some trouble with some Montville kids, suddenly anything having to do with Montville is off limits. I mean, like, Meg, it's a fucking *basketball* game, okay?"

Though Lark tried constantly to force Lucinda to clean up her language, Meg had only once pointed out to Lucinda that to substitute the word "fucking" for all the millions of adjectives available showed a certain paucity of imagination, and she then gave up on the subject. It was obvious to her that almost of all Lucinda's bad behavior was used for shock value, and to overreact was just playing into her impossibly needy hand.

"There's more to it than that, I suspect," Meg said as they made their way past Ethan's looming darkened studio and then up the final slope to the house. With its long, latticed white porch and double brick chimneys, its picket fence around the vegetable gardens in the back, and the vine-covered well, Ethan and Lark's home was the epitome of the picture-perfect New England farmhouse. The fact that, on closer inspection, it wasn't at all perfect—the front steps needed repair, a porch railing was missing, the entire interior could use a fresh coat of paint—made the place all the more endearing to Meg. She had always loved this house that Lark had so fondly reworked over the years into a real home. Though Meg owned her two bedroom co-op in the city, this in many ways was where her heart resided. Five pumpkins and a basket of Mums stood sentinel up the front steps. She was glad that she had already made her decision to tell Lark about Ethan. It would have been utterly impossible, she realized now, to enter this house with the question still unresolved. Then she heard his voice as he opened the front door.

"Meg? Is that you? This damned front porch light is out again."

"Yes. Me and Lucinda." Ethan leaned in to kiss her on the forehead. She almost stumbled as she took a step back, and he grabbed her arm.

"Let go!" she cried, pulling away from him. "I fell on my way up the drive."

"Are you okay? Let me see. Lucinda, take her bags upstairs and ask Lark to come down."

"Don't order me around," Lucinda said, but she did as she was told, stomping up the stairs with Meg's two weekend totes slung over her shoulder, just as Lark was hurrying down.

"Meggie? What happened?" She was an inch shorter than Meg and, after three children, a little plumper. But the five pounds she had put on with each of the girls had gone primarily to her breasts and hips, giving her at last the kind of sexy curves the slender and underendowed Hardwick sisters had longed for as teenagers. ("Breast-feeding," she had confided to Meg. "If those Hollywood starlets only knew—plastic surgeons would go out of business overnight.")

Though Lark's features were less finely drawn than Meg's—her nose slightly smaller, her lips a bit larger and fuller—and though Meg's eyes were a deep hazel tinged with gold and Lark's were the blue of October skies, there was no question that the two women were sisters. If you didn't notice the similarity of their postures (a tilt of the chin, the arms crossed below their breasts), or failed to hear the same inflections in their voices (a quick delivery, high and slightly twangy), their laugh would have given them dead away.

"For heavens' sakes," Meg said, pushing Ethan aside to hug Lark and hoping that in the confusion of the moment her sister wouldn't notice her husband's concentrated gaze. "Will you all stop hovering! I just took a spill on your damned driveway. I really don't think it's life-threatening."

"But you should put a little something on it," Lark said, after examining Meg's elbow. "Some arnica or comfrey leaves. Let's see what I've got." With her arm around Meg's waist, Lark led her sister into the pantry where she kept an old pie cupboard full of oils and ointments, infusions and tinctures. Drying flowers and herbs that she'd grown or collected hung in garlands and bouquets from the ceiling. Lark was a committed homeopath and her growing understanding of natural medicines had turned her kitchen into a kind of free local out-clinic for the town's various aches and pains. Meg's initial skepticism of Lark's healing techniques had been overcome one summer afternoon when Lark had rubbed crushed garlic onto a nasty wasp sting on Meg's neck and the swelling pain had—within two minutes—subsided.

"That'll do it," Lark said stepping back after she'd wound gauze around Meg's elbow to keep the compress in place. Ethan had gone upstairs to help his three younger daughters finish up their bath. Lark and Meg were alone.

"Well, you look okay," Lark said.

"Yes." Meg moved her elbow back and forth. "Feels better already."

"Actually, you look kind of fabulous. Meggie—it *is* a man, isn't it?"

"Lark, I—listen . . ." Meg felt her heart pounding. After everything she'd promised herself and despite her resolutions, Meg was now facing Lark unable to find the words that would indict Ethan. The familiar pantry, her sister's smiling face, the delicious promise of dinner wafting in from the kitchen—everything felt so normal, so loved, so safe. It seemed impossible suddenly that the man clomping around upstairs singing silly songs to his daughters could be the person who'd been stalking her the last few weeks. She felt blood rush to her cheeks as she tried to regain her resolve and sense of urgency.

"Meg—I can't believe it—you're actually blushing! It *is* somebody. And it's serious, isn't it?"

Meg felt her sister's eyes upon her. Lark was able to

read Meg's emotional terrain like a map. She knew where each hidden heartbreak lay. Where each romantic triumph took place. She had been there for every high and every low. And, always, she'd been on Meg's side. Whispering instructions. Suggesting alternate battle plans. She'd always been so eager to help, so hopeful that Meg would find the same kind of happiness Lark shared with Ethan. Or thought she shared. Meg felt her eyes misting.

"Okay." Meg sighed, looking down at the cracked tiled floor. "Yes, yes, there is someone. But it's very weird and confusing."

"I'm happy for you!" Lark hugged her and then stepped back to look at her. "But why do you seem so upset? Tell me about him—is he . . ."

"Please, Lark." Meg swallowed hard, cursing herself inwardly for her cowardice. She had all weekend, she reminded herself. This was just not the right time or place to tell Lark what was really happening.

"Damn, I bet he's married. Am I right?" Lark tucked in a stray hair behind Meg's ear. Her mothering instincts came flowing out whenever someone she loved was in danger of being hurt. "Kids?"

Meg, trying to clear her thoughts, shook her head and took a deep breath. "I'm . . . I'm not really ready to talk about it yet, baby. Even with you. Can you believe it?" Without warning, she felt her eyes spill over with tears.

"Oh—I hate to see you in any kind of pain," Lark said, pulling her sister close again. "But I understand. Really I do. Just know that I'm here when you *are* ready. And you know what? Speaking from experience, if two people are meant for each other, nothing—not even a marriage—is going to be able to stand in their way."

"I feel so egotistical, throwing a party for myself." Lark remarked over that evening's dinner of home-made spinach linguine with roasted eggplant and bell pepper. She was feeding Fern, in the high chair beside her, little spoonfuls of mashed spinach. The dinner party that Lark had been planning for weeks to cele-brate the sale of her children's book was to be held the following night. "But, hey, Ethan got a party for his opening. I think I deserve a little something, too."

"Of course you do, sweetie," Ethan said, his smile lingering on Meg.

"Who's all coming?" Meg asked, not looking in Ethan's direction.

"All my favorite people in the world," Lark went on. "You guys, Abe, Francine, Matt, and Janine—"

"That fart-face," Lucinda muttered just loud enough for the whole table to hear, causing Brook and Phoebe to snicker gleefully.

"Luce—" Ethan warned.

"Like you think she's attractive?" Lucinda's face darkened. "Of course, you—"

"That's enough, " Lark said. "Don't be like that with Meg here."

"So what's on the menu?" Meg asked.

"Smoked oysters!" Phoebe sang out before collaps-ing into a fit of giggles. She was six, blond and blue-eyed like her mother, with a round, cherubic face and the temperament to match.

"Corn pudding, stuffed peppers, brussels sprouts with chestnuts—" Lark was not one for half measures when it came to entertaining.

"I hate brussels sprouts," Brook announced matter-of-factly. Tall for her nine years, slender as a reed, Brook had inherited her father's hair—a wild mane of brilliant golds and reds. She was naturally quiet, thoroughly self-possessed. Lark had confided proudly to Meg that Brook was at the top of her class in every subject without seeming to put any effort into her studies. She had her aunt's hazel eyes, and something about her strong, determined character reminded Meg of herself as a girl.

"Three big free-range chickens, stuffed with lemons and rosemary," Lark went on as if uninterrupted. "Creamed onions, green beans with slivered almonds, and, what else?"

"Lord, I think that's enough," Meg said.

"Mashed potatoes!" Phoebe cried at the top of her little voice. "With gravy!"

"Phoebe," Ethan said. That was all it took with the younger girls—that tone from Ethan, or a shake of the head from Lark. It always amazed Meg what good parents Ethan and Lark had somehow, naturally, become. The girls were raised with a firm, loving hand, the two parents rarely disagreeing on points of discipline. It helped, no doubt, to have Ethan working in the studio just a few hundred yards away. He was around the house—and in their lives—as much as Lark was. And, even now, despite Meg's outrage at Ethan, she had to admit to herself that he was wonderful with his daughters—fun-loving and imaginative, thoughtful and patient.

After the dishes were cleared and done and Lucinda had sullenly gone out to "see some friends," they all sat in the living room in front of the open fire, reading and talking. It was so warm and comfortable by the fireplace, the mantel decorated with dried gourds and Indian corn from the garden, Meg could almost believe that this circle of family—all aglow in the flickering light—was as it had always been. Innocent. Loving. Indivisible. But then she would feel Ethan's eyes upon her, and she would flush with a terrible secret anger.

Around ten, and only after Meg had promised to read them yet another story if they agreed to go to bed, Brook and Phoebe finally trudged upstairs. Lark carried Fern up behind them and Meg could hear Lark humming a lullaby to the sleeping baby. Though they had separate beds, Brook and Phoebe curled up together for Meg's reading of "Sleepy Hollow." It was a long story, and Meg had forgotten just how frightening it was. Rather than ease them into sleep, the story jarred them into a nervous wakefulness. Afterward, Meg had to promise Phoebe several times that it was "all make-believe," that the headless horseman was not going to come barreling up the driveway and grab her. Then, as an antidote to the first story, she read them their old favorite, "Goodnight Moon." Twice.

"I had forgotten how scary some of those children's stories are," Meg said as she came back down into the living room. The fire had collapsed into a bed of glowing embers. Lark and Ethan were talking on the couch. There was something about the way they were sitting and the low, tense tone of their voices that made Meg feel she was intruding.

"Did they give you trouble?" Lark asked, looking over Ethan's shoulder at Meg. Ethan didn't turn; he seemed to be staring intently at the dying fire. "We were just getting ready to go up ourselves."

"Me, too," Meg said. Usually, after the girls were in bed, Meg would sit up with Lark and Ethan for another hour or so, catching up on their lives. The three of them had once been so casual, so easy in each other's company. Ethan had ruined all that now. Though it felt odd and a little awkward to go to bed so early, Meg was relieved. Meg realized that they were waiting for her to leave before continuing their conversation. "I'm heading up then," Meg said, turning to the stairs.

"See you in the morning, sweetie," Lark called after her.

"'Night," Ethan added. He still hadn't turned around.

Usually Meg slept better at Lark and Ethan's house than anywhere else in the world, including her own apartment. She was always given the guest bedroom at the top of the stairs that faced out on the side yard and downhill to the river. With one of the three large-paned windows open a crack, the soft white curtain stirring in the breeze, Meg could lie in bed and hear the sound of the rushing water below. It would carry her gently into sleep and she would remember nothing more until morning.

Tonight, though, was different. The temperature had dropped precipitously after nightfall and the bedroom was freezing. Meg closed all the windows and pulled a spare army blanket out of the closet. But once under the covers, Meg felt too hot, and the full moon flooded the room with a weird white presence. Meg's elbow began to ache again, and she had a hard time finding a sleeping position that didn't hurt it. The old house creaked and moaned and made other odd noises. Just as Meg drifted off at last into a troubled sleep, a distant bang—a shutter in the wind? the sound of gunfire?—would jar her awake. Sometime in the middle of the night, Meg woke to hear someone knocking softly on her door. She lay in bed, every muscle tensed, staring at the door through the drifting darkness. But it did not open. Finally the sound stopped, and Meg heard footsteps creaking on the floorboards. Or was it just the house shifting on its beams? At some point, she finally fell asleep. But her dreams were fragmented and nerve-racking. In one, a headless horseman galloped through a moonlit night.

8

" ... for Her mercy is forever, Amen," Francine Werling's deep voice was calming and self-assured. Though Meg found some of Francine's ultrafeminist mannerisms clichéd, she grudgingly respected the minister of Red River's Congregationalist Church. Francine, who had led the town's congregation of two hundred souls for the past fifteen years, seemed to Meg to be a tireless champion of all that was liberal-minded, environmentally correct, and socially responsible. She'd arrived in Red River from an assistant minister posting in upstate Vermont with a two-year-old son, no husband, and no questions answered—either then or as the years went by—about her son's father.

Matt looked nothing like his mother. He was tall and lanky, with a splotched complexion and dark, somewhat greasy hair that he wore in a ponytail.

Though tall herself, the prematurely gray-haired Francine was solid, almost matronly, whereas Matt was whippet thin. Francine's usual—and, Meg thought, somewhat studied—expression was open and beaming. Matt wore a perpetual scowl behind his light-sensitive rimless glasses. He had the appearance of someone who spent all his time indoors, which, in fact, he did, glued to a computer screen and wired into an Internet world that seemed far more vital to him than his own. Matt rarely went anywhere without his laptop. He'd arrived behind his mother for Lark's dinner with the computer case slung over his shoulder and had spent the hour or so before the meal curled up on a window seat as far away from everyone as possible, absorbed in his computer games.

As in all small towns, Red River's most thriving industry was gossip. For years, the rumor mill had been busily speculating about Francine and Matt. Was he illegitimate? Was she a lesbian and he one of those test-tube babies? Just who was the father and why was she so closemouthed about it? Someone had even contacted the Vermont congregation where she had last been posted, but Francine had arrived there with a six-month-old Matt from somewhere in New Hampshire, and the Vermont congregation had as many unanswered questions as the Red River community did. There were no questions, however, about Francine's abilities as a community leader and spiritual counselor. And so, because they admired and needed her, Red River let Francine publicly keep her secrets. Privately, the unfinished triangle of Francine, Matt, and unknown father sparked enough curiosity and interest to keep it one of the top five or six topics in town, right behind Lucinda McGowan's most recent outrage.

"Thank you, Francine," Ethan said somewhat formally. He was at the head of the table, the enormous, perfectly roasted chickens waiting to be carved in front of him. Francine, two seats down from him on the left, gave Ethan a curt nod. Though there no overt animosity passed between them, Meg had noticed over the years that Ethan and Francine were hardly friends. Meg thought she understood why. She could see how Ethan might object to the unusual closeness Francine and Lark shared. The two women had so many interests in common and were both so dedicated to their pet causes that, together, they headed up every important committee in town: the Red River Environmental Awareness Group, the Youth Fund, Red River's Women's Caucus, and the local New York Democratic Club. Between meetings, fund-raisers, and just attending to the details of getting things done, Lark probably saw more of Francine Werling than she did of anyone else in Red River, including Ethan.

If their relationship had ended with friendship, Meg suspected that Ethan might have tolerated, even encouraged, the bond. But Francine had become something of a spiritual mentor to Lark as well. They spent hours together in deep conversation. They'd organized a women's reading group that studied and discussed books on inner light and universal oneness. They rarely let a day pass without taking a moment to "share" with each other on the phone. Ethan had always kidded Lark about her tireless campaign for self-awareness and enlightenment. Over the years, she had embraced every philosophy that had come down the pike—EST, Sufism, the New Age flavor of the year. With Francine, Lark had finally found a soul mate and fellow seeker—a situation that was bound to irritate the confirmed agnostic in Ethan.

Francine no doubt sensed Ethan's reservations and harbored some of her own. Ethan didn't come to church with Lark and the girls and rarely participated in the church functions—the chicken frys, bake sales, and contra dances—that were at the heart of Red River's social life. Once, at Lark's and Francine's urging, Ethan had given a lecture in the church basement about the art of glassblowing, but he had talked in such abstractions and at such length that the twenty or so people who attended the evening left far more baffled than when they arrived. Meg learned from Lark that Francine believed Ethan had been obtuse and difficult on purpose. In any case, he had never been asked to talk about his work again.

Besides Francine and Matt, the other invited guests were Abe—who had called earlier to say he was running late and to start without him—and Janine and Clint Lindbergh. Janine, seated between Francine and Ethan, was blond and large and capable-looking. She could have been an early pioneer woman, driving a Conestoga wagon across the sweltering plains. In her mid-forties and too heavy to be considered beautiful, her skin was nevertheless soft and translucent, her eyes the palest of blues, her teeth very tiny and white. Her dimpled smile was simply part of her natural expression. She favored dresses that were far too young for her—floral prints with lace edging and puffy sleeves. For all Janine's sweetness—or perhaps because of it—Meg had always found her a bit grating. Janine didn't seem to notice how often she was stepped on by Ethan or Lark—left to clear the dishes, wait by the phone, or baby-sit Fern, while everyone else did as they pleased. Of course, Meg would have to remind herself, Janine and Clint were in the awkward position of being both employees and friends.

Clint, however, seemed to handle it better. A big, bearlike man, with a full red beard now dusted with gray, Clint was slow-moving and relaxed. He had a great belly laugh and, when pushed, a wonderful way with a story. When not working for Ethan, he helped Francine out doing janitorial work and playing—very badly—the church's old pipe organ. Kind and always game, he was a favorite of the girls, who called him "Uncle Clintbones" and climbed on him, swinging from his broad shoulders as if he were some kind of jungle gym.

With Janine, who did housecleaning and baby-sitting for Lark in the afternoons, the girls were less responsive. Brook, especially, seemed to take against her. "She's like a big dumb cow," Brook confided to Meg. "I've been able to beat her in Scrabble for the last three years."

Lucinda, for her part, kept up a nonstop, one-woman smear campaign against Janine. She made constant fun of her and called her nasty names behind her back—"Gigantic Janine," "Little Dough-girl," "Earth Pig"— often loud enough for Janine to hear. When Janine had finally complained to Lark about Lucinda's behavior and Lark had done what she could to keep the difficult teenager in line, Lucinda had simply continued her name-calling on a more clandestine but no less consistent basis. Perhaps that explained Janine's puffy eyes today, Meg thought, and her new nervous habit of biting her lower lip. For the first time since Meg had known her, Janine was beginning to look her age.

"Well, I'd like to make a toast," Clint announced after everyone had been served. Seated at the foot of the table beside Lark, he pushed back his chair and lumbered to his feet, his wineglass raised in his right hand. "To our beautiful hostess—much success with her new book. And," he turned to Ethan, "our generous host. Congratulations on your show. We're—Janine and I—very proud."

"Thanks, Clint," Ethan called down the table. He raised his glass. "To the Lindberghs. Who keep the joint running." Flushing with what seemed to be sudden embarrassment, Clint sat down abruptly, and tucked into the full plate in front of him.

"I have a toast as well," Lark said, though she didn't rise. Dressed in a red corduroy jumper, black wool turtleneck, and black leggings, she could almost pass for the college girl Ethan had fallen in love with. Her blue eyes glistening, she raised her glass to Ethan. "To family and friends. Hearth and home. Here and now."

Meg, sitting across the table from Francine, saw the look and smile that passed between husband and wife and she felt her heart leap. All day, Ethan hadn't given Meg so much as a glance. Though not distant in a way that anyone else but Meg would notice, he seemed to have completely shut down on her. And she couldn't have been more relieved. If he needed to be dismissive of her, fine, thought Meg. If he needed to be angry, moody, nasty even—Meg would welcome it all. If only he would continue to leave her alone.

Perhaps to compensate for his coldness toward Meg, Ethan was being as jovial and attentive as possible to everybody else. As the meal progressed, Meg watched him talking to Janine, who was seated to his immediate left. It was almost as if he, too, had noticed Janine's unhappy state because he made a point of kidding her and making her flush and giggle. Then he turned his attention to Brook and Phoebe, who were seated next to each other on his right, and before too long the head of the table was in hysterics.

"Dad- Dad-dy stop!" Phoebe was laughing so hard she started to hiccup.

"What's so funny down there?" Lark asked.

"Daddy was telling us about the re—" Brook began to giggle herself and turned to Ethan, touching his elbow. "You better tell it."

"I'm not sure what all the fuss is about," Ethan began, straight-faced. "I was merely filling them in on the steering committee that the chickens have formed to discuss—"

As Ethan was speaking, the front door opened and then was slammed shut. Everyone looked up. Abe appeared between the French doors leading into the dining room.

"Why didn't any of you people tell me about Becca's plans?" he demanded, speaking in a voice Meg had never heard before. His usual ironic poise was gone and in its place was undiluted anger. "Christ, I thought you were my friends!"

"We are your friends, Abe," Ethan responded quickly, with a glance down the table to Lark. "Don't blame us for what happened between the two of you."

"Two of—?" Abe started across the floor toward Ethan.

"Not in my house." Lark said. She rose quickly, grabbing his arm as he passed. In his anger, he started to shake her off, then seemed to realize what he was doing. He hesitated and Lark seized the moment, adding: "Not here. Come with me." She pulled Fern out of the high chair with one arm and, with her other, took Abe by the elbow and drew him down the hall to the kitchen.

"What in the world . . . ?" Meg, forgetting herself, turned to Ethan, but he was occupied trying to soothe Brook and Phoebe.

"It's okay, guys. Abe's just a little mad, is all. Happens to the best of us."

"So he's heard the news," Francine said, shaking her head.

"Heard what?" Meg asked.

"About Becca," Clint replied. "She took her divorce money and bought those ten acres north of town on the other side of the river that Eddie Soneson has been trying to sell forever. She's going to build a house there."

"I thought the agreement was that she had to leave," Meg said, repeating what Lark had told her.

"That's what we all thought, including Abe, obviously," Francine said. "Becca let him keep the country house—all of it, without any kind of struggle, though she fought him on everything else. He must have assumed, as we all did, that she intended to leave Red River."

"Poor Abe." Janine sighed.

"Hey, it's a free country," Clint pointed out philosophically. "The lady can build where she likes. But that property's straight uphill and all tree-covered. I'm not sure where she's going to squeeze in a house."

"She's already contracted with Hawkins and Lee, the architects who designed the Yarrow place in Montville," Ethan said, carving himself another slice of breast meat.

"Where'd you hear that?" Francine asked.

"I ran into her on the train when my Jeep was in the shop, and she gave me a ride back from Hudson. She showed me the plans. It's going to be a hell of a beautiful place. Abe must have handed over a wad of cash."

"I didn't realize you were still in touch with Becca," Francine said in a lowered voice.

"She gave me a ride home to save Lark from having to make the trip. I'm sorry, Francine, but you weren't there so I was unable to ask your permission."

"Okay, kids," Clint pushed back his chair and stood up. "Who's going to help Uncle Clintbones clear?"

"When did you start smoking again?" Meg asked Lark. Everyone had gone home and Ethan had taken the girls up to bed. Fern was already tucked in for the night. After looking all through the downstairs, Meg had finally found her sister on the top of the five wooden steps that led from the kitchen to the backyard. Lark was wrapped in an old bulky sweater of Ethan's.

"Oh, I've always sneaked them from time to time,"

Lark said. She held up the cigarette for Meg to get a better look. "These are organic, if that makes it any better."

"Doesn't bother me," Meg said, sitting down next to her. "But speaking of being bothered—what happened with Abe? Did he leave after the two of you talked?"

"I'd hardly say we talked. I listened to his tirade. It's scary when someone who's usually so self-contained really loses it. But this business with Becca—you heard what she's planning?"

"To stay here . . . and build a new house?"

"Yeah. Right up the river. It's driving him nuts. It's kind of horrifying to hear just how much he hates her. You know what he told me? After the split, he piled everything Becca had ever given him—clothes, books, CDs, anything that could remotely remind him of her—and donated it to Francine's last tag sale. He just couldn't stand having it around. And today, when he walked into the dining room? Already half-crazed because of what he'd learned about Becca's plans? He saw poor old Clint wearing a shirt Becca had given Abe for his birthday last year. Clint and Janine pick up half their clothes at tag sales. It made Abe sick—just seeing that damned shirt again. Imagine what it's going to be like for him running into Becca every time he turns around."

"Poor Abe," Meg said. They were both silent for a moment. It was a chilly night, the air clear and dry, the stars filling the sky above with their cold, puzzling beauty. This would be the perfect moment to talk to Lark about Ethan, Meg thought. But, how to begin? *Speaking of feeling sorry for people, Lark . . .* No, how about just coming straight out with it: *Ethan's been harassing me, Lark, I just thought you should know. . . .* Meg found her brain spinning with words, none of them convincing, no tone anywhere near right.

Finally, sensing the silence had stretched on too long and having nothing else to fill it with, Meg said, "That was an incredible meal. I've never eaten so much in my life."

"You always say that. And yet I watch you, and you're always so careful about what you eat. You took maybe two bites of that apple pie. That's why you still look so great. Slim, stylish."

"I didn't know I was such an object of scrutiny. And if you're in any way comparing the two of us— believe me, I'd give anything for your body."

"Oh, let's not do this, sweetie. What's the point?"

"No, there isn't any point." Meg put her hand on Lark's knee, feeling her heart expand with love and pity for her sister.

"I mean, we're just different, you and me. It's hard to keep that in perspective sometimes because I feel so close to you. But we're not the same—we've different bodies, different minds. Want different kinds of lives. But, you know what? Ever since the book got bought, I feel that I understand you better. It's a wonderful feeling—totally exhilarating—to be acknowledged as a success. Complimented, wooed by important people. Now I think I kind of know how you must feel, running your own business, dealing with real problems in the real world."

Meg squeezed Lark's knee, encouraging her, though these were not the revelations she had hoped for.

"You know, for so many years now," Lark continued, "I've felt like I was in your shadow. I was always comparing myself with you. Weighing what I had against what you had. Competing—I guess they already have a word for it. But now—it's like this weight's been lifted—I don't feel that way anymore. We're equals somehow. Different, but both successful. Oh, Meggie," Lark said with a laugh, turning her head up and looking at the stars, "I just feel so great."

Clearly, Lark didn't know what was happening with Ethan. Probably didn't even suspect. Whatever Ethan had been going through, he'd been keeping it from his wife. And wasn't it better that way? Meg asked herself now. Ethan's fixation—like a kind of high, hallucinatory fever—seemed to be breaking up. He'd been careful not to see Meg alone all day. He'd barely spoken to her through dinner. Of course their relationship was hardly back to normal and it would probably take years to regain their old, easygoing footing, but Meg felt that the worst was over.

Ethan, after all, had made it clear to Meg that this was his personal hell. So wouldn't it be wrong, actually, for Meg to intervene—now that Ethan was finally trying to deal with the crisis on his own? Meg wasn't shirking her responsibilities as a loving sister, she told herself, she was simply adjusting her decision to a changing situation. Besides, she'd never seen Lark so confident and proud of herself. Surely, Lark deserved her moment in the sun. Perhaps that was why Ethan had decided to keep his emotional turmoil hidden from Lark. In time, Meg promised herself, the long episode would no doubt seem like just a bad dream.

For now she'd let it stay *her* bad dream. What was the point of making it Lark's nightmare?

"I'm happy for you," Meg said finally, putting her arm around her sister. For a time, they sat there in silence together, looking up at the vast beckoning sky.

"Funny, we've both said that to each other this weekend," Lark said. "Isn't it too bad that everyone can't be as happy—and happy for each other—as you and I are?"

9

The town of Red River was settled by English and Dutch farmers in the early 1700s. Built on a wide curve of the river the Indians had called Rocquonic for the water that would run red every spring with the rust-colored silt from upriver, it sat in the midst of a narrow, fertile valley, nestled in the heart of rolling hills. Though hardly isolated, it was not a stop on any important route. When the railroads were laid in the mid 1880s, Red River was bypassed for the more accessible Montville, and so the town itself never expanded far beyond its original configuration: the Rocquonic Inn, the general store, the grange, the First Congregational Church, the post office, and the two-story white clapboard building that had once been the blacksmith's shop and that for most of this century had served as the town hall and library combined.

Woodstock and the Summer of Love washed far enough north and east to spill over into Red River. Communes sprang up all over upstate New York in the wake of the peace movement, and hippies, in a mass return to nature, started to homestead the old family farms, some of them left fallow since the Depression. Red River, like so many small towns, became an odd conglomeration of old and new, permanent and transitory: hardscrabble farmers, long-haired artisans, and always—from the late 1800s on—weekenders and summer people, visiting from the cities with the same approximate migratory patterns as the bird population. The town would start to fill up in late spring with New Yorkers and grosbeaks alike, the twitter of exotic birdsong along with chitchat of Wall Street and the Yankees drifted on the summer air, but by mid-November there was no longer a run on the *Times* in the general store and the local chickadees and titmice once again held sway at the feeders.

When Ethan and Lark bought the old Rensselaer mill and farm in the late 1980s there was already a well-established network of artisans in the area. With the news that Ethan was converting the mill into a working glassblowing studio, the McGowans found themselves invited to the many low-key functions that served the artistic community: poetry readings in converted barns, art openings in abandoned churches, and open-air New Age music concerts in the cow pastures of working farms. For a time, as they were first becoming established, they became something of a fixture at these events: the blond, glamorous McGowans, holding hands throughout the evening. But as Ethan became more involved with his work and the demands of motherhood started to restrict Lark's evening hours, they joined in less and less frequently.

"When will they figure out that I'm not a fucking *craftsperson*," Ethan complained in disgust as he crumpled up a letter soliciting his work for an upcoming fair and tossed it out the window of the jeep. It was the Monday morning of the Columbus Day holiday, and Ethan, Lark, Meg, and the girls had driven into town to pick up the mail and some groceries at the general store. They were on their way home, Fern up front with Lark and Ethan, Meg and the two girls bouncing along in the back.

"Ethan, please," Lark scolded, as she started to nurse Fern. "You're as bad as Lucinda."

"*Excuse-moi, Madame,*" Ethan replied in a haughty tone. It was one of several voices he used to kid around with Brook and Phoebe and now it coaxed giggles out of both of them.

"You're undermining me," Lark murmured in a voice so low Meg wasn't sure she heard her correctly.

"Yeah, you're right, sorry," Ethan replied, pulling the jeep up to the house and hopping out, the engine still going. "Okay, guys, hippity-hop." As Lark and Fern climbed out the passenger side, he quickly lifted first Brook and then Phoebe from the backseat. Meg started to climb out on her own, but Ethan took her arm, steadying her as he slipped a folded piece of white ruled paper into her hand. She looked at him, startled, but he turned from her to help Lark with the groceries.

Ethan had been absent from everyone that weekend, retreating to his studio all day Sunday and late into the night as the sisters and the girls kept themselves busy baking shortbread fingers and gingersnaps for the church bake sale. Meg had always been aware that Ethan had "his moods," as Lark called them, but she'd had no trouble simply ignoring them in the past. Now, for most of the last day and a half, Meg had felt responsible for the trouble he was going through and, at the same time, filled with a growing sense of relief: Ethan was working his demons out on his own. But the whole household seemed infected by Ethan's unhappiness. Fern had become colicky again and cried intermittently. Lucinda clomped in and out of the house, headphones buzzing with angry rock music. Nobody seemed to be sleeping very well. Meg woke up several times Saturday and Sunday nights and twice thought she heard someone tapping at her door.

"See you all for lunch," Ethan said, as he climbed back into the jeep and wheeled it around toward the studio.

In the house, there were groceries to be put away, dishes to be done, laundry to be sorted. Brook wanted to show Meg her growing butterfly collection and Phoebe wanted to be everywhere Meg and Brook were. But at one point Meg was able to steal away to an upstairs bathroom for a few seconds where she read Ethan's note. In his all-capitals, forward-slanting scrawl, he'd written:

PLEASE COME SEE ME AT THE STUDIO LATER. WE MUST TALK—ONE LAST TIME.

He was probably right that they should talk things through, Meg thought, as she flushed the note down the toilet. In some ways Meg was surprised that Lark hadn't already noticed that something was seriously off between her sister and husband. If Meg was obviously uncomfortable around him, Ethan was downright uncivil to her. He hadn't addressed a single comment to her since Friday night. He looked through her when they were in the same room. Meg saw clearly that the friction between her and Ethan had generated the unhappiness permeating the household. It was probably best that these problems were sorted out before the weekend was over. Eventually they would have to find a way to ease back into a normal relationship.

Clint and Janine came back to the house with Ethan for lunch, as they frequently did. And when Ethan returned to the studio after the meal and Clint drove down to Hudson on errands, Janine stayed at the house to do the lunch dishes and take care of Fern and the girls so that Lark could work on her book. It was easy enough then for Meg to slip out the kitchen backdoor, down the steps, around through the woods, and along the riverbank now slick with fallen leaves.

Ethan's studio had been a grist mill once, built on the river, and while its barnlike interior and three-story arching roof remained basically intact, Ethan had lovingly refurbished the slatted wood walls and slabbed marble floor. The south side of the studio, which had once housed the stalls of unshucked corn and storerooms for barrels and shipping pallets, Ethan had converted into offices for Clint and Janine. The bulk of the mill, north-facing, was now the huge open area he had made over into the glassblowing studio, keeping the old mill stone in the center of the room for a tempering table. Seven-foot-high open wooden shelves ran along the south side of the studio, stacked with recently fired glassware, each piece etched on its base with the Red River Studio logo. Although most of Ethan's art pieces were down at the Judson Gallery, what Meg assumed were two new sculptures sat on a separate raised platform next to the shelves. They were squat cubed masses of primary colors, composed of intricate, wildly convoluted glass tubing.

He was working on one of his glass sculptures that afternoon; sections of the piece, foot-long angry squirts of red and yellow, lay like salamanders in the sun on the iron hot plate on the worktable next to the annealing oven. Meg stood for a moment in the doorway watching Ethan as he rotated the long pontil in the blasting furnace and then blew on the rod with the gentleness of a father kissing a baby. He moved with the slow precision of one totally comfortable with a difficult medium—like a ballet dancer or a concert pianist—his mind and the body fused in intense concentration.

Over the roar of the furnaces and fans Ethan could not possibly have heard Meg enter and yet something made him turn as she started across the sun-filled room toward him. He was standing in front of an open furnace, rotating a pontil in the heart of the flaming gas jets. When he saw Meg, he slowly withdrew the rod, revealing the molten fist of glass on the end.

"So, you came." He examined the tip of the pontil before returning it to the fire, rotating it the entire time. He was wearing tinted heat-protective glasses and a faded blue T-shirt soaked with sweat.

"Yes," Meg said. "I think you're right—we need to talk." She thought he looked odd in the glasses, sinister almost, the light of the ovens casting a bright pinkish glow over his body.

"*Damn* you, Meg," Ethan spat out the words as he whirled around to face her now, the blazing rod between them like a sword.

"Ethan!" Meg took a few steps back in alarm.

"Lark told me about your new *boy*friend," he said. "What the fuck is going on?" He turned back to the furnace and tossed the rod into it as if it were a piece of trash, sending sparks flying out of the hole. He tore off the glasses and threw them on the metal table; they skidded across the surface with a metallic twang.

"Please, just calm down," Meg said. "What exactly did she tell you?"

"That you're seeing someone new," Ethan said, facing her. His hair, damp with sweat, curled in ringlets on his forehead. The heat from the ovens or his own outrage had flushed his face a dark red. "He's married. No kids. What's the point of this? Or do you enjoy torturing me?"

So, Lark had passed Meg's cowardly lie on to Ethan; that was why he'd been so distant. He hadn't given up on his fantasy about her—he'd just twisted it into an ugly new shape in his mind.

"Lark kept asking me what was going on," Meg replied slowly, as she tried to size up Ethan's state of mind. "I hadn't been talking to her much these last few weeks—because I didn't know what the hell to say. You kept promising me you'd tell her the truth. And you haven't. You've lied to her, and you've been lying to me. What I did was cover for you, damn it."

"You mean ... it's not true?" he asked, staring at her hungrily.

"Of course, not," Meg said. "But what difference does that make? You've got to deal with this thing, Ethan. You've got to talk to Lark."

"Oh, Jesus," Ethan said, throwing up his hands. "I've been such a total fool. I've been utterly, absolutely insane with jealousy ever since Lark told me Friday night about this guy. And the whole time ... he was me!" Ethan started to laugh as he took a step toward her.

"No, he's *not!*" Meg cried. "Listen to me. I feel *nothing* for you. You have to face the fact that this whole thing—it's unreal on your part. It's delusional."

"Meg, please, don't be like this," Ethan said, suddenly gripping her hands in his.

"Let me go, Ethan," she said evenly, though she felt trapped. When he didn't immediately release her, she struggled against him. The firestorm of the furnaces seemed suddenly louder. He stepped toward her, forcing her arms to his waist, her fists balled in impotent protest.

"It is me you love, Meg, *me,*" Ethan whispered, as Meg tried to wrench her arms free. Ethan tightened the pressure on her wrists to keep her from pulling away. "Why can't you just admit it?"

"You're hurting me," she cried, twisting from him, the pain underscoring the awful reality of her situation: he wasn't going to let her go. She no longer knew who he really was, let alone how to reason with him. Now, though she was inches from him, she would have been hard-pressed even to describe him. He seemed to loom above her, casting her in shadow. Meg felt her strength dissolve under the sudden rush of a sensation almost unknown to her. Fear.

Then Meg heard the noise in the front office—a door or window slamming. Ethan heard it, too, turning toward the sudden distraction.

"Let me go. Now," Meg said, trying to keep her voice steady.

He looked down at her with the uncomprehending stare of someone emerging from a dream. Then he nodded, releasing his grip and stepping back from her.

"Oh, Meg. " He sighed, running his hands through his hair. "What am I going to do?"

"You're going to tell Lark what you're going through," Meg said, the blood rushing back through her fingers. Her uncertainty hardened into resolve. Ethan was out of control, hell-bent on a path of self-destruction that threatened to take with him everyone Meg loved most in the world. The time for doubt and temporizing was over.

"I will," Ethan said, turning to met her gaze. The anguish in his eyes did not touch her heart at all this time. Her pity for him was now overwhelmed by her fear for the rest of them. He had become such a powerful, dangerous force, and yet Meg was the only one who could see the threat he posed, the tornado spinning them into its devastating spiral.

"You'd better," Meg said, as she walked away, leaving him standing alone in the middle of his self-made inferno. "Or, believe me, this time I will."

10

"She's hardly a kid any-more," Meg said, trying again to reassure Lark that Lucinda would be all right. It was the Friday morning after the Columbus Day weekend and Lucinda had been missing since Monday night. Through Meg's intervention, Lucinda had been allowed to attend the basketball game in Montville. She had not come home. Tom Huddleson, the police chief, had asked around town and discovered that Lucinda never attended the game. The household in Red River from Tuesday morning on had been in an uproar, overrid-ing, for a time at least, all other concerns. Huddleson had put out an APB on the teenager, but there was very little anyone could to do besides that. Except wait. And worry.

"In some ways, yes," Lark said. "But in others, I guess because she's just so screwed up, she *is* a little kid, Meg. She's so damned needy. Lord, I can see her hitchhiking and being picked up by some awful guy and—"

"Stop it," Meg cut in. "She's not an idiot. And remember, she probably acts very differently with you than she's does with her friends."

"Friends! Like she has any around here. I mean, they've all been perfectly polite to me, but it's clear none of the Red River kids can stand her. And the Montville crowd? Tom and I have gone over there and tried to talk to the one or two who sometimes hang around with her—Tom knows who they are because they're constantly in trouble—but they're not nice and they claim they haven't seen her since early October. Goddamnit—where is she? I haven't got a thing done on the book all week worrying about her."

"I know how you feel, believe me," Meg replied, swamped by worries of her own. As far as she could tell, Ethan still hadn't spoken to Lark and, under the circumstances, she didn't quite know what to think. Was Ethan just waiting for Lucinda to be found—and that problem resolved—before confronting his wife with another crisis? Or was Ethan stalling again—seizing this as an excuse to spin out his fantasy even longer? "What does Ethan say?"

"Ethan's been in one of his moods—well, you know what he's like when he's upset. He's holed himself up in the studio. I'm just letting him be for now."

"Oh, baby," Meg said, hating the uncertain situation Ethan had left them in once again. "I wish there was something practical I could do to help."

"Thanks, Meg, but you help just by being there. I always feel better just talking to you."

After Lark hung up, Meg took a deep breath and tried to clear her mind. Now was not the time to think about Ethan. Or to wonder again if Lucinda had spied on Ethan and her that Monday afternoon in the studio and seen things that made her want to run away. Lark's comment about Lucinda hitchhiking and being picked up by the wrong kind of man had only reinforced Meg's own worst scenarios about what might have happened to the wayward teenager. Meg suspected that Lucinda, despite her tough exterior, was not nearly as experienced as she made herself out to be.

Meg took another deep breath and tried to put her personal problems out of her mind for the time being. She had enough worries to contend with at work. She began to mentally sort through everything she had to get done before the SportsTech presentation at three that afternoon. Between Lark's call and a last-minute screwup with one of the ad designs, Meg felt seriously behind, and even as she was talking with Lark, she could hear the phones ringing out at reception almost nonstop. From her glassed-in corner office she could see just enough of the bull pen to know that all three of her art directors and their assistant had, miraculously enough, made it in before ten-thirty. But then, preparing a new business pitch was like getting ready for combat. Troops had to be ready, and battle plans reviewed.

Hardwick and Associates, with fifteen employees including Meg, was not a large agency. The offices themselves were not particularly chic. As Meg's small enterprise had grown, she'd simply rented space adjoining her original closet-size office in a rather dilapidated turn-of-the-century building, and broken through walls to create one large, oddly contoured studio next to four smaller rooms: Meg's office, a tiny conference and lunchroom, Oliver's reception area, and the cubicle office of Eduardo de Marquez, the creative director. The bathrooms were, inconveniently, public and down a long hall. The elevators were temperamental. The cleaning service sporadic at best. But the reasonable monthly rent and the location—in the heart of the Fashion District—made it ideal.

It was a busy shop, the kind of place where people tended to stay put, not because it was particularly good for their careers, but because it was as freewheeling and noisy and slightly crazy as a large, loving family. It was a warm, welcoming place in the middle of a tough and competitive industry. Though Hardwick had a great reputation, fashion clients came and went as they did in all industries—each change of upper management prompted a housecleaning that often resulted in a switching of agencies, deserved or otherwise. Meg had been very lucky. Over the course of the eight years she'd been in business, she'd lost only one account to management changeover. Lately, though, she'd been facing another bane of Madison Avenue—bad debt.

Frieda Jarvis, Inc., a high-end, funky woman's-wear line based in Los Angeles, had been, up to six months ago, one of Meg's favorite accounts. Frieda herself was as wacky as her clothes—loud and flamboyant, a transplanted New Yorker who could talk her way onto the most reluctant buyer's order form. Then Frieda, with the encouragement of a new husband, decided to take the small, growing company public. Donna had done it. Calvin as well. Why not Frieda? Meg, personally, had given her about sixteen reasons why it was a terrible idea, the foremost being that Frieda's clothes were too special, too "nichey" to appeal to the kind of mass market the stock market expected. But Frieda seemed to have acquired, along with the new husband, a hankering for quick money and splashy stories in the business sections.

The initial stock offering had gone up to thirty by the end of its first two weeks and Frieda, flush with her new paper wealth, had Meg run the most expensive nationwide Frieda Jarvis campaign in the company's history. The orders poured in. The factory in Mexico worked overtime. The fall Jarvis line was featured at the front of every major department store and in the windows of all the best boutiques. But the average working woman, alarmed by the jarring color combinations and unfamiliar cuts, didn't even try the clothes on. By the end of August the stock had fallen to four, and Meg was unable to get Frieda's comptroller on the phone to discuss the invoices that had been overdue since June.

With the recent ominous article about the Jarvis stock in the same business section that had touted the offering just six months before, Abe began pressuring Meg to sue for the overdue funds. But Frieda had been one of Meg's first accounts. And a friend, besides. So despite the debt that had slowed Hardwick and Associates' cash flow to a trickle, Meg had opted for tersely worded letters and threatening phone calls. What she needed instead, Meg had decided, was a new, healthy client, with a pristine D&B, and ready cash. So when SportsTech put their account into review, Meg had jumped on the prospective-agency bandwagon.

SportsTech wasn't really Meg's type of client. The hugely successful New Jersey–based company produced midpriced sports- and action-wear for the whole family. Eminently practical and decently made, but with an uninspired logo and ho-hum packaging, SportsTech had the brand awareness of tap water: it wasn't anyone's first choice but it was everywhere and always within reach. Initially, when Meg had asked to be considered in the review, the SportsTech marketing director had expressed surprise . . . and concern. Meg was known for flashy, trendsetting creative.

"I'm not sure we're really your kind of product line," Vincent Goldman had told her.

"Of course you're not sure," Meg had replied. "That's why you're looking at new agencies. But at some point you decided you wanted to try something different. Let me just come out and show you what that might look like."

"You mean pitch it? Right away?"

Usually, at the beginning of a review, competing advertising agencies presented their portfolios and credentials and only after the field was narrowed to the three or four top contenders did agencies prepare full-fledged creative pitches for the potential client.

"Yes. Because you're right, Mr. Goldman—if I show my current portfolio to your management, they'll have a collective coronary. But I'm interested in broadening my client base just as you're looking for something a bit more innovative. I'd say we have enough in common to at least meet one another."

It was a meeting that was now less than four hours away, including the forty-five-minute ride out to

Paramus, so when Oliver buzzed Meg on the inter-com, she told him:

"I can't take any calls now. I'll be with Eduardo going over the—"

"There's someone here to see you," Oliver inter-rupted her.

"I told you I can't—"

"I think you'd better come out to reception right now."

At eleven-fifteen in the morning, Lucinda, who stood leaning against the reception desk shakily smoking a cigarette, looked totally wasted. Her burgundy-dyed hair was matted and greasy. Her face appeared pale and blotchy without makeup. Her clothes—army jacket, blue jeans, oversized flannel work shirt—were rumpled and shiny and gave off an unpleasant aroma of overuse. Sometime over the past few days Lucinda had acquired a nose ring, and the skin around the left nostril where it had been pierced looked infected.

"Where the hell—?"

"Please don't start with me." Lucinda sniffled and Meg realized that she was trying to hold back her tears in front of Oliver.

"Okay, into my office," Meg said, pointing down the hall. She said to Oliver as Lucinda began to follow her, "Tell Eduardo to go ahead and have the artwork mounted on foam core in the order we discussed. And you'd better reserve a car for two-fifteen."

"It's like a regular, I don't know . . ." Lucinda had dropped her backpack on the floor in front of Meg's desk and was looking around the small, cramped room. A filing cabinet, too full to close properly, stood sentinel to the right of the door. A long, faux–wood

covered table sat next to it, stacked with fabric swatch-
es and sample books in plastic binders. Behind that,
taking up most of the wall, was a bulletin board
pinned with active print ads and storyboards in various stages of production.

"Like a regular office?" Meg finished for her, closing the door behind them. "You were expecting
something more glamorous?"

"Yeah. Guess so." Lucinda slumped into the armchair opposite Meg's desk. "Okay, so go ahead and
scream at me. I'm ready now."

"Well, I'm not," Meg replied, sliding into the one
luxury piece of office furniture she'd allowed herself:
a black leather armchair with more adjustable positions than the bucket seat of a Jaguar. "I'm not one of
your parents who, by the way, are totally out their
minds with worry. I just got off the phone with
Lark."

"Lark's not my mom, okay?"

"Oh, give it a rest, Luce. She cares about you. She
and Ethan are sick with worry. You've gotten their
absolute attention, all right?"

"That's not what I wanted," Lucinda mumbled,
chewing on a thumbnail. "I don't give a fuck about
them or their fucking concern."

"Fine. Point registered," Meg said, picking up a pen
and tapping it on the desktop. "Where have you
been?"

"Like . . . around," Lucinda said, looking down at
the badly chipped polish on her nails with sudden
interest. "With some friends."

"Okay," Meg said, trying to keep her patience. In
the past, she'd found that pushing Lucinda for a

clear explanation of her moods or motives only made her shut down even further. "So, just what exactly are you doing here? As you can see, I'm in a middle of a busy, if not particularly glamorous, workday."

"I need a place to stay. I ran out of money," Lucinda's words came out in a rush. "And you told me once that I could come stay with you, remember, like, over Christmas? But so, okay, I'm a little early—"

"That was if you stayed sober. If you pulled yourself together. I'd hardly say—"

"Fine." Lucinda lunged for her backpack. "Thought I'd give it a try. But I can see you're just like the rest of them."

"Oh, sit down," Meg said. "It's not as if you have a million options. Lord, just look at you, sweetheart. Where the hell are you going to go? Without any money. A shelter? Yes, I suppose, you can spend the night."

"Just the night? I was hoping . . ." Lucinda's voice trailed off along with the sentence.

"But we have to call Lark right now," Meg, added. "Let her and Ethan know you're here."

"Oh, fuck that!" Lucinda said, bolting up again. "I'm not talking to him—that asshole."

"I'll call Lark," Meg said, picking up the phone. "You sit there and see if you can't manage to scrounge up a little gratitude for me."

* * *

The meeting had gone well. Very well. Vincent Goldman turned out to be middle-aged and balding, with a basketball-sized paunch. After some initial posturing as a total company man, he began to vent his true feelings about the new corporate VP who had put the account in review against Vincent's better judgment.

Vincent and Meg talked for over an hour about the problems of upper management. About the squeeze so many middle-aged managers were feeling from all these whiz kids with their computers and their MBAs and hot-shot marketing buzzwords. Anyone could sit around yakking about "vertical marketing" and "brand awareness" but it was the Vince Goldmans of this world who actually got the work done. At around four-thirty, Meg was finally able to slide some of the comps across Vincent's desk, showing the three that most closely resembled the company's current approach but with a cleaner, more contemporary graphic look. And Vince had responded with obvious enthusiasm and even further confidences: the SportsTech annual advertising budget would edge six million the following year, not including collateral.

It was past five by the time Vince had wound down enough for Meg to gracefully depart. She settled into the backseat of the livery cab feeling hopeful for the first time all week. An account the size of SportsTech would more than offset Meg's concerns about Frieda Jarvis. Lucinda had resurfaced, seemingly not too much worse for the wear, and Lark had been relieved to the point of tears by the good news. Now there was just the Ethan problem and, with these other positive events behind her, Meg felt newly confident that she could solve that as well. An hour later, between rush-hour traffic and a tractor-trailer accident on the Triborough Bridge, Meg's car was still a mile from the entrance ramp to the George Washington Bridge.

She called Oliver on her cell phone.

"It doesn't look like we're getting back into Manhattan this century. Any fires there that need putting out?"

"No, just a few messages. Nothing business-wise that can't wait until Monday. Lucinda called from your place, as you'd asked, said she's gotten in okay."

"Good. I shudder to think what my kitchen looks like about now."

"Well, I'd certainly count your silverware before she leaves again," Oliver suggested with a smile in his voice. Then he added, "Oh yes, and Ethan phoned right after you left. That's about it."

"So close up shop. And thank everyone for me. I have the feeling we're going to bag this one."

"I knew that kid was trouble the minute I saw her." Salvatore Arigato had been the super at Meg's apartment for the last fifteen years. Short, burly, and opinionated, Sal had a confrontational macho manner that grated on Meg's nerves. She'd long sensed that Sal didn't think any woman should be allowed to live on her own, let alone in one of the best co-op apartments in his building. He accosted Meg by the mailboxes as she came in that evening.

"Are you referring to my niece?" Meg asked, pulling out the mail and then letting the metal door slam shut. She started back down the hall to the elevators, Sal trailing after her.

"Kid with the nose ring. Yeah."

"Need I tell you she's my guest here?" Meg said, straightening to her full height, which made her easily a foot taller than Sal. "I invited her to stay."

"Well, she's gone now. Made a hell of a lot of noise doing it, too. Don't like that kind of craziness around here, Miz Hardwick."

Meg tried not to show her concern as she stepped onto the elevator and pushed the button for her floor. She couldn't imagine what kind of trouble—let alone commotion—Lucinda could make in her apartment. It didn't occur to her until she was hurrying down the hallway from the elevator that, if Lucinda had indeed taken off with Meg's keys, she wouldn't be able to get into her own apartment without having to enlist her insufferable super's aid. She rang her buzzer anyway, mostly out of irritation, and was relieved to hear movement inside. Sal had to be wrong—Lucinda was still there. The door opened, and Meg found herself confronting Ethan.

"I needed to see you," Ethan said. "I tried to call."

"But I phoned Lark. Weren't you still there? Didn't she tell you?"

Ethan leaned against the wall and shook his head, his eyes clouded with worry. It was like some bizarre mirror image of the night of his opening—the two of them facing each other in her front hallway. Only this time when she closed the door, she moved quickly past him and he followed her into the living room.

"Tell me what happened," she said, looking around the room. The doors to her audio unit were open, a dozen CDs stacked in front of it on the carpet. Something had left a slimy path of brown liquid across Meg's good Pakistani carpet. It took a moment for her to see that the trail ended with an open can of Diet Coke lying on its side under the coffee table.

"I had to talk to you. I needed to see you. Lucinda running away like that really threw me. I began to think that maybe it was her the other day in the studio when we heard that noise—maybe she was watching us, hearing me bleating on like some sick ram. I began to see myself through her eyes—objectively, coldly. I hated what I saw, Meg, and I—"

"What happened *today*, Ethan," Meg cut him off, furious that once again Ethan seemed incapable of seeing beyond his own pain and problems. "*Here*, with Lucinda?"

"Well . . ." Ethan began to pace. "I drove down here, figuring you'd still be at work, that I'd wait in the hall until you got home. But I heard music playing in your apartment. I rang the bell."

"And Lucinda answered."

"Yes. And when she saw me she just went ballistic," Ethan paused, looking down the hall to Meg's front door. "She told me to keep my dirty hands off of you. To just leave you—and her—alone. She was seriously nuts. I tried to calm her down." Ethan tapped nervously on the back of Meg's couch.

"So she *had* been spying on us in the studio?"

"Yeah, she told me she saw the whole thing. Accused me of trying to rape you. That wasn't true, I told her. I was just trying to reason with you. To get you to see—"

"Where did she go?" Meg demanded, the anger

ringing so clearly in her voice that Ethan stopped and stared across the room at her.

"I don't know. She slammed out of here, that's all I can tell you. What a mess," he said, running his hands nervously through his hair. "What a fucking—"

"Ethan." Meg stopped him. "We've got to tell Lark what happened."

Meg made the call.

"But I don't understand. . . ." Lark finally replied after she'd heard Meg's explanation. "Ethan left me a note saying that he had to go down early to the gallery. What was he doing at your place?"

"He was . . . there was . . . there was something he needed to talk to me about." The hesitancy in Meg's tone explained far more than she actually said. The silence was a palpable thing, a negative presence, like the dark of night.

"Oh, Meggie," Lark said, as she hung up the phone. "Not you, too."

11

Meg had debated with herself through a long, restless night after that conversation with Lark. She kept waiting for the phone to ring—for Lark or Ethan to call back and say they'd talked it all through. That the truth was finally out. Instead, she'd heard nothing. She'd woken up feeling nervous and ill and decided that the only thing that could set her right would be a good long run in the park. But the run hadn't helped, and soon any hope Meg had of averting the crisis was ended for good. The disaster struck.

I have something to tell you, Meggie. . . . Ethan's dead.

Meg called Abe as soon as she hung up with Lark, but his answering machine informed her that he could be reached upstate that weekend. The radio was delivering severe thunderstorm warnings with gale-force winds throughout the afternoon and into the evening. The air had turned sultry, the sky a dull, ominous green. On the way to pick up her car at the garage on Eighty-eighth Street the wind whipped grit into her eyes, and leaves swirled around her ankles.

The thunderstorm broke again just north of the city and then howled around Meg with a hungry fury almost the entire way up to Red River. Her hands were slick with sweat, her body hunched forward over the wheel straining to see ahead through the sheets of rain and wind. The roads were flooding under the downpour; water slopped against the tires and splashed onto the windshield every time another car passed. She drove as slowly as she dared. She tried to keep her thoughts focused on Ethan and the hell he had created over the past weeks, even as the meaning and extent of the calamity that had overtaken them all washed over her in an enormous wave. Feverish, she felt chilled to the bone and flushed at the same time.

Meg found herself at one point trying to pray, the words swimming unbidden into her consciousness: *Our father who art in heaven.* A few miles later, she heard herself crying "No, oh, please, God, no." Tears streamed unchecked down her cheeks. She was aware of a pain in her chest that wouldn't cease, as though some heavy object were pressing on her diaphragm and interfering with her breathing. It took her a while to realize that there wasn't anything physically wrong with her. Simply put, she was feeling guilt. She'd been weak. She'd been afraid to tell Lark about Ethan's problems. In her attempt to protect her younger sister and let her think that all was right with the world, she'd allowed the very life she hoped to shelter to become disorganized, chaotic.

She had long disliked Ethan's controlling, egotistical tendencies, and yet, looking back over the past long weeks, she realized how closely her own behavior had resembled his. Where had her loyalties been? Her trust? Her respect for her younger sister? From the beginning of Ethan's onslaught, Meg had simply decided that Lark didn't have to know the facts—even worse, perhaps, couldn't handle them. Instead, she'd allowed Ethan to set the pace and control the situation, while they both left the woman who stood most to lose by their actions totally in the dark. Ethan never should have lied to Lark, this was true. On the other hand, Meg should never have allowed him to do so.

How much, even now, did Lark know about the man she'd married? Had Ethan finally told his wife about his feelings for Meg? Had he discussed the emotional whirlwind that had been driving him to extreme behavior over the past few weeks? It was this force, this madness that Ethan had unleashed, that had swept Meg up in its ugly path, and that Meg now believed had pushed Lucinda into an act of blind fury.

Lucinda. Angry, frightened, needy. Lucinda, who saw Meg as a friend and perhaps something of a mentor. Almost from the moment Meg had met Lucinda over a year ago, they'd shared a special rapport. Meg had sensed that the teenager, who frequently complained about having to live out in the sticks, admired Meg's stylish Manhattan wardrobe, her expensive haircut, the overall gloss of city life. After slowly circling Meg for a few weekends, Lucinda had begun to draw closer.

"Cool car," Lucinda had said last summer when

Meg drove up in her newly leased Acura. She'd chosen it primarily for its reputation as a safe, well-built car, and she'd been able to write off half its monthly cost as a company expense.

"Hop in," Meg had invited her. "I've got thirty-six thousand miles to spend." Lucinda had opened up to her for the first time that afternoon, though Meg still wasn't sure why. Perhaps Lucinda thought that Meg's more sophisticated lifestyle would make her a more forgiving listener. Or, more likely, the lonely teenager desperately needed an older woman in whom to confide.

"So, do you have a man friend or anything in the city?" Lucinda had asked after complaining about the idiot geeks who passed for boys in the Red River area. Glancing at the overweight teenager, Meg suspected that Lucinda's difficulty in finding a boyfriend might not be entirely the fault of the male population. Her badly cut dyed hair and poor complexion would no doubt put her somewhere near the bottom of the social food chain.

"I've just broken up with someone," Meg confided in return. This was a month or two before Paul Stokes appeared on her horizon, and she was in her own desperate state about men.

"I bet you get asked out a lot, though," Lucinda replied.

"Oh, I keep busy. But, honestly, I haven't had much luck in the love department."

"Like, you're probably too good for most of them," Lucinda had replied, and Meg felt touched by the younger woman's uncritical support.

"Not necessarily," Meg had said, trying to be truthful and also hoping to give Lucinda some honest advice. "I really believe that a lot about love is a matter of luck. You know, being in the right place at the right time."

"Yeah, but that's the problem," Lucinda said. "In Red River, like, I'm in the wrong fucking place all the time."

That had been the first of many such conversations between Lucinda and Meg. Gradually, Meg began to notice Lucinda's defenses come down and her honesty quotient shoot up.

"You know, it's because I'm fat that no one likes me," she told Meg earlier that past summer. "But I eat because it makes me feel good. Sometimes I can do a whole box of Oreo cookies in one sitting. "

"And that takes—what?—about twenty minutes? That's not a lot of time to feel good, as far as I'm concerned. But I think you're right, Luce. Lose a little weight—you're nice and tall—and the boys will come around."

"I'm not saying that the boys don't, like, come around, Meg," Lucinda said slyly. "There's other ways of attracting attention, if you know what I mean."

Meg made a policy of not lecturing Lucinda directly; she knew the teenager wouldn't listen if she tried. Instead, she tried to make her points by speaking in generalities. Lucinda was smart enough to draw her own conclusions.

"You know, I've always thought that no one's going to like you if you make it clear that you don't much like yourself. Giving it away for free is a mighty clear sign that you're discounting the merchandise."

Whether Lucinda ever acted on her advice, Meg
didn't know. She did keep tagging along behind her
on weekends when she visited. Lark pointed out that,
unlike other Saturdays nights, Lucinda always made a
point of sticking around for dinner if Meg was there.
Meg was well aware that Lucinda's behavior when she
wasn't around was far from stellar: her drinking and
delinquency at school were only worsening with
time. But Meg knew that Lucinda trusted her, probably more than she did anyone else in Red River.
Trusted and liked her. And by not stopping Ethan
weeks before, by allowing his feelings to spiral so out
of control, she had exposed Lucinda to something the
girl never should have witnessed. Afterward, when
Lucinda ran away, it was Meg she ultimately sought
out. Looking for a haven. And it was Meg who had
allowed Lucinda to open the door to the girl's worst
nightmare: Ethan.

Like an avenging angel, Lucinda had performed the
act that Meg should have done weeks ago herself—she
stopped Ethan from doing any further harm. Lucinda's
impulsive deed, however, had been fatal. Whether or
not she intended to kill her stepfather, she had surely
destroyed her own chances. And, right now, as far as
Meg could tell, no one but Meg really knew why.

The rain began to ease by the time she turned off
the highway. When she finally drove through Red
River, Meg allowed herself a moment of wild disbe-
lief. The town looked the same; it had all been a bad
dream. Ethan would be waiting at the house—clomping across the front hall as he flung open the front
door. Lark and the girls would be behind him, laughing and welcoming. Lucinda would be skulking

somewhere close by, unable to suppress her welcoming smile. But the illusion lasted only as long as it took her to turn into the McGowan's drive and see how many people had already come to console the bereaved family.

Meg recognized Francine's Chevy pickup, parked at the top of the hill by the house behind Abe's black Saab; a dozen or so other cars and trucks were pulled off along the driveway. Meg had to park near the studio, which, flanked now by police cruisers, was lit up against the slowly clearing sky. The rain had finally stopped, but Meg had to slog through mud to reach the front steps to the porch.

The house felt empty and cold—as if no one had bothered to turn the heat up that morning. Meg added her dripping boots to the jumble outside the front door, her parka to the pile of coats on the chair in the front hall. Generally, when Lark was entertaining, she cleared the downstairs coat closet for the guests. She liked to give the house at least a semblance of order, a center of gravity amidst the pandemonium created by the children. Meg had once seen Lark carefully align a pile of magazines on the coffee table when the entire living room looked like an uncharted sea of Barbies, Scrabble pieces, and abandoned homework assignments.

Meg followed the murmur of voices down the long hallway past the living room to the sun porch that ran the length of the house at the back and overlooked the river below. Though Ethan and Lark had wanted to keep the nineteenth-century farmhouse essentially true to its original function and design, they'd both felt that the downstairs rooms were dark and the low ceilings claustrophobic, especially during the long winter months. The sun porch had been Lark's idea, but it had quickly turned into one of Ethan's elaborate projects. The room was his design. It was two stories high and almost all windows; facing the river was a wall of diamond-shaped panes of the palest green cast that he had handmade in his studio. Many panes contained stained-glass murals of a flower, leaf, hummingbird, or frog. When the sun streamed through the bare trees as it did that afternoon, the room swirled with pinpoints of brilliant refracted color. Meg stopped at the door, her view slightly blocked by the broad shoulders of a man she didn't know.

Lark, her face blotchy from crying, sat next to Francine on the low-slung red corduroy couch. Phoebe was nestled next to Lark and sucking noisily on her thumb. Brook was perched beside Phoebe, her back very straight; her red-rimmed eyes traveled from adult to adult with the conversation.

Janine rocked in the wicker rocker kitty-corner to the couch, sniffling into a wad of tissues. Abe stood next to a man Meg recognized as the town's retired postmaster, nodding emphatically to something the older man was saying. Though Meg didn't know all their names, she recognized most of the other dozen or so adults, neighbors and friends, whose casseroles, breads, and cookies cluttered the long French picnic table. An aluminum twenty-four-cup electric coffee urn—Meg thought she recognized it from Francine's chicken roasts and bake sales—stood in the middle of the table. Hot paper cups and matching napkins printed with smiling teddy bears were stacked next to it.

"Well, as far as I'm concerned you went above and beyond," Meg heard Paula Yoder say as she entered the room. Paula who, with her husband Mike, ran the general store, knew everybody's business and possessed a wide-ranging and frequently enumerated inventory of opinions. Her dislike for Lucinda, who had twice been caught stealing cartons of Marlboros from the storeroom, was well-known. "Way, way beyond."

"I think we all agree on that," Francine added with finality. In the past, Paula had not been above declaring that Lark let Lucinda run wild, that she didn't know how to discipline the teenager. After the second petty theft incident, Paula had filed a formal complaint with Tom Huddleson and refused to allow Lucinda in the store.

"Some people are just ... sometimes there's just nothing ..." Ivar Dyson, who ran a goat farm that abutted Ethan and Lark's property to the north, had been a longtime friend of Ethan's. The two men could not have been less alike: Ivar was terse and politically conservative, a card-carrying member of the NRA. Though Ethan often poked fun at the straitlaced dairyman, it was obvious that he also respected Ivar. And the girls loved the rolling pastures of Dyson Farms and its ever-growing herd. When Ivar was shorthanded, Ethan would help with the milking. Afterward, under the fluorescent lights in the milking shed, the two men would play chess. They were an evenly matched pair and sometimes the games would go on for hours.

"We know, we know," Francine said comfortingly when it was clear that Ivar was choking up. "It's unfair. It appears to be unjust, terribly so. But we'll never fully comprehend why things happen as they must, what makes people turn out the way they do."

A sudden wave of dislike for the minister swept over Meg; Francine, Meg thought, was definitely in her element. Her arm draped protectively around Lark's shoulders, her more-than-ample body weighing down the lumpy couch, she was the stolid center of the situation. Death, misery—this was *her* business, her longsuffering expression seemed to say. Francine Werling was the expert, dispensing advice and comfort as needed to the poor, stunned amateurs in her midst. What bothered Meg was the sense—and today was not the first time she'd felt it—that Francine secretly enjoyed these times of tragedy. She gloried in her power to comfort, her ability to be articulate and wise when those around her were struck dumb with grief.

"Meg, when did you get here?" Abe saw her hesitating at the door and called to her over the hubbub.

Lark called to her. "Meggie . . ." Meg walked across the room and knelt in front of the couch as Lark leaned forward to embrace her. "Oh, Meggie . . . What will become of us?" Lark whispered as Meg tried to pull her closer. Though it looked as though the two sisters were holding each other warmly, Meg could feel the resistance in Lark's body. Her muscles were so taut they seemed to vibrate with tension. After a few moments, Meg tried to look her younger sister in the eye, tried to gauge the depths of what she knew, but Lark's gaze kept skittering away. Her eyes had an overexcited glitter, darting around the room, not focusing, and her smile was fixed.

"Meg, dear, could you check to see who might like some more coffee?" she asked in her best hostess's voice.

"Actually, perhaps Meg might be more useful taking care of Brook and Phoebe," Francine suggested. "The weather's finally cleared, and they haven't been out of the house all day."

"I'd be happy to," Meg replied, though she hardly needed Francine to tell her that the girls needed some attention. Phoebe hadn't taken her thumb out of her mouth since Meg had arrived and Brook had the stunned look of a wounded animal.

"Hey, guys, let's go for a walk," Meg said, her voice falsely cheerful even to her own ears. But the girls nevertheless followed her obediently to the mud room beyond the kitchen where she helped them pull on boots and jackets. Outside, though the temperature had dropped at least ten degrees, the sky had lightened, and to the west the last of the sun streamed dramatically thought the departing banks of cloud. The trees dripped with leftover rain, and the swollen river roared between its banks. A family of chickadees swooped and chattered around the elaborate array of handcrafted feeders that Ethan had constructed in the backyard. It felt wrong to Meg that the afternoon had suddenly turned so calm, so normal. She wanted everything to stop. To be silent. To feel as damaged and different as she did.

The three of them walked along the bank of the river, the mud sucking at their boots with each step. Meg tried to think of something comforting to say, something to stave off the confusion and pain in their young hearts. Without any warning, Phoebe suddenly raised the stick she'd been trailing and slashed it into a large pile of soggy leaves.

"That's what Lucie did to Daddy, right?" Phoebe

said, turning to Meg for confirmation. She looked so like Lark as a child—the heart-shaped face, bright blue eyes, a sweetness that either a child was born with, or wasn't. Brook, on the other hand, didn't have Phoebe's sunlit nature; neither had Meg at her age. Brook was more cautious, more curious, demanding proofs and answers. Phoebe had always jumped right into life, laughing, ready for anything, come what may. That's, why, Meg thought, it hurt so much more to have Phoebe ask the question rather than Brook.

"We don't really know for sure," Meg began, looking from Phoebe's wide eyes to Brook's lowered gaze. She could not lie to them. "But it looks like that's what happened."

12

By Sunday evening, Meg was beginning to think that the guests would never leave. She hadn't slept much the night before—nobody in the household had—and she'd spent most of the day on her feet. She was trying her best to handle the kinds of household things that Lark would usually have attended to. Francine had made an announcement from the pulpit that morning about Ethan's death, asking the congregation to pray for peace and forgiveness and suggesting that neighbors offer whatever help they could to the bereaved family. It seemed to Meg that the help consisted primarily of casseroles and sweets that only the visitors themselves had the appetites to consume.

Over the course of the afternoon, the flow of guests increased dramatically. Each new arrival brought yet another covered dish or cookie tin and Meg had to see to it that everything was properly heated, set out on the long planked table on the sun porch, and, when necessary, the empty dishes removed, to make room for the new ones waiting in the kitchen. Even the smallest task seemed to take an enormous amount of effort on her part. It didn't help that Lark was doing her best to ignore her, turning to Francine, Janine—anyone but her sister—for the emotional support Meg would have so gladly supplied.

Later on, Abe drove Lark into town to meet with the police. Janine helped Meg attempt to feed the girls in the kitchen. No one ate much of anything. Francine became the de facto hostess, welcoming new visitors with a serenity Meg found particularly grating. And something about the milling, chattering group began to take on the feel of rubberneckers crowding around the scene of an accident. As she stacked yet another load of dishes in the washer, she overheard snippets of conversations taking place in the hallway:

"There was blood all over the place, I hear."

"Poor old Tom. He's never had to handle more 'n' a traffic ticket before in this town."

"Deputy Voberg told me Tom called up the state police so fast his head was spinning."

"Yeah, I saw the cruisers down by the studio."

Lark and Abe came back a little past eight-thirty, and Lark went up to see the girls, while Abe sought Meg out in the kitchen.

"I don't know how Lark's managing to hold herself together," he said, helping himself to a cup of coffee. He looked as tired as Meg felt, the skin under his eyes smudged with fatigue. "Huddleson was nice enough, but those state detectives are all business. They're already all set up in the clerk's spare office above the police station."

"To do what?" Meg asked. "Everybody knows Lucinda killed Ethan."

"But it's a homicide case, Meg," Abe explained. "There has to be an investigation no matter what the circumstances. And a town this size just isn't equipped to handle that kind of thing. That's what this state crime unit does. The detectives come in with all the latest forensic training and equipment. They've sealed off the studio."

"Yes, I know." Meg said. Wearily, she turned back to the sink. Though the question weighed heavily on her mind, she asked with forced lightness, "Did you see Lucinda? Has anyone spoken to her . . . since it happened?"

"They took her to the medical center over in Montville," Abe said, setting his coffee mug down on the counter and picking up a towel to help her with the dishes. "She's still in pretty bad shape, I understand. Bad burns on her hands. And hungover as hell from whatever she was on. Tom told me she was really out of it when they took her in."

"Oh God, Abe." Meg sighed, leaning on the sink for support. "I just feel so . . . so . . . ." When Abe put his arms around her, Meg finally found the permission she needed to give in to the distress that had been building within her all day. She wept. Abe guided her over to the kitchen table and pulled out a chair, taking a seat beside her. In the middle of the round wooden table, Ethan and Lark had years ago carved their initials in a big heart and, when the girls were old enough to spell, they'd been allowed to add their names to the battered oak surface. Reaching for the tissue Abe held out to her, Meg saw the uncertain spidery letters spelling BROOK chiseled into the wood and she felt another wave of sorrow break within her. Ethan's murder was more than a loss of one life; it signaled the end of innocence for his daughters, as well. Today's events would forever change the carefree little girl who'd carved her name. Just as it had destroyed all immediate hope for Lucinda to find the love and acceptance she needed.

"You okay?" Abe asked, tucking a strand of Meg's hair behind her ear and leaning in to look at her.

"Not really," Meg answered. She found herself longing to confide in Abe, to pour out her feelings of guilt and regret. He had always been a good listener, fair-minded and realistic. She sat across from him now, trying to think of the right way to begin. "Everyone's so furious with Lucinda. I hear such hate in their voices. Am I the only one who feels sorry for her at all?"

"Well, this town's pretty upset right now," Abe said. "They're thinking about themselves—the danger Lucinda represents in their minds. It'll calm down eventually."

"I hope so. I've been listening to Francine all day, preaching tolerance and forgiveness. The whole time I've had this sneaking suspicion that she's . . . I hate to say this. She seems perfectly okay with the idea that Ethan's dead—and that Lucinda killed him."

Abe sat back in his chair and folded his arms across his chest. Even in his faded flannel shirt and jeans it was evident he wasn't a local. His hair was fashionably cut. His skin had the smooth pallor of someone who worked indoors. He carried himself with the confidence of a man who knows his place and value in the wider world. "Not everybody in this town felt the way you did about Lucinda and Ethan."

"Meaning?"

"A lot goes on in a small town like this that you—visiting every few weeks or so—never see. It looks like a place Norman Rockwell would have painted, doesn't it? Everyone's so friendly. So different from the city. You begin to think that the people are genuinely *nicer*, and somehow *better* here than in other places. Don't kid yourself, Meg. Human nature doesn't change with location."

"People were jealous of Ethan? His success with the studio?"

"Jealous, maybe . . . but . . ." Abe thought better of what he was going to say. "Listen, it's late. We're all tired. I'll try to roust that crowd out of there so you and Lark can get to bed."

"Wait, Abe." She touched his arm. She hesitated a moment, examining the face before her, etched with exhaustion. Her own problems could wait. "Are you trying to tell me something that I'm not getting?"

"Maybe just to watch your step the next few days . . . and watch your temper, as well. Things might be said . . . you may hear some things that you won't like. Remember, this isn't your town, Meg. Or Lucinda's. And, in many ways, it was never Ethan's. When all is said and done, he was just visiting, too." Abe rose. "I'll talk to you tomorrow."

Not surprisingly, Francine was the last to leave. Lark walked her to the front door and Meg saw them embrace. Francine whispered something urgently in Lark's ear and gave her one last hug.

"Goodnight, Meg," Francine called over her shoulder as she zipped up her jacket. "You've been a tremendous source of strength." Lark closed the door behind her. The night before, Lark gone to bed with a tranquilizer. Today she had been busy with her children, visitors, endless phone calls, and the police.

Now, for the first time since Ethan's murder, Lark and Meg were alone together.

They sat by the fire—now just a pile of smoldering embers—in the living room, Lark curled up in a corner of the couch, Meg in the wooden rocker nearby. Lark appeared strangely composed, until she lifted her hand to brush back her hair and Meg saw that she was trembling.

"Long day," Meg said.

"Yes. Horrible. And weirdly wonderful at the same time. Everyone has been so loving. Open. There for me. Us. And these aren't people who show their emotions often. Francine says it was cathartic. For everyone."

"Cathartic? Ethan's *murder*? I can't believe you really feel that way."

"Don't tell me how to feel." Though Lark's words were stinging, her tone was controlled and emphatic, as though she were reciting from memory. "I'm trying to cope with this . . . this *evil* . . . with love. I'm desperately trying not to wallow in anger. To stay above the horror of what has been inflicted on me. My family. I know precisely what we're *talking* about."

"I'm sorry."

"Oh, I'm sure you are," Lark said. "I can only imagine how terrible you must feel. But I don't want to hear about it. Your feelings. Or what happened between you and Ethan."

"So Ethan told you," Meg said, confirming what she had suspected from the moment she'd seen Lark the day before—when she'd resisted Meg's embrace. Lark turned away from her now, pulling the afghan throw off the back of the couch and drawing it over her shoulders.

"Ethan told you that *nothing* happened, right?" Meg went on, trying to help her sister deal with the pain and humiliation of her husband's emotional betrayal. "I still don't understand what he was going through, exactly. I think it was some kind of midlife crisis—some kind of fixation."

"He felt vulnerable about my book getting published," Lark said. "He was having a hard time handling my success. It was a way of building his ego. I think it's pretty simple."

If only Ethan hadn't first approached her before he even knew that Lark had sold her book, Meg thought. But tonight seemed the wrong time to try to correct Lark's conclusion—there was too much else to cope with. But Meg was determined to help Lark face the truth someday; no good had come from letting her sister make up her own version of reality.

"Perhaps," Meg said gently, rocking back in her chair. "But he was definitely working through some real conflicts, some serious problems. I'm afraid I was just too shocked by his behavior to be of much help."

"It wasn't your role to help," Lark replied tersely. "I didn't want to get into this, but I think now that I'd better. I know my husband is—" she hesitated and Meg saw her hands shaking again as she pulled at the afghan, "was enormously attractive. He had women throwing themselves at him. But I never for a moment thought that you—my sister—"

"What are you talking about?" Meg stopped rocking.

"How you felt about Ethan," Lark said, staring blankly at the fire. "I don't know why I should have been surprised. He's so—that amazing appeal. And you're lonely, you've been so disappointed—"

"Stop right there," Meg said, standing up. "I never for one moment reciprocated Ethan's feelings. Did he tell you that? What the hell did he say to you?"

"Please, Meg," Lark shook her head. "Don't shout. The children . . ." She hugged her knees to her chest. "Ethan was one of those men whom women just feel naturally feel drawn to. I've known this—I've dealt with it for years. It's not a big deal for me—"

"Well, it is for me," Meg interrupted again, crossing to the couch and sitting down. "I can't have you thinking for even a moment that I felt anything for Ethan besides a—a sisterly kind of love."

"It's okay, Meg," Lark said sadly. "It's so relatively unimportant compared to what's happened. God, this thing with Lucinda. My mind just can't seem to process everything. The whole chain of events." She paused. "Did you realize that Lucinda stole money from you? Off your dresser for a bus ride home?"

"No. I guess I was too upset to—"

"She took the bus to Albany," Lark went on. "Called me from the station to pick her up. This was about an hour after you and Ethan had called. So I already knew what had happened when I went to get her." Lark leaned back in her chair. "We had a good talk on the way home. It's funny, but that's the only decent conversation I think I've ever had with her. We bonded. We both agreed that men were shits. That you couldn't count on them. You had to forge your own existence. We only spoke in general terms. She didn't mention you and Ethan in particular. I assumed, of course, that she was upset about the situation for my sake. I was touched. I remember thinking that I really had never given her the chance she deserved. . . ."

"You did everything you could—" Meg tried to reassure her sister, but Lark seemed determined not to let her have a say.

"No, wait! Listen. This is all much worse . . . more complicated . . . than you think." Lark took a long, deep breath. She exhaled slowly, and said: "Lucinda was pregnant. She had a miscarriage last night in jail. That's one of the things the police wanted to talk to me about this afternoon."

"Oh my God."

"Yes. Indeed." Lark stared at the dead fire. "Though it's hard to know at a time like this whether you really want there to be a God or not. I mean, what kind of a God would let things get so totally screwed up? I was telling Francine that the only way I know I'm still alive is because I'm so angry. It really feels as if my blood, my breathing . . . has turned into pure burning rage."

"But what does Lucinda being pregnant have to do with her killing Ethan?"

Lark was silent.

"You don't actually think that . . ." Meg couldn't finish her thought.

"Yes. I think it is possible that Ethan was the father

of Lucinda's poor little ... Remember, Ethan was Lucinda's *step*father, not her real father, and—according to Ethan, anyway—they'd always had this very weird, strained relationship. She acted like she hated him, and she made such a display of her dislike. It was a very complicated kind of love-hate. In the last couple of months, she became so needy and aggressive. Hormones totally out of control."

"I don't believe it."

"You don't know what it was like here, Meg. Lucinda could be very provocative. She'd wander out of the bathroom half naked. And she'd taunt him constantly. Make fun of his ego ... his manhood. I can imagine Ethan getting mad. And yes, I can even imagine him getting aroused. And, well, poor Ethan. He can't resist." Lark shut her eyes for a second. "Couldn't."

But Meg could conjure up a very different scenario. She recalled the Ethan she had grown to fear: his raw power, his sudden bursts of emotion and need. She imagined Lucinda thoughtlessly provoking him—and Ethan losing control. She remembered his fierce grip, the feeling of utter helplessness when she realized that Ethan overpowered her. Meg had been lucky enough to escape. But if Lucinda hadn't, if Ethan had indeed assaulted her, Meg could only imagine Lucinda's rage, the dark underside of need. The hand groping blindly for the pontil—

"Lark, listen to me." Meg touched her sister's arm. "Nothing happened between Ethan and me ... but I went through enough to realize he could be very aggressive and—"

"I told you I don't want to hear about it." Lark's eyes flashed, and Meg saw the anger under the calm exterior. Meg had long thought she understood Lark better than anyone else in the world. Each sister, without having to say word, seemed always to know what the other was thinking. And over the years they'd developed their own shorthand way of communicating—a raised eyebrow from Lark had more meaning for Meg than a long, impassioned argument from someone else.

Yet tonight, trying to read Lark's gaze, hoping to gauge the depths of her sorrow, Meg had to face the fact that Ethan's death and the events leading up to it had severed the vital, intricate bond between them. The murder had hit their relationship hard, destroying connections, wiping out naturalness. Meg had been waiting for two days to be with Lark, to share her sorrow, to pour out her grief and love. But at that moment she might as well have been sitting across from a stranger.

"I need you too much right now to hate you, as I'm so tempted to do," Lark finally told her. "The only thing that keeps me from it . . . is knowing that you don't—didn't—really understand Ethan and me at all."

It was the most wounding thing she could have said.

13

Montville was the largest town in the county, though that hardly meant it ranked as a major metropolis. The summer visitors nearly doubled its population, but at the height of the season, that amounted to no more than fifteen thousand people. Its wide maple-lined downtown avenues had undergone a major face-lift during the last decade when the booming stock market had brought an influx of second-home buyers along with a fresh infusion of capital. Clothing boutiques, a gourmet cookware store, a wine merchant, and an ever-changing selection of restaurants now lined Main Street. The railroad station, abandoned for decades, had been converted into a mini-mall. Montville was the county seat, and its courthouse, an elaborate 1880s brick edifice, looked out behind its curving entranceway and well-tended green with the gracious, slow-paced solidity of a long-forgotten era.

Up the hill behind the courthouse, the Montville Medical Center, a modern, full-service hospital, served the neighboring communities with well-deserved acclaim. At ten-thirty on a Monday morning the visitors parking lot was half full.

"You're coming in with me?" Meg asked Abe after he'd parked the car near the front entrance. He'd already done so much for the family, stopping by the house first thing that morning with sticky buns for the girls and some legal advice for Lark and Meg. Lark had confided the facts of Lucinda's miscarriage to Abe after the police interview and, though Lark's anger toward Lucinda had now all but hardened into hatred, Abe had been able to convince her that Lucinda deserved a good criminal lawyer going forward. He'd suggested a friend of his—Peter Boardman—who worked out of Albany, and Lark reluctantly agreed to the suggestion.

"Yes," Abe said, as he climbed out of the driver's seat. "I want to get Lucinda hooked up with Boardman. And you look like you could use the support."

Meg was not surprised to hear she appeared shaky. She had hardly slept again the night before, obsessively rethinking the events that led up to Ethan's murder . . . and her role in them. Her passivity during those weeks haunted her—her procrastinating, her justifications. Though physically and emotionally exhausted, Meg wanted to spring into action, get things moving, try to right the wrong she had allowed to be done. At daybreak she decided that she had to visit Lucinda and hear her side of the story. She stuck to her resolve even when

Lark announced coldly that she could really use Meg's assistance around the house. Ethan's funeral was scheduled for the following afternoon and she needed help with the girls, the arrangements, the visitors who continued to stop by. Lark was clearly unhappy when Abe suggested that he and Meg drive over to Montville together.

Despite her determination, Meg was feeling nervous and uncertain about her meeting with Lucinda. What did she possibly think she could do to help at this point? And though she wanted Abe with her, at the same time she wished she'd had the chance to tell him about her own complicated problems with Ethan on the way over in the car. But he'd spent the twenty-minute drive on his cell phone with Boardman, filling him in on the details of the case.

They learned from the ground-floor receptionist that Lucinda was being held in a special ward on the second floor under a security watch. Following a phone call from the receptionist, a policewoman came down to escort them to Lucinda's room. After they'd been searched and cleared by the officer, Meg and Abe followed the nurse through swinging doors into the infirmary. Lucinda was at the end of the room, past a row of empty beds. Her hands, bandaged in gauze, lay on her stomach like two white boxing gloves. An IV stand stood beside the bed.

"Visitors, Lucinda," the nurse announced, as they approached.

"I don't want to see anybody," Lucinda muttered, turning her face to the wall. Though Abe hesitated at the foot of the bed, Meg went quickly around and crouched down beside Lucinda, her heart aching as she took in the teenager's clearly terrified expression.

"Hey, Luce," Meg said.

"Go away," Lucinda said. Her face was a puffy mask of tears. She tried to squirm down under the sheets.

"Sit up," the nurse ordered her sharply. "You'll pull out the IV."

Whimpering, Lucinda obeyed, and the nurse and guard moved off together to stand by the door.

"Lucinda," Meg said again. "We're not here to blame you. We just want to understand . . . what happened."

"I can't. I really can't." She screwed her eyes shut. "I don't remember." Tears oozed from under her lids and slid down her chin. She kept biting her lower lip, and Meg saw that it was bruised and bleeding slightly.

"Listen, Lucinda," Abe tried. "This is not a game. It's very, very serious. You've got to tell us what happened Saturday morning."

"I'm sorry." Lucinda began crying in earnest.

"We know," Meg said. "We know you are." She sat on the edge of the bed. She brushed back Lucinda's dirty bangs from her forehead.

"I mean, I'm sorry . . . I don't remember." She wept almost silently, though the sobs shook her whole body.

"Listen, Luce," Meg began, trying to keep her voice calm while thinking how best to phrase what she had to say. "I think I understand a little better now about Ethan and you. I mean, what he did to you . . . I understand that what you did—it was a moment of a kind of insanity. And I think everyone can recognize, can somehow sympathize if not forgive, knowing that

Ethan . . . I mean the fact that you were pregnant."

"But that's what I'm trying to tell you, Meg. I didn't know. I didn't know what was happening to me."

"You didn't know you were pregnant?" Abe demanded.

"No," Lucinda said. "Nobody told me until it was . . . gone."

"But then, why?" Meg asked. "Why did you . . ."

"I don't *remember*," Lucinda said, pawing at her cropped hair with bandaged hands. "I remember deciding to go down to the studio. I was going to confront him, you know. Tell him to stay away from you. That you were better than that. I was going to finally tell him, face-to-face, what I thought of him. What he did to my Mom. To Lark. Then to you. I couldn't *believe* he'd go after you. I was so pissed. Okay, I admit it. I was also totally drunk at the time so my thinking wasn't entirely, like, clear."

"What about *you*, Luce?" Meg persisted, "What did he do to you?"

"Ethan? That's what you all think, right? That Ethan fucked me—got me pregnant—and so I murdered him?" Lucinda began to giggle, her shoulders shaking.

"This isn't funny, Lucinda." Abe said, pacing beside the bed.

"Oh, yes it is! If you only knew—the idea of Ethan fucking me! You can forget about it. Ethan thought I was a pig—big and ugly. He made that plenty clear. Couldn't stand to even touch me for chrissakes. Though there were plenty of guys in that town who liked me just fine. Thought I was pretty okay. Even if my stepfather thought I was hideous. I guess that his stinking attitude toward me was enough reason to hate him. And I'm not saying that I didn't hate him. I did."

"But you didn't kill him?" Meg asked.

"I don't think I could have, though I'll tell you right now I wouldn't be sorry if I had. In fact, I think I would've been almost proud of myself. But, the truth is, I don't have it in me. I literally can't hurt a fly. I like lift them up by their wings and all and take 'em outside to let them go free. You know what I mean? I can't even begin to imagine having the guts to drive that thing through Ethan's heart."

"Luce, they found you holding the pontil," Meg said sadly. "It was in your *hands*. Look at your bandages."

The three of them stared at the white wrappings around Lucinda's palms.

"You know what I was thinking?" Lucinda finally said. "What if I, like, found him that way? You know, with that thing, the pontil, already there?" Her words were coming out in a rush, the scenario obviously something she'd already played over in her mind already. "What if someone else killed him before I came in? And I see this pontil and Ethan, you know, like, *dying*. And I pulled the damn thing . . . out?"

"Is that how you remember things now?" Abe asked, skepticism clear in his tone.

"No." Lucinda sighed heavily turning away from Abe and looking straight into Meg's eyes. "I'm not going to lie. I know the shit I'm in here. I don't remember a thing after draining that fifth of vodka and throwing the bottle under the studio. I don't even remember walking up the back steps. It's just—a blank."

"You swear to God that Ethan never laid a finger on you?" Abe said.

Lucinda nodded her head, her eyes welling again with tears.

"Luce, do you think you might have done it," Meg hesitated, glancing at Abe, then looking back to Lucinda again. "Do you think you might have done it . . . because of what Ethan tried to do to me?"

"Like I said. I went there to warn him off, you know? Not to fucking kill him. There's a huge difference. I don't know what happened exactly except for one thing: I didn't murder Ethan. And if it wasn't me, Meg, whoever did kill Ethan is walking around right now hoping nobody's going to believe a word that comes out of the mouth of a total fuckup like me. You've got to believe me. You've got to help me."

"We've hired a lawyer for you," Abe said. "He'll be coming down from Albany tomorrow to visit with you. We'll call him before we leave and give him your number here."

"I don't care about a lawyer," Lucinda said, looking frantically from Abe to Meg. "I need your help, Meg."

"I'll do whatever I can," Meg said, standing up to go. She patted Lucinda's shoulder. "But it's really out of our hands now."

"No, Meg, don't say that," Lucinda cried. "You've got to listen. You're the only person involved who wasn't at Red River that morning. You *couldn't* have killed Ethan. Meg, you're the only person I know who doesn't have any reason to want to pin this thing on me."

*　*　*

"She could actually be telling the truth about blacking out," Dr. Sutphin, the chief resident, told Meg and Abe when they met with him afterward in his corner administration office on the ground floor. The psychiatric counselor, a Dr. Fredricks, joined them in the book-lined, sun-dappled room.

"That's correct," Dr. Fredricks added. He was a slight, balding man, with a pair of distinctive thick red-rimmed glasses and, it seemed to Meg, fidgety gestures. "In fact, I'd be alarmed and suspicious if she *did* claim a clear memory of the events leading up to the murder. She was still thoroughly intoxicated when she arrived here. Easily an hour and a half after she was charged."

"She was drunk?" Abe asked. "You verified that?"

"We took blood immediately. She was high on vodka and Percodan. An extremely potent combination. Frequently toxic. Occasionally fatal."

"It was a primary cause of the miscarriage," Dr. Sutphin added. "That and a lack of sleep. Not eating correctly. The body can take just so much abuse— even a teenager's—and then it just rebels."

"Tell us about that," Meg said. "What happened, exactly?"

Dr. Sutphin glanced at Dr. Fredricks.

"I'm not here on the weekends. So perhaps Dr. Fredricks can . . ."

"Actually, I wasn't on the premises myself. You know, we rotate into the prison ward. I'm on call Saturdays and . . ." the doctor began, but Meg interrupted, saying:

"Can we find someone who *was* here? We'd really like to know firsthand what took place."

"I was thoroughly briefed," Dr. Fredricks said. "And I can certainly walk you through the chain of events with authority. Lucinda had been admitted. Her routine physical at that time showed that her blood alcohol level was through the roof. We sent the blood sample to the lab for further testing and for a more definitive breakdown of alcohol and drugs, et cetera. No one at that time suspected she was pregnant, though the lab tests would, of course, later confirm the fact. The nurse saw that she had begun to bleed and assumed it was the beginning of her normal cycle. She gave her a menstrual pad."

"Nobody thought to ask?" Meg demanded.

"Actually, they did. It's a routine question here. She told them she wasn't pregnant."

"The bleeding worsened through the night, apparently," Dr. Fredricks continued. "The nurse on the floor thought it was just a particularly heavy period. Lucinda, by the way, gave her no reason to think otherwise. She even demanded a painkiller at one point, complaining about her cramps."

"But she didn't alert you that it could be more serious than that?" Abe asked.

"Frankly," Dr. Fredricks replied, "from what the staff has told me, she was incoherent, profane, and extremely rude. No, she made no mention—in word or deed—of her condition."

"Surely you understand how critical some of these issues are to us," Meg said.

"Look, this is a busy hospital," Dr. Fredricks said. "We were shorthanded on Saturday night, doing the best we could."

Meg stood up. She glanced over at Abe, who hadn't

moved or spoken in several minutes. He was looking thoughtfully from Meg to Dr. Fredricks.

Dr. Sutphin also rose, and walked around his desk. He took Meg's elbow and started to lead her gently to the door. "Let us know if we can be of any further help. You can call me directly any time."

Abe got up to join them and they had opened the door to the corridor when Meg stopped.

"I've a question," she said, looking back at Dr. Fredricks. "What happened to the . . . baby?"

"Excuse me?"

"When Lucinda miscarried?" Meg asked. "What happened to the fetus? We are trying to determine who the father actually was."

"As I told you before," Dr. Fredricks said slowly, "the nurse on duty thought Lucinda was simply experiencing a particularly heavy menstruation. It wasn't until a resident examined Sunday morning that we realized she'd in fact had a miscarriage."

"So where's the fetal tissue?" Meg demanded. It was the crucial question. If Ethan was the father, and Lucinda had lied about their relationship, then she could very well be lying about the murder, as well. "Apparently," Dr. Fredricks said, "from everything we can ascertain . . ." He cleared his throat and continued, "we don't think she really knew what she was doing at the time, but Lucinda flushed it down the toilet."

14

Abe and Meg weren't five minutes out of Montville before he asked, "You want to tell me about you and Ethan?"

Abe had a stare that could be disconcertingly personal, Meg decided, as though he was appraising your net worth as a human being.

"I've been wanting to for a while," Meg replied. "It's just not easy explaining that your brother-in-law is coming on to you."

"He was the man Paul saw you with at lunch that day, right?" Abe said, turning back to the road. The storm that had swept up the coast the day of Ethan's murder was to be followed, according to local forecasts, by a series of unstable, possibly dangerous weather systems over the next few days. The wind was ripping the last of the leaves off the trees and, though it was just noon, the sky was the lowering gray of early evening.

"Yes." Meg sighed. The blocks of quiet homes circling Montville had given way to acres of farmland and rolling, wooded hills. She looked out over the rural landscape and wondered if she would ever be able to respond to its beauty again. "It started the night of his opening. We'd all had too much to drink. Lark wasn't there. He saw me back to my place. He kissed me and he tried to—God, Abe—I just assumed he was drunk at the time."

"And you responded . . . how?"

"With a lot of anger."

"You mention it to Lark?"

"At the time it seemed unnecessary, hurtful even. I thought he'd just gotten drunk and sort of lost it."

"But it was more than that?" Abe asked, slowing down as they neared a diner at the intersection of two county roads. It was a popular place that catered to local farmers and truck drivers, and Abe suggested that they stop there for lunch. With a subtlety that attested to his skills as a lawyer, Abe drew out the rest of the story from Meg over sandwiches and coffee.

"And you didn't think to tell Lark yourself what Ethan was up to?" he asked after she had described her conversation with her sister the night before. "You two seem so close. That surprises me, Meg. Why were you protecting him?"

"Thinking back on it now," Meg said, fiddling with the edge of her napkin. "I believe I just didn't want to be the one to hurt her. It was *Ethan* who was causing the pain, damn it, asking for trouble. But, you know how Lark is about him—she's still so smitten. Or was . . . I just can't seem to get used to thinking about Ethan in the past tense. Anyway, I sensed she would somehow end up blaming me for it. And it turns out that I was right."

"I've known and admired Lark for many years," Abe said as he looked out the window at the half-filled parking lot. "Her feelings for that son of a bitch are, as far as I'm concerned, the one flaw in her character."

Meg had forgotten about the bad blood between Abe and Ethan, capped in her mind by the scene at dinner over Columbus Day. But when she thought about it, she realized that Ethan and Abe had been at odds for several years. When had it started? Why? Too much to drink over a long holiday weekend? A difference of opinion about art or politics? They were both competitive, ambitious, and proud in different ways. Neither tended to keep his opinions to himself. But recently it seemed that they were disagreeing over just about everything. Whether it was tax reform, or the rightful place of the Grateful Dead in the rock and roll pantheon—you could almost count on Abe and Ethan taking different sides. The contempt in Abe's voice when he talked about Ethan was palpable.

"I think he really managed to convince her that *I* was after *him*," Meg said finally, breaking the silence. "And that makes me so angry. What a blatant manipulation of the facts! She was blind to what he was doing, what he was really like. Lark actually told me that other women—even Lucinda—'threw themselves' at Ethan."

"In Lark's defense," Abe replied evenly as he signaled for their check, "Ethan was obviously very charismatic. Women did come on to him. I've seen the dynamic in action. He clearly had a certain appeal—a very strong one. And I'm not saying Lucinda's lying about her feelings toward Ethan. But it's impossible to say she's telling the truth about what happened—she can't remember what the truth is."

"But she's being honest enough about Ethan's feelings toward *her*," Meg insisted. "And she'd be better off letting people think he *did* molest her. That would give her a motive that everyone could at least understand."

"Explain her flushing the fetal tissue down the toilet, please," Abe said, his direct question unsettling her.

"She didn't know she was pregnant," Meg said quickly, uncertain herself about this piece of the puzzle. It did look suspicious that Lucinda had destroyed the one piece of evidence linking her to the father. "She made that very clear."

"Maybe too clear?"

"You're just so quick to blame her." Her tone sounded defensive, even to her. "As far as Lucinda goes, forget any presumption of innocence."

Abe reached across the table, touching Meg's hand.

"Listen to me, okay?" he said. "We've hired an excellent lawyer for Lucinda. There's a whole team of detectives combing the crime scene for evidence. It's going to take a couple of months for them to complete their work and present their findings to the D.A. But I know Arthur Pearson, the D.A. He's tough and demanding. He'll make sure there's an airtight case, one way or the other. The trial, if there is one, is many months off."

"So what are you saying?" Meg asked.

"Let the professionals do their job. Stay out of it."

"Do nothing. Close my eyes. Hope for the best,"

Meg said. "That's exactly what I did with Ethan. That's precisely why we're here now. Because I didn't have the courage—the strength—to stand up against what I knew was wrong."

"I see," Abe said, shaking his head. He picked up the check the waitress had slipped under his plate and tapped it sideways against the tabletop. "Ethan's murder is all your fault, right? You're just as responsible as Lucinda because you weren't able to reform Ethan's character in time? It wasn't possible for you to rid the world of evil and pain, therefore you should be blamed for its multitude of wrongs?"

"Please, you know what I'm trying to say, Abe," Meg told him.

"Yes," he said, standing up to go. "You feel sorry. You feel guilty. And you're so used to being in charge of your life—your problems—that you can't handle the fact that this one is out of your control. Lucinda's just going to have to live with the consequences of her actions. Justified or not."

"But, it's not fair, Abe," Meg said, walking with him to the register.

"Meg Hardwick." Abe laughed, a bit sadly. "When did you ever start thinking life was fair?"

A cherry-red car was pulled up in front of Lark and Ethan's house when they arrived.

"Oh God," Meg heard Abe mutter under his breath.

"What's the matter?" Meg asked, leaning forward to get a clearer view.

Ignoring Meg's question, Abe turned off his engine as he said, seemingly to himself: "I'm not going to let that woman drive me away. This is my town, too. My home. I told Brook we'd have a game of Scrabble when I got back and, damn it, we're going to."

By then Becca Sabin was already walking toward the car. Stalking it, was a more precise description, Meg thought, as she watched the tall, dark-haired beauty approach. Her hair was shoulder-length, ebony, cut in a classic pageboy, glossy as mink. She'd been a model once, or so Meg remembered hearing, and she certainly had the height and the lean, loose-limbed build for it. It was a tall boy's body, slim-hipped, angular, but with generous, low-slung breasts.

Meg used to think that Abe and Becca made a stunning couple—both dark, lean, and intense. Becca didn't have Abe's sense of humor, or his flashing intelligence, but she did possess a self-assurance and an innate sense of style that complemented his more substantial personality. He had adored her, and he'd been unembarrassed to show it. She was easily ten years his junior, and he tended to treat her with the absurdly lavish affection a father shows a favorite daughter. Theirs had been one of the most physically demonstrative relationships Meg had ever witnessed. They were forever kissing and fondling one another in public. They'd had a seemingly endless litany of pet names for each other, "snuggle bunny" and "snuggins" being two that Meg had always found particularly cloying.

What had gone wrong after five seemingly idyllic years of married bliss Meg had never really discovered. Lark had once hinted to her that there had been "someone else" in the picture, not surprisingly on Becca's side. Whatever the cause, the breakup had been explosive, immediate, and irreparable. It was obvious to everyone that Abe was the injured party. His pain and anger had been terrible to see, made worse by his refusal to discuss the thing that was clearly eating him alive.

Meg had never been able to get close to Becca. She had tried to do so in the beginning, when Abe was proving to be so generous and helpful to her professionally. Meg had suspected that Becca was jealous of the friendship she had with Abe. Their shop talk. The inside jokes. But she had come to believe that Becca saw any unattached, attractive female as the enemy. *Hands off*, Becca's narrowed gaze had told Meg while Becca cooed into Abe's ear at cocktail parties.

Meg didn't trust women who treated men like territory, or wives to whom marriage was a form of ownership. So she'd learned to stay out of Becca's way, keeping up her friendship with Abe primarily in the city. Frankly, she preferred Abe when he wasn't around Becca. It bothered her to see how hard he'd had to work to keep Becca happy and entertained.

"She's a high-maintenance type, all right," Ethan had declared during a late-night post-party discussion with Lark and Meg.

"Hey, she's a beautiful woman," Lark responded in Becca's defense. "And Abe was totally aware of what he was getting into when he married her. He told me when he first met her that he knew she was difficult. I think he sort of thrives on the challenge of her."

"No, *you're* a beautiful woman," Ethan had corrected his wife. "She's only an excellent replica of a beautiful woman. I'm not sure she actually has blood in her veins."

Blood in her veins, Meg remembered, as Becca marched right up to Abe's side of the car and made an impatient circling motion with her right hand indicating he should roll down the side window. He opened the door instead and stepped out, so quickly in fact, that Becca stumbled getting out of his way. Their first terse words were inaudible. Then Becca's voice rose above the slamming doors as they all scrambled out of the car.

"Happy now, you bastard?" she demanded. She attempted to hit him on the chest, but he stepped deftly aside.

"Spare me the histrionics, Becca," he told her, and Meg was disturbed to see that he was smiling.

"Feel like a man again?" Becca hissed, fighting his grip. The whole exchange took less than a minute, yet it seemed to compress months of intense loathing. Meg had always believed that couples have one or two core arguments—about money, family, or ambition— that they keep recycling and refining over time. Meg felt that she'd just witnessed that between Becca and Abe. An ugly little morality play right there on the front lawn. It was the first time Meg had seen Abe and Becca together since their breakup, and it was clear to her that the marriage hadn't just dissolved—it had ignited into hatred.

"Abe, Becca—" Meg hadn't noticed Lark come around the side of the house, carrying a basket of salad greens in one arm and Fern in the other. Brook and Phoebe trailed along behind her. "I can't believe you're fighting here."

"I'm sorry. " Abe came to his senses, glancing around at the circle of women. "I better go. We'll make another date for Scrabble, Brook," he said as he opened the car door. "Call me if you need anything, Lark."

"Meg, would you take the girls back to the house?" Lark asked as Abe drove off, handing the basket to Brook and giving Meg the baby. Turning to Becca, she said, "I was going to make a salad for lunch. We've been living off these cakes and cookies people have bought us."

"I'm sorry, I didn't think to bring anything," Becca apologized, as Lark took her by the arm.

"Meg? You'll make the girls lunch, please?" Lark said dismissively as she and Becca walked slowly back to the car.

A dispiriting mix of stale cooking smells and damp ash hung in the front hall. The house felt neglected, as though a coat of dust covered everything. But the truth was, Meg thought, that no one was actually living there at the moment. Each of them was existing in her own locked room of sorrow, in a cold gray dimension parallel to the full-color one they used to inhabit.

No one had any appetite either, though Meg put together a big salad and heated up one of the casseroles. Once Brook and Phoebe were seated and picking at their macaroni and cheese, Meg carried Fern back down the hall and slipped into the front dining room, which offered the best view of the turnaround. Becca had turned on her car's engine and exhaust was pluming down the driveway. The windows were fogged and it was hard to see, but it looked as though both women were smoking. They'd been talking for over twenty minutes. About what? Meg wondered. Didn't Becca have enough sense to know that this was not exactly the time to burden Lark with her troubles?

Though Meg was never able to make much headway with Becca, Lark had become her closest confidante in Red River. It wasn't that the two women were friends exactly, sharing time and laughter. It seemed to Meg that Lark was more like Becca's amateur therapist, or non-denominational Mother Confessor. In the same way Lark turned to Francine for advice and guidance, Becca depended upon Lark. There appeared to be one main problem that they were dealing with, but when Meg had once asked what the hell Lark had been talking to Becca about on the phone for over an hour, Lark had been evasive.

"She just needs someone to listen to her," Lark had replied. "I know we used to call her Beautiful Becca and all but, believe me, that sort of perfection comes with a price. There's a good, giving person hiding somewhere under all the hard nails and high gloss. I'm trying to help coax her into the open."

Lark, the healer. Lark who would do anything, go to any lengths to make the world a better place. As Meg watched, the passenger door opened and Lark emerged from the car, and she felt her heart constrict with love for sister. How pitiful, how sad, that now—when Lark herself most needed comfort and love—Meg was cut off from giving it to her.

Her uselessness was made even more evident later that evening when Francine came by to finalize the plans for Ethan's funeral the next day. The evening had been filled with phone calls and visitors. Clint and Janine had dropped in, bringing a fully prepared dinner, and Janine had stayed on after Francine had arrived to do the dishes.

"Can I help?" Meg asked Janine, as Lark settled the girls upstairs. Francine was waiting alone in the living room.

"Not really, Meggie honey," Janine said, her face rosy from the steaming water. "It does me good to be *doing* something. I baked all afternoon just to keep my mind occupied. I'm making some tea now. Perhaps you can take it in to Frannie with that cookie tray?"

Frannie. It seemed an unlikely, girlish nickname, Meg thought, for such a substantial and serious woman. But then Janine tended to cuten up everything around her—from people's names to the little smiley face she drew in the upper loop of the *J* in her signature. No one seemed to mind it, because, Meg thought, nobody really bothered to notice. She worked so hard at pleasing others that it was easy to forget that Janine, too, must have emotions and needs.

"How are you taking all this?" Meg asked.

"Oh, I'm just—" Janine's high-pitched voice warbled and broke. "It's just . . . so sad." Janine was shaking her head, and, though her wide back remained resolutely turned, Meg could tell that she was crying. Not only had she lost a good friend, Meg realized, but her livelihood had been wiped out with that fatal blow. Ethan's designs and masterly technique were what made the Red River studio so successful. It seemed unlikely that Clint and Janine could carry on without him.

"I'm sorry," Meg said, taking a step toward her,

though something kept her from reaching out a comforting hand. "It's a tough time for everybody, I know."

"No-no-nobody can know how hard it is." Janine sighed and visibly made an effort to pull herself together. "But it's kind of you to at least ask."

Lark had joined Francine in the living room by the time Meg came in with the tea.

"Thank you," Francine said, as she reached for a mug.

"You've done so much today, Meggie," Lark said quickly. "You must be exhausted." Meg was being dismissed, she realized. Lark would be turning to Francine for the comfort Meg would so willingly have given. She felt Ethan's long shadow following her up the stairs as she went up to bed. Even from the grave, his powerful presence had managed to come between her and Lark. Unwilling to tell his wife the truth, perhaps unable to face up to it himself, Ethan had implicated her in his own wrongdoings. And now the seeds of doubt and jealousy he had sown were taking root . . . and spreading.

Much later, when she woke up and heard Lark crying downstairs, Meg started to get out of bed. Then she heard the sonorous rhythms of Francine's voice, though she couldn't hear what she was saying. Francine seemed to talk on endlessly, intent on some explanation or instruction. And Meg lay awake, listening to the meaningless river of sound, feeling herself overtaken by an intense, irrational fear. She was certain now that Lark had told Francine about Ethan and her—had passed on the lie that Ethan had started and that now Meg was unable to set right.

Francine seemed, in some way that Meg couldn't explain, to know about all the dark, complicated workings of the town. The minister looked out over her congregation, heads bowed in prayer, and knew the sins and secret thoughts of every worshiper. Meg felt chilled. Now that Francine had the leverage to do so, she was afraid that the minister would try to drive the wedge between Lark and herself deeper and deeper—until the mistrust and the pain that Ethan had so selfishly inflicted robbed Meg of the one heart, the one home, where she once thought she would always be welcome.

15

The First Congregational Church of Red River had been built in the mid–1880s and was a fine example of classic nineteenth-century New England religious architecture: white clapboard frame and steeple, red arched double doors, simple, stained glass windows, a pipe organ behind the pulpit and choir chapel. The pews, divided by one main aisle, were crafted of local maple and hemlock. A needlepoint banner of gold thread on burgundy velvet, sewn by a group of female parishioners in the 1920s, hung above the organ as the visual centerpiece for the altar. It was composed of two doves holding aloft the scripted letters: THOU WILT SHOW ME THE PATH OF LIFE.

Although the church had always been well-supported by the town, Francine Werling had, during her tenure, enlarged the parishioner base even further by introducing community-oriented programs such as after-school care and meals for the elderly and homebound. Built on a hill, the church basement was actually the first floor, accessible from the large macadam-paved parking lot. The church basement had become the social center of the town. Wedding receptions, town meetings, bake sales, chicken roasts, reading groups—the weekly schedule of events was posted on the glassed-in bulletin board to the right of the double front doors.

Though a school- and workday, the church was packed on the afternoon of Ethan's funeral. The morning had dawned cold and windy and by two o'clock, when the service was scheduled to begin, the first sleet of the season was gusting through the town. It sounded as though handfuls of pebbles were being thrown angrily up against the large stained-glass windows. The wind howled each time the doors were opened in the entry hall at the back of the church; it whistled down the aisles and fluttered the ribbons on the funeral wreaths grouped around the altar. Bad weather would have done little to deter country folk from coming, though there were people in the congregation that afternoon who hadn't set foot in the church for decades. Ivar Dyson, Ethan's neighbor who owned the goat farm, was one, dressed in the only suit he had ever owned, now several sizes too small for him.

A town like Red River, still steeped in agrarian tradition, never failed to stop for death. A life, like nature itself, had its seasons. A murder, however, was something else again. That Ethan's existence was cut short so tragically was the equivalent of the tornado that ripped through the valley in the early 1970s. It was unnatural and terrifying. The congregation that afternoon was subdued and tense. There had been a lot of angry talk about Lucinda's bad behavior and her disrupting influence on other teenagers in town. Some stated privately that the family brought the tragedy on themselves.

"Maybe Ethan and Lark were trying to do the right thing," Meg had overheard Paula Yoder confide to several customers in the general store that morning. "But they put us all in jeopardy with that girl running wild." When Paula had blocked Lucinda from entering the store after she had been caught stealing cigarettes, Lucinda told Paula that she'd "be getting hers someday." It was a threat that Paula was now taking too much to heart. In any case, there was a general sadness and confusion in the crowded church, a need for answers and reassurance.

The front right pew had been reserved for the immediate family. At two-fifteen, when people were standing five deep in the back of the church, Clint Lindbergh stepped quietly into the small office off the entranceway where Meg, Lark, and the girls had been waiting. Meg hadn't seen much of Clint since the murder, though she was aware that he had been running errands for Meg and Francine and had done a yeoman's job getting the church arranged for the funeral and reception. As the church organist, he usually hit as many sour notes as pure ones, but he was a dutiful and well-meaning musician, putting up with the gibes and insults that his playing prompted with his usual unruffled humor.

"You guys ready?" he asked gently. He was wearing a black suit that looked suspiciously like a slightly altered dinner tux, though the jacket fit his barrel-chested frame with surprising elegance. He'd trimmed his beard and neatly parted and combed his thinning hair; he looked almost handsome. Though he smiled at them all and patted Phoebe's shoulder affectionately, his red-rimmed eyes gave away his true emotional state. And Meg thought she caught a whiff of beer on his breath.

"I'm going to go around to the organ loft now, and when you hear the first couple of chords of the Bach piece, just start down the aisle."

One can't really anticipate a moment—how it will actually feel, the exact combination of impressions that will add up to the reality. Meg thought she'd be able to get through the funeral just fine. This wasn't her town. She wasn't a part of all this. And yet, as she walked behind Lark, who was carrying Fern, and Brook and Phoebe, who were holding hands and crying, she found how much she *did* belong to Red River. In the moment, her aching heart suddenly bursting within her—demanding that she face the truth. Before her were many people she knew from town . . . and others who'd come up from the city. Hannah was there. Becca . . . Janine . . . Abe . . . Seeing them all, and then the flowers at the altar, and then— why hadn't she been prepared for this?—the coffin with Ethan's body inside, it really hit her. Ethan was dead. Ethan was gone. And though her feelings for him had changed radically over the last month, he still remained an essential part of her life. Over the last few days, his death had seemed impossible, and therefore, somehow, something she could deal with later. Now it was irrevocably true. It rose before her like a dark mountain. And she knew she had no choice but to climb it.

"Friends." Francine held her arms up, embracing them all. "Dear family." Francine nodded to Lark. The minister was dressed in a white robe with a red satin mantle and gold-corded sash. When she looked out over the congregation above the half lenses of her reading glasses, her luminous gaze seemed to meet each and every eye.

"Ethan McGowan was not a religious person." Francine looked down at her notes and then up again. "He was not the kind of man you could label easily. For some in this town he was a good friend. For his daughters . . . he was the best father you could ever ask for. And for Lark . . . I think we all understand how special Ethan and Lark's marriage really was. . . ."

She was trying, Meg thought. Francine was making a real effort to sound the appropriate notes of sorrow and affection. But it was only after she had paid the necessary tributes to Ethan, only when she had moved on to her prepared sermon that Francine's face took on its characteristic beaming glow and her words—always carefully crafted—found a life of their own. Meg listened to her tone as much as to her message—the lulling, almost hypnotizing promise in her voice.

"But what are we to do with the injuries his death has left—the torn ligaments of our lives that were once so effortlessly attached to his? How do we attend to the horrible injustice that has ripped him from us . . . that has sundered this town?"

Francine took a step back, as if affronted. She let a

moment of silence follow the question before she went on, "Friends . . . Family . . . This, this loss was not God's doing. It was not Her will. Death in many ways is a noble thing, a natural process, a homage to life. Death is, as a famous poet once wrote, the mother of beauty. But *this* was not such a death. This was an aberration. And its burden is much harder to bear. Its message is much more complicated—darker and more difficult to comprehend. . . ."

Meg could feel the congregation listening as one. And though there were many small children in the church, there was not one cry, one cough. Francine's voice held them spellbound.

"We must take heart and draw courage from the fact that even the vilest acts of man and woman are perpetrated under God's all-seeing eye. We must recognize that there is a grand design to our lives . . . to all of life. We must believe that there is a method in what we sometimes perceive as madness. God saw the hand raised in hatred against Ethan McGowan. She saw it . . . and She did not halt it. She *allowed* it. . . . But why. *Why?*"

The question came out as an urgent whisper—angry, outraged. Francine's nostrils flared and she closed her eyes. She bowed her head and shook it back and forth. Then, slowly, she raised her head again and looked out over congregation.

"We may never have the one, complete answer. But I believe there are many answers and each of us carries a slightly different one within themselves. Each time we feel hate in our heart . . . each time we experience a twinge of jealousy . . . each time we slight another . . . each time we lie . . . we know that we, too, have acted against God. We, too, are capable—as Cain was, as Judas was, as Ethan's assailant was—to lift up our arm in anger against another. And every day, each moment of our lives, we choose—to walk on God's path . . . or to follow our own. God *lets* us decide. She must let us decide. Because She knows, as every parent here today knows, that the only way children really learn is by trying, by failing, and by trying again."

Francine looked over at the coffin resting among the frozen wands of gladioli, carnations, and lilies.

"But what *do* we do with the terrible fact of this man's death? How do we learn from what seems to be such a senseless act of violence? Where do we turn for answers and guidance? Let me tell you, friends, do not look into your hearts. Do not follow your instincts. For the raw, emotional, immediate response to murder is . . . more bloodshed. An eye for a eye. Revenge, blame, blind justice. Let us all beware of what our hearts clamor for. Let us hold our fire. For as the Bible warns us: 'Judge not that ye be not judged.' There is not one person among us today who is without sin. . . . Friends, family . . ."

There was a singsong finality to Francine's words now. "We must put aside our anger. We must walk out of the shadows of our despair . . . and into the light of God's wisdom. We must understand that Ethan's death is, in a way we may never truly comprehend, a part of God's plan. We must allow justice to take its course. We must not lay blame."

Francine ended the address, as she did every sermon that Meg had heard her deliver, with the evocation: "I will lift up mine eyes unto the hills, from whence cometh my help. My help cometh from the Lord, which made heaven and earth."

After the prayer, Francine kept her head bowed in silence. Meg had been moved by the power of her words, encouraged by her moral support for Lucinda. Yet during the sermon, she kept sensing that something was missing. It took her until the very end to realize that while Francine had praised and mourned a life, it wasn't really Ethan's. She had made no attempt to evoke the charisma—his laughter, his voice, his outsized, sometimes outrageous enthusiasm. She had spoken about him only through the eyes of others—Lark and the children, his friends and neighbors in town. She had praised Ethan's work in the community, his accomplishments as an artist, and though she touched on all the finer points of Ethan's character, it was as though Francine were speaking about a man she had never met. Of the powerful, opinionated man himself—the man with whom Francine had clearly had her differences—she made no mention.

Meg was so lost in her own thoughts that she didn't realize right away that the silence was stretching on far too long. The congregation was waiting for Clint to start the Bach Fugue he always played for the processional, but nothing happened. A baby started to cry. Meg could hear people whispering behind her, a rustling of clothes as neighbor turned to neighbor. Francine stepped out of the pulpit and looked questioningly up at the organ loft.

Just when it seemed obvious that something had gone wrong, Clint began. Note after note, phrase by phrase, Clint's playing was strong, purposeful, and, it seemed to Meg, uncharacteristically—almost eerily—perfect.

16

The basement was so crowded that it took Meg several minutes to make it down the stairs at the back of the church. It didn't help that Janine had set up the three refreshment tables directly to the right of the steps. Though this location was conveniently close to the kitchen and supplies, it meant that the crowd waiting for soft drinks and pretzels kept backing up into the stairwell, and newcomers had to nudge and squeeze their way down the steps.

"Excuse me," Meg said as she edged around the congested area, stepping, as she did so, on the heel of the woman in front of her.

"Quite all right," the woman replied, the familiar voice prompting Meg to look at her more closely. Black velvet cloche. Pearls with the trademark Mikimoto butterfly clasp. Tailored black crepe suit.

Meg had scuffed up a pair of pumps that she estimated were easily worth three hundred dollars.

"Hannah?" Meg asked.

"Yes?" The close-fitting hat had obscured her hair at the back. She turned slightly, blocked by the crowd from facing Meg. "Oh, it's you! I was just looking for you, Meg. You know ..."

The noise level was so high, Meg could only pick up bits and pieces of what Hannah was saying: "Awful sleet ... van spinning out ... I only just made it in time ... desperate mood ..."

At one point, Meg thought to ask, "What's going to happen to Ethan's show now? There's been so much on my mind, I didn't even think about you and the gallery."

"What?" Hannah demanded irritably. "I can't hear a damned thing you're saying."

"I can't either," Meg admitted. "Let's try to find a quieter spot." Meg pointed to the far corner by the coatracks.

"What a crush!" Hannah cried when they'd finally reached their destination. "Who *are* all these people?"

"They're from the town mostly," Meg told her, looking around the packed basement and seeing Ethan's friends and neighbors through Hannah's eyes. The majority were in their thirties and forties, over-weight and badly dressed by Manhattan standards. A woman nearby had on a pale blue jersey pantsuit with pink piping—the kind of outfit New Yorkers wouldn't even jog in—and beat-up white Reeboks. She wore her dyed blond hair pulled back in a thin ponytail. Meg had seen her around town, a load of kids in the back of a Chevy van. She was probably in her early thirties, but she had the worn-down look of someone much older.

"Oh, I see," Hannah said, her green eyes scanning the room. "It's very interesting. Different from what I expected. Ethan always painted something far more dramatic, you know. Nature in all its wildness. I passed a Stop 'n Shop not fifteen minutes from here."

"You came through Montville then," Meg said and, wanting to justify Ethan's view against Hannah's urban scrutiny, she added, "Red River is still very rural. Some of the farms up here are the size of small counties. It's a pretty tough life. A lot of hard work. And people just getting by."

"I can see that," Hannah said.

"This has hit them pretty hard," Meg went on. "It's a quiet town. A close one. Murder is something that just doesn't happen here."

"It's hit everybody hard, Meg."

"Yes," she said and they were silent for a moment while the noise surged around them. Released from the solemnity of the church service, children raced through the crowd, their laughter drowned out by dozens of conversations, many conducted at shouting level. Meg strained to hear the snippets of conversation as the room filled to overflowing.

"I just saw him last Wednesday, at the Agway with the girls. . . ."

"Her mother's a druggie. That's what I heard."

"The first wife . . . Totally messed up. They had to put her away, right?"

"Yeah. And that kind of thing runs in a family, you know. . . ."

Suddenly Meg realized that Hannah was speaking

to her. She felt Hannah's warm breath in her ear, as the woman leaned in closer to say, "I knew about you and Ethan, Meg."

"What?" Meg turned to stare at Hannah. For the first time she saw the fine web of wrinkles around her eyes, the grooves bracketing her mouth. Meg couldn't have heard her correctly.

"Ethan told me a little bit about what was going on before—before he was killed."

"Going on?" Meg cried over the noise. "*Nothing* was going on. It was all in Ethan's head." Meg felt her heart beating rapidly. The room was far too noisy and hot. Her head, too, was pounding—with anger, she realized. How easy it must have been for Ethan to imply that she had responded to his overtures. A slight smile on his part, a shrug to a certain question from Hannah, and the picture would be quickly painted: How could a single, lonely woman resist a man like Ethan? For someone as experienced and sophisticated as Hannah, the fact that Meg was Ethan's sister-in-law was probably just a minor concern.

"Meg, don't worry," Hannah said, touching her elbow. "You can trust me. I'm really very discreet. And, God knows, I totally understand about Ethan. He was such a powerful presence—in my life, as well. From the moment I first saw him. I knew. He had that certain something—that life force that draws others to him."

"That may be the case," Meg replied. "But I was never drawn to him in that way. I don't know what he told you, Hannah, but it simply wasn't true."

Hannah took a sip from the plastic cup she was holding, appraising Meg as she did so.

"You're overreacting," she said soothingly. "I really only brought up the subject because I assume you'd be upset. I thought you might want someone to talk to. I guess I've come to think of you as Ethan's friend. And, by extension, my friend. I hope I haven't upset you. But, quite frankly, I've been devastated by all of this, too. It was such a shock. He'd just been to see me Friday night, you know. He told me then that you two had had something of a lovers' quarrel. . . ."

"Hannah, we were *not* lovers," Meg hissed, glancing quickly around the closely packed room. Nobody seemed the least bit interested in their conversation. Meg and Hannah were outsiders and, at any other time, would have been objects of intense curiosity. But that night there was only one subject among the residents of Red River: Ethan McGowan's murder.

"Whatever you say," Hannah whispered back. "Whatever you *need* to say. I understand your position. Really. All I want you to know, Meg, is that I do understand. More than you realize. I know what a special kind of man Ethan was. And, well, if you ever feel the need to talk to me about it . . . "

The basement was a burbling sea of voices. Meg realized that Hannah was still talking to her. She saw other mouths moving: people drinking, chewing, talking, laughing. She smelled bourbon. She felt sick, as though she'd been drinking herself. The room had a precarious list to it, as though everyone were going to slide off to the right at any moment. She needed balance.

"Are you okay, darling?" Hannah asked.

"Yes, I think . . ." Meg turned toward the double doors leading out to the parking lot. "I'm going to get some air."

The storm had passed, but night had already started to settle in and it was barely four-thirty. Meg could see stars through the branches of the old sugar maple trees that clustered around the church. The parking lot was still full, the surfaces of the cars aglitter with a hard coating of frozen sleet. Ice crackled like broken glass under her heels. It was damp and cold and she hadn't bothered to find her coat. Though she was wearing nothing more than a lightweight black wool suit, she didn't feel anything when she first started out except a kind of lulling numbness—as though not just a limb, but her entire body had gone to sleep.

She found herself walking aimlessly along the edge of the parking lot, clutching her arms to her chest to keep herself warm. She had to get some perspective on what Hannah had said. She had to come to terms with the ugly impression that Ethan had left behind. Ethan was gone, but the force that had driven him to such extremes of passion was still at work. The small lies Ethan had dropped—in front of Lark, and then Hannah—were rippling out across the lives that had intersected his. He probably had not intended any real harm. Meg could almost hear him justifying his actions now: He'd simply implied that she had responded a bit to his flattery—not such a big thing, really, hardly a sin. His ego couldn't handle the truth, so he had changed it. He'd recast the facts to a shape more pleasing to himself.

But now Ethan's offhand half-truth had blossomed into something Meg only seemed to make more substantive by denying. It had taken on a malevolent life of its own—undermining her relationship with Lark, producing an unwanted ally in Hannah. If Ethan were still alive, she would have asked that he retract the falsehood. But with him gone, she was left with a situation that was growing ever more complicated and dangerous.

The parking lot was bordered on its northern edge by an old graveyard, separated from the macadam by a lichen-crusted stone wall overrun with weeds and vines. No one had been buried there since 1918 when the flu epidemic of the First World War had—within the space of a few years—doubled the number of graves. The new cemetery—where Ethan would be buried the next day—lay to the south of Red River and boasted manicured lawns and neatly cared-for shrubbery.

Several years before, Ethan had made a number of rubbings from the worn headstones behind the church. He'd framed the charcoal impressions—sad-eyed cherubs and sailing ships—intending to hang them along the hall leading from the entryway to the kitchen. Lark had objected.

"They're gruesome," Lark had said during the argument Meg had witnessed at that time. "I don't want to be reminded of death every time I walk down my front hall."

"I disagree, my love," Ethan had replied. "I think they're funny as hell. Like comics. Man's little joke on himself. As if angels will be singing as the big ship death pulls into the heavenly harbor. I think it's hilarious that people can't stand the thought that when they die they'll simply be dead. Ashes to ashes, dust to dust." Meg had forgotten how the rest of the argument had gone, but the rubbings ended up hanging in Ethan's studio.

The small cemetery was slick with sleet, the gravestones leaning drunkenly, one or two broken in half and tented carefully on their respective graves like oversize place settings. Meg could hear the noise coming from the reception behind her. She wasn't sure what had drawn her here. Moonlight played through the wands of the gnarled willow tree whose roots had heaved up several gravestones at the southeast corner of the walled-in plot. Meg's fingers traced the ghostly lettering of a headstone. Pale light illuminated the first name, MARY ELLEN, but time and the elements had erased the rest.

Meg tried briefly to imagine who this woman had been, what she had yearned for, what had made her laugh. But it was impossible to know her, or to know anybody. Other people's lives—even Ethan's, in which Meg had played such an integral part—were, in the end, mysteries. Ethan, who had lived so large and demanded so much of the world, was soon to be nothing more than a name, like this one, chiseled on a headstone. All that passion and need and ego—the fires that blazed and burned—were no more now than the memories he'd left behind. The chaos he'd created was for others to sort through. But trying to understand the dead, she knew, was as difficult as reading worn stone letters. Like those carvings, Ethan's life was dissolving into the pieces of a puzzle that she needed desperately to decipher and fit together. Once again she ran her fingers over the gravestone, searching for an impression that was hardly there.

17

"I'm just saying we don't need a lot of outsiders telling us what we know already," Lester Friedlander said, his words slow and slightly slurred. He stood in the belligerent, shoulders-back stance of a man asking for trouble. An overhead light at the bottom of the steps leading down from the church to the parking lot illuminated the scene. Lester, who had his own construction company; Willie Skylar, the part-time manager of the town's transfer station and full-time handyman; and half a dozen other men stood in a loose half-circle around Willie's pickup. A keg of beer gleamed in the back of the truck. It seemed obvious to Meg, who came upon them as she made her way back to the reception, that the group had been helping themselves liberally to the keg's contents. She stopped just outside the circle of light to listen.

"You just don't like cops," Carl Yoder, Mike's younger brother, shot back. "Ever since Tom hit you with that D.W.I. last year."

"That's not what I'm saying," Les continued, stumbling a little in an attempt to keep his macho pose. "This has nothing to do with me personally, okay? It's got to do with all of us. My point is this: Who do you think is paying for those state guys to come in here and take up half the rooms at the Rocquonic? Who's paying for them to pick through the dust balls and shit at Ethan's studio? We are, folks. That's who. It's our hard-earned tax dollars at work, that's what. And for what purpose? We already know what the hell happened."

"Hey, it just needs to be investigated by professionals, Les," Willie said as he refilled his plastic beer mug.

"Like we need some fricking state seal of approval on this thing?" Les demanded. "Come on, that's just ridiculous. Lucinda McGowan was found with the murder weapon in her hands, for chrissakes. We need Columbo and Matlock to help Tom track down the killer?"

"Well, my observation is that old Tom has a difficult enough time tracking down his reading glasses," Theodore Weisel observed. A math teacher who lived in Red River and taught at the Montville secondary school, Theo always tried to sound wry and knowing. He was obviously pleased by the round of laughter that followed his comment.

"He sure had them on when he was interviewing Becca Sabin," Willie observed, smiling as he shook his head. "Should've seen the guy helping her out of her car down at the police station yesterday—like she was some kind of visiting dignitary."

"I wouldn't mind helping her with a few things myself," Carl Yoder commented. "That woman has some body, if you know what I mean."

"Those state guys were getting an eyeful, too," Willie added. "I was over there to pick up my hunting license when Becca came by for her interview. They were just falling all over themselves to get her coffee and whatnot."

"And that plays exactly to what I'm saying." Les, a bit steadier on his feet now, had also found his voice—and everyone there knew just how much Les enjoyed the sound of his own words. Les paused for dramatic effect and went on in a more measured tone. "I mean, can't you just hear those state detectives talking up Becca Sabin? 'And what were you doing, ma'am, the morning that Lucinda McGowan drove a flaming hot metal rod into her stepfather's chest? Sleeping in, eh? And what were you wearing, please? No, it's very important to the progress of this case that we get an exact description of your red silk negligee. . . .'"

To general laughter, Theodore Weisel observed, "Ethan could have provided them with one."

"That's for sure," Willie said, chuckling.

"Ethan probably could have given them a pretty good description of a couple of bedrooms in this town," Carl added.

"Yeah, including your brother's," Les said, prodding Carl Yoder with his elbow. A silence fell on the men and Meg could almost hear them thinking, *Les Friedlander and his big mouth. When he has a bellyful of beer in him, he just doesn't know how to keep his yap from flapping.*

Carl took a step away from Les. "What are you try-ing to say, Les?"

"Just what the rest of us have known for years," Les replied defensively, though he sensed with a quick look around at the others' faces that he was alone on this one. "What you Yoder guys are just too holier-than-thou to admit to yourselves. Paula had a thing for Ethan. A big one. And, knowing the man the way we all did, I'd say he took ample advantage of Paula's tender feelings."

Without any warning, Carl Yoder rammed his right shoulder hard into Les Friedlander's chest. Les's beer mug flew up in the air and landed on the windshield of a nearby car. The two men fell to the icy macadam and rolled against the back wheels of Willie's truck. Meg couldn't see them, but she could hear their angry curses and ragged gasps as they grappled with one another.

"What's going on here?" Francine had emerged seemingly from nowhere, the bulky parka she had thrown on over her clerical garb giving her a slightly comical look. There was nothing funny, however, about her angry tone of voice.

"Nothing," Willie Skylar muttered, stepping between the beer keg and Francine's line of vision. "Just a little friendly misunderstanding. Right, guys?" Les and Carl grunted as they pulled away from each other and crawled out from under the rear of the truck.

"Willie Skylar, have you actually brought beer onto church property without my permission?"

"Now, Francine," Willie began in his slow, sincere-sounding way, "the keg was already sitting there in the back of the truck when I came to the service. I didn't bring it specifically for any purpose. And we all just got talking out here, you know, waiting for the wives and kids, not wanting to break things up in there. Didn't think it would do any harm."

"You grown men should be ashamed of your-selves," Francine replied, though Meg could sense her anger seeping away. "Get that keg out of my sight and get yourselves on home now while you can still see straight. The roads are slick and I don't want any of you idiots rolling drunk into a tree. I've had about as much trouble these past few days as I can stand."

"Yes'm," Willie replied, as Carl and Les brushed the ice shards off their coats. "Sorry to have caused any trouble."

"And Les?" Francine added. "Sometimes I think that they left out an eleventh commandment: 'Thou shalt mind thine own business.' Do you understand me?"

Meg hesitated in the shadows, not wishing to be caught eavesdropping, as the group broke up and Francine turned and went back to the reception. She overheard one last comment as Willie Skylar climbed up into his truck.

Just before he turned on the ignition, he rolled down his window and called over to Les who was scraping ice off his windshield, "It's fitting, don't you think, that Ethan got it with a poker? I mean consid-ering how many he's poked in his time?"

Les and Theo Weisel, who'd overheard the com-ment, laughed out loud in the damp, cold night air.

*   *   *

"Meg, I need to get the girls home." Lark came up to her as she walked back into the basement. The reception was winding down, the crowd now massed around the coatracks. A row of small children, ornery with fatigue, sat on folding chairs as parents tried to get them into their snow boots. Meg had watched Lark sail through the funeral and reception with a luminous calm. Her eyes glistening, her head high, Lark, publicly at least, was handling her husband's murder with dignity. Detachment. With the "love," Lark had told Meg she wanted to display. But now Meg couldn't help but wonder what was behind her sister's forbearance. Clearly, Ethan was not the husband or father that Lark pretended he had been. Meg was obviously not the first or only woman he had tried to seduce. It didn't make her feel any better that Ethan hadn't singled her out, but it did make her question everything she thought she knew about her sister's marriage. It had been far more complicated and compromised than Lark had ever let on. Lark, who had confided to Meg the smallest minutiae of her daily life, had managed to gloss over what was surely her biggest problem: her husband.

"I'm ready to go, too," Meg replied, trying to read her sister's expression, but Lark didn't meet her eye. Looking tired and irritated, she scanned the departing crowd.

"Actually, I'm going to ask you to stay and help Francine clean up. I was counting on Janine to do it, but apparently Clint's had too much to drink and she's got to get him home. Where the hell did all the booze come from?"

"Willie Skylar had a keg in his truck," Meg began.

"There was a fight—" Though she wanted to confront Lark with what she knew, she thought better of it when she realized that Brook and Phoebe were following sleepily in their mother's wake.

"These men," Lark said disdainfully, but then her expression softened as her eyes fastened on someone across the room. Meg followed her gaze to where Abe was struggling with an armload of coats.

"Okay, guys," Abe said as he passed Brook and Phoebe their parkas. "Time to saddle up."

"Abe'll help me get us all home," Lark told her. "Francine offered to drive you back when you're done here."

Meg knew she had no choice but to do Lark's bidding, though she felt her anger welling. Lark had purposely made Meg feel guilty and miserable—while keeping her sister in the dark about so many things. The haven of love that in Meg's mind had been Lark's beloved home had collapsed as swiftly and completely as a house of cards. She thought of the anguish she'd endured on Ethan's behalf—all of it in an attempt to save Lark's marriage and family. But now she knew that her sister's married life had been no better than her parent's ill-fated union. All those years that Meg had envied what Lark possessed—could it really have been nothing more than a trick of the heart?

Meg didn't know the two other women in the congregation who stayed on to help with the cleanup. They knew how to operate the three large industrial dishwashers, so they concentrated on the kitchen while Meg and Francine picked up the main hall, folding chairs, bagging trash.

"Shall we do the tables?" Francine asked when the

chairs had been stowed away in the storage room behind the coatracks. Meg helped Francine ease the first table over onto its side and then unclasp and push the metal legs inward. They hadn't exchanged more than ten words over the twenty minutes or so that they'd been working together, though it didn't surprise Meg when Francine finally spoke. It was as though they were already in the midst of a long, ongoing conversation on the subject.

"I saw you out in the parking lot. I saw the look on your face, Meg. Could it be true that you really didn't know about Ethan until tonight?"

"Well, I knew—from personal experience—that he had his problems, but I guess I didn't realize the extent of them."

"You couldn't see it for yourself?"

"When I first met Ethan—a decade or so ago—I had my doubts." Meg looked down the edge of the table at Francine and felt for the first time the gentleness of her pale, disarming gaze.

"Yes." Francine nodded, encouraging her, "Lark told me about Bennington."

"But, over the years," Meg continued, feeling the release of confession, "as their marriage lasted, as the girls were born, I guess I came to believe in him. In them. More than that, I grew envious. They seemed so united, dedicated to each other and the girls."

"Ah . . . yes. I see," Francine said, nodding, as they started to collapse the next table. "The grass is always greener. Need, desire . . . they can be such positive driving forces. The emotional fuel to get us from place to place. And yet, so often when we get there, what do we find? Well, life is never what we expect, is it?"

"So everybody in this town knew the truth about Ethan?"

Francine drummed her fingers on the table as she met Meg's eyes. She hesitated. "Truth? When it comes to the actions and motives of mankind, I sometimes think the word truth just doesn't apply. God deals in truth. We seem to traffic in something much baser. But, to answer your question, I can at least give you facts. You're sure you want to hear them?"

"Yes."

"Ethan McGowan seemed to make a hobby of going after the most desirable and prominent women in this town. How many over the years that I've been here? My guess is half a dozen. Regardless of marital status. Or emotional stability. I suppose he couldn't help himself. Some people claim it's an addiction—like alcohol or drug dependency. There's actually a support group in Albany for sexual addiction. I suggested once to Ethan that he try it. You know what his response was? He laughed at me. In my heart, I have examined the question countless times: Should Ethan be absolved of his actions because—like some down-and-out drunk—he can't help himself?"

Meg noticed that Francine was talking about Ethan in the present tense, the intensity of her feelings bringing him back to life.

"You didn't much like him, did you?"

Francine stared back at her, but Meg felt as though the minister were staring through her—at something beyond the reach of the human eye.

"When I first met Lark and Ethan," Francine said, shaking her head at the memory, "I was so taken with them. As you just said, they seemed perfect—but not

in any cookie-cutter kind of way. They were gen-
uine—intelligent, artistic, and committed, I felt, to
living *good* lives. Lark and I—from the beginning we
could talk for hours. Ethan and I were friendly then,
too. I realized, of course, that he was an agnostic, but
out of real conviction rather than laziness. We used to
have such intense arguments. Ethan knew his stuff—
Kierkegaard, Ortega y Gasset, Spinoza—and he was
an exciting, challenging sparring partner. It was a real
pleasure, debating him. . . ." Francine broke off with a
trail of dry laughter.

"He walked me home one summer night and,
halfway there, right past the Lindbergh's house at the
end of the driveway, he pulled me into his arms and
kissed me. Oh Lord, yes. Kissed *me*. I was so
shocked. But . . . I wasn't horrified. I'd never—I'm
not a particularly sensual person. His, his . . . passionate nature took me by surprise. Eventually I pushed
him away, told him not to be ridiculous and never to
do it again. But he told me that he'd longed to kiss me
from the first time he saw me—that he'd fallen in love
with . . . *my mind*! You see how smart he was? He
knew that I would never believe he'd long for me
physically—but I might just go for the idea that he
had this great intellectual passion for me. And I did.
For several days."

Meg held her breath. It was eerily like what Ethan
had said to her.

"Then, a night or two after that, a young woman in
my congregation, newly married, came to see me.
Local girl. Farming family. Pretty, buxom, a redhead.
She was clearly troubled about something and eventually—it took nearly an hour—she confessed that

she'd fallen in love with someone other than her husband. Well, why drag this out? You know who it was, of course. Ethan. Though, with her, he'd taken a different course of action. She liked to paint in watercolor. Fancied herself an artist. Seems he'd started giving her lessons. Told her she had a special talent. That she needed to develop it. Of course, her brute of a husband didn't understand. But Ethan did all right. You see, he'd fallen in love with her *artistic* nature. And that, Meg, was the beginning. . . ."

"And they came to you," Meg said, imagining how it must have been for Francine. "To pour out their hearts."

"Those in my parish, yes," Francine continued. "Even after Ethan had developed something of a reputation in this town. It didn't matter. He was that good. He had this uncanny sixth sense of where a woman's weak spot might be—where she might have hidden the one little weakness or small dream that he could exploit. Ethan wasn't content with physically seducing someone—he had to do it emotionally as well. He wanted your body, of course, but even more than that he wanted your heart. He did everything he could to ensure that you loved him, had fallen totally in love with him, body and soul, casting off husband, children, whomever, and given yourself over entirely to him. Then he moved on to his next victim."

"You hated him," Meg said.

"Yes. It is my worst sin. I've hated Ethan McGowan with all my heart for years now. I've hated him as I would hate the devil himself."

18

The clear weather held through Tuesday, and they were able to bury Ethan in the new cemetery south of town. Only Lark, Meg, Clint, Abe, Francine, and the cemetery workers were in attendance. Lark, deciding that the girls shouldn't be exposed to any more of death's unhappy details, had left them at home in Janine's care. It was a brief ceremony. As Francine recited the Twenty-third Psalm, electronic pulleys lowered the casket into the prepared grave.

"Yea, though I walk through the valley of the shadow of death . . ."

Meg listened impassively, dry-eyed, unable to feel much of anything except bone-weary exhaustion. She knew that it would take her a very long time to understand—if she ever would—the man they were burying that day. For so many years, Ethan had been such a familiar part of her world that she hadn't really *seen* him, hadn't acknowledged him as a man, separate from Lark and the girls. Then, suddenly, out of nowhere, he'd ripped through her life, leaving behind a trail of emotional chaos. Only now, with him gone, could she see the devastation he had caused. Meg glanced around the semicircle of mourners, assessing the damage.

There was Abe, standing beside Lark, dressed in an expensively tailored black suit and overcoat that looked out of place against the rural countryside. He'd told Meg before the ceremony that he was heading directly down to the city after the burial because of pressing business concerns. She sensed that he'd only stayed on to help Lark, who'd increasingly turned to him—as she'd turned from Meg—over the last few days. Though Abe and Lark had always been friendly, she had never noticed how close they'd become until this past weekend. He was good with Brook and Phoebe, who clearly adored him, and thoughtful and gentle with Lark. Meg felt a pang of envy when Abe put his arm around Lark's shoulder as the workers started to shovel a mixture of dirt and snow onto the casket.

Abe had been perfectly cordial to Meg over the past few days, though from time to time she'd caught him so deep in his own thoughts he didn't even realize he was being watched. This was unlike Abe, who was usually the most observant person in the room. He'd been by the house a lot, helping Lark deal with the funeral home and cemetery, doing what he could to keep the girls' spirits up, but Meg felt his bantering good humor was forced. Of course, they were all under a lot of pressure—sorrow had the tendency to make the world feel like it was lodged directly on one's shoulders, but she sensed a deeper undercurrent of unease in Abe.

Lark was crying, her whole body shuddering with silent sobs. A few brief days ago Meg would have been torn apart by the sight. Now she felt only confusion. How could Lark care about a man who had been cheating on her for years? Why should she feel anything but relief that he was gone? Of all the questions surrounding Ethan's life and death, this puzzled Meg the most: How could Lark have acted so much in love with Ethan when she must have been so terribly disturbed by what he was doing to her and to the family?

Clint looked terrible, his eyes puffy and his face flushed red. He stood stiffly beside Francine, holding her purse as she read from the Bible, his wispy hair blown about by the wind. Meg had overheard him ask Lark if he could come by the house after the burial.

"There's something Janine and I need to talk to you about," he'd said in the cemetery parking lot while they waited for the hearse to arrive.

"Of course," Lark had replied. "But you needn't be so formal about it, Clint. You've been dropping in and out of the house since I've known you."

"Well, this is kind of important," he'd replied. "I'd prefer to make an appointment."

They were going to tell Lark they were leaving, Meg guessed, watching Clint bow his head as Francine began reciting the Lord's Prayer. Of course, the two of them would be moving on; their whole lives had been tied to the Red River studio. They'd worked behind the scenes for nearly a decade—Janine handling the shipping, invoicing, and inventory, Clint assisting in the studio and helping with the heavy lifting and maintenance work that Ethan couldn't be bothered with—and what did they have to show for it? Meg doubted if Ethan had set up any kind of retirement fund for them, or if they themselves had ever considered what would happen to them if Ethan wasn't there to run things. She felt bad for the Lindberghs—two more people left in the rubble of Ethan's careless life and senseless death.

And there was yet another sad victim of Ethan's recklessness. Lucinda, alone in the hospital—indicted already in the eyes of the town. Rebellious, confused, unloved, Lucinda had been handed over to Ethan and Lark at a most difficult time in her life. Hoping for shelter, she had found in the rural quiet of Red River a stepfather who, having already abandoned her mother, was now deceiving his own young family. She had to deal with the fact that the only father figure in her life was ... a monster. At an age when most teenagers were worrying primarily about their complexions, Lucinda had been forced to confront the most complicated of adult issues—lust, adultery, betrayal. Meg thought of the weeping mess of a girl she'd seen in the hospital and felt her heart harden even further against Ethan.

"... And forgive us our trespasses, as we forgive those who trespass against us."

Francine's deep voice was steady and clear—but Meg wondered just how sincere she could be. If Francine hadn't been able to forgive Ethan while he was alive, Meg doubted that death would suddenly absolve him of all the trespasses Francine had witnessed during his lifetime. Francine paused and looked around the circle of mourners. Meg met her eyes with a wan smile.

Francine nodded back.

"Amen," she said, and shut the Bible with a thump

Clint followed them back to the house, and as Lark was pulling into the driveway she turned to Meg and said, "I'd appreciate it if you'd sit in on this thing with Clint and Janine. I'm not sure what they want, or what Ethan might have promised them at some point. Whatever it is, I could use some advice on what to do with the studio." It was the first time since Ethan's death that Lark had really turned to her for help, and she felt both relieved and apprehensive. Now that her sister had reopened communications, Meg knew she'd have to restrain herself from offering unwanted words of caution and concern.

They sat around the kitchen table. Clint had brought a thick manila folder with him. Lark immediately lit up a cigarette. Janine coughed, waving her hands in front of her face.

"I'm sorry," Janine said in an apologetic voice. "I'm allergic, you know."

"And I'm a nervous wreck," Lark replied sharply, "so it's a draw."

"Of course," Janine said, letting out a little sigh. "I totally understand. It doesn't really matter."

"Now the thing is," Clint began without preamble, opening the file, "Janine and me know how to run the studio. And you need someone to run it for you. We've talked about it—Janine and me—and we think we've got a good plan for keeping things going more or less as they were. Without the artistic pieces, of course."

"How?" Lark asked. "Ethan was a master craftsman. I don't mean to be unkind, Clint, or sound ungrateful. But Ethan left some pretty big shoes to fill."

"I knew you were going to say that," Clint said, nodding his head and looking down at the papers in front of him. "But, in reality, I've been turning out Red River Studio glasses—all three varieties—as well as vases, plates, and whatnot on my own now for nearly two years."

"Clint, is that true?" Lark sounded shocked. "Ethan never told me. . . ."

"We didn't think you knew," Clint replied. "I guess Ethan kept imagining it was going to be a temporary sort of thing. That he'd get back to the glasswork himself. Once the show happened, though, he pretty much turned the day-to-day work over to me. He told me to keep quiet about it. I guess he was afraid that customers might feel cheated if they didn't think the master craftsman oversaw all the stuff himself. But I never understood why. The pieces are all produced from Ethan's designs. And they all feature his techniques. That's what matters, after all, that's what can't be duplicated. I know plenty of other studios where the assistants do most of the work. In any case, I've been doing it for a while now and it hasn't hurt business any that I can tell."

"And what was Ethan doing?" Lark asked.

"His art pieces," Clint replied. "I think we all know that that's what he really cared about. When he saw that I could do the other, the commercial stuff, he just kind of turned it over to me. For a while I guess I felt a little cheated, I mean he didn't raise my salary or anything, but then I began to see it as a blessing in disguise. I learned the trade, you see. Believe me, I wouldn't be offering to take on the studio if I didn't think I could do a good job of it. I'm not that kind of person."

Silently, Meg agreed with Clint's assessment of himself. Like his wife, Clint might be self-effacing and uncomfortable in the spotlight, but he was a conscientious man, determined and hardworking. It struck Meg that Clint's conclusion about learning the trade applied to Lark's circumstances as well: it was a secret blessing. Ethan's growing disinterest in the commercial side of his studio had left Lark with a manager capable of carrying on in Ethan's stead.

"It's certainly worth thinking about," Lark replied.

"We've done more than think," Clint continued, laying a neat stack of typed pages in front of Lark. "Here's our proposal. It's something I've been considering for a while now. I would have approached Ethan directly with it at some point, if . . . "

Lark flipped quickly through the pages. "What's this about a retail outlet?" she asked, pointing to a line item halfway down the second page.

"It's, well, sort of a store that we'd open, with an area for various workshops and classes," Clint replied, sounding unsure of himself for the first time since the conversation began. "We could sell pieces there, and make extra money giving classes, sort of promoting interest in glassblowing in the community."

"I doubt if Ethan would have allowed that," Lark mused. "He hated anything that commercialized something he considered an art form."

"In his hands," Clint said, nodding quickly in agreement. "But for others—for me—it's just a skill. A job. I'm not an artist, Lark, I've never pretended to be. The kind of things I can make—the tumblers, the simpler paperweights and vases—I won't be able to charge what Ethan did for his finer pieces. We'll need to generate money in other ways to compensate. Through the store. The classes." He leaned over and tapped the pages in front of Lark. "It's all spelled out in here."

"We'll give you fifty percent of everything we make," Janine added meekly. "That's sales, you know, not profits. So it would be up to us to handle expenses."

"But you'd expect the use of the studio as part of the agreement, right? And you've always paid minimal rent for your house. I don't know. . . ."

"But, Lark," Meg broke in when she saw the Lindberghs' disappointed expressions, "it's a terrific solution for everyone. I can't imagine why—"

"I need a little time to think about it," Lark sighed, lighting another cigarette. "Everything's been happening . . . so quickly."

"We understand," Clint said, rising to go. He pulled Janine's chair back, forcing her to stand as well. "We just want you to know, though, that we've been in touch with a crafts center in New Hampshire. They said they might make us an offer; they were going to think about it, they said. So we'll need an answer soon."

Lark squinted up at him through her cigarette smoke, and Meg thought she saw tears in her sister's eyes. "You'll have it within the week."

"Okay, I give up," Meg said when she returned from showing the Lindberghs out. "I was under the impression that you wanted my advice. So what the hell more can you ask? If Clint ran the studio, you'd have enough income to keep working on your children's books. You could go on as you were. . . ."

"It's not what *I* might want," Lark said, "but what Ethan would have wanted. He knew he could make more money if he had a store, if he gave classes, if he turned the studio into a kind of commercial center. He knew all that, but he was adamant about not going that route. He wanted to keep his work pure. You start giving classes to people in this town, or to tourists during the summer—everybody begins turning out the same cookie-cutter bud vases—it diminishes the real work, dumbs down the whole art of glassblowing into something that anyone can learn in one easy lesson on a rainy afternoon."

"Okay," Meg said. "But isn't a little diminution of integrity better than total loss of income?"

"You don't lose your integrity in little bits. Once it's up for grabs, it's just gone, okay? Ethan knew that. He believed very deeply in what he was doing. I don't think you really understood that about him."

"There was a lot about Ethan I didn't understand. Until this past weekend. But I'm finally beginning to get the picture. No thanks to you."

"Meaning?"

"You talk to me about integrity, Lark. Ethan's *integrity*? For chrissakes—he screwed around on you with every attractive woman he could find. How can you talk to me about wanting to honor the memory of someone who would do that to you?"

Since Ethan's murder, Meg had noticed that her sister seemed to have a hard time focusing her gaze. Now, looking distractedly at Meg, Lark said, "You don't know the first thing about Ethan and me."

"That's because you've been doing everything in your power to keep it from me," Meg said. The time had come to open up on how she really felt about her sister's so-called happy marriage. "You knew perfectly well what Ethan was up to behind your back. He apparently had a long history of it. But I had to learn the dirty truth all by myself—and then I had to learn how long it's been going on from Francine and others in this town—from near strangers. Not from my own sister—the person closest to me in the whole world. I can't believe you've been concealing this from me for all these years."

"I knew you'd never understand." Lark got up from the table and walked over to the sink. She leaned against the counter and gazed out the window at the monotone landscape. "You . . . Francine . . . nobody can possibly know what it was like. What Ethan was really like. How loving. Protective. We were his nest. His family. We were everything he worked for. Everything he truly loved."

"I don't mean to be cruel, but if that was the case, how can you justify all those other women?"

"They didn't *mean* anything to him. I knew that.

He kept reassuring me, but he didn't have to. I believed him. Listen, I know that Ethan was far from perfect. He had his demons. He had something in him—a drive, a fire, a kind of desperate passion that nobody, that nothing, could seem to satisfy. We talked about it a great deal, especially in the beginning. It did hurt me some then—those episodes. Initially, I saw them as you probably do now—infidelities, betrayals. But, we kept talking, kept trying to figure things out, because I also knew how much he loved me. How much he adored the girls."

"And me, too, Lark, remember? He certainly made a point of showing how much he cared about me. Listen, he basically tried to rape me, okay? And if you believed for a single second that I 'shared' his attraction, you'd better think again. I was never more humiliated and afraid in my life."

"I loved Ethan." Lark began to cry. "I loved him more than anything in the world."

"And he betrayed you. Over and over again. Baby, I'm asking again. Why didn't you come to me? Why didn't you tell me about this?"

"What? You, who'd warned me that he'd break my heart?" Lark shook her head. "Remember, that's what you predicted would happen? And when it began to appear that you were right—I just couldn't face you. I wanted you to believe in me. I wanted you to respect us. I couldn't begin to explain it to you. To anyone. Except him. So we talked. We analyzed. We came to realize what it was. Why it was. It had to do with his creativity. His need to mold, to possess. It was his way of working things through. These women . . ."

"Were just a part of his creative process?" Meg said

bitterly. "Like firing an oven? Or rotating the pontil? 'Excuse me, dear, but I have to go out now and fuck some unsuspecting girl so that I can keep my creative juices flowing?' It was okay because Ethan was an *artist*?"

"You see?" Lark replied quietly. "You don't understand. I knew you wouldn't. I don't really expect you to. What Ethan and I shared … it was beyond the bounds of what most people experience. I let him go his own way, I gave him complete freedom, because I understood finally that that was the best way for me to show him how much I loved him. You can't cage a man like that. You can't put limits on the kind of marriage we had."

"God, you should hear yourself! Justifying Ethan's outrages so calmly … so patly!" Meg moved her chair backward, scraping it along the floor. She stood now, too angry to sit any longer. Lark also rose and retreated to the pantry. Meg watched as she shuffled through an untidy drawer, pulled out a packet of rolling papers, and started to lay out a row of cigarettes on the counter.

"He really had you fooled, didn't he?" Meg continued. "Francine told me that he had a kind of funny way of knowing just which buttons to push with a woman—what her secret longings were, where they were hidden. He knew yours all right— he knew how you fancied yourself a free spirit— unconventional, undemanding. And if you were so free with your spirit, why shouldn't he be free with his love? But, you know what, Lark? I don't believe for a single minute that it was okay with you. I think it must have killed you a little bit inside every single time you discovered he was screwing around with someone new."

"What Ethan did on his own time was his own business," Lark said. "It was separate from me, from us. I didn't condone it, Meg. But I could forgive it. We were a *family*." Her voice was wobbly but Meg couldn't decide if it was from conviction or anger.

"And Lucinda? Wasn't she a part of that family? Look at her now."

Lark lit a cigarette, inhaled deeply, her eyes roving over the pie cupboard, its shelves stacked neatly with tiny blue and green bottles of homemade tinctures, the bouquets of dried herbs hanging upside down above the old porcelain double sink next to them. She turned to face Meg. The fact that she had lost weight since Ethan's murder didn't surprise Meg; Lark hadn't been eating much of anything, subsisting, it seemed, largely on a diet of herbal smokes and green tea. But now she noticed that Lark had lost something else as well. The glowing eagerness that once infused her face was gone. Her features seemed to have congealed into a dark mask of uncertainty and deep sorrow. Though Lark was mother to three young girls, Meg had always thought of her—up until Ethan's death—as a girl herself. Spontaneous and carefree, Lark had been the confiding, giving, almost ridiculously optimistic one. All that had been snuffed out. The woman who faced Meg now would never laugh with the abandon of pure happiness again. And though Lark no doubt thought that her world had started to collapse with Ethan's death, Meg now believed that the damage began the day Ethan McGowan walked into her sister's life.

"I was asking for your advice," Lark said after a moment. "Not your approval."

"Okay." Meg touched Lark's shoulder. Lark didn't flinch and Meg kept her hand there. She said, "Let the Lindberghs take on the studio for six months. See how it goes. You can always change your mind later if you think it's not working out."

"Maybe you're right."

"That way you can concentrate on your own work—the book, the girls. You can get on with your life."

Meg knew that she was offering the most banal of platitudes, but Lark nodded her assent. They stood there together for a moment, an arm's length away. And then, sighing, they walked into each other's arms. They might never be able to forgive or truly understand what had happened between them but they still needed one another, Meg knew. And that was all that mattered now.

19

Meg hadn't planned to stop and see Lucinda on her way back to the city the day after Ethan's funeral. Usually, she took the scenic, meandering back roads down to the parkway. But she needed to make it back to Manhattan by early afternoon to deal with work that had piled up at the office, so she opted for the more direct route through Montville. When she found herself near the hospital, she pulled in. At the time she told herself it was purely an impulse. Later on she realized that she'd probably put herself there on purpose. She had so many questions on her mind, and she knew that she needed to resolve the most pressing one first: Did she believe Lucinda's claim of innocence? That the girl hadn't killed Ethan?

According to the nurse who had met Meg at the elevator and led her to the infirmary, Lucinda was still on the IV because of an infection that had spread from the third-degree burns on her palms. This sort of thing wasn't at all unusual, the nurse assured Meg, but they'd needed to take precautions nevertheless. The intravenous feeding had caused Lucinda to drop some weight. That, combined with a new short haircut the state provided the patient free of charge, had dramatically altered Lucinda's appearance. Her complexion remained pasty and uneven, there was a pimple on her chin, but the weight loss bought out the structure of her face: the high cheekbones, the wide expressive brow. With the red dye nearly gone, her hair was now a thin mousy chestnut color. Short bangs accentuated the liquid amber of her brown eyes. There was a new vulnerability in Lucinda's expression, the stripped down, raw, and authentic look of someone who had little left to lose.

"Meg? Thanks so much for coming..." Lucinda said, her eyes widening with surprise as Meg approached. She tensed when Meg leaned over and kissed her forehead. This, too, was something different—Lucinda was grateful. Meg noticed that the bandages on Lucinda's hands were far less bulky than when she had visited two days before; the taut bands of gauze looked something like the fingerless gloves pop star Michael Jackson used to wear.

"How are you feeling?" Meg asked.

"Terrified," Lucinda whispered. "I think that they're out to get me, Meg. And I think they're going to do it."

"Boardman's an excellent criminal lawyer," Meg reassured her, repeating what Abe had said. "He's done a lot of juvenile cases. You're in good hands."

"Oh yeah?" Lucinda had tears in her eyes when she said, "He was here yesterday, and we had a big old talk. I went through the whole thing with him again. As far as I can tell, he has me signed, sealed, and delivered. He discussed term stays with me. Good behavior. How everyone is looking for leniency. Well, you know what I think? I think you all should spend some time looking for the fucking truth."

"And what do you think the truth is?" Meg asked her, pulling up a chair and sitting down by the bed.

"I don't know," Lucinda said. "I keep going over in my head all the people I know in that town who didn't like Ethan. There were plenty, Meg. I think I knew more than most people did about the uglier side of Red River. Everyone saw me as a troublemaker, a bad seed, you know? And one of the main reasons they didn't like me—I mean, right off the bat—was because they knew I was from Ethan's past. Forget the fact that I wasn't even *related* to the bastard. It was guilt by association."

"Is there any one person, though? Anyone with a clear-cut motive you can think of?"

"Well, let's start with all the husbands of the women Ethan fucked. That already gives us a list about as long as your arm."

"Yes, but all of those affairs were in the past," Meg pointed out. "From what I can tell, Ethan went through women one at a time. And we both know where he'd turned his attention before he died. I can't think why a husband would suddenly get jealous—enough to put him into a homicidal rage—months after the fact."

"Well, how about the women themselves?" Lucinda

asked, sitting up a bit in the bed. "Maybe one of them still had a thing for Ethan. Maybe she was pissed that he'd moved on, you know."

"That could be. But she would need to have been really furious with Ethan—and seriously in love with him. I don't know . . . would you really murder someone because he didn't love you anymore?"

"Are you thinking what I'm thinking?"

"You mean Lark?" Meg said, meeting Lucinda's troubled gaze. "I've been thinking about her since you told Abe and me two days ago that you didn't kill Ethan. You see, when Lark told me you'd had a miscarriage—and implied Ethan had been the father—I was convinced you'd murdered him. And I totally understood why. I knew how aggressive and manipulative he could be. I would have gotten on the stand to testify as such. But when you said Ethan hadn't so much as touched you . . ."

"Meg, I'll swear on a stack of Bibles," Lucinda said eagerly.

"I've a feeling you'll have to swear on at least one," Meg said. "The thing is—I suddenly realized that your scenario made sense. Also, why would you be holding the burning end of the pontil? I think your hands were burned because you did pull it out—that you did try to save Ethan's life rather than take it."

"So, you really do believe me, Meg?" Lucinda's eyes were brimming, her face bright with expectation.

"I think I do, but I still have a lot of questions. Why did you flush the fetus down the toilet, Lucinda?"

"Because I didn't know I was pregnant?"

"I wish I could believe you. But I don't think I do. That's the one thing you're holding back, as far as I can tell. You did know you were pregnant—and you were relieved when you lost it. You thought no one would be able to tell what had happened to you. You hoped that you were flushing something away you'd never have to deal with again."

Lucinda, her eyes squeezed shut, couldn't keep the tears from slipping out. She lay back on the pillows and, with her eyes still closed, said with a sob, "It's not any of your fucking business, okay? All you need to know is that Ethan had absolutely nothing to do with it."

"I know," Meg said gently. "I believe you about that. And for now, at least, I won't ask you anything more about it. But at some point, Luce, I'm going to have to know. Everything. If you want my help—I'm going to need your total honesty."

Lucinda's eyes flew open.

"You're going to help me then?"

"I don't know how yet," Meg said, "but, yes, I'm going to try."

In some ways, Meg could understand why so many people wanted to blame Lucinda for Ethan's death. It would be so simple and somehow appropriate to have this troubled outsider be the culprit. Knowing what everyone certainly did now about Lucinda's miscarriage, they could assume what Lark had already insinuated: Lucinda killed Ethan because he'd gotten her pregnant. Good riddance to bad trash, the town could declare with impunity. Two birds killed with one stone. It would have been easier for Meg, as well, because the murder would then make sense and Lucinda would be seen as a victim herself in the eyes of the law. The leniency Boardman predicted would be forthcoming. Yes, Lucinda would no doubt have to spend some time in prison. But, with good behavior, she'd be out in time to pick up the pieces of her life and move on. Just as Red River would have moved on—quickly, quietly, smoothing over whatever ugly truth they all seemed so determined to hide.

All the way back to the city Meg turned over the next question in her mind, and it was a far more complicated and dangerous one. If Lucinda didn't murder Ethan, who did?

Meg considered the people she knew personally who didn't like Ethan. Francine and Abe came immediately to mind. But they'd both been so free and frank about their objections to Ethan; surely, if either one had been driven to kill the man, he or she would have not been nearly so forthcoming. Then Meg thought about those who cared for Ethan, those who seemed to have loved, or at least admired him: Hannah, Clint, Janine. Ethan was a man who inspired strong emotions in others—who provoked response. Arrogant, demanding, charming, impossible, he either loved you or dismissed you. He had no patience for the middle ground. And there seemed to be no one close to Ethan who didn't respond to him with the same degree of passion. Meg reminded herself then how easily love could turn to loathing, admiration to anger.

A murder victim's spouse is always the most obvious suspect, she knew. And, in this case, she was well aware that once the police began interviewing people in the town, the facts about Ethan's philandering would lead the authorities to go back and requestion Lark. Yes, Lucinda had been found with the murder weapon in her hand. But it was Lark who had come up with the motive—she'd started the speculation about Ethan being the father of Lucinda's miscarried baby. Why had Lark done that? Lucinda had made no bones about her promiscuity. But it was a big leap from promiscuity to sleeping with one's stepfather. Had Lark meant to mislead? Or had she simply jumped to the wrong conclusion during a time of extreme emotional stress?

As Meg thought about these problems, she returned again and again to the most important question. Did she have enough strength, enough determination, or enough courage to look for Ethan's real killer . . . even if it meant she might find her own sister?

20

It was over forty blocks from Meg's offices off Bryant Park to the Metropolitan Museum of Art, but once she realized that she would never be able to get a taxi at rush hour and with nearly an hour to spare before she was scheduled to meet Hannah at the museum, Meg decided to walk. She cut diagonally through the park behind the New York Public Library and crossed the great rectangle of lawn, the high windows of the office buildings surrounding the park glittering through the gathering dusk with an alluring intimacy. She loved the city at night, especially during the week, when one could almost feel the pulse of urban life— the commuters running for the subway, the theater-goers hurrying off to an early dinner, the worlds within worlds ebbing and flowing around her. The collective power of crowds had always moved her; listening to the national anthem in a stadium full of fans sent a shiver down her spine. She found comfort in numbers, in knowing that others were there beside her, in recognizing that everybody knew the same words by heart.

And Meg had decided to take comfort these days anywhere she could find it. She stopped briefly in front of the bench where she had sat with Ethan. It seemed utterly impossible now that it had been only six weeks ago. Her world had changed in so many ways since then. No, she corrected herself, *she* had changed. In almost every area of her life, she could feel herself being more cautious. She thought twice before voicing her opinions. She took more time to think about problems at the office. She was now aware of things that she had previously taken for granted: her staff at the agency, the business itself, her friends, and, probably more than anything else, her family.

Since returning from Red River after the funeral, she'd spoken to her sister on the phone at least a dozen times, sometimes for hours on end. She tried her best to feel Lark out about her feelings toward Ethan—the anger, the humiliation that might have led her to kill him. But Lark assiduously avoided any subject that was the least bit depressing. These calls were like their old conversations, rambling digressions, mostly about Lark's day-to-day concerns—the girls, the Lindberghs, the studio, her writing.

"It's so hard to get back into it," she'd confided to Meg during their phone session that afternoon. "I've been through so much . . . and my little characters are still exactly the same. They seem so innocent, so cute—I feel like kicking them in their adorable butts."

"I know what you mean," Meg said. Ethan's murder had also altered some of her relationships in subtle and sometimes subversive ways. She had been talking to an old college friend who had complained about problems she was having with her longtime boyfriend: He didn't know how to be truly intimate; he was spending too much time at his brokerage firm; he'd forgotten their two-year dating anniversary. Had Meg really listened to this kind of whining with interest before? She just wanted to scream: "Grow up! You have no idea what real problems are like."

The old Meg would probably have responded with much less concern to the ongoing bad news about Frieda Jarvis. The new Meg was growing increasingly alarmed. While her phone calls to the wayward fashion designer went unanswered and her letters were ignored, three more articles on Jarvis appeared in the business and trade papers, each mentioning that the financially troubled apparel company was looking for prospective investors to staunch its hemorrhaging cash flow. The best-guess earnings that one of articles had given for Jarvis's most recent quarters were a mere half of what Meg had been owed for the past six months. This finally made her pick up the phone to call Abe.

"What if there's no money left?" she had asked Abe, "I kept thinking that she was just slowing down on paying me because she knew I would be more lenient than her other creditors. Now I'm afraid I've waited too long."

"Welcome to the real world," Abe said. "I won't say I told you so."

"Oh, come on, you know you just did. But listen, Abe. I'm worried. I've been putting off suppliers for a couple of months now. Haven't paid some of the bigger media, hoping they won't notice. But I can't go on like this. Bad credit for an advertising agency is the same thing as a death knell."

"We'll have to sue her," Abe said without hesitation. "Believe me, I'm sure others are lining up to do so as we speak. But you're out a lot of front money here, more I'd guess than any of her other vendors. We'll rush the papers through. We should have everything in order by the end of the week."

When Meg didn't immediately respond, Abe continued in a more conciliatory tone: "I'm sorry about this. I know you two began as friends. But there's literally no other recourse at this point than the law. I'm sure this is hard on you, but—"

"The only thing that's hard on me is the realization that I should have listened to you three months ago."

"Getting tough."

"Gotten," Meg said. "About a lot of things."

"You know, one of the qualities I've always admired in you," Abe said, "is that you've conducted business on your own terms. It's true that you haven't been particularly hardheaded. You've given people the benefit of the doubt when you probably shouldn't have. But you've been strong without losing—you're going to have my head for this—without losing your femininity. I think that's one of the reasons so many of your clients are loyal. You're *you*. Not some by-the-numbers advertising exec."

"And by this you're trying to say?"

"Don't get too tough."

After the mob scene at Fifty-seventh and Fifth, the crowd began to thin out. At the Plaza Hotel, Meg crossed over to the east side of Fifth and walked north along one of the most expensive stretches of real estate in the world. Doormen nodded to Meg as she strode past the canopied entranceways, chandeliers gleaming behind them in the marble-covered lobbies. Meg had the look of someone who might belong there. With her good eye and access to the sample sales of all the top designers, she dressed with conservative flair. Blacks and beiges and navy blues. Cashmere, linen, silk. The lines were what mattered, the magic of a perfect bias cut fluttering at the knee, the jacket collar resting on the shoulders like a mantle.

Money. You could smell it on the chill night air. A subtle perfume, nothing too strong or memorable but lingering, elusive, like the cushioned interior of the chauffeur-driven Mercedes that stopped as Meg passed. The car door opening, the gloved hand on the upholstered handle, the casual way the occupant's black leather heels touched—one, then two—the sidewalk. Money. And leisure.

Leisure—Meg didn't have it. The nonchalance of the brown-and-white striped Bendels shopping bags, the perfect posture of a woman who never had to make a deadline in her life. The surety that the world would wait for you. That when you were ready, someone blew a whistle, and a limo or taxi pulled up to the curb. Nothing had ever simply *been* there for Meg. She had to drive herself to go out and get what she wanted. She had to learn what it took to get things done. There was in her very walk a certain competence that comes only from working—and working hard. It was an attitude that would forever separate her from the woman who emerged from the Mercedes and, without a word to the driver or a smile for the doorman, sauntered through the gleaming double bronze doors.

Don't get too tough, Abe had said and yet, though Meg had always been a firm believer in creating your own destiny, sometimes life just blindsided you. That's what Ethan felt like to her now: a bad accident that had left her both physically and emotionally damaged. Meg, who had never been afraid of anything or anyone, was now more than a little wary of the one person she thought she could always count on: herself. How she'd allowed herself to be duped by Ethan, how she had actually come to believe he was good for her sister she would probably never understand. It didn't help that she hadn't been alone in misunderstanding Ethan's true character. The fact that he'd manipulated countless women over the years did not make it any easier for her. Because Meg had always prided herself on knowing about men. She could generally size up a man within the first three minutes of meeting him. And she had rarely been wrong. So how had her signals gotten so disastrously crossed with Ethan? How had she let him insinuate himself into her life? This destructive man had left an enormous amount of damage in his wake—a trail of distrust, betrayal, and emotional pain, the extent of which Meg was only beginning to fully comprehend.

Meg had promised Lucinda that she would help her—though she'd admitted that she didn't know how she would go about doing so. Red River and everyone associated with the murder were two and a half hours north of the city. Though she planned to visit Lark over the upcoming Thanksgiving weekend, she didn't have much time these days for more than the occasional morale-boosting phone call to Lucinda, who remained in the hospital, mending slowly. For the time being, her hands were tied, though her mind kept returning to the subject of the murder and its aftermath.

Recently she had begun to think about Hannah Judson. She had seemed so eager at the funeral to talk to Meg about Ethan—perhaps Hannah herself could cast some light on Ethan's final weeks. She'd called Hannah and they'd chatted on the phone. At the end of the conversation, the gallery owner had invited Meg on a private tour of a new exhibit at the Metropolitan Museum.

"Boucher and Fragonard mostly," Hannah had told her with a slightly bored air. "Mid–eighteenth-century French paintings. Not totally my cup of tea, but a friend of mine is a curator there and she'll let us tour the collection after hours on our own. It's bliss to see this sort of thing without all the crowds."

She met Hannah, as arranged, at the Eighty-third Street service entrance. With her was a tall, willow-thin woman in her late forties, sallow and oval-faced, her long black hair in a thick braid to her waist. Hannah introduced her to Meg as Frederica Gomez, "an old, old dear, dear friend" but when Meg held out her hand to shake Frederica's, the curator seemed not to notice and led them without a further word down a long marble hallway. The exhibit was on the second floor, and even before Frederica nodded them into the stately high-ceilinged rooms, Meg could feel the giddy pleasure of the billowing, heaven-washed canvasses: the cerulean blues and salmon pinks, the carousing nymphs and satyrs, and the multitudes of chubby, for-ever-laughing putti.

"You've about an hour," Meg heard Frederica mutter to Hannah.

"Thank you, darling," Hannah replied, and the two women gave each other air kisses, European-style, one blown to each side of the cheek.

"I do adore her, but . . ." Hannah said when Frederica was barely out of earshot. She took Meg's elbow and led her to an enormous canvas that acted as the introductory centerpiece to the show. "She is so very intense. Incredibly knowledgeable, though. And totally connected. She knows simply everybody."

Meg couldn't help but wonder who "everybody" consisted of and whether she herself was included among Hannah's chosen ones, but she refrained from questioning Hannah's snobbishness. There was no point in antagonizing someone she wanted to understand. They wandered slowly from room to room, examining the seductive landscapes of Boucher, Fragonard's dramatic views, the intimate scenes of Chardin. From time to time Hannah would comment knowingly on a painting or artist.

"They say that Chardin began to paint these domestic pictures," she told Meg when they stopped in front of a portrait of two women sewing, "because he was annoyed when someone said painting a still life was easy. Thank God for the idiot who made that pronouncement. I adore Chardin's interiors."

Meg kept trying to find a way to introduce Ethan

into the conversation. But as they entered the final gallery and stopped in front of a large, richly colored Fragonard, Hannah did it for her.

"I've been thinking a lot about Ethan lately," Hannah said, as they took in the canvas before them. It was a bedroom scene. A red velvet canopy unfurled from somewhere above and outside the painting, its deep color and soft fabric taking up almost the entire left side of the canvas. White sheets and pillows, slightly mussed, shone darkly beneath the lush fall of velvet. The right half of the painting depicted a man and a woman, their eighteenth-century dress in dishabille. The man had his left arm around the woman's waist. She was arching back from him, her blond, powdered head seeming to draw away from his body and yet, if you looked closely you could see beneath the folds of her satiny gown that her legs were spread and her hips just starting to curve toward his tautly muscled thighs. This half of the canvas was brightly lit, a semicircle of intense white heat, accentuating the movement of the man's right hand just as it found the tip of the bolt on the bedroom door. The woman's hand, reaching blindly beneath his, was stretching to find the lock as well, but it was difficult to tell if her gesture was one of protest or complicity. It was a passionate, complexly textured painting, infused with ambiguity. How easy it is to misread other people's signals, Meg reflected.

"I imagine we all have been thinking about him," she said.

"I was recalling our conversation at the funeral," Hannah went on. "That dreadful noisy basement. You were surprised, Meg. That Ethan would confide in me about your affair."

"No, I was surprised that you'd thought there had even *been* an affair," Meg corrected her.

"It struck me later that you didn't know about Ethan and me," Hannah continued, "that you didn't realize we had been lovers, too."

Meg turned and stared at the older woman, her expression obviously revealing her surprise. In her mind, she had for some reason confined Ethan's affairs to Red River.

"Please, don't look so aghast." Hannah laughed nervously. "Knowing the kind of man he was I can't imagine why you'd be surprised, unless it was my age. And that, frankly, I'd find insulting."

"I'm sorry," Meg said, trying to pull herself together. "But I didn't know. And you're right—it should have occurred to me."

"I'm relieved to have it out, one way or the other," Hannah told her. "Though I suppose a small part of me had hoped that Ethan had told you—that he'd talked to you about me . . . about us." Meg could not help but hear the hurt and regret in Hannah's usual plummy and unemotional voice.

They had a dinner at a northern Italian restaurant on upper Madison that was so new it didn't yet have a sign. Hannah assured Meg that the food was delicious and that they'd better enjoy it now because the *Times* was scheduled to review the place glowingly the following week. Over a glass of wine before they ordered, Hannah told Meg about how she and Ethan had first met.

"He'd come by to drop off slides of his work," Hannah said, smiling thinly. "Just a cold call. He was looking for representation and I generally never see anybody like him—I mean anyone with absolutely no connections. My secretary was at lunch and I was at the reception area. He pretended he thought *I* was the secretary and went on and on about how he heard how wonderful Hannah Judson was, what an eye she had, a sixth sense about talent. Of course he knew that I knew what he was up to ... but, Lord, he was so charming. I looked at his work just to appease him. I was quite surprised to see how good it really was."

"And you could tell? Just from a slide?"

"Well, of course, in the beginning it was a little confusing. Ethan himself is ... was so vital ... and disarming. I'll admit that in the beginning, I cared a great deal more about him than his work. That first month? When we were talking about mounting the show, what to include, how to display the pieces? I began to see how closely he was tied to his art, how to a very large degree he *was* his work. It's what gave him fierceness, his passion. And I began to see what *he* saw in the pieces—the compressed energy, the risk, the masculinity."

"And if he'd been less ... appealing? Would you have given him a one-man show like that?"

"Oh, probably not. But the line between talent and personality has always been rather blurred, don't you think? One feeds on the other, fires the other. I mean, think of Picasso or Hemingway? Surely their looks, their sex appeal have played a part—an important one—in keeping their cult status alive. A strong, brooding photograph of an artist sells just as much as a glowing review. People want to see, to feel an artist's creativity—his pain, his loves, you know. People, buyers, want to have that—whatever it is that drives the process—sometimes as much as the art itself. And Ethan? He was a walking embodiment of an artist. He had my clientele just eating out of the palm of his hand."

"A regular poster boy for creativity."

"That's a bit cynical. I'm just saying the two things—talent, personality—are simpatico."

The meal, as Hannah had promised, was delicious.

"Did Ethan know all this?" Meg asked after they had finished. They had both ordered espressos, and Meg waited until after the two little white cups arrived before adding, "I mean—how you really felt?"

Hannah produced her strange, carrying laugh. "And how *did* I really feel? I've told you a few things, because you've asked. But it's just a rough sketch, Meg, hardly the full truth. I took Ethan as a lover because he seemed so wild—so fresh—only to find he was also a truly talented man. So what does that say about us? We were adults. On a certain level I think we both knew exactly what we were doing—and what we could do for each other. But, no, I don't think he ever realized that it was more for me than that. He was such a passionate man." Hannah toyed with her spoon. Under the restaurant's flattering light Hannah looked younger and more vulnerable.

"Didn't it bother you to learn about his other women?" Meg asked. "Weren't you jealous when you heard about his feelings for me?"

"Sad, perhaps. But I understood what Ethan was like from the beginning. And why should I hold him to a standard different from the one I set for myself? I believe in life in its fullest, most unrestrictive way. I look at nature as my guide—the animals, the seasons, the cycles of dormancy and renewal. I say, jump in, take what you can, give back what you will—take pleasure in it all. I like that part in the beginning of Genesis when God ends each 'Let there be' . . . with 'and he saw that it was good.' It *is* good, Meg. And it's meant to be enjoyed."

"That's how you interpret what Ethan was doing? Simply taking pleasure in life?"

"Exactly. He did what every man really wants to do. He just had the nerve and the energy to do it. That's why I loved Ethan so. He had such drive! He was a romantic, in the truest sense of the word—thoroughly emotional, larger-than-life, a lord of nature."

"Think of all the people he hurt," Meg said. "The women whose lives he ruined. The marriages he wrecked."

"So, what were they—lambs to the slaughter? Is that how you see it? A hoard of innocent, dumb girls, without any say in the matter, without any power, going under Ethan's ax? Please! Don't be so naive. These women—whose lives you say Ethan ruined—as far as I'm concerned, they were asking for it. And I wouldn't be surprised if Ethan was the single most exciting thing that happened to each and every one of them."

The waitress came by with their check, and Meg picked it up. "I can't say I shared your enthusiasm for Ethan's charms."

"Of course, you didn't," Hannah replied. "But then you never knew what it meant to love him, did you?"

21

"When did all this happen?" Meg asked Abe, as he showed her into a handsome wood-paneled conference room. The requisite shelves of legal tomes took up one long wall. A Rothko-like lithograph of richly hued rectangles hung on the far wall at the head of the long bird's-eye maple table. The lighting was recessed and subtle. This room, the new reception area, and the row of offices leading down the hall from Abe's corner suite had all been added and renovated since Meg's last visit. Though she spoke to Abe on the phone about business matters at least once a week, it had been easily a year since she stopped by his offices in Rockefeller Center.

It was nearly six o'clock on the Wednesday night before Thanksgiving, but it seemed to Meg that most of Abe's staff was still working. Phones were ringing.

The whine of a fax machine and the rhythmic swishing of a copier could be heard down the hall.

"I'm sure I told you we were remodeling," Abe said, pulling out a buttery soft leather-covered chair for Meg next to him at the table. He closed the glass door on the noise from outside.

"And expanding? And adding staff? I saw the names of at least two new partners on your masthead."

"Well, yes." Abe sighed, dropping a legal folder in front of him as he sat down at the head of the table. "It's been one of the few beneficial side-effects of divorce. You get to devote all your energies to work. And, happily for me, we are living in highly litigious times. So it's now Sabin, Reinhardt, Tuchman, and Herrington, and we're all making money hand over fist."

"You don't sound particularly happy about it," Meg replied, trying to interpret Abe's tone. He was often hard to read—his cynicism kept people off balance and slightly at a distance. He hadn't always been so inscrutable. When both Meg and Abe were starting out in their different businesses, Abe has been far more open and affable. The day she'd first moved into the offices on Fortieth Street he'd sent her a huge bouquet of garishly colored helium balloons each carrying the preprinted message CONGRATULATIONS! It had been a long time, Meg guessed, since he'd done anything so spontaneous and whimsical. Sometimes when he smiled or laughed Meg could still see the boyish optimist she recalled from those years, but more often now, Meg saw only a serious, somewhat troubled man.

"Happy?" Abe tipped back in his chair, his hands folded behind his head. "In college, I remember we used to have these long philosophical discussions about happiness. Aristotle versus Plato. You know the sort of thing—what is the ultimate end of mankind? That's what happiness seems to me now— a concept, an argument, an *abstraction*. So what's real? I suppose I'm able to feel proud of all this, Meg," Abe said, nodding at the beautifully appointed room. "It gives me a sense of accomplishment. I'm moving forward. Moving on."

"From Becca?" Meg asked, without thinking.

"Now, about Jarvis." Abe sat forward abruptly.

"Oh, Abe, I'm sorry."

"You're on the clock here, and my rates have gone up. I hate to waste your money on personal chitchat."

The papers that Abe had prepared on the Jarvis lawsuit were incomprehensible to Meg, written in a legalese that made her want to nod off in the middle of each sentence. But she read through the twenty or so pages of complaint nevertheless and scanned the evidence sheets, mostly the approved schedules and consequent invoices that Jarvis hadn't paid. The conference room phone rang several times while Meg was reading, and she listened with half an ear while Abe fielded the calls.

"No, no, Jacob. This is *just* the moment to keep a cool head. They're hoping you're going to run scared. Just sit tight and don't sign a damned thing until we have a face-to-face with them next week."

A few moments later the phone rang again.

"It's for you, Meg."

"I'm so sorry to track you down like this," Lark

said. "But Oliver told me you were at Abe's, and I didn't know exactly when you were coming up this weekend. Will you be here in time for dinner tomorrow?"

"Sure. I already told you I plan to be there by midmorning," Meg glanced over at Abe, frowning. "That's all you wanted to know? When I'd get up to Red River tomorrow?"

"No, Meggie. I just needed to hear your voice. I'm . . . I'm kind of shook up."

"What's the matter, baby?" When Abe heard Meg's tone, he got up from his chair and came around and leaned against the front of the desk. Meg looked up at him while Lark explained.

"I've spent the whole afternoon down at the police station. This is the third time they called me in. Tom wasn't even there this time, it was those damned state detectives. They kept asking me the same things. Over and over. They know all about Ethan. . . ."

"Calm down now," Meg said soothingly. "It's going to be all right. They're just being thorough."

"Thorough! They've gathered every dirty piece of gossip about Ethan that they could find. Every ugly little thing that they could lay their hands on. And they have the nerve to play it all back to me, saying: 'Now tell us, Mrs. McGowan, did you know that your husband came on to your own sister a month ago?' "

"So they know about me?" Meg asked, as Abe shook his head in sympathy.

"That little tramp must have told them," Lark said and Meg could hear tears in her voice. "I'm so upset. I can't believe they're still asking questions. They want to talk to you, too, Meg. Next time you're in town, they said. I didn't tell them when you'd be coming."

"It's okay. I'll leave here first thing in the morning. . . ."

"I'm driving up tonight," Abe cut in, and Meg was startled by the urgency of his tone. "Right after work. You'll come with me."

There was hardly anyone on the road by nine-thirty when they finally left. Abe had been detained at the office and Meg had gone back to her apartment to pack a few things. She'd met him at his garage near Lincoln Center. The drove in companionable silence for the first half-hour, listening to Abe's favorite jazz station from Newark.

"Lark didn't say anything to you about Lucinda's hearing, did she?" Abe finally asked as the station's frequency began to fade. He clicked off the radio.

"No. Neither has Lucinda," Meg said, turning to him in the dark.

"So, you've been in touch with her?"

"Yes. I stopped by to see her on my way back after Ethan's funeral. And we talk on the phone."

"So she's told you that she and Boardman are not exactly hitting it off."

"She calls him an old fart. I think that's a pretty good indication of how she feels about him."

"He's a very smart lawyer, Meg," Abe told her. "She's lucky to have him. But she's giving him very little to go on. Can't remember anything the day

Ethan was murdered. Didn't realize she was pregnant. Doesn't have any idea who the father is. If you're trying to help her, then give her some advice, tell her to work with Boardman."

"I don't think she's trying to be difficult. I think she really can't remember. She blacked out. Either because she was so high or because she saw something that was so terrible her mind just couldn't cope with it."

"You've been giving this a lot of thought," Abe observed. He turned to look at her, then looked back to the road.

"Enough to think that Lucinda didn't kill Ethan."

Abe was silent for a moment. Then he asked, "And the argument for the defense is . . ."

"What she told us that day we both visited her. She went down to confront him about me . . . and found him with the pontil already in his heart. Already dead. Her hands were burned pulling the pontil out."

"She could have gotten burned when she drove the pontil into him, you realize. He was a big man, you would need a lot of force, plenty of momentum to puncture his clothes, skin, ribs. It could have slipped in her hands when she was killing him. Don't let that one piece of this puzzle convince you of anything."

"It's more than that," Meg said. "It's Lucinda herself. What's her motive? She was going down to the studio simply to tell him to leave me alone. Yes, she was angry. Upset. But not homicidal."

"So she tells you," Abe said. "There's still the question of the pregnancy. There's just no proof one way or the other that he didn't rape her. And it was Lucinda, after all, who destroyed the evidence."

"I know. A case can be made both for and against

her. But I happen to believe she's innocent—viscerally, instinctively, that's how I feel. Maybe I'm wrong, but the question I keep asking myself is why am I the only one who seems to be on her side?"

They were silent for a time as Abe concentrated on driving. A new moon cut a fragile scythe in the clear starlit sky above the gently rolling hills. The tires sang on the highway.

"It's not that I don't share some of your concerns," Abe said. "Or agree with some of your conclusions. But if I were you I'd be very careful about this business of taking sides."

"Meaning?"

"There are really only two of them. The prosecution and the defense. And if you take Lucinda's side, you're going to be staring across the courtroom at your own sister. Is that something you're prepared to do?"

"Do you really think it's going to come to that?"

"It could. The hearing to set charges and bail is coming up soon. I just want you to know what you're doing, Meg. Once the town knows your feelings about Lucinda, you'll find yourself sitting on a powder keg."

Lark had left the front porch light on, but the rest of the house was dark. Abe pulled into the turnaround and let the car idle as Meg reached into the backseat for her overnight bag. She thanked him for the ride and was about to climb out of the car when she thought to ask him a question that had been troubling her.

"Why did *you* hate him, Abe? Because he was a womanizer? Some might say that Ethan just did what every man secretly longs to do."

"Sleep with a lot of beautiful women—yes, plenty of guys would be made very happy by that. But manipulating them? Coercing them into believing that somehow love is involved? Sex, I can understand. Fucking around with someone's mind? That's despicable."

"I still can't believe I was so wrong about Ethan. That I just didn't see things."

"You know, I hear that sort of thing every working day of my life: 'I can't believe that I didn't know my business partner was robbing me blind,' or 'Why didn't I realize that my wife was having it on with my kid's soccer coach?' People see what they want to see, what they *need* to see. On a certain level you have to trust your fellow man—your best friend or your wife or, in this case, your brother-in-law—that the face he presents to you is the real one. You can't live your life being suspicious of everyone. The thing to be aware of is this: every once in a while you're going to come across someone like Ethan—someone very smart, very good at his game, very dangerous."

"But how *will* I know, Abe? That's my problem—I feel that if this happened with Ethan again tomorrow, I'd react in just the same way."

"At some point with Ethan, didn't a little bell go off inside you? Somewhere deep inside? I don't mean all the moral considerations you must have been dealing with because of Lark and the kids. I mean, a warning about *him*. Didn't something inside you whisper 'beware'?"

"Years ago, yes."

"Remember that next time. Trust that early warning signal. Listen to your instincts. After all my years as a lawyer and all the hard luck stories I've heard, I've come to believe that people always know when they're being screwed, they just don't want to believe it. They can say they didn't know, but they knew. Your wife comes home late smelling like she's just showered? And you think: isn't it great that she always smells so clean. Isn't it wonderful that she'd such a clean, hygienic person! I'll tell you what. Even as you tell yourself all that, you know. She's dirty as hell."

Later Meg would realize that Abe wasn't just talking about his experiences as a lawyer. What he'd learned about betrayal, he'd learned a much harder way. But at that moment all her thoughts were stopped by the pressure of his hand on her shoulder as she started to climb out of the car.

"What?" she turned back to him. He drew her closer. He reached over and touched her left cheek, the tip of her chin. Then in a swift, impulsive movement his arms were around her. They'd kissed before—quick hellos, pleasant thank yous—and this was not that. She hadn't realized until that moment just how much she missed being held, feeling someone's body against hers, knowing in an immediate and intimate way that she was wanted and desirable. It took her totally unawares, and yet, strangely enough, she wasn't surprised. It almost felt as though she'd been waiting a long time for this. For the pressure of his lips . . . the taste of him on her tongue. A deeper, stronger need stirred beneath it all.

"Nothing," he said, sitting back finally, stroking her cheek. "Just be careful, okay? I don't want anything but good happening to you from now on."

22

When Meg looked out her guest bedroom window on Saturday morning, she saw a white Ford minivan parked in front of the house. JUDSON GALLERY was scripted in elegant teal letters across its side panel. Meg showered and dressed. The house had been busy and full of people since Thanksgiving, friends and neighbors stopping by to lend support and catch up on the latest gossip. Though Meg kept hoping to see Abe's Saab among the cars pulling into the turnaround, she'd remained disappointed.

It wasn't yet nine-thirty by the time she followed the voices onto the porch, but the sunlit room was already filled with visitors: Hannah and Clint were sitting with Brook and Phoebe at the long farm table. Fern, smashing bananas with a plastic spoon, was perched kitty-corner to the foot of the table in a high chair. Lark came in from the kitchen with a platter of French toast, Janine right behind her with a pitcher of orange juice in one hand and a bottle of maple syrup in the other.

"Meg, hey, I didn't want to wake you," Lark said as she handed Clint the platter. "Hannah's here with some news about Ethan's work."

"I thought it more fun to tell you all in person," Hannah said, smiling around the table. Fun? Meg knew that Hannah was simply not the kind of woman who would travel two and a half hours first thing in the morning for such a lighthearted reason.

"Come on, everybody dig in," Lark said, as she sat down beside Fern, wrested the spoon from the infant, and attempted to actually deposit some of the mashed banana into her daughter's mouth. Meg watched with amusement as Hannah tried not to look horrified when Phoebe, seated to Hannah's left, picked up a piece of French toast with sticky fingers and plopped it down on Hannah's plate.

"For you," Phoebe said, smiling proudly up at Hannah.

"Why, thank you, darling," Hannah replied. "But I've already had my breakfast. We'll make this yours, and I'll just have a little juice."

"We can't wait a minute longer," Janine said in her little-girl voice. She seemed to have put on much more weight since the last time Meg had seen her. Though her complexion remained luminous, with a peaches-and-cream richness, a roll of fat overflowed the collar of her shirtwaist, and gaps were visible around the buttons on her floral-printed dress where her breasts and stomach stretched the material. "What's your news?"

Hannah Judson was not a woman to be hurried. She reached for the juice, took a careful sip and put the glass down again. She dabbed her perfectly clean lips with a paper napkin. Clearing her throat, she looked across at Meg as she said, "The Guggenheim has decided to take one of Ethan's pieces."

"The Guggenheim *museum*?" Lark mused. "How did this happen?"

"They believe your late husband was a unique innovator in his field," Hannah replied, enunciating as though she were talking to someone hard of hearing. Meg could tell that Hannah had expected her news to be greeted with far greater enthusiasm.

"That's wonderful," Meg said. "And it must mean that Ethan's artistic stock goes up as well. Along with the prices for his work, I'd imagine?"

"Of course," Hannah said. "This is a pivotal moment in any artist's career. The sad thing is that with Ethan . . . well, now that he's gone . . . his work is even more valuable. The old question of supply and demand. I've had several buyers call already asking what else I might have by him."

"There're at least twenty other pieces in the icehouse by the studio," Clint said. "Taking up a lot of room we could use for the new store outlet."

"I'd love to see whatever's left," Hannah said, turning her perfectly groomed smile on Clint. Meg could feel how much she wanted to get her hands on the rest of Ethan's work, and she doubted it was just for the money the sales would generate. Hannah, Meg knew, believed that she had discovered Ethan, had given him his big break, had helped to create him. There had been a tone of personal pride in her announcement

about the Guggenheim sale. And, even more troubling, a sense of entitlement as she asked to see
Ethan's remaining glass sculptures.

"I don't think you've had the chance to inventory
them yet, have you, Lark?" Meg asked, trying to
divert Lark's attention from feeding Fern to the more
pressing subject at hand.

"I'd be happy to help you," Hannah put in smoothly,
giving Meg a quick glance. "I brought a printout with
me of Ethan's recent sales. We should talk at some point
about a new pricing strategy. I don't want to be
accused of gouging, but the five thousand dollars we
were asking before is simply too low in light of the
Guggenheim sale."

"Five thousand per?" Clint asked, and then whistled between his teeth when Hannah nodded. "Jeez,
that already seems like a lot of money to me."

"Well, Ethan had a lot of talent," Hannah replied.
"And I must say that it's a tremendous relief to me
that I'm no longer entirely alone in my saying so."

It was not unusual in Red River, and especially at
the McGowan's, for people to wander into the house,
unannounced. Francine Werling felt enough at home
to stop and pour herself a mug of coffee in the kitchen
before joining the others on the sun porch that morning. Matt, carrying a large Kmart shopping bag, followed behind her, his headset pumping with angry
rhythms.

"Hannah." Francine extended her hand; Hannah
flinched under the minister's bone-crunching grip.
"Good to see you again so soon."

"Indeed, you as well."

When Francine dismissed the news of the Guggenheim sale with a quick "that's nice," Meg sensed Hannah's animosity toward the minister growing. It didn't help that Francine immediately monopolized the conversation. No matter where she was or what she was doing, she was somehow always in the pulpit, above them all, dispensing advice, casting judgment.

"Matt and I are going into Montville." Francine said, smiling. "We're going to visit Lucinda. Take her a few things. We've been collecting some books and magazines we thought she might enjoy."

"That's thoughtful of you," Meg said, glancing across the table at Lark. She was looking over her daughters' heads, out the window, her gaze unfocused.

"I don't understand," Hannah said. "Why would you be bringing that girl gifts? I wouldn't think you'd want to reward her behavior."

"I wouldn't think so, either." Lark's words came out in a rush.

"God is merciful, Lark," Francine said, looking at her. Sometimes Francine's serenity could be almost frightening; her calmness overcontrolled. Meg could sense the enormous reserve of emotion Francine held in check and wondered what would happen if she ever let it break through the floodgates. "We must learn to follow Her example. We must not ever forget, as the Bible tells us: 'Judge not that ye be not judged.'"

"The Bible also said something about an eye for eye," Lark said, scraping her chair back and getting up. She crumpled up her paper napkin, threw it on her plate, and started to clear the table.

It seemed to Meg that Clint entered the conversation at that point primarily to diffuse the tension building between Francine and Lark. He'd been in charge of Ethan's business for only a few weeks, but already he seemed more confident and grounded. He'd always been big and somewhat lumbering, but now his bulkiness seemed more pulled together. It helped that he'd recently gotten a haircut and had his beard trimmed as well.

"I was going to ask about Luce. What's happening with her?"

Meg waited until Lark left the room before she said, "Abe told me that there's a hearing scheduled for next week. To review the case and, I guess, rule on further hospitalization and mental status."

"Does she need to stay in the hospital?" Janine asked.

"Her burns became infected," Meg explained. "But I don't think it's too serious."

"An infection is the least of her worries," Matt said sourly. He hadn't sat with the rest of them at the table, slouching down instead on the low-slung couch facing the river, a plate of French toast balanced on his lap. He spoke up so seldom that Meg at first didn't recognize his voice. Deep and mellifluous, it immediately gained his listener's attention. And it was unmistakable that he was his mother's son. Everyone at the table turned to him as he spoke.

"Only God can know her true state of mind, Matt," Francine said, turning back to her coffee and away from her son. "We really must make a concerted effort not to judge for ourselves." Snorting laughter from Matt followed Francine's pronouncement, and he stood up abruptly. He was a tall, rangy boy, with an insolent bounce to his walk. There was a sense of menace in the way he approached the table and dropped his empty plate down next to Meg's place.

"Are we going? Or are we going to sit around and chew the fat all day?" he said.

"We'll be going in a moment," Francine said. "I just wanted to ask if there was anything we could bring Lucinda from here?"

"I'm going to lend her my Archie and Veronica comics," Phoebe announced, slipping off her chair.

"She won't want them, silly," Brook said, trying to stop her little sister. "And besides, I don't think Mom would like—"

"What wouldn't I like?" Lark asked with a forced smile as she carried a fresh pot of coffee into the room along with, Meg sensed, an attempt to be more cheerful.

"Us giving stuff to Lucinda," Brook told her.

"It's the charitable thing to do," Francine said when she saw Lark start to frown. "We've talked and talked about this. Now is the time to act. To turn the other cheek."

Lark put the coffee on the table and wiped her hands on her jeans.

"I can hear what you're saying, Francine," she said, looking directly at her friend and adviser. "I know you mean well. But, I'm telling you right now—if one single thing goes out of this house for Lucinda . . . it will be over my dead body."

"A tooth for a tooth," Matt said into the silence that had taken hold of the room.

"Matthew!" Francine snapped. She looked from

Lark to her son. "Behave." It was the same tone of voice one would use to discipline a recalcitrant puppy, and Matt, hanging his head, responded in much the same way a puppy would have.

"C'mon," he said to his mother with a whine in his voice, "Let's get the hell out of here."

23

After Francine and Matt had left, Lark and Clint walked Hannah down to the old ice house by the studio that Ethan had used for extra storage space. Clint was already working on the old wooden structure, repairing its walls and patching its sagging roof. This was where Lark had agreed to let the Lindberghs set up the retail end of their business. The studio, as Clint pointed out, had too many bad memories associated with it. And, for the time being, it remained sealed off by the police. Janine stayed at the house to clean up after breakfast and look after Fern and the girls. Meg, alone for the moment, dialed a number posted in big bold letters by the kitchen phone.

"Red River Police Department. Huddleson speaking."

"Yes, I'm Meg Hardwick, Lark's sister. She told me you wanted to speak to me."

"Meg, sure," Huddleson said. "We've met a few times. It would be great if you could come by. When's good?"

"How about right now?"

"Well . . ." he hesitated a moment. "The other two men on the team are over in Montville this morning, but I think I can handle it on my own. If you don't mind me having to get the phone from time to time. This is pretty much a one-man show on Saturdays."

It was a ten-minute walk into town. The morning was chilly and clear, a blanket of frost covering the fields and lawns. A quarter mile beyond the turn-off to Lark's drive, a concrete bridge spanned the Rocquonic, leading into the town proper. Here the two-story white clapboard houses sat on half-acre lots, a clutter of bicycles and toys in every other driveway. Without the flattering leaf cover of the maples that lined Main Street, it was clear that many of the storefronts and homes needed a fresh coat of paint or new shingles.

Though far from wealthy or prestigious, Meg knew that Red River was a pleasant, quiet place to bring up a family. Children could roam freely, play in each other's yards, come home after sunset without parents worrying about anything happening to them. Everybody knew everybody else—a glance would place you as so-and-so's child. There were no strangers here, though it often took a while for new people to feel welcome. Once you were known and liked, however, as Lark and the girls clearly were now, you became a part of a community as close-knit and caring as a large, extended family.

Then there were those, like Ethan, who were never really accepted. He hadn't tried, of course. He'd moved to Red River primarily because the farm had been a good buy and because it was a perfect location for a glassblowing studio. The town itself, its unique character and inhabitants never meant that much to him. Except for the more attractive women. No, Meg decided, as she passed Yoder's general store with its rank of pickups out front, Ethan had never been liked—and would not be missed.

Lucinda, on the other hand, had been actively despised. She'd been disruptive and disrespectful from the moment she'd come to town. Once she got a reputation for wildness and promiscuity, parents discouraged their children from speaking to her. In a town the size of Red River, the bad news spread quickly. Lucinda managed to chalk up one outrage after another during the past year. It wasn't surprising, Meg realized, that Red River had turned its back on her now. Lucinda McGowan had managed to make herself into the perfect scapegoat.

The police station was located in the middle of town. The American and New York state flags hung limply on either side of the well-scuffed front door.

Tom Huddleson, alone in the station, sorted through papers at a metal desk. In his fifties, running a bit to fat, he had a thick head of steely gray hair and the well-lined face of a veteran sportsman. The front office contained a cluster of wanted posters and a series of shelves sagging under the weight of heavy binders. A garishly framed portrait of the last police chief shaking hands with the governor hung above the fax machine.

"Sorry about the mess," Huddleson said, lifting some papers off a swivel chair next to his desk and nodding Meg into it. "Cup of coffee?" The smell emanating from the two-pot electric coffeemaker in the corner made Meg suspect that the coffee had been sitting there for several hours.

"No, thanks," she said, taking a seat.

"I've a few questions for you," Huddleson said. He pulled a file out from a row of folders behind his desk, opened it, and drew a yellow legal pad toward him.

"We've been told by several people that Ethan and you..." The police chief had a deliberate way of speaking, weighing each word, thinking through every sentence in advance. "... you had been, uh, seeing each other."

"Ethan tried to seduce me—and failed," Meg corrected him. "The first time was the night of his gallery opening in Manhattan in late September. Then he kept at it right up until the time of his death. At no point did I respond in a positive way."

"I see." He wrote something down in a chicken scratch that looked impossible, from where Meg was sitting, to read. "You were upset with him because of this?"

"Yes. I was furious. I didn't know until later, until after the murder, that he had a reputation for that sort of thing. I was horrified, in any case. He was my brother-in-law, for heavens' sake."

"Of course." Huddleson nodded sympathetically. "But then you know about Lucinda's miscarriage, right? And the possibility that Ethan was the father? Lucinda came to you in the city after she ran away. What did she want?"

"Money. A place to stay," Meg replied. "Months ago I promised her that she could come visit me—if she cleaned up her act a bit."

"But you were aware that 'her act' wasn't exactly together?" Huddleson looked over his half glasses at Meg. "You knew that she was pregnant?"

"No, I didn't. I had no idea until Lark told me about the miscarriage."

"Lucinda did turn to you for advice from time to time, didn't she? Confide her feelings and such?"

"Yes, I'd say she felt comfortable telling me things."

"She tell you about her feelings for Ethan? Go into that at all with you?"

"They had a strained relationship, I know. She never gave me chapter and verse on it, though."

"But she was pretty upset when she discovered that you had become the object of Ethan's affections, right?" Huddleson scanned the file in front of him. "That happened at your apartment down in the city when Ethan came by and Lucinda was there instead of you."

"Yes, she was upset," Meg said, realizing that Lark must have gone over all this ground already with the police during her various interviews.

"Very upset from what we heard. In a jealous rage."

"No, she wasn't jealous. She was upset that Ethan was coming on to me."

"I'm sorry, but that sounds like jealousy to me." Huddleson said. He put down his pen, pulled off his reading glasses, and massaged the bridge of his nose.

"No, that's not how it was at all," Meg, sitting forward, tried to explain: "Lucinda didn't want Ethan screwing up my life—the way he had her mother's. She was upset because he kept cheating on his family— Lark and the girls—and, by extension, Lucinda herself.

But it wasn't a sexual jealousy—it was an emotional outrage. She felt betrayed by him—and concerned for me."

"And how do you know all this? Did she tell you how she felt?"

"Not in so many words," Meg answered truthfully. "But she did tell me that Ethan would never have tried to seduce her. He didn't even like to touch her. She told me that he thought she was ugly."

"And this was when?"

"When I saw her in the hospital."

"*After* the murder."

"Yes."

"And where were you when he was killed?"

"I must have been running in the park—in New York," Meg said, thinking back."

"Anyone see you there? Anybody able to verify your whereabouts?"

"My neighbors' kids," Meg said, remembering the Edleson twins skating past her. "And Lark, of course. She called me right after Ethan was found. Am I a suspect?"

"No, not unless we find out that you're lying about being in Manhattan at the time of the murder." Huddleson closed the file and stood up. "My counterparts from the state may have a question or two, though I think we've pretty well covered it. I'll just need to take your prints, if you don't mind."

"You seem to be running a very thorough investigation," Meg observed, attempting to defuse the forced intimacy she felt as Huddleson helped her slowly roll her fingers through the cool black printing ink. There was a sour smell of coffee on his breath.

"Got to. The D.A. in this county hasn't lost a case in years. And he doesn't intend to lose this one, I can tell you that. It's up to me—and my friends from the state—to make sure he's got the goods to convict."

"Convict Lucinda, you mean?" Meg asked. He handed her a moist towelette, and she worked at the stains on the pads of her fingers until they were clean, though she felt tainted in a deeper way by the interrogation. Despite her best intentions, she knew that her interview had done nothing but add to the mounting circumstantial evidence against the teenager.

"I know why you're worried," the chief said kindly, as he walked her to the door. "The state detectives have been putting your sister through the ringer. They just go by the book, you know, for them its just another job. They can't see what I see—I know this town and the people in it like the back of my hand. I've known and admired Lark for many years. And you'd have to have been blind not to see how much she loved Ethan. These state detectives couldn't know that. They just see a wife who's been cheated on for a lot of years."

"They think Lark killed Ethan?"

"You want to know how it is?" Huddleson looped his thumbs in his belt and for the first time Meg noticed he was wearing a gun. "These guys think anybody might have done it—they make no assumptions. They're looking for evidence. They're gathering alibis. Shipping hair and skin samples off to the forensics lab upstate. To them, it's like science. A kind of math problem. To them, all they need to do is get the numbers all lined up and—there you go—the face of the murderer comes up. Like looking at some X ray on a light box. Now, I'm not saying they're wrong. It could very well be that clinical. But in my mind, solving this thing is a lot more like a religion—you take everything you know, add to it everything you believe, factor in history and experience. You end up with a kind of inevitable sense of what is true—a kind of faith, I guess."

"You're convinced Lucinda did it?"

"I'm not saying that." Huddleson held the door open for her. "I'm not coming out and saying that, you understand? All I'm telling you is that you can go back and tell your sister not to worry. This town knows what she's been through. We know things instinctively—in our hearts—that strangers like these state detectives can't know. Let them work their science. Let them run their tests. In the end, I believe it's all going to add up to the same thing. We're going to get her . . . coming and going."

24

The Lindbergh's cottage reminded Meg of the series of worn-down rentals she'd lived in growing up. On her way back from town, Meg caught sight of its fading white facade through the now leafless woods—and was drawn to it. She turned off the main driveway and followed the short dirt road down to the two-story shingled Cape where Clint and Janine had lived for the last ten years. Though the nearly hundred-year-old cottage was in need of a major overhaul, Clint had recently patched the roof in places and reinforced the gutters with metallic tape. Meg knew enough not to try the front of the house. In Red River, most of the front doors hadn't been opened in twenty years. Instead, she went around to the side door that led onto a small porch attached to the kitchen. Janine, working at the sink, saw her before Meg had the chance to knock.

"Meggie!" Janine turned her name into a surprised little squeal. She wiped her hands on a dish towel and added in a more contained voice: "Everyone's still up at the big house."

"Actually, I wanted to talk to you, if you have a second," Meg said, looking around. The kitchen was warm, sweet with the smell of something baking in the oven. Apart from that, Meg thought it was a depressing sight. She hadn't been in the house for several years, and its state of repair had only deteriorated in that time. The linoleum floor was clean but heavily scuffed and the oval rag rug in front of the sink didn't quite cover the area where pieces of the flooring had been ripped out for some plumbing repair and never replaced. The veneer cupboards were chipped in spots, pressed wood showing through like skin beneath ragged clothing. Taped with pictures of animals and flowers that Janine had cut out of magazines and old calendars, the refrigerator wheezed unevenly. An overhead fluorescent light gave the room a bright, slightly bluish cast.

"Sit here," Janine said, pulling out one of four mismatched kitchen chairs for Meg. "It's so nice, so unexpected to have you visit. I was just making some coffee, or would you rather have tea? The water's boiling in any case so either one is just as simple as can be!"

"Is Clint around?" Meg asked.

"Why, yes, he's upstairs washing up for lunch. We don't get to have our noonday meal together here, you know, because usually I'm needed up at the big house. But Frannie took the girls so that Lark could help Hannah. Wasn't that sweet of her? Do you want

Clint? I could call him if you like, though he should be down any minute now. But I'll call him anyway. Cli-int! Cli-int!"

Her high-pitched voice had an immediate effect. A door slammed above them. Heavy feet sounded on the stairs. Clint, his flannel shirt half unbuttoned, burst into the room. He was clutching a towel in one hand.

"What—?"

"Honey, look who's here," Janine said, beaming at her husband and then at Meg.

"I thought something was wrong," Clint apologized, nodding to Meg as he buttoned up his shirt. "The way you were screaming, hon."

"Clint's such an alarmist," Janine said, going to the cupboard and taking down three green glass cups and saucers; Meg recognized them as Red River Studio originals. "He worries about every little thing. Is coffee all right with you, Meggie? Or would you rather have tea?"

"Oh, no, thanks so much, I'm fine," Meg assured her. Clint and Janine sat down across from her. There was an awkward moment when the only sound was that of spoons hitting glass as Clint and Janine stirred sugar into their coffee.

"What can we do for you, Meg?" Clint asked at last. His expression was one of concerned goodwill.

"I spent the last hour down at the police station. Going over everything again with Tom Huddleson. I guess he's talked to both of you as well?"

"Oh yes," Clint replied, stroking his beard. "Together. Separately. Tom. The state detectives. They've had an awful lot of questions. We've being doing everything we can to help. Though them taking over the studio has put a real serious dent in our plans. But, we understand they've got a job to do."

"How do you . . ." Meg hesitated a moment, glancing from Janine to Clint "How do you see that job?"

"What do you mean?" Janine asked.

"I guess, what I'm asking is—are you convinced Lucinda killed him?" Meg asked Janine directly.

"I saw her with my own eyes with the pontil in her hands," Janine replied, her voice falling to a whisper. "I was the one who first saw her."

"So you were there?" Meg asked. "You were both there all the time? Would you mind telling me what happened?"

Clint and Janine exchanged a look.

"What's your interest?" Clint asked. "We've been over this ground plenty already."

"Yes, I know," Meg said, stalling for a moment as she tried to think of a way to allay their concerns. "It's just that . . . well, I haven't really heard the whole story from anyone. And I can't bring myself to ask Lark about the details. You know, with everything else she's going through. All these questions Tom was asking me—well, I began to think I'd really like to know more myself about what actually happened. So I thought, maybe you two wouldn't mind helping me a bit."

"About what exactly?" Clint asked.

"Did anyone else come by the studio that morning? Besides Lucinda."

"Well," Clint tipped back in his chair, resting the back of his head in his cupped hands. "Okay, one more time: It was Saturday. Janine had breakfast with the girls and Ethan up at the big house and I went over to Yoder's for my eggs and bacon. I like to hang out with the boys there sometimes, you know."

"I got back to the studio before you, hon," Janine said. "And I started in on the mailing list merge and purge. I remember because I'd been putting it off for so long and was proud that I'd finally just buckled down to it."

"That's right," Clint said, sitting forward again. "You were at the computer when I got back from town. And a little while after that someone did come by. I thought it might be a delivery so I started to go into the studio but Ethan called out that he'd taken care of it."

"Did he usually do that?" Meg asked. "Handle the deliveries on his own?"

"State police asked me the same thing," Clint replied. "And what I told them was this: no, not as a general rule. Ethan expected us to do all the routine work. But I don't remember it seeming like a big deal that he did it himself that day."

"Did you see the car?" Meg continued. "Do you remember what it looked like?"

This time Janine answered. "I saw it. I got up and went to the side door and took a look. It was a sort of plum-colored car. A beemer, I think."

"A BMW?" Meg asked, and Janine nodded. "Why'd you bother to check?"

She looked flustered for a moment, the color rising easily to her cheeks. "I guess because I wanted a distraction. Anything. I really didn't want to do the mailing list. And I also wondered if it was Becca, if she'd come early for some reason. But Becca doesn't own a beemer."

"Becca Sabin?" Meg asked. "Was she a customer?"

"Depends on what you mean by that," Janine replied. "Ethan sure had something that Becca wanted."

"Now, hon," Clint warned.

"I'm not saying anything that everybody in this town doesn't already know. Has known for years. Becca was sick in love with Ethan McGowan. I mean, she was crazy with it. Even after he'd dumped her. Even after he told her it was over. She couldn't give him up. She refused to believe that he didn't want her. Someone as beautiful as her. But—"

"Janine, just stop it" Clint's voice was sharp and sobering. "Meg doesn't want to hear a lot of tired old gossip. And neither do I. There was the one delivery that morning. And then, a half-hour or so later, another car drove up—and as I recall, it went on to the big house. That's it. That's what I told the police." Clint pushed back his chair and stood up. "Now, unless there's something else, I've a lumber delivery to pick up in Montville."

"No, really, thanks," Meg said, her mind taken up with the news about Ethan and Becca. "You've been so helpful, Clint."

"Now, hon," Clint said as he fished a fist of keys out of the back pocket of his jeans, "I've a feeling Lark's wondering what's happening to you. Time to get a move on." With a nod to Meg, he left.

"I'll help you clear up," Meg said, standing and starting to gather up the cups and saucers. It occurred to her that she'd get more out of Janine with Clint gone. She followed Janine to the sink.

"Oh, I can handle all this," Janine said as she turned on the faucet. Meg heard the grumble of Clint's pickup truck receding down the drive.

"I know what Clint was saying about gossip," Meg observed, leaning against the counter as Janine washed the dishes. "But you knew, of course, that there was a lot of truth about Ethan and his—"

"Other women?" Janine asked with a nervous giggle. "Of course, I knew."

"How did you feel about it?"

"That it wasn't any of my business." Her prim response didn't jibe with her earlier venting about Becca. "Ethan was our employer. And he was a good one. He gave us this house to live in. He taught Clint the craft. We have nothing but gratitude for everything he did."

"You know that others in this town feel differently?" Meg asked.

"I don't understand all this talk against Ethan," Janine said, staring at the stream of running water. "He was a good man. Thoughtful, generous. He took good care of us—and Lark and the girls, too. You know that, Meg."

"Yes, I know," Meg replied. "I also know that he had his passions. And that he sometimes couldn't control them. Did he ever . . . approach you, Janine?"

"Me?" Janine turned to Meg, her face flushing a deep pink. "No. Absolutely not. He was always a gentleman with me. And doesn't that tell you something? I mean, despite what people say, don't you think that perhaps it was really these women who approached *him*? You know, he was so attractive. And some of them, like Becca, just couldn't get over him. Lost all sense of decency."

"Maybe," Meg said, deciding it wasn't her place to set Janine straight about her former employer.

"Meg, there *is* something that Clint didn't see." Janine turned off the faucet and reached over to dry her hands on the dish towel. "Something that I told Tom Huddleson, but nobody else."

"Do you want to tell me?" Meg said

"It's about the car Clint mentioned that drove by after the beemer," Janine said. "The second one. It didn't drive past to the big house like Clint thought. But it didn't pull into the driveway, either. It went up and turned off into the woods where nobody would see it. But I saw it. I was watching. I recognized it, of course. I was expecting it."

"And it was?"

"Can't you guess? Becca."

25

Lark's studio was on the third floor of the house, facing north, a small, beamed room that had once been part of the attic. Its ceiling followed the steep slant of the roof. Lark had painted it a bright yellow and, with the first draft of the illustrations for her book tacked in progression to the wood supports that girdled the room, it gave off the bright slightly disordered cheeriness of a nursery. The final flight of stairs was uncarpeted and rickety, and Lark must have heard Meg's ascent from her first step. But she didn't turn when Meg, breathing a bit heavily from the climb, hesitated at the open doorway.

"Francine's brought the girls home," Meg told her. "And Janine came back with me. We put Fern down for her nap."

"Thanks," Lark said, dropping a paintbrush into a glass of discolored water. She arched back in her chair, stretching. "We finally got Hannah squared away. I saw Fran drive up. I can see all sorts of things from here. You have a nice talk with the Lindberghs?"

Though the dormer window that Lark's drafting board faced was small, the view it offered was generous and broad; without the obstruction of leaf cover, one could clearly see the turnaround in front of the house, the studio, the scaffolding around the ice-house, and the Lindbergh's front yard.

"You do have quite a view," Meg said, walking across the room to stand behind Lark. "You sit here and watch Becca Sabin come visit with Ethan every afternoon?"

"Janine's mouth has been flapping away again, I take it."

"Lark," Meg squeezed her sister's right shoulder, but it was tense and unyielding, solid as stone. "Why didn't you tell me?" Meg asked. The two sisters were alone together, just as they had been for most of their lives.

"Because I didn't want you to know," Lark said. "All the others were bad enough. But Becca . . . Becca and Ethan . . . that was just the worst."

"Listen, baby," Meg sat down on the little footstool next to Lark's drawing board and took her sister's hands in hers. "Talk to me now, okay? Tell me what happened."

Lark looked down at their joined hands for a moment, then away into the middle distance out the window. With a deep sigh, she began: "Becca Sabin looked like trouble to me from the moment I first met her. She seemed so full of disdain for this town, despite the fact that Abe just loved it here. It helped a little that the house Abe had built ended up being featured in the pages of the *New York Times* magazine. That kind of thing—appearances, awards—mean so much to her. I remember that at the housewarming party Abe and Becca threw when the construction was finally completed, Becca had propped the magazine article open on the large glass cube they had for a their coffee table."

Meg saw Lark frown as she paused, remembering the scene.

"It was late Indian summer weather that night— sultry, unsettled," Lark went on. "The other women at the party had on the kind of thing I usually wear— you know, floral print dresses or black pants with silk shirts. But Becca! She was in full Manhattan regalia: a fuchsia-colored slip dress, a real curve-hugger. Bronze-dyed high-heeled sandals, a heavy gold chain-link necklace. The one thing she wasn't wearing was a brassiere.

"I saw Ethan watching her. I saw him kind of slowly circling around her. About halfway through the evening, he found a way to approach her. I could see them starting to talk to each other. Then I watched her really begin to take him in. The way her hips started to sway. And you know how Ethan used to run his hands through his hair? I always recognized that as one of his signals. I could just tell he was getting turned on by her."

"Oh, baby," Meg squeezed her sister's hands as Lark shook her head sadly.

"Well, Meggie, you know by that time I was pretty accustomed to turning a blind eye on Ethan's little 'things.' That's how I used to think about them. I was used to these infatuations—they'd only last a few weeks, maybe a month, always accompanied by a lot of intense activity in the studio. I came to the conclusion that this was simply Ethan's way of working. Flirtation, sex, his artwork—it was all the same to him. Ethan always came back to us in the end, refreshed, relaxed. I felt that these episodes somehow freed him from his inner demons. So when I saw Becca and Ethan moving toward each other that night, I thought I knew what was going to happen. Ethan had been restless for several months at that point. He'd been increasingly difficult and demanding. Bad moods flaring up at unexpected times. I'd tried everything I could think of to help him out of the black hole he'd fall into at times like that—but I was beginning to feel pretty damned helpless. It seemed to me that these affairs—as meaningless as he always claimed they were—tended to release him. I knew the women meant nothing to him. That helped me get through it each time I sensed he was starting up with someone new."

"I hate to think of you going through this alone," Meg said. Lark's tone was so resigned and matter-of-fact, Meg couldn't help but wonder how her sister had dealt with her anger.

"Well, at least I'd become somewhat inured," Lark replied, giving Meg a brief smile. "Poor Abe had no such understanding or help for his humiliation. He told me later how he'd blown up after the last of their guests had gone. He'd accused Becca of doing everything but unzipping Ethan's fly. He'd begged her not to take it any further. Apparently, Becca had been known to stray a bit before this—that's one of the reasons Abe wanted them to spend more time in the country. Becca would go off on shoots or runway work, get high on coke and screw around on him. He thought Red River could solve their problems. I guess, for a time anyway, it helped. Then Becca met Ethan.

"Becca told me later that she tried," Lark continued, her gaze moving back to the window. "Not to see Ethan, I mean. Not to think of him. But, you know how it is up here, Meg. We all get invited to same the parties, run into each other at Yoder's every other day. You can't help it. And at some point, Becca didn't want to help it anymore. She moved up to Red River for the winter, then spring and summer, while Abe commuted from town on weekends. Poor Abe. He thought she was trying to please him, do her bit to keep the marriage together.

"Instead, she began to put herself in Ethan's line of vision as often as she could. She figured out when he usually picked up the mail, and she'd be at the post office at the same time—juvenile things like that. But she was hooked on him. Janine was right, it was a kind of insanity, because she was so used to getting what she wanted. Becca the Beautiful. But there was one thing about Ethan that she didn't know. He hated to be pursued. He liked romance to be a mystery, a dance, a series of slightly obscure signals, like lightning bugs on a summer's evening: 'I'm here, where are you?'

"The illusion of the chase." Lark shook her head. "That's really what he thrived on. Like the high-wire act he did with his sculptures—not knowing, until the penultimate moment, how, or if, the whole crazy thing would turn out. And there was Becca—giving the surprise ending away. Ethan ignored her, stepped around her. He even complained to me that Abe's wife was becoming something of a nuisance. So when we were invited to a Labor Day party at the Aldridges and he heard the Sabins were going to be there as well, Ethan actually thought about refusing to go. You know the Aldridge place up on Edencroft Road? That gorgeous colonial on the hill with perennial gardens that go on forever? Owen Aldridge is a big muckety-muck on Wall Street, and he and his wife Myra poured millions into fixing up the house and grounds. It was going to be the first time any of us saw all the renovations. Catered. A swing band from Boston. I was the one who talked Ethan into going.

"Everybody who was anybody in the county was there: all the wealthy weekenders, the local elite, a couple of TV stars who had been doing summer stock in the Berkshires. It was a beautiful, crystal-clear night. Tons of stars. I remember seeing them all reflected in the Olympic-sized swimming pool the Aldridges had put in. Dinner and cocktails were served around the pool. Dancing on a raised platform under a striped tent. It was truly elegant. Ethan and I steered clear of the Sabins, which wasn't all that hard to do as there were so many people.

"After dinner, we danced. He's—he was—a very good dancer. He had that grace. We were happy, having such a good time, and then Abe asked if he could cut in. I learned afterward that Becca had put him up to it. Abe had actually forgotten or—who knows?—repressed what had happened the night of *their* party. That had been nearly a year before. We were all getting to be friends now, or so he thought.

"I don't recall what Abe and I talked about, but I

remember thinking how much I'd come to like him. My personal barometer for judging people these days is the girls—if they go for someone I just automatically trust that person. Brook and Phoebe adore Abe—well, you've seen them all together. And Abe can always make me laugh, even when things are really bad. Whatever happens, I get the feeling with Abe that he's already been there—whatever down place you're at—and he has great empathy, I think that's the word. That's why it was so awful to see his face, to feel his whole body go kind of dead, when he saw them. Talk about making love on a dance floor; Becca had plastered herself against Ethan, moving her hips in that way. And Ethan, well, I can't pretend that he was exactly pushing her away, but she was definitely all over *him*, rather than the other way around. People were staring. And laughing a little to each other. I was so hurt and embarrassed, I just wanted to cry. But Abe—he saw it all in a flash and he lost control. He went after Ethan right there on the dance floor.

"And Abe is, what—three inches shorter than Ethan was? Twenty pounds lighter? It was a joke. Ethan overpowered him from the start, but Abe wouldn't give up. It was awful. Abe took a real beating. Of course, Becca and I tried to stop them. Finally Owen and two other guests pulled them apart and Owen asked us all to leave. It was pretty terrible. But that was just the beginning of it. Ethan was furious with Abe for accusing him publicly like that of coming on to Becca when she had spent the past nine months or so throwing herself in his path. So he got his revenge the one way guaranteed to hurt Abe the most."

"He started up with Becca," Meg said for her.

"With a vengeance. About two really intense months of it. Just enough to totally destroy the marriage. Not that the Sabins weren't heading for the rocks before Ethan came along. But he made sure the thing shattered for good."

"So that's why they divorced. And why Abe hated Ethan."

"They wouldn't have lasted anyway. I've gotten to know Becca and Abe awfully well through all of this—and that marriage was definitely a case of opposites attracting—for a time. Becca is totally self-involved—to her, nothing is more interesting or important than the drama that is her life. Initially, I think, Abe liked that—the intensity, the self-absorption. Abe thought Becca was high-strung, a bit neurotic, you know—this overly sensitive, exotic flower. But he also thought she loved him, when what she was actually responding to was his love for her—the flattering, comforting reflection in the mirror.

"Ethan was the first man Becca ever knew who pulled her out of herself—who forced her to look at herself and wonder what was lacking. It made her nuts, in the beginning, when he rejected her advances. But it also made her think. Take stock. She came to realize that she didn't want to simply be adored. She wanted to be *known*—ravished, diminished, redeemed—all the things that a deep physical passion can do. What she was really after, and I see this now, was to grow up. And Abe kept wanting to protect her, to keep her this sheltered special woman-child. It was just the opposite of what she needed."

"Janine said that Becca couldn't cope with Ethan

ending the affair. That she continued to pursue him when everybody else knew it was over," Meg prodded.

"Janine." Lark frowned. "There's a twelve-step word for her: co-dependent. She's gotten so into this family that all of our dysfunctions have become her own. She sort of feeds off us—emotionally, I mean. But that's her choice. And, yes, she's right—when Ethan threw Becca over for a second time, she had a really bad time dealing with it. She couldn't believe it, after giving up her marriage for Ethan, that he didn't seem to care. He'd been cooling way down on her for months and then, after he got the Judson show, he just cut her off.

"There was a lot in New York to keep him occupied," Lark went on, looking down at her hands. She picked up a rubber band from her drawing board and started twisting it tighter and tighter as she spoke. "And nothing in Red River to keep Becca going, to keep her from obsessing about the whole thing. I got to hear all about it. She turned to me for comfort. Me, of all people. But, you know, Francine and I had been talking a lot about forgiveness and forbearance, about learning to live with the world as it is given to us. I decided that I could actually help Becca. I knew what Ethan was like. Once he was through with some-one—that was it. I wasn't jealous of Becca anymore. And the more I listened to her pain, the more I felt sorry for her. She was so pathetic, Meg. This beautiful, glamorous woman—groveling for information about Ethan. She kept asking me if there was someone else. Someone new. Who could it be? Who?"

"How in the world did you stand all of this, Lark?" Meg said. "I think I'd have killed Ethan, if . . . "

26

It was Sunday morning and Meg could hear Lark and the girls getting ready for church, Brook admonishing Phoebe to hurry up because they were all going to be late again. Meg had begged off going to the service the night before. She'd told her sister that work was running her ragged and she just needed a morning to sleep in. Now, she could hear her sister whispering to her daughters on the stairs to be quiet—Aunt Meg was still sleeping.

Actually, Aunt Meg had been wide awake for several hours. She'd been lying in bed, staring at the ceiling, thinking through everything she knew so far about Ethan's murder. But her thoughts ended up leading her around in circles, spinning uselessly through motives and opportunity, going back to a question that she'd raised with Lucinda: Would you kill someone because he'd stopped loving you? Could

Lark, or could Becca have murdered Ethan for that reason? Would you destroy the object of your passion—or try ever harder to win him back? And then the question of passion had led Meg's thoughts in an entirely different direction.

Abe. *Abraham Leonard Sabin*. She remembered examining his business card when he first suggested years ago that she call him if she needed advice on starting her agency. They were both in the early stages of starting their own companies then. The very next week she had taken him up on his offer.

After an exasperating meeting at her bank, Meg said to him, "They want to know what kind of business I'm going to have. I said an advertising agency, but apparently that wasn't what they meant. I need to file something or other with the state. They told me a lawyer would know."

"And luckily, they're right," Abe said, laughing. "There are different kinds of corporate entities— Chapter S, sub-chapter S. Come on in and we'll go over the details. It's pretty simple really."

He'd made it fun as well. He was able to explain things—her office lease, the eventual credit line from the bank, the papers of incorporation—in a way that was clear without being condescending. The first year she was in business, she called him at least twice a month on one issue or another.

"This new client, Jonas Sportswear, wants to know when I'm going to send over the contract agreement. I haven't got one Abe—you know me, I prefer to conduct business on a handshake."

"Jonas puts you in the big leagues, now," Abe pointed out. "And it's probably time we drew up a standard contract. I'll call their lawyers and see exactly what they have in mind. And I also think it's time I started charging you my regular rates."

"Jesus, Abe, how the hell much money do you lawyers make?"

"It's disgusting, isn't it? But then I saw your third-quarter financial statement. I'm not exactly going to bankrupt you.

Most of their conversations over the years had been about business. The news. The goings-on in Red River when Meg shared a ride up there with him. Gradually, as he became a close friend of Lark's, and especially after his marriage to Becca, she began to open up to him about some of her problems with men.

"I'm beginning to think I was born without that radar most women seem to have," Meg had told him after the fiasco with the sports broadcaster. "You know, the ability to properly read male signals. They can be literally right on top of me before I realize that I'm seeing some triple-timing egomaniac."

"Were your parents happy?" Abe had asked. "There's an awful lot of learned behavior that we pick up from them. I'm beginning to realize that I'm just like my father."

"Which means what about you, Abe?"

"I'm a romantic. I fall in love like a ton of bricks."

"I think that's wonderful," Meg said, curious about his rueful tone of voice.

"Sure, until you hit the ground."

They were both older and wiser now. Meg doubted that Abe could have any illusions left after Ethan stepped in and tore his marriage apart. And Meg?

After what she'd been through recently, could she really still believe that she'd eventually find the real thing? After what she now knew about the only married couple she'd ever respected—did she honestly think that a good marriage was even possible?

Probably not. And yet . . . since Friday evening, the thought of Abe had been lingering behind everything else she'd been going through. She could taste him on her lips. Feel his touch on her cheek, his breath in her hair. Of course, he knew that she'd been through hell lately. She'd been afraid. They were friends. He cared about her, no doubt. He'd kissed her as a way of reassuring her that everything was going to turn out all right. He had simply been trying to be kind. And he'd probably be horrified, Meg decided as she finally got out of bed, if he realized the kind of passionate response he'd aroused in her.

There was one other person in Red River who Meg knew for sure would not be at Francine's Sunday morning service. For several years now, Meg had been hearing about Matt's refusal to so much as put a foot inside the First Congregational Church.

"He has to hear her preach every day of his life," Ethan had said last Christmas when Lark was bemoaning Matt's behavior. "That's more than any human being should have to endure."

The rectory sat up on the hill above the church, its western property line bordering Lark's and Ethan's extensive acreage. A roughly cut path through the woods joined the two households; it meandered along the riverbank and then climbed along the side of the hill. It was a shortcut that Lark and Francine often took when they visited each other. Meg easily found her way along it that morning through the still, leaf-less woods.

Like most of the houses in Red River, Francine's had been constructed in the mid-1880s of clapboard, though an effort had obviously been made to give this important residence some extra degree of elegance. Gingerbread woodwork decorated the front porch and eaves, and a diamond-shaped stained-glass pane graced the tiny window in the attic.

Meg rang the doorbell on the side entrance three times before she heard any movement from within. Finally, there was the thumping of heavy steps on the stairs. A clomping down the hall. The door was wrenched open.

"What do you want?" Matt fixed her with a heavy-lidded stare. His upper lip, smudged with a fuzzy attempt at a mustache, was twisted into a sneer.

"A moment to talk with you," Meg said. "I wanted to know how things went with Lucinda yesterday."

"Didn't get to see her," Matt retorted. "We just dropped the stuff off. That's all Francine really wanted, you know. Make the big gesture."

"Did your mother know you were sleeping with Lucinda?" Meg asked as he began to close the door. He stopped.

"How did you know?" he demanded, his deep voice straining with emotion.

"Actually, I guessed. I've spoken a lot to Lucinda since all this happened. We talk on the phone—at least once a week. Your name comes up just a little too often for me not to wonder what was going on."

"That so?" Matt stepped out on the porch and lit a cigarette, inhaling deeply.

"What about Francine?" Meg persisted. "Did she know about you and Lucinda?"

"Despite my mother's do-good posturing, she actually considers Lucinda beneath contempt. I'm sure you can understand why I wouldn't confide in her about having sex with Lucinda."

"But you could have been the father of Lucinda's baby. You could have spoken up and told us what was going on. You knew Ethan wasn't involved."

"That's true. But almost every other boy from here to Montville could have gotten her pregnant."

"She did imply that she was seeing a lot of guys," Meg agreed, but something in Matt's tone intrigued her. She thought she detected anger under his carefully modulated words.

"That's an understatement," Matt went on. "It was like her way of being validated, as Francine would phrase it. She knew what Ethan thought of her—and that really hurt her. Sleeping around was her way of showing him that guys found her attractive. That she was worthwhile, you know."

"And you thought she was?"

"That's none of your business, is it?"

"I'm making it my business," Meg said. She looked out across the monotone landscape of trees, rooftops, chimneys, and the rolling hills beyond and tried to think how she could reach the boy beside her. Though the more she listened to him, the more she realized how close he was to being a man. There was a depth, a maturity to Matt that she'd missed at first. She also sensed that he could be an important ally in her battle to get Lucinda a fair hearing.

"How is she?" Matt asked after a long silence.

"Scared stiff. How would you be?" Meg said, and then added more softly, "You care about her don't you, Matt?"

"I did at one point," he replied, looking away. "I thought the feelings were reciprocated."

"Are you sure they weren't?"

"Yeah, I'm sure. I was a jerk, okay? It meant a lot to me—more than I should have let it—being really close to someone, making love, talking half the night. People think Lucinda's so tough, but she isn't. She's just not a hypocrite like almost everybody else in this damn town. She's totally honest. You know, I would have given anything to have that be my kid. To have it live. Be a dad. I never knew who my dad was."

"I'm sorry. Francine has never told you who . . ."

"I think she likes to believe it was an immaculate conception. I mean, if she can't actually *be* God, bearing Her child might be the next best thing."

"I'm not convinced Lucinda murdered Ethan." Meg turned to face Matt.

"I see. Lucinda told you otherwise? Explained away some crucial evidence? She can be very persuasive when she wants your help."

"She *needs* my help, Matt," Meg told him. "Our help. I'm trying hard to understand why everyone's so willing to convict her. There are plenty of questions in my mind about exactly what happened in the studio that morning. Lucinda was not Ethan's only visitor."

"What do you mean?"

"Janine identified two cars, at two different times, not long before the murder."

"Yeah, well Ethan was working there, right? If he

had visitors, they probably just had some business with the studio."

Meg had been hoping to enlist his sympathy and support, but she sensed a real determination on his part not to be drawn in. She tried a different tack. "There are plenty of people in Red River who aren't particularly devastated that Ethan's gone."

"Exactly," Matt said, flicking the butt of his cigarette off the porch.

"What do you mean by that?"

"Why not lay it on Lucinda?" Matt replied. He turned back to the door. "Why not let everyone think that Lucinda killed her stepfather because he got her pregnant. They all hated Ethan. Thought he was capable of anything, even that. This town despised them both—father and daughter. Blame this thing on the two of them and don't look back. Don't look closer. Everybody knows how many people had it in for Ethan. Maybe everyone's afraid that someone close to them might have flipped out and done it." Matt nodded across the lawn and woods to the rooftops of the town. "Any one of us could've done it," he said, stepping back into the house and closing the door on further conversation.

No one had actually lied to Meg, at least, not as far as she could tell. And yet, everywhere she turned in Red River, with everyone she talked to, she had the feeling that no one was exactly telling the truth. A flicker of the eye. An intonation that was off. An emphasis that felt forced. As she rode with Lark and the girls down

Main Street later that afternoon on the way to the general store to pick up groceries, Meg saw a town that was intent on keeping its secrets, protecting its own. Of course, everyone gossiped, talk was cheap. But when you got down to it, when you asked the hard questions, you got a shrug, a mumble, an excuse.

When she walked into Yoder's behind Lark and the girls, suddenly, for the first time in Meg's memory, the chatter around the deli counter stopped. Meg felt the looks. She sensed what was being thought, and probably said. Meg was that outsider who was going around stirring up trouble. Suggesting they all consider *Lucinda*'s side of things, for heavens' sake. As though they all couldn't see right through that viper's story. Lark's own sister, can you beat that?

But if Lark sensed any of the town's hostility, she didn't show it. And if she was aware of Meg's growing belief that Lucinda deserved a fair hearing, she pretended not to know it. Meg now realized how often her sister willfully did not see what was right in front of her face. How good she was at living in a world of her own making. It was, after all, what Meg had taught her to do as a child.

"Thank you so much for coming up this weekend," Lark told her, giving Meg a hug as she was leaving later that afternoon. Abe was waiting for her in the car outside. Lark had been too preoccupied with her own concerns to have noticed—or at least commented on the fact—that Abe hadn't stopped by all weekend. "And for listening to me. And for just being there, big sister. Love you."

"I love you, too," Meg said, holding Lark in her arms, and then pulling her close. It had always been her role to be the responsible one, to think for them both. Now, for the first time in her life, she found herself torn between protecting Lark once again—and doing what she thought was right.

"Remember that, baby," Meg said as she stepped away. "No matter what."

27

"Would you like to come up for some dinner?" Meg asked Abe when they pulled up to the side entrance of her apartment house. It had been a strained, strange ride back to the city, with fits and starts of conversation that never went anywhere and long uncomfortable silences that neither of them seemed able to fill. Meg had spent most of the trip swept up by the insecurities that surfaced every time she started really caring about a man. Successful as she might be in business, she was a proven failure with romantic relationships. Not that Abe had that in mind when he kissed her the other night, she reminded herself. Not that he wanted anything more from her than an easygoing friendship— one she was in the midst of screwing up with her own ridiculous concerns.

When she wasn't dwelling on her limitations, she

was brooding about Ethan and Becca's affair—one so serious that it had devastated Abe's marriage. And yet, despite everything she'd poured out to Abe about her problems with Ethan, he'd never bothered to mention this disastrous episode in his life. Was he too hurt by Becca's betrayal? Wasn't this just confirmation that he still was in love with his ex-wife?

"You actually cook?" he asked, putting the car into park. "Last time I was at your place there was nothing but a jar of olives and a half-eaten yogurt in the refrigerator."

"Don't worry, I didn't say that I'd make it," Meg replied, releasing her seat belt. "I live in the best neighborhood in the world for take-out. I was thinking of Thai."

"I'm there," Abe said. "If I can find a parking space."

She was being utterly ridiculous, Meg told herself, as she hurried through the apartment, straightening up. She spent another five minutes in the bathroom, brushing her teeth and hair and in general behaving like a teenager. She was still rummaging through her drawer of take-out menus when he rang her front doorbell.

"I stopped at the corner and brought some decent beer, which you never seem to have," Abe said, walking down the hall as she locked up. He'd acted as her lawyer when she purchased the apartment and had helped her negotiate the mortgage. He'd been there many times for parties and dinner since, but for the first time Meg was sensitive to his opinion of it. She glanced around the living room, seeing it through his eyes, and decided that the little throw pillows had to go.

Abe came back from the kitchen with the beer. "Is everything okay? You've been so preoccupied."

"I'm fine," she said, reaching for her drink. But he put both bottles down on the side table instead and took her hands in his.

"I'm not kidding anybody here, am I?" His face was no longer friendly. She felt the strength of his grip.

"What do you mean?"

But he answered by kissing her. She felt the automatic kick-start of desire. She realized how much she had been wanting this—needing this—how he could be so tender and yet feel so tense, holding back, as if she were some fragile thing. He slipped his arms around her, pressing her up against the back of the couch. He kissed her lips. Then the tip of her nose. Then both earlobes.

"What's your radar tell you?" he whispered in her ear.

"What do you mean?"

"That sense you claim you don't have about reading men," he said, kissing her neck as he spoke. "Can you pick up any signal right now?"

"There's a scratchy kind of sound," Meg replied, smiling at him. She'd never seen his face so alive and open. "But it could be just my sweater rubbing against the couch fabric."

"We could always just take it off," he said, leaning away to get a better look at her.

"Abe! I'm not sure I'm ready for any of this," Meg said, more than a little nervous now that things had gotten this far. She couldn't help comparing her perfectly fine body to Becca's absolutely perfect one. But it wasn't just Becca that made her pause. She knew Abe so well in so many ways. There was already a sense of intimacy between them that made their coming together that much more intense. And she always failed at this game, she reminded herself again. Only this time she had more than just a new romance to lose, she had a treasured friendship as well. She should really have him stop right now, she told herself, as she felt him brush against her, already aroused.

"That's okay," he said, his lips finding hers again. "I'm not ready for it either." He ran his hands through her hair, down her shoulders and arms, around her waist, pulling her gently toward him. His kisses were deep and slow. He kept touching her—hair, shoulders, cheeks—as though not quite believing that she was really there.

Experience could be a dangerous thing when it came to sex, Meg knew. All too often, the shadows of former lovers would hover in the corners of her mind, reminding her of past pleasures or suppressed frustrations. No matter how much you liked someone, she realized, no one arrived in a relationship with a guarantee of satisfaction. Timing could be tricky. The one's turn-ons could be the other person's turn-offs. Often with Meg the whole thing seemed too much of a gamble. So it was her tendency to take over, as she did in business—guide the proceedings and carefully monitor the outcome.

Like most things in her life, Meg felt that she had her body under almost perfect control. She knew how to keep her appetite in check, how to force herself to exercise even if she felt lethargic. And when it came to sex, it was Meg who usually determined when—and how—she would be satisfied. Though she thoroughly enjoyed the shuddering bliss of making love—even at the moment of abandon—she was still in command.

With Abe, however, she almost immediately sensed that her authority was being challenged. No, more to the point, overruled. Initially, she tried to struggle against his taking the lead—the way he insisted on spending so much time just kissing her—she didn't need that. It really wasn't necessary. But he seemed so determined and ... after a moment or two, she thought, well, why not? And then, a little while later she realized that she had somehow lost her train of thought and given herself over to pure feeling. She relaxed in his arms.

"Abe ..." At one point she remembered there was something important she needed to ask him. Force him to clarify. It was about Becca and Ethan. But before the question could form itself into actual words, she found herself pulled down again by a strong, persistent undercurrent of desire. His touch was so gentle, so light, that at first she didn't realize what he was doing to her. It seemed harmless enough, the way he caressed the small of her back, the feathery kisses he planted on her neck. Who could object to his hands moving down her hips, then up again, to the way her body fit so nicely into his? And then, without warning, the tug of longing turned into a tidal force of need. Then, without knowing how, she realized that she had drifted far beyond the safety of her own senses. She was with him and they were rushing toward something. She felt herself holding on for dear life.

They found their way to her bedroom. He had stopped being gentle. They didn't speak. He guided her to the edge of the bed and tore back the spread and the sheets.

"No," he said, as she started to pull off her sweater. He knelt in front of her and with maddening slowness pushed the clinging wool up as he kissed her stomach and then the white straining fabric of her bra. He stood, pulling the sweater off in one eager movement, helping her unhook the bra, and then pressing her onto the bed, his hands cupping her breasts.

She watched him fumble with his own clothes—the shirt that must have lost a button or two in his haste, the belt that seemed to take forever. She smiled when she saw him naked—more muscular than she would have guessed and sweetly vulnerable with a full, bobbing erection.

"Oh God, you're laughing," he said, sitting on the edge of the bed and looking down at himself. "Is it that bad?"

"No," she said, as she watched him roll down a condom. "It's absolutely adorable."

They were hardly strangers to each other—and yet all of this was so new. His touch, the taste of him, the sweet outdoorsy smell of his skin. His body was such a pleasure to explore—leaner and harder than she would ever have guessed—with such lovely surprises: the salty terrain of his neck, the gentle pasture of his stomach, the taut arch of his back. She smiled in the dark as she heard the quick intake of his breath when her fingers found his erection. She circled her fingers around the shaft, making a tight circle, moving her hand gently up and down. He turned to her, kissing her breasts, and they lay side by side, exploring each other, learning about one another.

His lips moved from her breasts, down her stomach, and to her thighs. She could feel her legs spreading and she moaned when his tongue parted her, her hands gripping the sheets as his mouth closed over her. It didn't matter who they were separately—it was what they had become now together: touch, taste, desire.

"No," she cried, at one point, wanting everything, needing him inside her. She pulled him up, guiding him. And when he was fully within her, filling her, he began to slowly, very slowly, show her what this meant. It was not about one person taking pleasure. It was not about another being in control. It was about giving and wanting to give, about holding back, and giving more, and loving the sound of the other person crying out in joy, until, at last, there was nothing else in the world but the quickening, demanding, essential rhythm of two bodies moving together, moving as one.

A little after ten o'clock they finally got around to ordering their take-out, which they ate in a tremendous hurry, standing up in the kitchen. But they were both too hungry for something else to concentrate on the spring rolls and rice noodles, and they were soon back in the bedroom again.

"So?" She was curled up in his arms, her cheek resting against the curve of his shoulder. She felt wonderful and terrified at the same time. All her old worries had swept in again—not ten minutes after they'd made love for the second time. The questions she had about Becca and Ethan, about Abe not confiding in her about their affair had returned in full force. It was nearly midnight, but she felt jittery, jazzed with doubts.

"That's a loaded question," Abe said, yawning and stroking her hair. "If you're asking was all this good for me, I can't even begin to tell you how wonderful it was. Okay?"

"I guess I meant 'so' in the comparative sense," kissing his chest. He tasted of salt. She breathed in his deep, masculine smell.

"You mean Becca?" he asked and when she slowly nodded her head against his shoulder, he sighed. "You don't really want to go there do you?"

"I don't want to," Meg answered nervously. "But I think we'll have to eventually."

"Can we not make it tonight?" he asked, kissing her hair. "I don't want to spoil this."

"And talking about her would?"

"Damn it, Meg."

"I'm sorry, I just have a lot of questions."

"It's not one of your more attractive qualities," Abe said. "Let's get this over with—fire away."

But something about his tone, a bitterness that she hated to hear after so much affection, made her hesitate. He was right, she decided. Her questions about Becca and Ethan should wait. She hated seeing Abe's face close with anger, his lips tighten into a hard line. She reached out and traced the curve of his jaw, drawing his face toward her.

"Sorry," she said. "You're right. Let's leave all those unfortunate people behind us up in Red River. We only want happy people here."

"I wish you were right," Abe said, stretching. "But as it turns out, Becca's back in the city. She'd taken up modeling again."

"She call and tell you?" Meg asked, despising the jealousy she felt and hoping it didn't sound in her voice.

"No, her lawyer did," Abe said, settling back down beside Meg. "He said that Becca didn't want me to be caught by surprise if I ran into her. Didn't want any more trouble. She claims I verbally assaulted her in front of Lark's house the afternoon we came back from seeing Lucinda. You know I really thought that when the divorce became final—that would be it."

"But it isn't?" Meg asked, pulling the sheets up around them, taking comfort in the tone of his voice. His distaste for the subject of Becca was obvious.

"No, now I'm afraid it's just going to go on forever."

28

There were problems everywhere Meg looked now. Peter Boardman, the lawyer representing Lucinda, had called her the Monday night after the Thanksgiving weekend and asked if she would appear at the hearing the following week on Lucinda's behalf.

"What does that mean exactly?" Meg had asked.

"Lucinda told me that you believed her side of the story," Boardman told her. "And that the two of you are close. I need people I can call on—friends, family—who'll publicly support her."

Since then, she'd been trying to convince herself that standing up for Lucinda did not necessarily mean turning her back on anybody else. Surely, Lark and the girls would understand that Meg was just trying to be fair. Her desire simply was to help Lucinda, not hurt them. She had long conversations in her head with Lark on the question, but when they actually talked on the phone, Meg found that she was unable to raise the difficult subject with her sister.

Various crises loomed at the agency, as well. Besides all its regular work—and the fourth quarter was Hardwick's busiest season—the company was frantically preparing creative for a project SportsTech had dangled in front of Meg.

"The big guy likes to make people jump through hoops," Vince Goldman told Meg when he called to say that SportsTech had narrowed its search to three advertising agencies and that Hardwick was one of them. "So each of the contenders is going to be given a project to handle—start to finish. I'm giving you the plum assignment: the launch campaign for our new User Friendly line for teenage girls. I'm sending you over all the promo stuff and a half dozen samples. It's advancing well in the stores and retail says that with the right advertising campaign this could be our next big label breakout."

What Vince didn't realize, of course, was that everything Meg knew about teenage fashion could be written on a Post-it note. Hardwick specialized in upscale women's retail—the type of clothes that sold through Bloomies, Bendels, and Saks. Now the future of her business could very well depend on motivating a portion of the population that, as far as Meg was concerned, could just as well be living on another planet.

But the worst news came by way of Abe on Wednesday morning: Frieda Jarvis was filing for bankruptcy. This had forced Meg, already cash-hungry because of the Jarvis situation, to do something she absolutely hated: take out a loan. Meg's financially unstable childhood had turned her into a fiscal ultraconservative—and debt, until now, had simply not been in her vocabulary. It was her spotless credit history that had helped her secure a line of credit from the bank. It was Abe's friendship with the loan officer that had allowed it to go through so quickly. Within twenty-four hours of the news, Meg had a letter of agreement from the bank. But during the meeting with the bank officer and Abe on Thursday, Meg had been forced to sign over her co-op and her growing stockpile of investments as collateral.

Afterward, as Abe and Meg left the bank and headed back across town together, he said, "You understand, don't you, that if you can't get the business back on track the bank could take away everything you've worked so hard for."

"I know, but I'm going to be fine," Meg told him with as much assurance as she could manage. They'd spoken every day on the phone, but this was the first time she'd seen him since Sunday night. She was trying very hard to behave professionally, though she now felt a ridiculously childish wish simply to walk into his arms and ask that he hold her—tight.

"Not if you go on as you are."

"And just what does that mean?" Meg demanded, stung by his tone of voice. She needed comfort from him, not criticism.

They were standing at the corner of Forty-second and Fifth, the late lunch hour crowd surging around them. One woman with a portable computer case slung over her shoulder, pushed past Meg and snapped, "For heavens' sake, people, move your lovers' quarrel off the middle of the sidewalk!"

"Come on," Abe said as he steered Meg down the street to one of the side entrances to Bryant Park. The huge public space lay beneath a blanket of well-trodden snow. Except for a few homeless people slumped with their belongings on the benches and a gardener pruning ivy around the base of a sycamore, the park was empty. Meg and Abe cut across the lawn.

"I'm telling you this because I care about you, okay?" Abe began, the crusted snow crunching beneath their heels. "You've got to begin to take a good hard look at the people around you. Decide who you can really trust. Who you can count on."

"I know I should have been more on top of the Jarvis thing," Meg said, fully aware that Abe was right; she'd been far too lax. "I realized way too late what was going on. I consider it an important lesson—one I've learned from. I'll know how to handle it next time."

"Listen to yourself! Do you intend to handle everything on your own? Are you the only person you can really trust to do things right—and to do the right thing?"

"We're not talking about Jarvis now, are we."

"Boardman called me Monday night right after he spoke to you. What do you think you're going to accomplish by taking this on?"

"This isn't about me," Meg said, caught off guard by Abe's apparent anger. "It's about Luce. She's a scared kid who's going to lose any chance she might have to turn her life around just because she's so convenient to dislike—and blame."

"Convenient?" Abe stopped and turned toward

her. They'd reached the far south side of the park, twenty yards or so from the bench where she'd sat with Ethan. "She was stone drunk. She had the pontil in her hands. I'd hardly say that the world was being unfair suggesting she had something to do with Ethan's murder. Sometimes you're so damned sure of yourself, so controlling, you can't see the enemy when he's staring you right in the face."

"Lucinda begged me to help. . . ." Meg began, but Abe stopped her by bringing his gloved hand to her lips.

"I'm not talking about Lucinda. I'm talking about Ethan. I think you want to get back at him for everything he did to Lark—I think you're feeling guilty about Lucinda. That's what driving you, Meg. Can't you see that?"

"Yes, that's part of it," Meg said. She looked over his shoulder. On one of those benches running along the length of the lawn Ethan had told her that he'd been in love with her for fourteen years. She remembered the tears in his eyes. How thoroughly he'd convinced her that he was being sincere—and that she was putting him through hell because of it. When, for years, that was what he'd been doing to countless women: Francine, Hannah, Becca—manipulating them, using them, and then discarding each one in turn. Throwing them onto the annealing table of his outsize passions like pieces of his sculptures that didn't work—to be melted down and reformed for his next work of seduction. "I feel angry. I feel ashamed. And guilty. I can't begin to explain it to you."

"I'm not asking you to."

"What are you asking?" But she felt it before he said anything. She saw it in his eyes.

"Let this thing with Lucinda go," he said. He stepped toward her. She'd been missing him from the moment she woke up Monday morning and realized that he had slipped out of her bed earlier and left, letting her go on sleeping. In the chill air, his body felt so warm and comforting. His arms around her made her feel secure and strong. His kisses held the answer to all her worries.

"This isn't your problem, Meg," he told her. "And if you make it yours—believe me—you're going to end up losing a lot of people you care about."

In the hard early winter light she could see every detail of his face, the deep grooves around his mouth, the laugh lines radiating out from the corners of his eyes, the cleft in his right cheek from an early childhood fall that looked like a dimple and often lent his face a deceptively affable appearance. His dark, wiry hair had receded a little at the temples and his full, expressive brows were tempered with gray—but he would look boyish until the day he died. She was falling in love with this face, Meg realized—with this body, this mind, this man. She wanted nothing more than to make him happy and proud of her. She longed to kiss the frown line away between his brows. But it stayed there, as she knew it would, when she replied, "I've already promised Lucinda that I would help."

As usual, Oliver wrote down what he considered the important messages for Meg on pink "while you were out" slips and put the less pressing calls in her voice mail.

"How did it go?" Oliver asked, passing her a half dozen messages. "You look a little dazed. Is that a good sign, or bad?" Though Meg hadn't given Oliver any of the particulars of her problems with Frieda Jarvis or the agency's need for a loan, he was somehow able to pick up enough through phone calls and keen observation to put the pieces together for himself.

"We're not out of the woods," Meg replied, sorting through the slips—P. Boardman, re: court hearing. V. Goldman, re: package sent. H. Judson, re: gallery opening. Your sister, re: call as soon as possible— "But, to mix metaphors, the wolf is no longer at the door."

"I'll take that as good news. How, I wonder, should I interpret the fact," Oliver was scrutinizing her with a prim smile, "that you have lipstick on your chin? It's certainly a different look for you, Meg. Some sort of fashion statement?"

"You're an insolent, impossible person," Meg said jokingly, rubbing her hands over the bottom half of her face as she started down the hall to her office. "Mind your own business."

"I'm too busy minding yours!" Oliver called after her and then, in a gentler tone, added, "Somebody has to."

Meg found it a little disconcerting that P. Boardman answered his own phone—and on the first ring.

"Hey, Meg, thanks for calling back." He had a warm, reassuring voice that reminded Meg of Walter Cronkite. "You talk with your sister yet?"

"Lark? No," Meg replied, looking down at the messages Oliver had given her. The one from Lark had followed Boardman's by a few minutes.

"Well, I'm afraid I might have put my foot in it. I called Lark with some follow-up questions—I assumed the rest of the family shared your concerns about the murder investigation. I mentioned that you were going to be at the hearing. Supporting Lucinda."

"And she was upset?"

"That would be putting it mildly."

Lark, too, seemed to be waiting by the phone, and Meg could tell by the hoarseness in her voice that she had been crying.

"It's me," Meg said.

"Why are you doing this?"

"Doing what?"

"Oh, for God's sake, Meg! You're suddenly siding with Lucinda? Why? Because of what I said about Ethan and you? Are you that angry at me?"

"This has nothing to do with that, baby, I promise. It's about—"

"I'm not your baby, Meg. I'm you're sister. Your equal. Don't you dare condescend to me. I used to really look up to you. Think you were so much smarter than me. Hipper. More together. But you're not. You're being *had*, Meg. Lucinda lied to me from the moment she walked into this house. She stole from us. She came home stinking drunk—to a household full of young kids. She was manipulating, totally amoral. And she killed Ethan. Those are the facts. Plus this: now she's using you—your latent feelings of guilt, your suppressed desire to be a mother—to get her off. She's the smart one, Meg. Not you."

"Latent guilt? Who's feeding you this psychobabble? Francine?"

"Francine cares about me. She supports me. She would never go behind my back. She would never betray me. The way my own sister is doing."

"How am I betraying you? Why is everyone so eager to see this thing in extremes? Is there absolutely no question in your mind that someone might have murdered Ethan besides Lucinda?"

"None. And if you believed in me at all, if you accepted me as a thinking, mature adult—you wouldn't doubt my side of the story. You wouldn't go around digging up dirt about Ethan and me. What are you and this Boardman planning to do? Have every woman that Ethan ever looked at hauled into court to testify against his character? Don't you see how sick that is?"

"What makes you think that's going to happen? Who's planting these fears in your head?"

"Luckily, I'm surrounded by real friends here, Meg. People who love me and the girls."

"Lark—listen. Doesn't it seem at all odd to you that everyone is so willing to pin the murder on Lucinda? Doesn't it seem odd that no one, not one single person, wants to give her the benefit of the doubt?"

"No. What's odd to me is that *you* are the only one who's giving her that. I don't know what's driving you. I can only imagine that you must be more hurt than I ever realized about Ethan. And this is your way of striking back at me."

"You can't seriously think that—"

"It may surprise you, Meg, but I *can* seriously think. All on my own, without my big sister's help. And what I'm thinking now is that I don't want to see you, or talk to you, have anything to do with you so long as you take Lucinda's side in this. You deal with Boardman and that little slut. I wash my hands of the whole thing."

For the rest of the afternoon, Meg immersed herself in her work, though a part of her kept replaying the conversation with Lark—again and again and again. What a relief it was to be able to make simple decisions—and deal with problems that could be solved. She signed off on a pay increase for one of the account executives who she knew had recently been printing out her resume. After reading through a glossy sales brochure, she decided against upgrading the art department's computers until the new operating system went into effect. She was going over papers from the bottom of her in-box when Oliver knocked on her door around six-thirty.

"I'm off. All the ads closing today are out. You need anything?"

"No, I'm fine."

"Actually, I don't think you are. But I've a feeling there's nothing I can do about it."

"Can you strip me of my scruples?"

"You're asking the wrong man," Oliver replied. "Next to the little black dress, I don't think there's anything more flattering than a nice set of scruples on a woman."

If only it could be as simple as that, Meg thought, after Oliver had gone. You just stood up for what you believed in. Did what you knew was best. And the whole world admired your integrity. But now, though her every instinct told her she was doing the right thing, just about everyone she loved was trying to convince her that she wasn't.

She thought about what Abe had said. Just let it go. She still could. She could find some excuse not to make it to the hearing. She could call Lark back and tell her what she longed to say, that she loved her and would do anything to help her. She could let Abe know that she would heed his advice. She could feel his arms around her. The way his hand pressed against the small of her back. The quick intake of his breath when she pulled him closer. She also could see the way he looked at her when he stepped away—the question in his eyes. Can I trust you? Wasn't that always what two people needed to know most? Will you help me or hurt me? Love or hate?

She was still thinking about him ten minutes later when Boardman returned the call she made to him after her conversation with Lark. She was alone in the office and she picked up the night line.

"Would have called you earlier," he told her, "but I was consulting a doctor—an expert witness I often use—on the effects of toxic levels of alcohol and Percodan."

"And?"

"Blitzo. She easily could have blacked out."

"So she could be telling the truth."

"Yes, but it's a story that involves not remembering a damn thing. A tricky scenario. The hearing's next Friday in Montville at two-thirty to review the case and set bond for Lucinda. Did you talk to you sister? Can someone from the family come?"

"That's why I called you before," Meg replied. This

was the moment to explain that she'd changed her mind, that Lucinda was on her own.

The moment passed.

"I'll be there," she said.

"Great. You know, I might very well be able to get her out on bail if I can convince the judge that there's a responsible member of the family willing to take her in."

"I see."

"And?"

Meg had never intended to have things go this far. She'd just wanted to make sure Lucinda was treated fairly. The last thing she really wanted was to be saddled with the difficult teenager, to have her already pressure-filled life complicated even further by someone else's problems and needs. She hadn't asked for this. It had been the same thing with Ethan; she had never asked for that. He had pushed himself on her, demanded her attention, turned her world upside down. Her mistake, though, was that she hadn't had the courage to stop him. And so he had come between the two sisters—tearing to shreds their love for and trust in each other. It crossed her mind that if she did the right thing by Lucinda she could somehow make up for the wrong she'd allowed Ethan to do.

"Let's see what happens," Meg said finally, but she sensed that even Boardman understood that she had chosen her side. And there was no going back.

29

Though small, Hardwick and Associates had an excellent reputation within the fashion industry. Meg was known to be fair, a straight-shooter, someone to be trusted. Hardwick was viewed as up-and-coming. And it was essential to her business, she knew, that her agency continue to be perceived in this light. So she had made certain that no one knew the extent of her problems with Jarvis, while she'd helped spread the word—and gossip was like catnip in the fashion world—that Hardwick might land the big SportsTech account. That meant Meg was diversifying, moving beyond the smaller, chic labels and into the mass-market big time. Her billings would increase, her staff would need to be enlarged. Despite the usual backbiting and petty jealousies rampant in that tight-knit, insular business community, almost everyone agreed that Meg deserved her success.

Meg was loyal to the suppliers she worked with—the modeling agencies, photographers, printers, and post-production houses through whom Hardwick's layouts and storyboards were transformed into four-color print ads and television commercials. She'd made it a policy to work only with those she considered the best, even if it meant that her production costs were a bit higher than those of her competitors. Over the years, Meg's electronic rolodex had grown into a coveted "who's who" to the creative end of the fashion world—and when Meg made a call these days it was always taken.

"How have you been, Hilda?" Meg asked the head of one the modeling agencies she favored and a woman she'd been friendly with for nearly a decade. It was Monday morning, and Meg had spent a good part of the weekend wrestling with her conscience about making this call. Abe had flown out to LA the previous Friday for a week-long business conference, so she had plenty of time on her hands to wonder why he had kept Ethan and Becca's affair a secret from her. Meg was cut off from her sister, her nieces, the whole town of Red River, so she had two full days to mull over the fact that she was losing her family and several friends. Lucinda was giddy with the news that Meg was coming to the hearing, so Meg had far too many leisure hours to consider how in adequately equipped she was emotionally to handle Lucinda's needs and problems. All in all, she felt as though her personal life was devolving into a morass of worries and questions—and any hope she might have for happiness depended on her somehow solving them.

"Fine, Meg. What do you need?" Hilda said, all business as usual. "I hear you're pitching a youth line for SportsTech. I've three fabulous new girls—total unknowns and absolutely gorgeous."

"Actually, Hilda, I'm trying to track someone down. A model who left the business for a while, but who I understand is working again."

"Sure, hon," Hilda said. "I could get her for you freelance if she's not represented. And if *you* think she's that good, we'd give her a look ourselves."

"Becca Sabin?" Meg asked. "Name ring a bell?"

"I'm afraid so," Hilda sniffed. "Burnt-out case, Meg. And attitude that you wouldn't believe. Unreliable, is the word, I hear. And worse. I have a hundred girls you should see before—"

"It's not about a job, Hilda," Meg explained. "I just need to talk to her."

"Oh, well . . . Last I heard she was freelancing with that sleaze bag Randolph Perrolo."

"Wasn't he busted for—?"

"Of course, that's what I'm trying to tell you. He deals in dope as much as girls. Watch yourself, Meg. Perrolo's a real pig."

It wasn't hard to track Becca down from there. Though most modeling agencies carefully guarded their clients whereabouts and schedules, the talkative receptionist at Perrolo Girls seemed delighted to tell Meg where Becca was working.

"She landed the Sexy and Silky catalog," the breathy-voiced girl told Meg. "A week solid. What a great deal, huh?"

A hint at a possible job for an ad agency that Meg didn't even have to identity brought forth the details of the shoot in a happily confiding gush: "Danny Hallovan's studio down on Twenty-fourth and Eighth. You know the place?"

Yes, Meg did. But then everybody knew Danny. Talk about a burnt-out case, Meg thought, as she grabbed a cab downtown. Danny's problems had never been about drugs or alcohol—instead he managed to sabotage a very promising career as a fashion photographer with his uncontrollable moodiness. Danny didn't like to take orders. He bridled when art directors made suggestions about lighting or camera angles. He screamed if anyone—even an important client—dared to ask him to reshoot anything. Over the years, Danny's talent had been overshadowed by his temper, his reputation slipped, and agencies tiptoed away from him. He still worked, but now it was mostly for direct mail catalogs—the pay wasn't great but Danny could demand almost complete autonomy. Meg had heard that Danny made up some of his profits by hiring has-been models or girls just trying to break into the business—and taking a percentage of their pay.

Though she'd long ago stopped trying to work with him, Meg had managed to keep on friendly terms with Hallovan; the past summer, she even sent some work his way. Danny seemed as pleased as he ever got to see Meg that morning.

"What the *fuck* are you doing here?" he cried good-humoredly as Meg made her way toward him through the cables and reflecting stands that cluttered the echoing studio. Models in various stages of silk-clad undress lounged around a set that was composed of pillow-strewn couches.

"Hey, Danny." Meg let herself be embraced by the big bear of a man who insisted on wearing the little hair he had left pulled back into a tiny ponytail. "A friend of mine's working this. Thought I'd stop by and maybe take her to lunch."

"It's great to see your face, Hardwick," Danny said, as he fiddled with a filter. "You're one of the few decent people in this whole goddamned business. Hate this work, Hardwick. Look at these fucking clothes—I swear, I feel like I'm shooting pornography."

Meg looked around the room, searching for Becca's distinctive dark haircut. There were seven models on the set, but Meg didn't see her among them.

"Isn't Becca Sabin working on this shoot?" Meg asked.

"When she isn't in the ladies room doing you-know-what," Danny said, leaning over to peer into the camera lens. "I guess you could say she's working. Hey, Freddie, where the *fuck* is Becca? We're about ready to roll here."

Becca, when she finally appeared, looked ravishing. Perhaps a bit thinner than Meg recalled, but then that was only a plus for a model. Her dark helmet of hair shone. Her perfect, heart-shaped face looked as cool as alabaster. Her smile was disdainful and provocative at the same time. Meg didn't know what Danny was seeing, but Meg guessed that the camera adored Becca Sabin. They shot for a little over an hour, then Danny called a lunch break.

"Becca?" Meg intercepted the model on her way to the back of the studio where, Meg suspected, the bathroom was situated. Up close, beneath the heavy makeup, Becca's skin looked unhealthy. Her beautiful eyes were bloodshot, her pupils dilated.

"What?" Becca eyed Meg warily, taking a second or two to place her. "What are you doing here?"

"Oh, just stopping by to see Danny," Meg temporized. "We go way back."

"Good for you," Becca said, attempting to push past Meg. "I got thirty shitty minutes for lunch. I gotta go."

"It's great to run into you like this," Meg said, following her. "Let me take you out for lunch. I know a terrific sushi place right down the street."

"I'm busy," Becca said.

"That's too bad. When I saw you just now, I thought it would be good if we could talk . . ." But Becca kept walking

"About you and Ethan." Meg said.

This got her attention. She stopped and turned to Meg.

"What about Ethan?"

"You were lovers."

"So? The whole damned world knows that by now."

"It must be hard on you, Becca." Meg tried to sound sympathetic. "To lose Ethan in such a terrible way."

"Listen, Meg," Becca said, her tone turning nasty. "Don't bullshit me. I know from Lark about Ethan and *you*. And you know perfectly well that he dumped me for you."

"We weren't lovers."

"You can lie to Lark but don't think for a minute I buy that. I know Ethan. I knew . . . Ethan."

"I'm sorry, Becca," Meg said, surprised that she felt pity for the unhappy woman in front of her. "This is hard for you, I know."

Becca bowed her head. Her hands were shaking as she tried to wipe away the tears that suddenly filled her eyes.

"You have no idea," she said. "It's like I had everything, you know? My husband, our houses, our cars—all the great things—and I also had Ethan. My Ethan, my love. And then, Jesus, within a year, I've got nothing. It's all gone. My marriage is fucked. Ethan is dead. I'm left with hardly enough money to live on—"

"But Lark told me you did well in the settlement," Meg said gently.

"I bought all this stupid property in Red River. You know, so I could be near Ethan?" Becca's tone was bitter. "Then he's killed. And I'm stuck with this mountain of trees and rock. You wouldn't believe the estimates my architect gave me to build there. Now . . . I don't even want to. And I can't even sell it back for what it cost because of some goddammed capital gains thing. So here I am, back at work." They had reached the bathroom, and Becca turned to sneer at the empty set.

"Why were you at the studio the morning Ethan was killed?" Meg blurted out.

Becca looked at Meg, her arms folded defensively. "Why are you asking me all these questions? I already told the police all about that. I have nothing to hide."

"Why were you there, Becca? What happened?"

"It's none of your fucking business," Becca retorted. She started to pull the bathroom door open. Meg stopped her, wedging her foot against the doorjamb.

"I don't believe Lucinda murdered Ethan," Meg said. She watched closely as Becca's face registered surprise and then fear.

"But that's ridiculous. Everybody thinks she did it."

"That doesn't mean it's true."

"You don't honestly think that I—?" Becca shook her head slowly as she tried to read Meg's expression.

"I'm trying to find out what really happened that morning, Becca,"

"You didn't run into me here by accident, did you?"

"No, I didn't," Meg confessed. "But I wasn't sure you'd talk to me if you knew that I was looking for you."

"Well, you were right," Becca said, brushing past her. "I'm not talking to you. Leave me the hell alone. You've already fucked up my life enough."

30

When Meg first met Hannah Judson, she'd been intimidated by her super-glossy veneer and the boldfaced names that she dropped so casually into conversations. On closer acquaintance, Meg saw that the gallery owner was far from perfect. Though her beauty was dramatic—the high cheekbones, shock of silver hair, dark arching brows—her features were beginning to seem masklike and drawn. Although no expert in these matters, Meg suspected that Hannah might have had a face-lift. And Meg detected cracks in her personality as well. She was snobbish, intellectually arrogant, and—much to Meg's surprise—as needy as a child for attention and approval.

Ever since Ethan's murder Hannah had been plying Meg with invitations to gallery openings, to a little dinner party she was throwing, to a Whitney Museum fund-raiser Hannah thought Meg might enjoy. Though Meg was flattered by the older woman's attentions, she usually found a gracious way of saying no to the many tempting offers. When she called Hannah back on Wednesday night she was ready to decline yet another invitation.

"It's just a little vernissage for a marvelous new talent I've discovered," Hannah told her. "He works in latex rubber. Molded soft sculptures. Totally brilliant stuff."

"I'm sorry, I—"

"I haven't even told you when it is," Hannah cut her off. "I suppose I should just conclude that you don't really wish to be a friend."

"Hannah—" Meg began, but the other woman's directness surprised her. She decided to be equally frank. "I've just a lot on my mind right now. Lark's not speaking to me. I have to go up to a hearing for Lucinda in Montville this Friday and I'm not exactly looking forward to it."

"You seem to be losing supporters right and left, Meg," Hannah observed. "I'd think you'd be looking around desperately for new friends at the moment, rather than putting them off. What time are you due at the hearing?"

"Two-thirty."

"I'm scheduled to drive up to Cold Spring this week—there's an art gallery there I do some work with. If you like, I'll drive you on up to Montville afterward, it's not much further.

"That's very kind of you."

"You'll actually be doing me a favor," Hannah said. "I really don't enjoy driving that far by myself. And we have a lot to talk about."

*   *   *

Meg went into the office early Friday morning and worked for a few hours before heading back to her apartment, where Hannah had agreed to pick her up. She had her eye out for the white Judson Gallery minivan and was surprised when a car honked down the street and she saw Hannah waving to her from a double-parked maroon BMW sedan.

It was a sort of plum-colored car. A beemer, I think.

It was an unseasonably warm day for mid-December, the sky clear except for a haze of high cirrus clouds. Most of the snow had melted, exposing bright stretches of green along the highway, grass and underbrush that had not yet gotten the message that their season was over. There was something unsettling about the fine weather. Meg had become accustomed to the cold, bleak landscape; it had complemented her state of mind. Now, the strong winter sun made her light-headed and anxious—everything made worse by the certainty that Hannah had been lying to her. In a subdued and abbreviated manner, Meg filled Hannah in on how her championing of Lucinda's cause had alienated just about everybody else.

"I'm persona non grata in Red River now."

"I'm sure you find that upsetting," Hannah said, glancing from the rearview mirror to the road ahead. She was a fast and clearly experienced driver, weaving around slower moving vehicles with abandon. "And though I can hardly pretend that I like Lucinda, I must say I rather admire the way you're sticking to your guns. Defending the weak, et cetera. I never would have pegged you for someone with such strong convictions."

"You make it sound like some kind of disease."

"Well, really." Hannah laughed in the throaty way that no longer sounded strange to Meg. "I'm one to let sleeping dogs lie, you know. I just mind my own business and if that means the world is going to go to hell in a handbasket, so be it."

"Were you minding your own business when you visited Ethan the day he was killed?"

"Excuse me?" Hannah didn't take her eyes off the highway.

"This car. Janine saw it at the studio that afternoon. I think you were there. But the day of Ethan's funeral, you certainly made a point of pretending to me that you'd never been in Red River before."

"I object to your tone of voice," Hannah replied, glancing at Meg. Her thin lips were drawn in a disconcerting smile.

"But you were there?"

Hannah thought for a moment.

"Yes," she said.

Hannah told her that Ethan had left his jeep near Hannah's gallery the final afternoon that he was in New York, though she didn't realize that until later. They'd spent an hour or two together in the small apartment Hannah kept above the gallery, a one-bedroom that Hannah lent to visiting artists or dealers who needed a place to stay for a few nights.

"It was convenient for other things as well," Hannah said dryly. "And Ethan never lost an opportunity to take advantage of that fact." When Ethan left at the end of the afternoon, Hannah assumed he'd gone back up to Red River. She went out for her usual busy evening, a dinner party, as it turned out, in a restaurant a block or two from the gallery.

"A lucky coincidence, actually. Usually, at that time of night, I head back to my loft in SoHo, but I'd left my car in front of the gallery and walked back that way after dinner to pick it up. And there he was. He was a mess. I actually believe he might have been crying,"

Alarmed, Hannah had invited him back up to the apartment above the gallery, and he talked to her in a way that he had never done before.

"He let the emotional floodgates loose. Pouring out all this stuff about his years of cheating on Lark, all the women—his need for them, the high they gave him, the lift. It kept him sane, somehow, kept him above the dark abyss. Well, he knew that I of all people would understand. I just let the man talk, though I'm not very keen on confessionals anymore. But what could I do? He was clearly in pain. And finally he told me about you and what had happened with Lucinda. I have a feeling that you meant more to him than most. Why else would he react like that? I'm not a great judge of these things, but you seem to have put him, as they say these days, in touch with his feelings—and he suddenly couldn't cope with the unreal life he'd created."

Ethan was afraid of being alone that night, though he longed to get back home and have it out with Lark. Finally, Hannah agreed to follow him back up to Red River, driving behind his jeep in her BMW. She saw him safely to the house, then slept over at the Days Inn in Montville. In the morning, still worried about him, she decided to drive by the studio on her way back to New York.

"I suppose that's when Janine saw the car," Hannah said, as she made the turn off the Taconic to Cold Spring. "I went over all of this with the police, by the way. They'd also heard about my being there that morning, and they found my fingerprints in the studio."

Hannah's business with Self Expression, the gallery in Cold Spring, took less than ten minutes. Meg waited in the car, dissecting what Hannah had told her. By the time they sat down for a quick cappuccino at the café next to the gallery, Meg had her questions in hand.

"What do you mean about Ethan having it out with Lark that night?"

"He told her he was finally leaving. He'd had enough of all her passive-aggressive anger. Her setting him up to look like the devil so that she could play at being a saint. What bull!"

"Lark had every right to be angry," Meg protested. "I only wish she'd expressed it a lot more."

"Oh, please," Hannah said, sprinkling sugar onto the foam-topped coffee. "Lark was boiling over with rage, and she found every opportunity she could to stick it to Ethan. Not coming to his opening is a perfect example."

"That's ridiculous, Hannah. Fern was sick. Lark's a very caring mother."

"Well, Ethan told me that she could easily have left the children with Janine. She took care of them as much as Lark did, according to Ethan. But no, the fact of the matter was, Lark didn't want to see Ethan succeed. She wanted to keep him right where he was, in that tight little box of guilty infidelity. She thought she had him so tied up with remorse that he would never leave. She flipped out when he told her he was going. Totally flipped, he told me when I stopped by the studio that morning."

Meg was silent for a moment. Then she asked, "Did anything seem odd to you at the studio?"

"I'd never been there before so it's hard for me to say. But Ethan himself was odd enough. Emotionally raw, everything exposed. He seemed intent on truth-telling now that he was facing his demons, I suppose. He told me some interesting things. . . ."

Hannah looked down at her coffee and played with her spoon, running a finger around the lip of the silver oval.

"He told me that he'd never really been able to love anything deeply but his work. Or anyone—Lark, the girls, all those women. Me. That he kept looking and looking, but it, she, whatever—was always out of reach. Except the art. I really do think he was having some kind of breakdown. He called himself a monster."

Hannah signaled for the check.

"Was there anything else? How did you leave things with him?"

"You might as well know. He told me it was over between the two of us, as well. He said we were 'played out'—what an apt way of putting it. All we'd been doing anyway was playing when you think about it. Pretending, and having some fun, and—acting, really. He said he was done with all that now. That he wanted to start being real, stop all the games. So sad when you think about it. Considering how soon after that the games actually did stop."

"Did you mention all of this to the police?" Meg asked.

"That Ethan dumped me?" Hannah replied. "No, darling, I did not. They made me so nervous with all their questions. I'm not good at dealing with authority to start with. And then, they were so suspicious about my being in Red River in the first place that morning. I don't think they believed me when I explained that I drove up behind Ethan to make him feel safe—I think they thought I was stalking him or something. This whole thing has made me jittery. I've even hired a lawyer." Hannah saw Meg's expression and intercepted her next question.

"No, I didn't murder Ethan. The day I kill a man because he's stopped loving me is, I can assure you, the day I kill myself."

31

Meg didn't know exactly what to expect at the hearing in Montville, but it certainly wasn't this. A small crowd of protesters, cordoned off by metal barricades and watched by two police officers, had gathered to the left of the courthouse steps. They were chanting something that Meg couldn't make out as Hannah drove up the curving drive. Their hand-lettered posters carried slogans: KEEP OUR TOWNS SAFE and STOP TEENAGE VIOLENCE.

"Oh, no, she has to go!" was what they were shouting, Meg realized, as Hannah pulled up behind an empty school bus. Meg recognized Paula Yoder and several other mothers from Red River. There were perhaps thirty people altogether, most of them women.

"Do you mind if I don't go in?" Hannah said, turning to Meg. "I really don't feel like getting into the middle of all this. Or antagonizing Lark—for purely selfish business reasons."

"I understand," Meg said, noticing two photographers talking to each other across from the main entrance. A local news van was parked nearby. "But you don't mind waiting? I've no idea how long this is going to take."

"I'll be fine. So long as I don't have to talk to any more policemen," Hannah said, and then added as Meg started to climb out of the car, "Good luck."

Luck was not all she needed, Meg decided, as she started up the steps. A little chain mail would help. Or a bulletproof vest.

"Shame on you, Meg Hardwick!" Paula Yoder cried when she spotted her. Meg could hear the rapid clicking of cameras behind her. Hurrying now, she pushed against one of the heavy front doors and entered the stately lobby of the courthouse. There was a crowd here, as well, and she quickly scanned the faces, trying to find a friendly one. Peter Boardman had told her he'd be waiting for her near the front entrance; she'd know it was him by the dark blue bow tie he'd be wearing. But it was his calming, grandfatherly voice that she recognized first.

"You must be Meg," Boardman said, taking her elbow. He was a tall, stoop-shouldered man in his early sixties with thinning sandy hair and half-glasses. His eyes were a penetrating blue. "Let's get out of this zoo. We should be starting any minute now."

He guided her through the crowd, down the corridor to the main courtroom, a lovely old two-story wood-paneled room with high, bottle-green glass windows. The afternoon light streamed into the room, casting a pale green sheen. Meg spotted Lark immediately, seated between Francine and Janine. Francine whispered something to Lark, who glanced in Meg's direction, shook her head slowly and sadly, and then purposely turned away from her.

"There's Arthur Pearson, the district attorney," Boardman said to Meg, hoping to distract her. He pointed to a small, dapper man who was deep in conversation with two assistants—one male, one female—both of whom towered over him. Pearson had a head of black hair so full and perfectly groomed that Meg suspected it was a toupee.

"We're in luck, by the way," Boardman went on, speaking to Meg as though they'd known each other for years. There was something about his voice and manner that made Meg feel immediately at ease—and grateful that Abe had steered Lucinda to him. "I don't think Judge Marin has taken kindly to Pearson's publicity tactics." Boardman brought her forward to one of the front rows where Lucinda, free of makeup and looking wan, sat next to a court officer.

"Did he arrange for that little welcoming committee outside?" Meg asked, smiling at Lucinda. Someone, probably Boardman, had wisely suggested that Lucinda remove her nose ring. Only a few streaks were left of Lucinda's red hair dye and her new shorter haircut with its feathery bangs gave her face a waifish look. Lucinda, who once struck such a rebellious, in-your-face pose, seemed to cower in her seat. She looked young and vulnerable—and very frightened.

"I don't know," Boardman said. "But the local papers have certainly been giving glowing reviews of his crackerjack work on this case. I've heard rumors that he's running for state senate next year. And that's more good news for us. The judge hates politics in the courtroom."

"Hey, Luce," Meg said, as the teenager turned around, stood, and impulsively enveloped Meg in a grateful hug. Meg couldn't bear to glance over at Lark's side of the room, though she sensed now that everyone on that side of the aisle was watching her.

The judge, a woman in her sixties with a brisk, no-nonsense manner, took her place on the bench and, leaving Meg to sit behind Lucinda, Boardman went up to consult with her and the D.A. After a brief discussion, which involved a lot of head-shaking on Pearson's part, the proceedings began.

"You honor," Pearson addressed the bench. He had a big voice for such a small man—a carrying baritone that was fulsome with self-assurance. "What we have here is a clear-cut case of homicide. The defendant was found in actual possession of the instrument that has been identified as the murder weapon. She was at the crime scene at the time of death fixed by the coroner. She was arrested in a drunken stupor. She admits that she was too 'out of it' to even now be able to account for herself during the time of the murder. Over the weeks I've been investigating this case I've learned that this deeply troubled and difficult young woman—"

"Counselor," the judge said, interrupting Pearson, "kindly confine your observations about the suspect's character to facts, not speculation."

"Certainly," Pearson said with a smile, nodding his head and glancing down at one of the index cards he was holding. "The suspect has been truant at the local high school for a total of ten days this past semester. She has been suspected of defacing county property and causing a public disturbance—"

"Does she have an arrest record, counselor?"

"Not per se, your honor—" Pearson began, but the judge cut him off.

"I suggest we stick to the crime in question, which seems to me complicated and volatile enough. Truancy can wait for another day."

There was a titter across the courtroom which, more than any reprimand from the judge, seemed to upset the D.A.'s composure. He took a moment to consult with his two assistants before concluding in a forceful and self-righteous tone, "I believe that this is an open-and-shut case of murder in the second degree. I hold that the defendant is a danger to society and to herself. I request that she be remanded without bail, pending a grand jury presentation."

Meg didn't know when she'd put her hand on Lucinda's shoulder but, as the D.A. finished his statement with a hard stare at Lucinda, she felt the teenager start to tremble. Meg leaned toward her and whispered, "It's going to be okay. The judge doesn't like him. Just keep it together."

Compared to Pearson's polished and obviously prepared delivery, Boardman's statement was low-key and conversational.

"I happen to agree with the D.A.—this *is* an open-and-shut case of homicide. Who killed Ethan McGowan, though? In my opinion, that's a question that remains unanswered by any of the facts we've managed to gather thus far. There were no eyewitnesses. The circumstantial evidence that we all know about—the murder weapon in the defendant's hands, her proximity in time and place to the murder—can be fairly easily explained away.

"I'm not suggesting that the county is wrong in pursuing the question of Lucinda's presence in the studio that morning. We all have questions about it, including Lucinda, who cannot remember what happened. And why is that?"

Boardman had been strolling back and forth in front of the bench as he spoke, glancing at Judge Marin, looking out across the courtroom of spectators, nodding at the D.A. and Lark in a gently reasoning way. Now he turned and spoke to Lucinda, "Yes, she was drunk. And she was stoned. She was a seventeen-year-old attempting to deal with the kind of emotional firestorm even the most experienced adult shouldn't have to face. She was trying to cope with betrayal—at the very center of her life—and, yes, she was unable to. So she anesthetized herself, hoping to make herself stronger. But it didn't work. She failed at playing an adult, of coping like an adult. And now she's admitting to us that she can't remember what happened that morning in the studio.

"Let me tell you something: I don't believe Lucinda killed her stepfather. But, even if she had—which, I repeat, I do not believe is the case—she would have done so under extreme emotional circumstances and in probable self-defense. I'm not going to go into the murder victim's well-known reputation in the town, but—"

"I'd take your own good advice there," Judge Marin interjected. "I'd move your presentation along, please."

Boardman nodded at her. "Exactly. That's for a later discussion. I do not wish to introduce more rumors and innuendo into a case that is already loaded with hearsay. The facts are these: There were no eyewitnesses. The evidence is purely circumstantial and can be interpreted many different ways. And Lucinda McGowan had been put through hell for long enough. She is a danger to no one, she has no arrest record. Her only crime, if it is a crime, is that she was unable to shoulder an adult's burdens at a most unfortunate time and place."

Meg could feel Lucinda's shoulders shaking. Lucinda began to cry, her head bowed.

"Look up now, Luce," Meg said when she saw that the judge had asked Pearson and Boardman to consult with her. "Look the judge in the eye."

Lucinda dabbed quickly at her face and blew her nose, but then straightened up and did as Meg instructed her. Lucinda's cheeks were blotchy, her bangs damp and in disarray. But her look was direct and undefiant.

The discussion was long and obviously heated, and it was clear to those who watched closely, as Meg did, that the D.A. was losing an important argument with Judge Marin—and losing it badly. His face reddened with anger, his gestures grew cockier—hands on the hips, shoulders back, foot tapping. Finally, with an irritated wave of the hand, the discussion was ended by the judge.

"This is a court of law," Judge Marin said slowly, looking from Lark to the D.A. and then out across the room. "It is a place where we try to arrive at the truth—and then dispense judgment. We're conducting a preliminary hearing today. That's all it is. And yet, it seems to me, far too many people have walked into this courtroom this afternoon with their minds made up and their judgments rendered. There are protesters outside already turning this case into a platform for other agendas. I will have *no* one," and here the judge glared at Pearson, "using this terribly sad and difficult situation for his or her own purposes. My cases are tried in the court of law—never the court of public opinion."

The room was hushed as the judge added briskly, "I'm setting the bail at one hundred thousand dollars and I'm allowing the suspect to be released into the care of a responsible adult who resides in Manhattan. I'm granting the D.A.'s request that the suspect undergo a Section 730 psychiatric examination—and the defense has agreed to pursue appropriate counseling for his client in the city, subject to my approval. You will all be notified of the next court date by mail."

They weren't supposed to meet. Boardman had suggested that he take Lucinda with him to the back court offices while he arranged the bail by phone with a local bondsman. Meg was to find Hannah and have her pull the car up to the small personnel-only parking area behind the courthouse. Lucinda and Meg were meant to slip away quietly and without notice. But, as Meg was hurrying down the courthouse steps she ran into Lark and Francine coming down from the other door.

"You're actually taking her in?" Lark demanded, her voice breathy with anger.

"Lark, listen—" Meg tried to sound reasonable, "She has no place else to go."

"Oh yes she does. She can go straight to hell," Lark said.

Francine squeezed Lark's elbow. "Reporters are watching, Lark," she whispered. "You don't want to make a scene."

"Yes, I do. I have a right to start a riot as far as I'm concerned," Lark said, brushing Francine off and turning to Meg. "I can't believe—I just can*not* believe—that you're actually taking that little slut into your apartment. That you put up bail for her. That you are comforting her! I saw you put your arm around her—Jesus! It made me want to get sick—right there. How can you do this? You, Meg! After everything we've been through—a whole life together—how can you choose her, that viper, over me?"

"It's not a matter of choosing anyone over any—" Meg began, but Lark cut her off.

"That's where you're so wrong! You can't be wishy-washy about loyalty, Meg. There aren't any gray areas when it comes to whose side you're on. Not when it's something as important as this. Not when it comes to me and the girls. If you're not with us—then you're against us." Lark started back down the steps, but Meg grabbed her arm.

"That's not true," she said.

"I'm sorry, older sister," Lark replied slowly, the venom in her tone spreading with every word, "but you are no longer in the position to tell me what the truth is. And to think I used to worship the ground you walked on." Shaking Meg off, she continued down the steps, followed by a sad-faced Francine

*   *   *

"How are you feeling?" Meg asked Lucinda, turning in her seat to face her. Lucinda was staring out the window at the bleak strip of KFCs and Jiffy Lubes that lined the road out of Montville on the way to the interstate.

"Well, like, *tired.*" She sounded aggrieved.

"That infection cleared up?"

"Yeah." The gratitude that Lucinda had shown in the courtroom earlier was gone, replaced by a moodiness that Meg couldn't figure out. Was Lucinda intimidated by Hannah? Had the hearing taken more out of her than Meg had, at first, realized? No one spoke for the ten minutes it took to reach the state highway heading south. Lucinda lit up a cigarette.

"Not in the car, Luce," Meg said, turning around again. "And ask first, please."

"Oh, ex*cuse* me," Lucinda replied, holding her cigarette up between middle and index fingers with elaborate artifice as she pretended to look around for an ashtray.

"That's all right," Hannah said. "But open the window."

It was another ten minutes before anyone spoke again.

"Have you given any thought to what you might want to do in New York?" Hannah asked.

"Sleep."

"Luce, don't be rude," Meg said. "Hannah's been incredibly generous to come all this distance to pick you up."

"Yeah, I know. And brave, too, with all those fucking housewives wanting to put me away." The fear in her voice suddenly explained her belligerence.

Meg kept her eyes on the road ahead while she said, "You heard what the judge said, they're just trying to use this case to further their own agendas."

"Yeah, right, which I'm sure they'll eventually get around to after they lynch me.

"I think they plan to string us up together," Meg pointed out, trying to make light of a threat she felt was all too real. She remembered the look of righteous anger in Paula Yoder's face, the shocked outrage in Lark's parting words.

Lucinda drifted off to sleep twenty minutes later and slept soundly all the way back to the city. Meg, grateful for everything Hannah had done for them that afternoon, devised conversation that would please and flatter Hannah, asking questions about the gallery and Hannah's circle of artist friends.

They were back in the city by seven that evening— all too soon as far as Meg was concerned. She was beginning to realize how ill-equipped she was to handle what she'd suddenly taken on. Any teenager would have been a handful, but one with a troubled history and an uncertain future was beginning to feel to Meg like an impossible challenge.

Meg invited Hannah to join them for take-out pizza, but Hannah's horrified look almost said it all.

"Thank you, but no. I'm sure I can find dinner plans that don't involve eating with my fingers while crouching over a cardboard box."

The greasy but delicious dinner had a salubrious effect on Lucinda, however. As she polished off the last two slices of extra cheese, she said, "That's the best pizza I've had in a long time."

"Well, don't expect this kind of home cooking

every night," Meg said. "And speaking of expectations. I think we should set some ground rules."

"That's cool," Lucinda said, lighting up a cigarette.

"Such as, no smoking in the apartment."

"Oh fuck—" Lucinda glared at her.

"And no swearing. And no drinking. And no drugs.
And remember to clean up after yourself. We're going
to get along fine."

"Even Lark let me smoke, for chrissakes."

"I didn't see Lark on your side of the courtroom
this afternoon, or footing the bill for your bail. I'm all
you've got right now, Luce, so you better make an
attempt to make nice."

"Yeah," Lucinda dropped the lit cigarette into her
open can of Diet Pepsi; it sizzled out. "I hear you.
Don't worry."

"You'll sleep in the study. There's a futon in there.
I'll get you some sheets."

"Okay," Lucinda said, yawning. She made no move
to clean up after their take-out meal, but Meg decided
to let that slide. Lucinda looked exhausted and,
despite what she had said about her infection clearing
up, not particularly well. When Meg came back into
the living room to tell her that she'd made up the bed,
she saw that Lucinda had fallen asleep. She woke her
gently, and led her into the study.

"Thanks, Meg," Lucinda murmured after she'd
climbed in. Two little words. But Meg realized as she
got ready for bed herself how much she had needed to
hear them. It wasn't going to be easy having Lucinda
in her home, she realized that now. There had already
been awkward moments—when they were waiting
for the delivery and disagreed about what to watch on

TV, the business about smoking. Meg resented that her privacy was being usurped by Lucinda—the teenager took up space, both physically and psychologically, that she had come to treasure. But Lucinda's thanks—however grudging and belated—gave her a warm feeling as she climbed between the sheets. It lasted maybe a full minute, or just long enough for the phone to ring.

It was Abe. He'd been calling almost every night from Los Angeles.

"How did it go?" he asked. Meg had given him the date of the hearing.

"Good and bad." Meg hesitated. "Depends on who you are."

"I meant for you, of course. What happened?"

"Boardman was able to get Lucinda out on a bail."

"I told you he was good. So? Where is she? I can't imagine she's too welcome in Red River."

"That's exactly what I thought." Meg rushed her words. "And she needed to stay with someone close to her whom the judge could deem responsible. So—"

"Oh God, Meg—don't tell me—she's with you?"

"Well . . . yes."

"She's there now? She's going to be living with you? For how long?"

"I guess until the trial . . ." Meg hadn't gotten much further in her thinking than feeding Lucinda and getting her into bed. Clothes, school, counseling—over how many weeks, or even months—she hadn't begun to sort it all out.

"And no one else could have done this thing? There is no other responsible person in Lucinda's life besides you? I can only imagine how Lark is taking this news."

"Not well," Meg conceded. "I'm just trying to do—"

But he cut her off, his voice sounding tired and worried. "The right thing. I know, you've already told me. I know you well enough now to realize that I'm never going to be able to talk you out of anything. No matter how much I think it might hurt you—and others. I already warned you to be careful about picking enemies, Meg. I think you better start being even more cautious about whom you choose for friends."

32

Over the next week and a half, Meg discovered that Lucinda's moods could race and spin with bumper-car abandon—nasty and uncommunicative in the morning when Meg headed off to work, needy and confiding by the time they both arrived home in the evening. With Boardman's help, she'd found a psychiatrist for Lucinda on the Upper East Side whom the court approved for counseling. She'd also been able to get Lucinda placed as a temporary student in a public high school not far from Meg's apartment. But where Lucinda was tight-lipped about what went on during her therapy sessions, she was vocal in the extreme about her new educational situation.

"I hate it there," she declared at the end of that first week.

"I'm sorry, I know public schools in the city can be

on the tough side," Meg sympathized. She'd tried to get her into one of the private schools in the area, but there had simply been no openings.

"It's not that," Lucinda had pouted. "I'm as tough as they come."

"What's the matter then?" Meg had asked. Lucinda's bad-girl pose was Meg's least favorite of the teenager's ever-changing attitudes.

"Everyone looks at me funny."

"What do you mean?" Meg was concerned that somehow Lucinda's indictment had been discovered by her fellow students. She'd advised Lucinda to keep her delicate legal position to herself if she wanted to make friends and attempt a more normal existence in the city.

"I've got, like, nothing to wear," Lucinda responded sulkily. "I'm in the same ugly clothes every fucking day."

"Oh, for heavens' sake, Luce, is that all?" Meg was irritated and relieved at the same time. "I'll see what I can do."

She called Francine from the office the next morning, asking if the minister could possibly arrange to have some of Lucinda's clothes and other possessions sent down from Red River.

"I'm sure you're aware that Lark's not talking to me," Meg explained. "And I remember how kind you were to Lucinda when she was in the hospital. Besides, I have a sinking suspicion Lark doesn't want Lucinda's things in the house anyway."

"Meg, I'd love to help," Francine responded, though Meg could already hear the big "but" in her voice. "Things are extremely tense around here now.

After the hearing, the D.A. lit a fire under the police investigation, just when we hoped it was dying down. It's all anyone's talking about now. Matt's been called back in for further questioning. Apparently his alibi didn't hold up."

"Matt?" Meg had never seriously considered him as a suspect. Though, knowing what she did about his feelings for Lucinda, she wondered how she could have overlooked the possibility.

"He claims he was on the Internet that morning," Francine replied, her usually calm and steady voice reedy with concern. "But our phone records don't show any modem activity at that time."

"I'm sorry," Meg said. "And I'm sorry to add to your problems, but do you think you could talk to Lark about Lucinda's possessions?"

There was a moment of silence on the other end, and Meg could imagine the minister trying to weigh all the pros and cons, the good and bad, of her request.

"I can't, Meg," Francine finally replied. "But not because of Lark's feelings. I'm just so worried about Matt. He refuses to tell me what's going on—what happened that morning. I think he was with Lucinda. I know that he cares about her—probably thinks he loves her. That's the only reason I made an effort to reach out to her. Because, you see, I'm afraid my real feelings toward Lucinda are not . . . they just aren't very Christian."

Meg considered the news about Matt and decided not to mention it to Lucinda until she was in a better place emotionally. The following Saturday, Lucinda and Meg spent the day out clothes shopping—an exhausting and ultimately frustrating experience for Meg. She was generous with her credit card as well as her advice about what flattered Lucinda, but the teenager didn't even pretend to listen to her. The merchandise in Saks, Bloomingdale's, Lord & Taylor, was "totally uncool." Finally, in Macy's, after a quick stop at a nearby McDonald's for lunch, Lucinda spotted a pair of boots that she liked: hideous platforms with grotesque rounded toes and wavelike slabs for heels.

"Can I wear them now?" she asked as Meg was signing the receipt.

"If you think you can actually walk in them without falling over," Meg replied, but she saw in Lucinda's expression something she'd never seen before: an unguarded, childlike delight.

The shopping breakthrough came as they were passing the cheaper discount stores on the way to get the subway down to SoHo and some of Meg's favorite boutiques.

"Cool," Lucinda said, stopping in front of a window display. Slinky lime green bell-bottoms and matching tunic made out of some ultra-shiny fabric that Meg suspected was highly flammable.

"You've got to be kidding," Meg moaned.

"Like you would know what's really hot. Can I at least try it on? *Puh-leeze?*"

It wasn't until Lucinda proudly modeled the shimmering, cheaply made outfit, complete with her new boots, that Meg realized how close the clothes were to the User Friendly line that SportsTech had assigned to Hardwick and Associates.

"Whaddya think?" Lucinda asked with a big grin, though it was clear that she thought she looked pretty stunning. In truth, the soft fabric of the pants glossed over Lucinda's heavy thighs. And the top, though nothing special, was cut tight across the chest where Lucinda had the greatest bragging rights. Meg's speculative look obviously worried Lucinda, who hurriedly went on, "But it's like ten times cheaper than that crap you wanted me to buy at Saks."

"It's not the money, Luce. I was just wondering *why* you like these particular things, that's all."

"Because," Lucinda turned around to catch the full effect of her reflection in the three-way mirror, "it's what *everyone*'s wearing." And, when it became clear that Meg was going to buy the clothes for her, Lucinda went on to magnanimously describe who "everybody" was: the lead singer in a band whose latest CD Meg was ready to burn and the teenage star of an insipid TV show that Meg had been forced to watch with Lucinda on Wednesday nights. In other words, role models not unlike the '70s icons who had dictated Meg's fashion tastes at the same age. She remembered her mother's despairing reaction to the shag hair cut that Farrah Fawcett Majors had inspired her daughter to try.

They went on to three other similar discount outlets and ended up with six purchases altogether. Meg knew that it was a relatively cheap way of buying Lucinda's gratitude, but after the emotional whiplash she'd experienced living with the teenager for just a few weeks, she decided that she deserved a break. She had been working hard to maintain at least a surface equilibrium in her new life with Lucinda, but it wasn't easy. Nothing was these days.

The once familiar rhythms of her existence

upstate—her talks with Lark, her closeness to Brook and Phoebe, the frequent weekend trips to Red River—had all abruptly stopped. But like a person who continues to sense the motion of the waves after returning to dry land, Meg could still feel the disconcerting pull and sway of what she'd been forced to leave behind. The lilt of Lark's voice. The smell of freshly mown hay in the fields beyond the farmhouse.

Perhaps worst of all, she sensed the end—before it had even had a chance to begin—of her relationship with Abe. He claimed to be very busy. He'd returned to New York for a few days and then had to turn around and go right back to LA again. He said a few times that he missed her. And yet, Meg was enough a veteran of the romance wars to be able to detect when the opposing side was in retreat. Abe was backing off, she knew. And it filled her with such sadness and longing that she was almost grateful for the endless distractions Lucinda provided.

The new clothes sent Lucinda into an upswing. She was so infused with goodwill that she announced on the way back to the apartment that she would cook dinner that night, treating Meg to her one great specialty: turkey lasagna. Though it took Lucinda three hours and levied a heavy toll on Meg's little kitchen, the lasagna was very good—sweet tomato sauce studded with ground turkey and onions, soft layers of pasta and ricotta, a crunchy crust of browned mozzarella and Parmesan. Meg made a tossed green salad. They ate in the small dining alcove that adjoined the kitchen, a CD that they could both agree on—Sarah McLachlan's latest—playing in the background. Meg poured herself a glass of wine.

"Let me have some," Lucinda said.

"No way."

"I'm, like, fully grown, you know."

"Legally, you're a minor. One who happens to be out on bail."

"So what—you gonna tell the judge I had a sip of wine?"

"At the same time I tell her you're smoking joints in my kitchen." Meg had first noticed the smell of pot the night after Lucinda started back at school. In the middle of the night Meg had gone to the kitchen for a glass of water only to be confronted by an aroma that took her instantly back to her childhood—the sweet sad scent drifting up from downstairs along with the sound of adult laughter.

That shut Lucinda up for a moment. Then she said, "I can't sleep."

"So? Read a book. Do some homework. Have you spoken to Dr. Markowitz about it?" This was the psychiatrist the state had approved for Lucinda's therapy, and Lucinda's one chore every afternoon was to get to her sessions by four o'clock. Meg had heard directly from the psychiatrist earlier in the week that Lucinda was late half the time.

"Yeah, she says it's kind of normal after a trauma. Wouldn't give me any pills to help, though. I'm supposed to use the time to think. And try to remember. But that's like all I do. Sit around and try to remember something I'd rather totally forget. I don't want to keep going over that same fucking ground. We've been doing this hypnosis in the sessions, and I feel sick when I wake up. I mean it. Like I want to toss my cookies all over Dr. Markowitz's ten-thousand-dollar Persian rug."

"You tell her this?"

"Oh yeah. I tell her everything. She says it's all part of the process. My subconscious fighting my conscious or something."

"I'm curious how far back your blackout goes. Do you remember being with Matt that morning?"

"What do you mean?" Meg, seeing Lucinda's expression, knew her well enough by now to know she was trying to hide something.

"Francine told me that Matt's been called back in for questioning," Meg told her. "He can't seem to account for his whereabouts that morning. And when I spoke to him a few weeks ago in Red River he was very tight-lipped about you—and him—and what he thought about the murder. The two of you were together that morning: that's my guess."

Lucinda suddenly reached across the table, poured herself a glass of wine, and downed it in a single gulp. "Okay, okay, okay," she said, spinning the empty wineglass on the tabletop. "It's not like a state secret, but we decided not to tell the police. I mean, it had nothing to do with the murder though it looked kind of incriminating. I see that now. But, yeah, we were together. All night."

"This was after Lark picked you up in Albany? You sneaked out to see Matt?"

"Yeah, we did that a lot. We hung out in the woods—way back behind the studio, maybe half a mile up the mountain. There's this old abandoned cabin that Matt fixed up with lumber Clint had left around the place. We had a mattress and blankets there, a little cooler. We drank beer and talked. And we did other things, you know. It was, like, the only place I felt really good. That night, though, I was so wired. So burnt up about Ethan. I'd scored some Percodan in New York and Matt had ripped off a quart of vodka from Yoder's. We got totaled. I mean, really out of it. I spent most of the time just venting to Matt about Ethan. Really letting it all go. I remember falling asleep just when the sun was coming up—passing out is more like it, I guess. Then I kind of remember waking up with a bad headache. I took some more pills and washed them down with the rest of the vodka. I have this sort of vague vision of someone walking through the woods. The sounds of twigs snapping. The studio swinging in front of this weird cameralike view. I guess that was me—like staggering toward the studio. Then . . . well, blankness."

"And where was Matt?" Meg asked

"Behind me, I think," Lucinda said, frowning. "He must have been. I remember the sound of his laughter coming from somewhere back in the woods."

Two days later, a week before Christmas, Meg discovered the ongoing extent of Lucinda and Matt's relationship. Her monthly phone bill arrived and it was easily double its normal total: the increase due to late-night calls placed to Francine's number in Red River. She confronted Lucinda that evening.

"What the hell were you two talking about for," Meg glanced down at the minutes logged on the invoice, "sixty-five minutes on the night of December eighth? And then fifty-seven minutes the night after that? What's going on here, Luce?"

"Well . . ." Lucinda's normally chalky complexion took on a pinkish tinge. "We're just. Oh, Meg, he's been so . . . he's been the only one—besides you, of course—who's stood by me. All this time. He wrote me every day when I was in the hospital. Called me when he could—when the Godmother wasn't around to stop him."

"The Godmother?" Meg asked.

"That's what we call Francine," Lucinda explained. "She hates me, you know. Always has. But Matt and me—we don't give a damn. About her, or anybody. This whole thing—it's made us really tight."

"Are you telling me you're in love with Matt?"

"We're *together*!" Lucinda replied defiantly. "We're like . . . just *together*. Do you know what? He's refusing to tell the police anything about our all-nighter. He's holding out on them. He's trying to protect me, Meg. Isn't that just the coolest?"

"Listen, Lucinda," Meg said. "Absolutely *nothing* about this situation is cool, don't you get it? Ethan's murder has ripped apart my life—destroyed my relationship with Lark. Kept me from my nieces—whom I love dearly. It's cut me off from Red River—a whole part of my world has been ruined. And why? Because I'm trying to help you—and trying desperately to get at the truth of what happened that morning. How the hell can you even begin to think that lying about what happened and hampering an investigation—how the hell can you think that's cool?"

"That's the last fucking time I confide in you about anything," Lucinda said. "I stupidly thought maybe you wanted to hear about me—my feelings. I didn't realize that this is all about you!"

"How dare you say that! After everything I've done for you!"

"Oh boy. Here we go again. You sound just like

Ethan and Lark used to—everything you all have *done* for me. Like I'm a fucking charity case. Some sort of cause. I thought you liked me, Meg. I thought you cared about me. I don't know how I could have been so stupid to ever believe that any adult could ever really love me. This is just the fucking story of my life."

She left the apartment soon after that, slamming the door on her way out. Meg was in the kitchen alcove, paying bills, and didn't see her leave. She assumed that Lucinda was going out for a smoke, to calm down. They'd both let off a lot of steam, and Meg herself felt tired and unsteady. She didn't start to worry until half an hour later when Lucinda still hadn't come back. Meg pulled on her jacket and went out to find her. It was bitterly cold, the wind cutting in from the river. The sidewalk was empty. Meg hurried upstairs again and went into the study that Lucinda had converted into her bedroom. The closet was thrown open, the drawers to the desk ajar, Lucinda's new clothes gone. On top of the desk she'd left a scribbled note:

I'm sorry to have screwed everything up for you. It seems like I'm always doing that to people. That's the other story of my life. Sorry. Really.

Luce.

33

Lucinda did not return that night. Or the next morning. Meg called Francine: Matt was missing, too. The police put out APBs on both teenagers. Lucinda, who had officially jumped bail, was now a wanted fugitive.

"If you'd just left well enough alone, Meg," the minister told her later that day, after the police had stopped by the rectory. Francine sounded exhausted and deeply shaken. "If Lucinda had been kept in custody—safe from the town, and all of us safe from her. People are very worried around here. Concerned she's going to come back and do further damage. Paula Yoder's demanding police protection. Tom Huddleson asked me just now if I thought Matt was dangerous. They're treating my son like a criminal—and, I'm sorry to have to say this—but I blame it all on you."

The next few days were an endless series of phone calls: Boardman, Huddleson, two different state detectives, Francine, checking every few hours just to see if Meg had heard anything from Lucinda. Over the course of this hellish period, Meg saw Francine's benevolent facade dissolve and the raw, powerful love for her son become painfully exposed.

"I just want him back," Francine told Meg at one

point. "If Matt and Lucinda call you, tell him for me that it doesn't matter what he's done. I'll stand by him. None of this matters . . . so long as he comes home."

Though Meg was not a mother, she understood what Francine was going through—the guilt, the helplessness, the self-doubt. Meg had promised to take responsibility for Lucinda, and failed. She'd allowed herself to become provoked by the teenager, letting her temper get in the way of her better judgment. She'd let Lucinda down and now, like Francine, all Meg wanted was to get her safely back again. But, besides checking in with the police, there was very little that she could do. Except wait and worry.

Meg now felt more cut off from her normal life than ever. It didn't help that Abe hadn't called. Was he was too wrapped up in the trial in LA? Or had he heard about this latest crisis with Lucinda and decided to wash his hands of her and her problems altogether? Forfeiting the bail money only added to her continuing financial worries. And the new SportsTech presentation had been postponed until after the holidays. Everything in her life, it seemed, was in some kind of nightmarish limbo.

It was hardly the moment for Meg to think about the Hardwick and Associates annual Christmas party, but Oliver kept dropping hints about where they might want to hold it this year—and that time was running out. Meg usually hosted an interesting party for the agency in some quintessential New York City locale. Last year, she had taken them all to Radio City Music Hall for the Christmas Show and then to the Rainbow Room for cocktails, overlooking the dazzling skyline.

Thursday night, three days before Christmas, Oliver had knocked on the door of Meg's office with a handful of menus.

"I apologize for barging in like this, Mr. Scrooge. But, you know, tomorrow is your last opportunity to acknowledge that this season is one traditionally viewed as celebratory. Could we at least get a few six-foot grinders from the deli?"

Meg had gone for the enormous sandwiches, and she'd also sprung for sodas, beer, chips, and a conference room full of hilariously gaudy Christmas decorations that Oliver had found at a discount party-wares shop. Oliver covered the walls of the agency with shiny plastic Santas, strands of Christmas tree lights, and the pièce de résistance, which they hung above the audio-visual center in the conference room: a plastic frieze of the eight reindeer and sleigh, Rudolph leading the pack with a huge nose that lit up, blinking bright red.

Despite her depressed state, Meg couldn't help but be drawn into the spirit of the occasion. They all worked together so closely and often under such pressure that their camaraderie was not unlike that of an infantry platoon. And that autumn a certain siege mentality had taken hold of the group. Though Meg had tried to gloss over how seriously the Jarvis bankruptcy affected their business—or how much her personal problems were claiming her time and attention—she had the feeling that they all knew. Oliver wasn't one to keep secrets and the art department, though often catty and bickering, managed to share gossip with generous abandon. In any case, they had all come through for her: working long hours, keeping their tempers and heads when the computers crashed, and making the daily grind seem like fun. With the problems at Jarvis, the company had barely made money that year, but Meg managed to give everyone a bonus by taking a pay cut herself.

The party started at four o'clock; it didn't start to wind down until after six.

"That's okay, I can finish up," Meg told Oliver after he'd helped her collect empty cans and bottles and bag the trash. "I'm staying for a while longer anyway."

"What for?"

"Oh, just a lot of catching up to do."

In truth, she had nowhere else to go. For the last dozen years, she's spent Christmas up in Red River. The traditions of those long, snow-laden weekends were now so much a part of her thinking and memories, that the idea of being anywhere else for the holidays seemed impossible to her. After she finished cleaning up, she went back to her office and tried to concentrate on the files in front of her. Instead, her thoughts drifted . . . up to the town that now despised her.

The front porch of Yoder's store would be stacked with Christmas trees and hung with holly wreaths for sale, the gas lights on Main Street wrapped with red ribbons to look like enormous candy canes. The old blue spruce next to the War Memorial would be decorated by the VFW, and in front of the Congregational Church a nearly life-size crèche would be set up, all the principal papier-mâché players dressed in real clothes hand-sewn by the ladies auxiliary. Last year, parishioners arriving for Christmas morning services had been outraged to see Joseph wearing a Montville High football helmet.

Though it hadn't snowed for a week or two, a heavy storm was forecast. By Christmas Eve, Red River would be adrift, voices and footsteps muffled, the town seemingly cut off from the rest of the world for a time, and yet utterly safe. On Christmas Eve night, Francine held a family service. The last carol was always "Silent Night" and Clint would lower the lights, and the candles surrounding the altar would glow and flicker as the high, reedy voices of excited children filled the small church. It was a moment that never failed to send a shiver up Meg's normally straight and cynical spine. And this year she wouldn't be there to see it—to see Brook and Phoebe in the new dresses that Lark sewed for them each Christmas, their faces full of innocence and wonder, singing the familiar words.

Around seven-thirty Meg heard a noise in the front of the office. The cleaning service never got to Meg's floor until eight o'clock most nights and, though the building was generally considered safe, she often found the night security guard nodding off when she left past regular working hours. Meg was accustomed to living alone, her mental radar highly attuned to the constant warning signals of urban danger. Hers were the only overhead office lights still on, and they could easily be spotted from the reception area. So when she heard someone coming toward her down the hall, she felt an adrenaline rush of fear.

"Abe."

He was dressed for the office: black cashmere overcoat open at the front, tailored dark blue suit, custom-made shirt, preppy scarf draped like a mantle over his shoulders. His hair was slightly damp, and it occurred to Meg that it had started to snow. She also realized, in much the same carefully detached way, that she was very glad to see him. Too glad. She took a step back.

"You scared the hell out of me."

"Sorry." He was carrying a canvas tote, which he set down by the door. There were three packages in it, identical in size and gift wrapping. "I should have called, but I didn't get back into the city this morning. Been trying to catch up ever since . . . I was dropping off presents and got tied up at the Spellman party." He glanced around her office: the papers waiting for her on the desk and, next to them, the half-filled plastic glass of cola and little pile of pretzels left over from the earlier festivities. She taken off her heels and had on the reading glasses her vanity allowed her to wear only when she was alone. She thought she saw pity in the look he gave her.

"You all alone?" he asked.

"We've been so busy," she said, hoping to appear casual as she removed the glasses. "I'm trying to catch up on some of this damned paperwork." She hadn't actually seen him face-to-face since the afternoon he had kissed her in the park and it struck her how self-contained he seemed—not relaxed, but utterly in control of himself and aware of his surroundings. Ethan had been so expansive and dramatic in his movements—all muscle mass and brute force—often unaware of his own strength. Abe knew where he was every second. His gestures were formed by understatement. The raised eyebrow in the courtroom that could seed doubt in the most reluctant juror's mind. The hand, half-raised, framing the question to come—then dropped again to his side: questions too big to answer.

She realized how much she longed to feel those hands on her body, and she protectively folded her arms across her chest. Where had he been these last two weeks—a time when she'd needed him more than she ever had anyone before in her life? She wasn't accustomed to wanting something beyond her grasp, to being dependent on another person—and it made her feel vulnerable and confused. She wanted to demand an explanation from him—a full accounting of his unreliable behavior. At the same time, she wanted simply to be taken into the warm, comforting shelter of his arms.

He pulled out one of the wrapped gifts. Meg knew from other years past that it was going to be a very good champagne.

"Boardman told me about Lucinda a few hours ago," he said, handing her the gift. "I'm sorry."

"But you can't say you didn't warn me." Meg tried to smile, but suspected that she didn't look particularly convincing.

"How are you holding up?"

"Fine," Meg turned and put the gift on her desk. She didn't want him to see her face as she lied to him. "And you? Did you win the case in LA?"

"As a matter of fact, yes," Abe said, taking a step closer to her. "But with no thanks to me. My heart wasn't in it. Thank God, the opposing counsel was such a moron."

"Where . . ." Meg kept her back to him as she fiddled with the plastic bow on the top of the package. "Was your heart?"

"I think maybe you know."

She felt his hands on her waist, the warmth of his lips on her neck. He pulled her back toward him and then slowly forced her to turn and face him. She felt as if she could see right through him—to the longing, the disappointment. Looking at him now—the eyes that were too knowing, too old for his mobile, boyish face—it occurred to her that what he'd given Becca was the brightness of his love, untainted and idealized—without letting her share any of the dark recesses of his psyche. He'd given Becca everything—and she had trashed it all in front of him, and in the eyes of the world.

Maybe that was what he was afraid of now, why he had been holding back. Love, for Abe, had meant adoration. He'd put Becca on a pedestal—he'd revered her, but always at an arm's length. For many years that was all Meg herself had wanted from a man. But Ethan's murder had changed that. She could no longer be satisfied with just taking.

She didn't say anything as she pulled off his coat. She could hear his surprise—a quick intake of breath—when, holding his hand, she stepped to door and turned off the light. The reflected light from the reception area lit up certain objects in the room: the top of a stapler, the phone receiver, the metal handles on the filing cabinet. In the near darkness, the falling snow outside was now visible—soft flakes floating haphazardly in the darkness. Somewhere there was the distant sound of a vacuum cleaner, a muffled roar of traffic.

"I need to know something, Abe," she said, brushing his hair off his forehead. "Why didn't you tell me about Ethan and Becca?"

He looked at her for a long time. At first, just her eyes. Then her lips. It was a speculative gaze, troubled and probing.

"I thought you'd heard," he said at last. "I assumed Lark had told you. And when I realized you didn't know about Ethan, I just couldn't bring myself to go into it all. I wanted to escape it. Move on, Meg. With you."

She studied his face in the near darkness, hoping to find truth there. But this was a man who presented arguments for a living, who knew how to manipulate facts, how to shade reality for his own ends. Did he see the lingering doubt in her eyes? He leaned over and kissed her, pulling her against him. There was something fierce and demanding in the way he ran his hands through her hair, down her back, cupping her buttocks to him.

"Abe . . ." she pulled away, alarmed by the strength of his need. "What is it?"

"I tried to stay away."

"Why?"

"Because everything is just too complicated right now. Too intense." He told her unhappily. "And I wanted us to take this slowly. I want so much . . . for this to work."

"And it can't now?"

"I don't know. There are so many others things to think about. So many dangers—"

But, before he could finish his thought, her lips hungrily found his again. And, despite the fact that he was right—this was the wrong time and place for what was happening to them—very soon they forgot everything but the here and now, touch and breath, of two people discovering and delighting in each other again.

"It's going to be lonely up there without you."

"It's going to be lonely here. It's been—I don't know—years, since I've spent the holidays anywhere else. I need to stay around—in case Lucinda calls. Not that I'm welcome anywhere else at this point.

"I'd stay in the city, Meg, but I promised Lark that I'd come for dinner—for Brook and Phoebe, you know. And then there's the Lindberghs' opening." Meg knew from Hannah about the wine-and-cheese reception on Christmas Day that Clint and Janine were hosting in the renovated icehouse to celebrate their new workshop and small gallery. Hannah advised the couple on how best to display the studio's wares and, in fact, had taken a real interest in their venture. Hannah herself was planning to attend the party. It occurred to Meg that everyone would be there but she and Lucinda and Matt.

"How is everybody? I miss them all so much. I can't begin to tell you."

They were sitting on her small, lumpy office couch, watching the thickening snowflakes. His arm was around her shoulders. He leaned over and kissed her temple. He kept his lips there as he said, "I'm sure they miss you, too."

"Francine told me the girls are not allowed even to mention my name."

"I'm not going to put myself in the middle of this. Between you two. Especially not now."

She knew that he was right to say that, but she had wanted to hear something else.

"You know, I'm as much at fault about Lucinda taking off as—"

"Don't even say it," Abe warned her. "Lucinda's leaving was unconscionable."

"We had a fight," Meg tried to explain. "I said some things I probably shouldn't have."

"Please, Meg," Abe laughed, but it was not a happy sound. "I know you're worried sick about her, but don't kid yourself. She screwed you over—and herself in the process."

Her head rested in the crook of his arm and she could hear his heart beating through his shirt front. The soreness between her legs felt good. He had surprised her with his lovemaking, and she had surprised herself. It seemed to her that once again something extraordinary had taken place between them, that sex had been just a minor part of it. She wondered what he was feeling, but wouldn't ask him.

Her body felt lighter than air. It seemed impossible considering how remarkably *alive* she felt, but she must have fallen asleep very briefly. She heard only the tail end of something he'd asked her.

"What?"

"We can leave my number up there on your machine in case she calls. We'll take the dirt road in from Montville."

"To Red River?"

"Why not? Nobody will even know you're there."

"I'd love to Abe . . . but—"

"Why not?" Abe agreed. "It can't be doing you a lot of good—sitting around your apartment worrying, all alone. You've been to my place. I rattle around in the damn thing these days. And I've that whole mountain where nobody goes in the winter. We can get some fresh air, maybe do some skiing, try to work out where Lucinda and Matt might have gotten to."

Though Meg tended to prefer older homes—farmhouses like Lark's, or the big boxy Colonials that dotted the New England landscape—if she had to live in a modern structure, she would have chosen Abe's. A series of rectangles composed of glass and wood, the house was set down on the portion of the mountaintop to offering the widest possible view of the river, the town, and the rising mountains beyond. Small rounded decks and screened porches skirted the north and south side of building, but the east side of the house was a glass wall two stories high, unobstructed by anything but the beckoning horizon. Meg remembered how clean the night air had smelled on the one occasion she'd been there with Lark and Ethan for a party, how close the stars had seemed.

Taking her silence for hesitation, he continued, "It's in the middle of nowhere, Meg, and no one has to know you're there. I promise, you'll be perfectly safe."

34

The snow continued through the long drive up to Red River that Saturday morning, throughout the rest of the day after they arrived at Abe's place, and into the night as they sat around the two-story fieldstone fireplace and played Scrabble. Meg had a hard time concentrating on the game. She was too busy trying to see Abe in a new, somehow surprising context—this showplace home with its gleaming hardwood floors and lush oriental carpets. Though he'd turned up the thermostat as soon as they walked in and though the fire had been blazing all evening, Meg felt a draft circulating through the airy, pristine rooms. At first she thought it was caused by the snow, piling up in drifts against the big windows in the living room. Then she realized that what she was sensing wasn't a real chill. The house simply *was* cold—a beautiful shell, filled with lovely things, where nobody seemed to be living.

She yearned for the comfortable disarray and nois-
iness of Lark's living room. The books and magazines
scattered across the beat-up coffee table. The throw
pillows that were actually used for throwing when the
mood overtook Brook and Phoebe. The couch that
could double as a trampoline or transform itself into
a sailing vessel depending on the needs of the
moment. Abe's long white leather sofa with its elegant
lines and small tightly packed armrests was one thing
and one thing only: a place to sit, preferably with back
straight and a cocktail glass in one hand. Meg couldn't
imagine children careering through these rooms, and
that thought made her sad.

"I have a feeling you're not very interested in the
game," Abe said at one point when he got up to put
another log on the dying fire.

"And I thought I was being so discreet," Meg said.
"How can you tell?" She enjoyed watching him
move. He was wearing jeans, and a faded work shirt—
though the toughest physical chore he probably faced
was transporting logs in from the woodpile. Abe's
energy differed from Ethan's. There was a sense of
premeditation in everything he did. Abe seemed to be
a man governed by his thinking. And it was a mind,
Meg was beginning to realize, that never stopped
working. Though they had kept the conversation
light and humorous throughout the day, she had been
aware of Abe's intense, inward concentration. And
even as they argued amicably enough through dinner
about the political shenanigans in Washington, she
sensed that his thoughts were really elsewhere.

"That's the second time you've made the word

'rice.' You could at least have opted for 'icer.'" He sat back down beside her. "I keep my eye on the little things. They reveal a lot."

"Is that how you found out about Becca and Ethan?"

She had meant to bring it up gracefully—or let it emerge on its own over the course of the weekend. Abe had given her the short answer to her question the night before. But the complicated circumstances of Becca's betrayal had been haunting Meg ever since Lark had told her how Becca had thrown herself at Ethan. How could any husband handle such humiliation? Let alone someone as intelligent and observant as Abe. She realized now how much she wanted to hear his side of the story.

"You don't have to talk about it if—" Meg began to say.

"I don't?" He turned to her, dark brows raised ironically. "Really? You'll happily spend the weekend in the house that Becca helped design and decorate, that has her taste and personality stamped all over it—without really needing to learn what happened? You'll sleep with me in the king-sized bed she picked out? The black designer sheets she had specially made?"

"Lark told me you threw out everything that was hers—or that she gave to you."

"Well that's the hard part, isn't it?" Abe replied, getting up to tend the fire unnecessarily. "What was strictly Becca's? And what was ours? Half mine. There's never any clear division. This house?" He turned and raised his arms to the soaring cathedral ceiling. "We both had it built. Made decisions together about the bird's-eye maple cabinetry, the Moravian tiling—I'd have to tear the whole damn thing down now to really get rid of her."

"So you kept the sheets."

"I'm not answering your question, am I?" he said, getting her point.

She tilted her head and smiled.

"You look so relaxed, so lovely right now," he went on. "Do we really have to talk about such an ugly thing?"

"I thought I made it clear to you. If we're going to give this thing a try, I want it to be real. I've dealt with way too many lies and half-truths lately."

"Well, then, let me ask you something," Abe said, folding his arms across his chest. "Do you like Becca?"

"I hardly know her."

"That doesn't mean anything. I know what you're like. You have instant reactions to most people. The first time you met Becca. What did you think?"

"That she was absolutely stunning. Really. She's a truly beautiful woman. With a lot of grace, as well. Natural elegance."

"But you didn't like her."

"I don't think she gave anybody room to. She was too busy concentrating on herself. But who could blame her? Or you? I can imagine what it was like. I mean, it was probably enough just to look at her most of the time."

"It was," Abe said, smiling to himself. "Like having a Monet water lily painting living with you. There was so much I could project into her—so much I saw there. I loved her beauty, as much as I've loved any- thing in my life. I know that doesn't speak very well of my character, but I couldn't think beyond her smile, those eyes. And, you see, the important thing for me was the realization that *she* was *mine*. This business of ownership. I felt so proprietary. This incredible masterpiece was hanging in *my* living room. I didn't want anyone else looking at her. That's one of the reasons I wanted to move up here. To isolate us. Keep others from staring."

"But you also loved this part of the world," Meg interjected, wanting to deflect Abe's criticism. "And you and Becca were having problems. Lark told me."

"Becca was still modeling. Mostly runway work in Europe. We fought about it because I hated having her be away from me and because she always came back on a cocaine high. Every damn time. I'd help her clean up her act just in time for her to go flying off again—in both senses of the word. The thing was: she promised me when we got married that she wanted to have children, too. And here we were, trying, and she was doing coke. Yes, you could say we were having our problems."

"I didn't know you wanted children."

"That's how I finally learned about Ethan. Though I knew subconsciously—had known for a long time. For one thing, I felt this new rapport with Lark. I could feel her—at parties, at Yoder's, the post office—making herself available to me, sort of hovering. I didn't know why. I didn't understand that it was a part of the amazing sympathy, this unbelievable support, she gave to Ethan. At one point I even misread the signals, thought she was coming on to me, and I tried to gently tell her how much I loved Becca. I think back on that now—that sad, knowing look she gave me—and I want to just cry."

"When did you find out?"

"Becca told me she had been pregnant about a year ago."

"Pregnant?"

"Had been. She wasn't sure if it was Ethan's baby or mine—but she didn't want it. For some reason, I was the one who got the bill from the clinic. Typical insurance paperwork screwup—Becca had already paid for the abortion the day she had it."

"Oh, Abe."

"Yeah. Poor, dumb Abe," he said, turning back to the fire. This time, it did need his ministrations, though Meg sensed that he took longer than was necessary fanning it back to life. "When I confronted her with the evidence, she didn't flinch. Told me the truth. Straight out. She thought I already knew most of it. How she'd been carrying on with Ethan for over a year. She was surprised that I was so shocked. Thought I'd been aware of the whole thing and had just turned a blind eye. That we had an 'understanding.'"

"I'm sorry."

"You see, she knew then she was losing him," Abe went on, as though he hadn't heard Meg. "She didn't tell me this. Lark was the one who filled me in later. But he'd already moved on, had grown tired of her demands. I've no doubt Becca loved Ethan. I can even feel truly sorry for her now. The fact is he played her as much for a fool as she played me. She had the abortion, of course, because she knew Ethan was looking elsewhere and she didn't want to lose her figure, not when she needed to appear at her best to win Ethan back. I don't think she thought for a single instant about what say I might have in the matter."

"I went to see her the other day," Meg told him. "I needed to ask her what she was doing at the studio the morning Ethan was killed."

"You went to see Becca?" He frowned down at her.

"I found out where she was working. On a catalog shoot. She was using cocaine pretty heavily from what I was told. She wasn't in good shape."

"She hasn't really been in her right mind since, well, I suppose, since Ethan was killed," Abe said. "She was really at the studio the morning he was murdered? How do you know?"

"Janine saw her, though it's hardly a secret. Becca herself told the police."

"I wonder what she was doing there."

"She wouldn't tell me. But from what Lark and Janine said, I don't think Becca ever gave up on the hope that she could somehow win Ethan back."

"Except for now," Abe pointed out sadly. "She's given it up now."

Periodically throughout the day and evening, Meg had checked her messages hoping to hear from Lucinda. There were calls from Peter Boardman, Hannah, and Francine, and various clicks and silences, but still nothing from the person she wanted most to hear from. Now she followed Abe up the beautiful curving wooden stairs wondering under what diminished circumstances Lucinda would be sleeping that night.

Abe had been wrong about one thing: knowing what happened between Becca and Abe didn't make it any easier initially for Meg to sleep in the bed they had once shared. Like everything else in the house it was selected with impeccable taste: a low-lying teak box frame, a delicately patterned blue and white Japanese print coverlet, and the as-advertised black sheets and pillowcases. She'd been looking forward all day to being with Abe again but, as she waited in bed for him, she realized that her passion had been deflated. Naked beneath the sheets, she thought she was able to pick up a faint scent of perfume—a lingering citrusy aroma. It was like Becca herself, so ingrained in the structure and fiber of Abe's life that he would never be free of her. The question that was bothering her, though, was—did he really want to be?

"What?" he asked after he'd climbed in beside her.

"Was this her side?"

"Yes."

"Then let's switch."

It was better after that, and soon it didn't matter. Abe, perhaps sensing some of Meg's reservations, seemed intent on making her feel loved. Slowly and tenderly, he kissed and caressed the length of her body. She writhed in pleasure as his mouth closed over her right breast, then her left. Every fiber in her body felt tensed, ready, fired with longing.

"Please . . ." she murmured. "Please, Abe . . ."

"Are you begging me, Meg Hardwick?" His eyes were black with desire. Catching him off guard, she wrestled out of his grasp and, laughing, turned quickly and straddled him. Her hair tumbled around her shoulders. He was erect, as aroused as she was. He moaned as she took him into her mouth, and he arched back against the pillows in pure pleasure.

"It's my turn to beg," he said, looking up at her with a languid smile. After he put on a condom, he guided her onto him gently, his hands on her hips. Slowly, at first, she moved up and down on him until they were moving as one. Finally, as their pace quickened, as she felt herself losing control, he pulled her down so that she was beside him, and he pulled her knees up around his waist and penetrated her. They came together, looking into each other eyes—Abe's smile lingering long after the shuddering climax was over.

He curled up against her, arms around her waist, his face nestled in her hair. She could feel his breathing start to deepen.

"Abe?"

"Hmmm?"

"How do you feel about Becca now?"

"It's a little late for this, isn't it?"

"Not for me."

He was silent for a moment or two and Meg could feel his arms tense, the alertness return to his body.

"I feel terribly, terribly sorry for her. She's lost the only person in the world that she ever truly loved."

Late into the night, the phone rang, its sound at first entering Meg's dream as church bells pealing. Lucinda! she thought, only half awake, struggling up, but by then Abe had picked up the receiver.

"No. I'm telling you, you're wrong." He was trying to keep his voice low, but Meg could hear the alarm in his tone. "This morning. No . . . just me. I'm sorry, but you're just wrong. And confused. It's you who needs—"

Abe gently replaced the receiver. He sighed.

"Who was it?" Meg asked drowsily.

"Crank call," Abe said, caressing her hair. "Nothing to worry about."

35

Christmas day dawned an opalescent gray, the sun shining through in patches behind the rolling cloud banks. The snow had finally stopped falling, but it still filled the air: shimmering in the morning breeze across the long field in front of the house, ticking persistently against the windows.

Meg was the first up, leaving Abe tangled in the sheets, curled into himself like a little boy. She made some coffee, then bundled up as best she could in the clothes she'd brought and a hat and extra gloves borrowed from Abe. She went outside. It seemed to be the only place big enough for her to explore her new-found happiness.

She was in love with Abe. She'd been too worried and preoccupied over the past few weeks to keep track of how often he'd crossed her mind. She'd been so cut off from so many people she cared about that she had been afraid to examine her feelings toward him. When had it started? That first kiss in his car? No, further back, she decided. For years, they'd enjoyed each other's company. Laughed at each other's jokes. Shared the private shorthand of people who work well together. But it had never been exactly a professional relationship, even then. Over the course of their many commutes back and forth to Red River, they'd told each other things—anecdotes of the workweek, plots to novels they were reading, reactions to a play they'd just seen. Things they probably didn't have the time to share with anyone else. There'd been no sexual tension between them then, because Abe was so clearly "taken." And if Abe gave her advice about men, it had always been done with a brotherly concern. It was he who had introduced her to Paul Stokes. But now she recalled his angry reaction to her breaking up with Paul—a man even Abe admitted was not her type—and to his hurt feelings when she refused to confide in him about the new man in her life. Had he been thinking about her even then—perhaps without realizing it?

Abe. The snow was deep and soft, sucking at her boots with each slogging step. Abe Sabin. It took a long time to reach the crest of the field to the north of the house. The limestone outcroppings, now covered with snow, had made construction here impossible, but it gave the best, most panoramic view of the town, the river winding through it, the lake nestled around its eastern perimeter, and the humpbacked mountains arching behind it with ghostly majesty. Behind Meg, rising like a slow wave, the rest of Abe's property built to a rock-ridged peak.

She knew it was too soon to think about where they might be headed. It had been decades since she'd lost herself in romantic daydreams. But something felt different about this. Unlike Meg's other ill-fated relationships, she knew who Abe was—his history, his character, his disappointments, his hopes. There were very few secrets left between them and yet, she sensed, there was still so much to discover. And share. With a giddy surge of joy, she recalled his telling her the night before about his hope for children. Could it be that after her long, hard search for a man with whom she could share her life, she had found him right here?

The first time Abe had kissed her she'd been surprised by how natural it seemed, almost inevitable. His touch steadied her. His kiss was gentle and knowing. Abe gave without asking anything in return. Meg had been able to control men all of her adult life—and sex had been just another weapon in her well-stocked arsenal. But with Abe there had been no sense of siege, not even the rising urge to compete. He made love to her with an intuition that left her completely without defenses.

She looked out over the long valley, the white steeple of the First Congregational Church, the smoke curling from the chimney of a farmhouse down the road, and she was struck by a feeling of déjà vu, as if she'd been here before and thought these things before. At that moment, her life stretched out as pure and unspoiled as the scene before her.

The ringing of the phone, a distant chiming across the snowbound fields, brought her back to the present and made her think of the call the night before that had half-woken her. She had a vague memory of Abe getting out of bed after that, of his going downstairs. Had he made another call? She'd fallen asleep again and woken up to find him sleeping heavily beside her, his body slack and unconscious, but his brow worried by his dreams.

By the time she got back to the house, Abe was up and drinking coffee in the kitchen. He was freshly shaved and neatly dressed: corduroys, a tweed jacket, blue shirt, and a darkly patterned tie that she had given him years ago as a birthday gift. And though it touched her that he had thought to wear that particular tie, the morning's brightness had begun to fade. Meg had conveniently forgotten that he was going to spend Christmas with Lark and the girls and then attend the opening party at Clint and Janine's new studio.

"Ah, the beautiful snow queen from the north," he said looking at her closely. How had she failed before to notice that cleft in his right cheek when he smiled?

"You're still going into town?" Meg asked. "The road's impassable—there's at least two feet of snow out there."

"I've a plow on my pickup," Abe replied, an apology in his tone. "And I promised Lark. But—just tell me. Would you rather I stayed?"

Of course, you idiot, she wanted to snap back, but Abe had this maddening way of bringing out the best in her. Especially this morning.

"No, really—you're right to go." Abe had handled the legal aspects of the Lindberghs' new enterprise. "And besides, wouldn't people think it odd if you didn't show up?" She walked over to him and pretended to adjust his collar and tie, though it was just an excuse to be near him.

"Probably," Abe said, putting down his coffee mug. "I'm sorry. You know I'd rather stay here, but Lark just called to make sure I was coming, and I accepted her invitation way before—" He stopped himself and shrugged, smiling down at her.

Meg followed Abe out to the garage after he'd put on his overcoat and snow boots. They were restricted by heavy wool and down, but he took her into his arms, backing her up against his truck.

"You," he said, kissing her neck. "Do you feel the way I do?"

"I don't know. Do you have a door handle jammed into your back?"

"Oh." He stopped, switched their positions, and started kissing her again, with renewed urgency.

"Abe?"

"What? I should stop this, right?" he said, taking a step back as he kissed the top of her head.

"I do feel the same way."

It was cold in the garage, and their breath came out in little puffs, like smoke signals. And what they were trying to tell each other was also like smoke signals— the disconnected words, freighted with too much meaning.

Meg tried to eat some breakfast after Abe left, but without Abe's banter and reassuring presence, the soaring rooms made her feel overly exposed and somehow vulnerable. The snowscape, which had earlier seemed so beautiful, now felt oppressive. Gauzy cloud cover replaced the patchy sunlight. By eleven o'clock, the day was completely overcast.

Once again, she called her apartment to check her answering machine. There were two new hang ups. No messages.

The snow started again a little after noon. Meg had been trying to read a novel, but found herself distracted by the thickening white landscape. She stood at the living-room windows and watched the horizon approach: the ridge of mountains fading, the tree line disappearing, and finally just a swirl of white—like static on an old television set—taking over the world. The day began to darken at three o'clock, the slow early evening collecting in the shadows behind the stairs. Again, she felt the essential coldness of the house, the sense of being exposed and—in some strange way that she knew was just her imagination— watched. She tried to build a fire to keep herself company, but it refused to take hold.

The first shrill ring made her jump, literally, a reflex action, her heart pumping wildly. She hadn't realized that there was a phone on the side table next to her. With the second ring, she laughed a little in relief. She was starting to see and hear things that weren't there. She wondered if she should answer after the third ring. It could be Abe, or even Lucinda—trying to reach her here. The message machine kicked in on the fourth ring. Meg recognized the voice immediately.

"I know you're there." Becca paused, waiting for the phone to be picked up.

"Listen, to me, Abe, I know you're *there*." The words were a little slurred. Meg heard ice clicking in a glass.

"Okay, okay. You go ahead and play your little games. But I'm telling you, you're not going to get away with it. Do you hear me, you bastard? I'm not going to let you get away with it."

Becca began to cry, the sobs echoing across the living room, the sound of deep, unstoppable grief. Meg fought down the impulse to pick up the receiver and try to comfort her. Becca was still sobbing as she said, "I thought it would be better for me if I kept my mouth shut, at first. But when Meg Hardwick told me that she didn't believe Lucinda killed Ethan—that was when I began to think that maybe the police had figured it out, too. I didn't want to lose your help, Abe—God knows, you're the only real financial support I've got. But I'm not going to lie for you either. You bastard, I saw you. I came back to try to get him to reason with me, listen to me, and I *saw* you. Standing over his body like fucking St. George slaying the dragon. Just like you said you would. I'm telling you one more time— Hold on a sec— Who's there? Listen, I got to go, but I'm warning you Abe. You tell them, or I will."

36

No, it couldn't be. Impossible. Not Abe. Not the man she had come to know and love. Throughout the terrible days after Ethan's murder, he had been so supportive. Concerned. Not just to Meg. He'd made such an effort to help Lark out at the house, playing with Brook and Phoebe, driving Meg to see Lucinda. Steering Boardman Lucinda's way. Listening. Advising. Standing beside Lark at the graveside, his arm around the shoulders of the new young widow. No, it couldn't have been Abe. No one could be that duplicitous. Becca was simply hysterical—angry, jealous, out of her mind with grief. This was just her way of getting back at the world.

Meg could feel Abe's comforting arms around her. The touch of his lips. She'd been moving around the house as she sorted through everything Becca had said . . . the trail of cause and effect . . . truth and lies. She put on her parka and boots. She had to keep moving, to do something, to find someone. To stop Becca's accusation from circling around and around in her head: *I saw you there, Abe.*

She found herself outside. Stumbling forward into the blizzard. The world was dizzy, whirling with white, and behind the snow, evening was closing in. She thought she was walking uphill, toward the spot where she had stood just that morning, when everything had seemed possible.

Love . . . need . . . passion . . . jealousy . . . hate. In most lives, these were emotions that ebbed and flowed, channeling in and out of the heart, shifting and ever-changing. But what if the passion—and the jealousy—kept building and need grew and wasn't satisfied . . . and hate became a constant? Meg tried to imagine loving one person enough to kill another. She remembered the fury in Abe's voice at Lark's dinner when he and Ethan almost came to blows. Again. They had fought with their fists before—Lark had recounted the scene to her—that night at the party when Ethan and Becca had writhed against each other on the dance floor. But, no, it couldn't be. Not Abe. Becca was a sick and unhappy woman. She was lashing out blindly—accusing, blaming—in the hope of easing her own pain.

Meg hadn't even thought about being cold before she realized that her fingers and toes had gone numb. She stumbled and almost fell against a stone wall that she hadn't remembered seeing before. An ice-coated power line drooped like a necklace between two poles and then looped off into the thicket of evergreens weighted with snow beyond the wall. She wasn't on the mountaintop. Two warm pools of light swam before her. She was so disoriented that she didn't realize they were car lights until the truck was almost on top of her.

"Meg! For chrissake—" Abe was lifting her up from where she had fallen. She saw now that she was at the bottom of the hill in the middle of the driveway. Before she had a chance to react to his being there, he had her back in the car and was rubbing her hands vigorously between his own.

"Where did you think you were going?"

"I was looking . . ." her words came out in a shiver, "for you. Abe—I was so worried . . ."

"It's turning into a really bad storm," Abe said. He put the truck in gear. "I left the reception early when I realized it had started up again. Told Lark I had to get back. It's crazy for you to have started out in this."

Abe built a roaring fire as soon as they got back to the house and made Meg stand in front of it, wrapping her in a throw blanket.

"You're still shivering," he said. He was standing behind her as she faced the fire, his arms circling her waist. "I'm going to run and get another blanket." It was when Abe was upstairs changing that the phone rang again. To Meg's ears, it shrieked through the downstairs rooms. Abe picked it up after the first ring. As quietly as possible, Meg lifted the receiver in the living room.

"—a terrible thing. I can't believe this is happening." It was Lark, her voice breathy and frightened.

"But how? When?" Meg could hear Abe simultaneously on the phone and distantly from upstairs—his voice urgent and angry.

"At the apartment she's renting near Montville. Whoever it was beat her up pretty badly. The police think her attacker left her for dead. She's in the Montville ER."

"Oh my God. Do you have any idea why?"

"It had to be because of what she was going to tell me. Becca was at the reception early on—before you got there. And she told me she had something important to tell me about the murder. But she'd been drinking and I didn't pay it much mind then. But any number of people could have overheard."

Meg waited until Abe had hung up before she put down the receiver. She then heard him play back Becca's message. Meg hadn't thought to erase it. She wanted to trust him. She needed to believe in him. There was a long silence upstairs after the cheerful beep-beep indicating that the message had ended. Then Meg heard Abe coming slowly down the steps. She turned to face him. His face was ashen, his eyes dark and disturbed. For some reason—in her fear and confusion—she found her gaze fastened on the tie she had given him so many years ago: the rich dark, criss-crossing patterns in the silk. Something about Abe's clothes, Meg found herself thinking, something about Becca and his clothes.

"Why didn't you tell me Becca had called?"

"I was going to," Meg told him, her mind on this other question, this piece to the puzzle. "But it seemed so bizarre . . ."

"It's not true." He stood before her, but she didn't look up at him. She found that she couldn't take her eyes off the dark blue and deep maroon diagonals. "What Becca said—it's not true, Meg. I don't know what's possessed her. She began about a week ago—I guess after you spoke to her—leaving me these messages. I think it must be the drugs, or her state of mind. But she now claims to have seen me there—in the studio—it's just absurd. Insane. Apparently she's starting to tell other people the same thing. And now—I can't believe this—that was Lark calling to tell me that Becca has been attacked. Someone apparently tried to kill her. I don't know what's going on."

"I think I do," Meg said suddenly, looking up at him. Of course, she understood it now. And she could see how Becca had made such a mistake—a nearly fatal one.

"What do you mean?"

"Becca wasn't lying. She actually does believe she saw you."

"What are you talking about?"

"It's going to take a little while to explain," Meg said. "And I don't have it all worked out. I'll tell you what I can in the car."

"We're not going out there again—not in this blizzard."

"Yes, we are. We have to. If Becca was attacked, then I'm afraid Lark is going to be next."

The three small-paned windows that faced the road glowed a warm welcome as Meg pushed against the heavy oak door of the icehouse and found herself in a small entrance hall. She followed the light. The large room, stained a rich hunter green, was lined with shelves displaying the Red River Studio glassware. A huge bouquet of dried flowers—pale blue hydrangeas, dusty pink echinacea, wands of bright red berries—sat on a wide wooden counter that also held a cash register. Two long banquet tables flanked the refurbished room. The white cotton tablecloths that covered them were slightly askew, the tops littered with the remains of the reception: dozens of Red River champagne flutes, crumpled cocktail napkins, leftovers hardening on a cheese board. Francine's large coffee urn sat on the far corner of the table on the right, its top removed, its electrical cord dangling like a loosened necktie from its base. A new large wood-burning open hearth lit the icehouse with the special glow of fire—a soft, flattering, flickering light that made the empty room seem filled with life. Meg could almost hear the clink of glasses, the murmur of voices.

And then she did actually hear a sharp groan. "Damn," Clint said as he rose from behind the counter, rubbing the back of his head. He saw Meg and froze. His flushed face suddenly drained of color.

"Clint?" Meg took a step toward him, and then stopped. She hadn't spoken directly to him since the afternoon she visited him and Janine at his house. She'd known Clint for many years, but he'd always been on the sidelines of her visits to Red River—a kindly, quiet presence with whom she really had nothing in common except her family. But he clearly adored Meg's nieces with an unabashed delight that made Meg feel as though she could see right into his heart. She'd watched him spend hours with Brook constructing a miniature wooden cottage for her collection of bright orange salamanders—then dutifully help her bury the same when Brook left the little home on a radiator overnight. When everyone else had wearied of one of Phoebe's endlessly repetitive made-up games, Clint could be counted on to hop around behind her in a circle clucking like a hen or ask "Who's there?" until even Phoebe's interest flagged.

"What's going on?" He'd regained his composure and strode towards her with a quickness that belied his heavy weight. He'd taken off his jacket, but Meg could see that he was still dressed for the reception in a starched white shirt, too-short but neatly pressed wool slacks, and the kind of brightly patterned suspenders that were briefly a craze among Wall Streeters. "Are you okay? You look frozen. C'mon—get over here." He guided her to the stove, his large right hand cupping her elbow.

"Take off your coat," he said, helping her pull off her snow-dampened parka. "Where have you come from? I didn't think you'd—uh—come up this year. . . ."

"Where's Lark?" Meg asked, letting him take her coat. "And the girls?"

"Up at the house," Clint said, staring down at her with his head cocked to one side. His smile seemed uncertain and he glanced around the room as if to confirm his statement. "Why?"

"Clint . . ." Meg began, searching his face. His wide forehead had crumpled into a frown.

"What is it Meg?" he asked.

"I know who killed Ethan."

"Oh, Meg," Clint said, stepping away from her. She

saw that he held his parka in his arms as if it were a child. "Let's not do this . . . Please let's not."

"But it wasn't Lucinda, Clint!" The fire was suddenly too hot, too close. She noticed that he seemed to be cowering, as if her words could physically hurt him.

"Please, no, Meg. I just can't stand it anymore."

"I know this has been horrible. For everyone. But it wasn't Lucinda."

"Please—" he swayed a little in front of her, his few strands of hair falling across his forehead. "Don't tell—"

"It was Abe."

"Abe?"

"He invited me to his place this weekend," Meg began, taking a step toward Clint. "When he came here for the reception this afternoon, Becca called the house. She left a message saying she'd *seen* him kill Ethan. She was there, in the studio, when Ethan was murdered."

"Yes, but Becca—"

"And I tried to get away. To get help. But Abe came back. That's when I found out where he'd really been. Not at the reception."

"But he *was* here," Clint interjected, rubbing his beard as he tried to take in what Meg was saying.

"For a time, maybe. But then he left and he attacked Becca. Lark called the house about an hour ago and I picked up downstairs. He pretended to be surprised. But I knew. He had to shut her up. She was demanding that he confess—that she'd tell everyone if he didn't. So, I don't know, I guess he'd just had enough from her. And now I'm so afraid—for everyone."

Clint was staring at her, his hand over his mouth, his head tilted as if he were trying to get a better look at her.

"Is Becca . . . still alive?"

"Yes, thank God. When did Lark go back to the house? We've got to make sure they're safe."

"Everyone's fine," Clint said soothingly.

"You don't understand," Meg said. "We've got to get to them—and to the police. We've got to stop Abe."

Something caught Clint's attention—a quick flash across the windows, a swirl of light along the glass display, a flickering gleam on the coffee urn. Clint swung around, dropping the parka on the floor, just as Abe, stepping into the room, said, "Stop me from what, Meg?"

37

"You killed Ethan," Meg found that her voice was surprisingly even, though he had startled her. She hadn't considered the possibility that he would follow her there. "And you tried to kill Becca because she was the only one who saw you do it."

"Everything's going to be okay, Meg," Abe said, as though he hadn't heard her. He looked at Clint, standing directly behind her.

"But Becca's been telling people she witnessed the murder," Meg went on. "She was going to tell Lark who it was. But we all know, Abe. Now what are you going to do?"

"Becca has been calling me night and day." Abe explained conversationally, taking a step toward them. "Ever since you spoke to her in the city, Meg. She's been calling me at the office. At my apartment. Up here. Haranguing me with these accusations. I thought she was going crazy. With grief, I thought. And she'd begun drinking too much again."

"She saw you, Abe," Meg retorted, her voice rising. She felt Clint's arm slide around her waist as if trying to protect her. She could smell his sweat and feel the dampness of his shirt against her back. She knew she had better not try to move away. "She saw you with the pontil, standing over Ethan."

"I know," Abe said. "She was drinking this afternoon at the reception before I got here, wasn't she, Clint? Drinking and whispering behind my back."

"I wouldn't know," Clint replied, squeezing Meg's waist reassuringly.

"I think you would, though. Lark told me that any number of people could have overheard her—she was not exactly being discreet. I think you were one of those people, Clint."

"Is that why you attacked her?" Meg asked Abe. "Because she'd started to tell everyone—what you wouldn't admit yourself?"

"You know, Clint," Abe went on, ignoring Meg's question, "I couldn't figure out why she was so sure it was me at first. Becca isn't dumb. She has a great eye. And I've never thought of her as particularly hysterical. Why would she be so convinced that it was me she saw with the pontil? Nothing I said could change her thinking when she finally decided to tell people what she thought she saw. This obsession she had that I'd killed him. Then, today, it all came together, Clint. Those ridiculous suspenders you're wearing. You know they used to be mine. Becca gave them to me."

"I don't know what you're—" Clint's arm tightened around Meg as he began to speak, but Abe interrupted him.

"You were wearing a shirt of mine the afternoon you killed Ethan. I remember now that I saw you in the general store that morning with it on. It's very distinctive: orange and yellow checks with ridiculous little green pineapples. Becca thought it looked sporty. I hated the thing. Never wore it. Gave it to Francine's rummage sale when Becca and I split up. But, of course, Becca wouldn't have known that. Becca thought that you were me."

"Don't be stup—"

"No, no, you're the stupid one," Abe cut him off again, edging toward them. "You probably had a good reason for killing Ethan. And, you know what? We all might have understood it, Clint. We might have helped you through it. If you'd had the guts to admit it. Instead you hung it on Lucinda. And then when Becca began to talk, oh—you bastard!" Abe picked up a glass, threw it against the wood-burning stove in an attempt to distract Clint, and lunged at them.

But Clint was stronger and just as fast.

"Don't," Clint said, pulling Meg against his side. Groping behind him with his other hand, he smashed a large glass pitcher against the tabletop and waved it in front of him—the jagged edges glinting dangerously. "Don't get any closer."

"Okay," Abe held both hands up. "Listen, okay. There's no need for anyone else to get hurt."

"I . . . tried to reason with Becca." Clint's voice cracked. "I drove over to her place when things were winding down here. Tried to get her to tell me what she knew. But she was so . . . snotty. Too good for the likes of me. Got it into her head that I was coming on to her. I just got so mad. Everything had been going so right, you know? Just as I'd hoped. Then she starts in saying she saw you kill Ethan? I worked it out, too, Abe. Of course—it was your shirt. And it was just a matter of time before the police figured it out, as well. I really didn't mean to hurt her so bad . . ." Clint's voice trailed off.

"But Ethan was a different story?" Abe said.

"You're damn right he was." Clint's tone hardened. "I had a reason to kill Ethan. I had years and years of reasons, piling up around me like garbage. You've got no idea. You people—you never bothered to notice me. Or Janine. All we did for him—and Lark and the girls. He dismissed every goddamned decent idea I ever had! He . . . he scoffed at my proposals for putting in the showroom, teaching classes. Oh sure, they pretended to care, like we were all friends. But underneath it all—who were they kidding? When you got right down to it, we were just the hired help. Even after I started doing all the real work around here. Kept the place running for him. So that he could do his art." Clint spat out the word as if it were a curse.

"Why did you stay?" Abe asked, from where he stood, six feet away. He made eye contact with Meg— one hard glance—and the briefest of nods.

"Because of her. Janine," Clint answered. His breath shortened with emotion as he went on: "She lived and breathed for him, you know. Lived and breathed. It was Ethan this, Ethan that. For years. She idolized him. Ethan, who could do no wrong. Maybe I should have been pissed off at her—caring for him so. But I'm not like that. I knew who we were, what we had. Ethan? He was just Janine's pipe dream. I knew nothing would ever come of it. He made her happy in a harmless kind of way. That's what I decided.

"But then I—we—gave up so much for that bastard and he never even knew. His ego was so huge—he didn't really acknowledge that we existed. We didn't matter. We were just the little people, not particularly bright or good-looking. I'll tell you the truth, I didn't mind her having this thing for him, so long as it was her secret, our secret. But when it all came out . . . and he just stepped all over it. Like it was nothing. Like she was—"

"What happened?" Abe asked gently. "What happened that morning in the studio?"

Clint didn't answer at first. He looked down at the broken pitcher in his hand as if he was suddenly unsure what it was doing there.

"He'd been getting worse," Clint finally replied. "His show made him even more self-centered. Totally focused on his own work. You could tell he didn't really even want us around. We were in his way, though we were keeping this place running for him. But he barely looked at my pieces. Signed off on the fall mail-order catalog without even reading the final proof. And he began to be away more. Down to the city every chance he got. And Janine hated that. Not that we ever talked about it. Not that she ever told me. She didn't need to. Janine and me—we had decided a long time ago not to talk about the painful things. We both understood. What was the point? But I'd always known about Ethan. How she felt. A blind man could see . . . and I'm not blind . . .

"I knew something was wrong that morning after

he got back from New York. He was slamming things around out here and cursing something awful. When Hannah came—I actually heard him crying. Couldn't believe it. Janine and me overheard all this from the back offices, Ethan wasn't bothering to keep any of it quiet. You should have seen the expression on Janine's face! It was like her world was falling apart, too.

"When Becca showed up, Janine crept out to the hallway. I saw her there, eavesdropping. She was shaking her head as she listened to all that cursing and weeping. And after Becca left, I remember suddenly feeling scared. It was too quiet. It was like I knew something was going to happen. Like I knew what was going to happen. I had to go out to get some fire-wood, and when I came in up the back stairs, I over-heard them. Janine had gone into the studio to see him. To try and comfort him. 'Ethan, what's wrong?' she'd said. 'What's happened?'

"And then he told her, 'Get the fuck out of here.'

"'But Ethan, I can't stand to see you in such pain.' She begged him to let her help him. Then he yelled at her. 'Don't touch me, you cow,' he said. 'Don't you dare slobber all over me—' He'd called her . . . a cow. My wife.

"There was just no question about it in my mind by then. I waited until she was back in the office. He didn't hear me. Or see me. He'd turned back to the table and I reached in and pulled out the hottest pontil I could find. I must have made a noise then, because he turned. He saw me coming at him. And it's a funny thing. . . . He had the time, and he was just as strong as me, but he did absolutely nothing to stop me. It was almost as if he'd been waiting for the blow—"

It seemed to happen in a second. The rapping on the window. The front door flying open. Clint whirling around to the see what was happening. The cold blowing in. Abe diving low at Clint, trying to pull Meg free. And Clint kicking Abe in the chest, then the face, holding Meg so tightly she could hardly cry Abe's name.

Abe was on his knees now, his hands and face bloodied, trying to struggle to his feet. Clint kicked him one more time, a horrible sound of boot connecting with bone and muscle, and Abe collapsed. Then three men in uniform burst into the icehouse, as Clint backed farther into the room. Tom Huddleson, his gun drawn, was flanked by two armed officers Meg didn't recognize.

"Hold it right there, buddy," Tom said, speaking calmly to Clint, his lifelong friend. "Just stop right there. Let Meg go. Nobody's going to get hurt."

Meg had thought that she could stall Clint in the icehouse, confuse him by pretending she believed Becca's story, keep him pacified until Abe could arrive with help. She hadn't factored in Clint's brute strength, or his violent reaction to finally being caught out—and cornered. She realized now that Abe would never have left her alone with Clint for very long, no matter that his return to the showroom had never been part of her plan. Or his getting hurt. Abe. She was more frightened for him now than for herself.

"Stay back, Tom," Clint said, his words coming out in dry sobs.

"C'mon, buddy," The police chief took a slow step toward Clint. "Don't make this any worse than it already is."

Clint bumped up against something solid—a wall, Meg assumed at first. Then Clint heaved the broken pitcher at Tom, caught Meg up in his arms, and pushed them both through the back door of the ice-house. At the top of the stairs Clint hesitated for a moment as he slid home the doorbolt and tried to get his breath—and it was all Meg needed. She kicked him hard in the right shin with her booted heel, and struggled free.

She ran. Down the rickety back steps. Into the snow-slicked underbrush. She heard Clint curse and start down behind her. She didn't turn around. It was slippery underfoot, the land sloping sharply to the river. Meg half ran, half slid along the bank. The snow had stopped falling. Stars glittered through the naked branches. She heard noises behind her—echoing through the still, snow-shrouded woods: Huddleson calling out to Clint to stop, the crackle of a walkie-talkie, and then the more distant but more familiar voices of Lark, Hannah, Janine, and—she almost stopped to make sure—Lucinda and Matt.

The river—a frozen ribbon—wound gracefully through the trees into town. Beyond it, the pond that Ethan had created glimmered beneath the starlit sky—an oval mirror. The voices followed her. Lark cried out her name and Lucinda shouted something. In the frigid air it was difficult to tell where they were coming from or what they were saying—and she couldn't stop to find out. Twigs and branches snapped as Clint plowed through the underbrush on the bank just above her.

She slid out on the river's glassy surface—and fell. Her full weight slammed against the ice. It held her, but she couldn't find purchase on the slick surface. She stood. Took a step. Slipped. Struggled to her knees. Stood and fell again. The pond was within her reach. But when she looked back she could see that Clint had reached the river's edge, was already taking a step to follow her across.

A gun shot—it sounded like a gun shot. A shot that echoed across the still night. And then another. And another. But it was the sound of ice cracking, the surface shattering. Then came the roar of the river, the ferocious river that had been waiting underneath— cold, hungry, and never-ending. It sucked Clint in. And down.

38

It was the last run she would probably ever take from her old apartment, Meg reflected, as she started off slowly down Riverside Drive. How quickly things changed. And yet, ten months after Ethan's death, the difficult period leading up to and following the murder seemed to Meg like something that had taken place in another lifetime.

"All our yesterdays have lighted fools the way to dusty death." Francine Werling had recited Shakespeare in church a few Sundays back. And yes, Meg had mentally agreed during the sermon, life was transitory, a flickering shadow, but not so much a poor fool strutting as a relentless army marching. Less than a year after Ethan had shuffled off this mortal coil, the lives of those he'd left behind had altered almost beyond recognition.

Lark's children's book, *Wally of Wall Street*, had been published in April and became an overnight hit. Like many of Dr. Seuss's works, Lark's simple lyrical story and charming illustrations resonated with adults as well as with children. Meg had been worried that all the publicity and attention would make Lark nervous, but her younger sister, on local television shows and at book-signings, had come across as naturally as if she been speaking from her own kitchen.

"Greed, the hunger for things and money, that's what everyone—kids and grown-ups—are struggling with these days," Lark had suggested to interviewers when asked why she thought the book was so successful. "That's what Wally learns about—and what we can learn from him."

Meg had helped Lark script her comments, just as she helped her sister deal with her unexpected success. There was money flowing into the Red River household for the first time—and it came at just the right time. After Clint's drowning, after the revelation that he had been the one who killed Ethan and assaulted Becca, Janine closed the studio and showroom and moved up to Vermont.

Initially, the loss of the income the Red River Studio had generated kept Lark up nights, worrying. But when the book took off, Lark's concerns were of a different sort. "I want to do everything all at once: fix up the house, turn the studio into a work space for me, invest the rest of the money in college funds for the kids. I don't know where to start."

"I can look into the investment end of things for you," Meg volunteered, talking to Lark from the agency during an unusually hectic morning. The new account executive she had hired to handle SportsTech had just poked her head in Meg's office with a worried look on her face—and new Mac computers were being installed in the art department. These days, though, none of these business concerns came before Meg's personal ones. "The other things—they'll all get done eventually."

"But you've given me a real deadline for getting this house in shape."

"Lark, really, I didn't mean for any of this to put you out."

"Your wedding reception putting me out? You've got to be kidding—it's the single most important thing you've ever asked me to do for you. Actually, Meg, it's one of the very few things you've ever asked for. And, believe me, it's going to be hands-down the most spectacular party Red River has ever seen."

There was still a tendency on Lark's part to want to make up for her treatment of Meg, and to try to hurry up the process that would mend the painful rupture that had so transformed their relationship. Lark constantly strived to make everything better, to help Meg forget that she had misjudged her, and Ethan, and so much else in her life. Though Meg had forgiven her sister long ago—and in many ways still felt responsible for the pain they had both endured—she knew that they should never allow themselves to forget what had happened. Ethan would always remain an important lesson in their lives, a reminder that love can blind anyone. That the best of intentions can lead to the worst mistakes.

Perhaps that was why she and Abe had taken things so slowly. Though he'd only suffered a broken collar bone and surface cuts, his confrontation with Clint had shaken him. For weeks afterward, he kept chastizing himself for not being able to prevent Clint from manhandling Meg. Though she repeatedly pointed out that she hadn't experienced anything worse than nervous shock, while he was the one running around with his arm in a sling, Abe was not easily appeased, "But it's what could have happened," Abe insisted darkly.

Yes, they had all narrowly escaped some pretty serious "could haves." Lucinda and Matt, who had holed up in a cheap motel in Montville after Lucinda had hitchhiked back to the area from Meg's, had been trying to piece together their own solution to the puzzle of Ethan's death. It was Lucinda who told Meg about that long, depressing week when the two teenagers came to the conclusion—indisputable in their minds—that Lark had killed her husband. On their way to Lark's to confront her, they had met Abe arriving at the house after he had called the police.

Francine had been so relieved to have Matt return in one piece that she managed to control her temper when he announced at his high school graduation party that he was going to be leaving home again. Boston University had offered him a full academic scholarship and, without telling Francine, he had accepted. And Lucinda was coming with him.

"I'm going to get some kind of a job," Lucinda told Meg proudly. "And I'm going to study for my high school equivalency exam."

"That's great. But aren't you two a little young to be living together?"

"What does age have to do with it? I think when

you find someone who makes you happy—no matter when, or where—you should just go for it."

Out of the mouths of babes, Meg thought, and, slowly, cautiously, she began to test Lucinda's advice. To a degree she barely noticed in the beginning, Meg's life began to revolve around Abe's. At first, it was just a toothbrush, hair dryer, and nightgown left at his apartment. They spent the evenings when they were together at his place—a spacious modern co-op in the west Fifties that was an easy walk to his law office. On the nights they didn't see each other, they talked for at least an hour on the phone. Most weekends they commuted to the house in Red River, every foot of which Abe had decided to redecorate. It was never said, but Abe's renovations felt like something of an exorcism to Meg: an attempt to finally excise the bitterness over Becca.

Becca, on the other hand, seemed to be the only one of them who wanted to keep the murder front and center in her life. Clint's assault on her and the reasons prompting it had made front page news in the local papers and had been picked up by a New York tabloid. Suddenly, Becca's career was hot again. She even managed to get on a television talk show about models who'd been stalked and slashed, though, as Abe pointed out, her attack had absolutely nothing to do with her vocation.

It seemed clear to Meg that Abe had put Becca behind him. Though Meg was beginning to believe that you never totally got over certain people. You moved on as the past stayed buried in your heart—a secret ache, something it was necessary to live with. Now, slowly, sometimes painfully, she was learning to live with, and for, someone other than herself. By late spring it seemed that Meg was stopping by her apartment only to pick up fresh clothes. In June, over dinner after an opening at Hannah's gallery, Abe asked Meg if it wouldn't be more convenient for her to move in with him.

"Is this a question of convenience?" she'd asked.

"No," he'd replied. "That was just a ploy on my part, appealing to your practical nature. Because I sense you are somewhat leery of the other 'c' word."

"Commitment? Is that what you want?"

"I'd better be clear with you. I want a lot more than that. I want a real marriage. I want a child, maybe even two. And I want them with you."

It wasn't just doubt on Meg's part. It was an all-encompassing, paralyzing fear. What Abe was offering—with such obvious love—was exactly what she had always longed for in the world. All she had wanted for as long as she could remember. Everything that she had long ago convinced herself she would never have. She realized now that something Ethan had pointed out to her nearly a year ago was actually true. She purposely entered into romantic relationships in the past knowing full well that they were wired to go wrong. Telling herself she wanted love and commitment, time and again she went for men who had only the most temporary of friendships to offer. She'd been looking for love in all the wrong places, knowing in her heart that she wouldn't find it anywhere.

Why? She realized now that she had been afraid. Early on in her life she had to face so many disappointments and shoulder so much responsibility that she'd learned to limit her expectations. If she didn't wish for too much—sober, caring parents and a normal, comfortable home—then she wouldn't have to be too let down when these hopes didn't come true. This way she was never too hurt. When you cared little about another person, then it didn't much matter when things didn't work out.

But now she found herself caring so much that all the old mechanisms that had kept her from really loving—fear of rejection, the terror of loss—simply broke down and lost all usefulness.

So she moved in with Abe and put her co-op on the market. At the end of July, when Abe officially asked her to marry him during a romantic weekend vacation in San Francisco, she said yes without hesitation. She took the plunge, and discovered that it meant she had learned how to fly.

Francine was to marry them in the First Congregational Church over the long Labor Day weekend. Brook and Phoebe were to be flower girls, Lark the matron—and Lucinda the maid—of honor. Abe's younger brother Jack, whom Meg found she liked enormously, was to be the best man. The ushers were an amalgam of Abe's and Meg's Manhattan and Red River male friends, including Matt, whom Abe had been trying to talk into pre-law. Hannah and her new flame, the latex rubber sculptor, were hosting a rehearsal dinner at Montville's fanciest restaurant. Frieda Jarvis, blaming all her financial and business problems on her now ex-husband, insisted on designing Meg's wedding dress—free of charge, of course. She would have to call Frieda about the design, Meg reminded herself; the dress needed a few alterations now.

Meg slowly jogged through the last half mile of the run. Though still early in the morning, the August sun was already beating down on the surface of the Hudson. And, though she felt strong and healthy, she knew shouldn't overdo it. She and Abe had a long day ahead, packing up the rest of her apartment. She was closing on the sale of the co-op in three days, and she had put most of her furniture into storage. Now they needed a new place to live. But there was no hurry, Abe had said, they had plenty of time to look around for something larger than his one bedroom.

Actually, there was less time than he realized. As she started her cool-down stretches, Meg felt the strange new flutter—part nausea, part excitement—in the pit of her stomach. She'd suspected it for several weeks now, and the bright blue plastic test tube had confirmed it just that morning: She was pregnant. She would to tell Abe that night, over dinner, when they celebrated the sale of her apartment. She could hardly wait to see his expression when she told him what else they had to celebrate.

She wondered what a child of theirs would look like, with her pale blond looks and his dark, intense coloring. What kind of a person they would make, between her drive and his sharp intelligence and both of their somewhat stubborn and demanding natures. As she walked into the lobby, the Edleson twins stepped out of the elevator, laughing and whispering about something. This summer they had outgrown their passion for skating. Now, they had polish on their fingernails. They passed Meg, with a quick "hi," too intent on their own conversation to notice much beside themselves.

They were growing up so fast, Meg reflected as she pushed the button for her floor. Well, aren't we all? she told herself with a contented smile, her arms folded over her wonderful new secret. The doors closed, and the elevator rose swiftly upward.